TI

Aelliana huddled w
gripping the rail so ti

Her brother turned

"Ah, yes, there was something else," he said with studied negligence. One hand moved; four coins flashed in the dimness, falling. "Your quarter-share." He smiled. "Dream well."

He was gone. At last she shut her dry eyes, listening as his footsteps faded down the stairs.

Aelliana sank to her knees on the thin carpet. Gods, how could she have been so stupid? Ran Eld would be delm someday; gods willing, not soon. But when he finally came into his rightful estate there was one task he would immediately set himself to accomplish: The annihilation of Aelliana Caylon, his old and bitter enemy.

He would kill her, she thought, shuddering. He would slap her face in company and fling her into walls for the pleasure of hearing her cry.

Gods, why had she never seen that every time the current delm stayed Ran Eld's hand, two blows were banked for later delivery?

I must leave.

The thought was so shocking, so perfect, that she raised her head, shaking tangled hair away from her face, the better to stare into the dim air.

She flung forward, scrabbling among the frayed rug-loops. Her frantic fingers found them quickly; she cradled their coolness in her hot palm, breathing fast and hard.

Four cantra. Not a fortune, certainly, though she approached seven, counting her hoarded bonuses. It might well be enough to buy her free of a future where Ran Eld was delm.

Clutching her meager treasure, she lurched to her feet. She would leave the clan, leave Liad, start anew among the free-living Terrans. She would go now. Tonight.

SCOUT'S PROGRESS

* A *
Liaden Universe®
Novel

SHARON LEE &
STEVE MILLER

A Baen Book

Baen Publishing Enterprises
P.O. Box 1403
Riverdale, NY 10471
www.baen.com

ISBN: 978-1-9821-9252-5

Cover art by Sam R. Kennedy

First Baen printing, March 2023

Distributed by Simon & Schuster
1230 Avenue of the Americas
New York, NY 10020

Library of Congress Control Number: 2022949305

Printed in the United States of America
10 9 8 7 6 5 4 3 2 1

For the binjali crew:
past, present and future

Authors' Foreword

YOU ARE HOLDING THE MORE-OR-LESS TWENTIETH anniversary edition of *Scout's Progress*, which is something of a shock all by itself.

Scout's Progress was written in 1993, part of an intended two-book set, featuring two brothers-of-the-heart—Er Thom yos'Galan, whose story was told in *Local Custom*—and Daav yos'Phelium, whose story is told in this book.

We never expected either book to be published.

Nineteen ninety-three was . . . an odd time in our lives. We were not at that point working writers, by which we mean that we weren't selling. Our first three novels had entertained "disappointing sales" according to their publisher. And yet that same publisher was in no hurry to revert the rights to us, the authors.

We may have been feeling just a trifle bleak in 1993, and questioning a whole lot of our life choices.

We say these things not to garner sympathy, but to set the stage for how we got to *Local Custom* and *Scout's Progress*.

In 1993 Real Life, Steve was managing a computer store; Sharon was working as a part-time office manager in the mornings, scrambling as a reporter/photographer for a small weekly newspaper during the afternoon and evenings, and writing a once-a-month science fiction review column for the local daily.

In his spare time, Steve set up and operated Circular Logic, the first computer bulletin board system in Central Maine, which essentially brought Maine into the rest of the then-infant internet. This may not sound like a big deal nowadays, but, trust us, back then, it was an Undertaking, involving multiple CD players, two large servers, interfacing with FIDOnet, to upload and download nightly message caches . . . Yeah, wow. Those were the days.

Sharon, being something of a one-trick pony— continued to write.

Previous to 1993, she wrote a non-Liaden space opera, *The Tomorrow Log*, which was roundly rejected by the SF houses. She then wrote an almost-cozy mystery—*Barnburner*, which was met with great editorial disinterest on the mystery side.

Which was when she decided to write—a Regency.

When we became a team, Steve had introduced Sharon to Georgette Heyer's Regency "romances." She fell in love, as had so many before her.

But Sharon didn't want to just write a Regency. She wanted to write a Regency without having to actually do the necessary research.

One of the Cardinal Writing Rules is: Write What You Know. So, Sharon set about telling the story of two brothers, alike in estate, though not in temperament, each of whom needed an heir to fulfill the demands of family and society. These brothers lived just outside of Solcintra, the premier city on the planet Liad.

We'd like to pause here and reflect upon how very,

very well Regency England, as portrayed by Georgette Heyer, dovetails with space opera. Heyer's task was to present her readers with a believable alien society operating by subtly different mores. The goal of space opera is to believably present alien societies operating under different, yet compelling, mores.

The Liaden Universe® operates under vastly different rules from Heyer's Regency Universe, but it is informed by the tenor of her narration, her phraseology, oh—and the clothes. Truly, we stand on the shoulders of a giant.

Returning to 1993, we had no expectation that *Scout's Progress*—or *Local Custom*—would ever be read by anybody but us. They were therefore written to amuse—*us*. Things that amuse us particularly are wordplay; dry, understated humor; a certain grace—of manner and of person; and protagonists with a strong sense of honor and right action, who are competent, though they may be flawed.

Improbably, *Local Custom* and *Scout's Progress were* published in February 2001, as original omnibus *Pilots Choice*, from Meisha Merlin Publishing. And is now being reissued by Baen Books, our publisher since 2008.

It's apparently Traditional on occasions such as these for authors to reflect on what they would have done differently, were they writing the work being celebrated today.

And our answer is? Nothing.

Daav yos'Phelium and Aelliana Caylon have become reader favorites, and more than that, true pillars of the Liaden Universe® supporting more than just their own happy ending.

Some readers, certainly, decry this novel, and *Local Custom*, as "Mills and Boone in space"—but we see that as a failure of their vision, not ours.

So, here we are, celebrating an unlikely anniversary. We hope that newcomers will enjoy Daav and Aelliana's story, and that those who have read the story before will be pleased to revisit old friends.

Sharon Lee and Steve Miller
November 2022

SCOUT'S PROGRESS

Chapter One

Typically, the clan which gains the child of a contract-marriage pays a marriage fee to the mating clan, as well as other material considerations. Upon consummation of contract, the departing spouse is often paid a bonus.

Contract-marriage is thus not merely a matter of obeying the Law, but an economic necessity to some of the Lower Houses, where a clanmember might be serially married for most of his or her adult life.

—From "Marriage Customs of Liad"

"SINIT, *MUST* YOU READ AT TABLE?"

Voni's voice was clear and carrying. It was counted a good feature, Aelliana had heard, though not so pleasing as her face.

At the moment, face and voice held a hint of boredom, as befitted an elder sister confronted with the wearisome necessity of disciplining a younger.

"No, I'm just at a good part," Sinit returned without lifting her head from over the page. She put out a hand and groped for her teacup.

"Really," Voni drawled as Aelliana chose a muffin

from the center platter and broke it open. "Even Aelliana knows better than to bring a book to table!"

"It's for anthropology," Sinit mumbled, fingers still seeking her cup. "Truly, I am nearly done, if only you'll stop plaguing me—"

"If you keep on like that," Aelliana murmured, eyes on her plate, "your teacup will be overset, and Ran Eld will ring down a terrific scold. Put the book aside, Sinit, do. If you hurry your breakfast, you can still finish reading before your tutor comes."

The youngest of them sighed gustily, and closed the book with rather more force than necessary.

"I suppose," she said reluctantly. "It is the sort of thing Ran Eld likes to go on about, isn't it? And all the worse if I had spilt my tea. Still, it's a monstrous interesting book—I had no idea what queer folk Terrans are! Well," she amended, prudently sliding the book onto her lap, "I knew they were queer, of course—but only imagine marrying who you like, without even a word from your delm and—and kissing those who are not kin! And—"

"*Sinit!*" Voni put a half-eaten slice of toast hastily back onto her plate, her pretty face pale. She swallowed. "That's disgusting."

"No," Sinit said eagerly, leaning over her plate, to the imminent peril of her shirt-ribbons. "No, it's not disgusting at all, Voni. It's only that they're Terran and don't know any better. How can they behave properly when there are no delms to discipline and no Council of Clans to keep order? And as for marrying whomever one pleases—why that's exactly the same, isn't it? If one lives clanless, with each individual needing to make whatever alliance seems best for oneself—without Code or Book of Clans to guide them, how else—"

"Sinit." Aelliana thought it best to stem this impassioned explanation before Voni's sensibilities moved her to banish their younger sister from the dining hall altogether. "You were going to eat quickly—were you not?—and go into the parlor to finish reading."

"Oh." Recalled to the plan, she picked up a muffin-half and coated it liberally with jam. "I think it would be very interesting to be married," she said, which for Sinit passed as a change of topic.

"Well, I hardly think you shall find out soon," Voni said, with a return of her usual asperity. "Especially if you persist in discussing such—perverse—subjects at table."

"Oh, pooh," Sinit replied elegantly, cramming jam-smeared muffin into her mouth. "It's only that you've been married an hundred times, and so find the whole matter a dead bore."

Voni's eyes glittered dangerously. "Not—quite—an hundred, dear sister. I flatter myself that the profit the clan has made from my contract-marriages is not despicable."

Nor was it, Aelliana acknowledged, worrying her muffin into shreds. At thirty-one, Voni had been married five times—each to Mizel's clear benefit. She was pretty, nice-mannered in company and knew her Code to a full-stop—a valuable daughter of the clan. Just yesterday, she had let drop that there was a sixth marriage in the delm's eye, to young Lord pel'Rula—and that would be a coup, indeed, and send Voni's quarter-share to dizzying height.

"Aelliana's been married," Sinit announced somewhat stickily. "Was it interesting and delightful?"

Aelliana stared fixedly at her plate, grateful for the shielding curtain of her hair. "No," she whispered.

Voni laughed. "Aelliana," she said, reaching into the High Tongue for the Mode of Instruction, "was pleased to allow the delm to know that she would never again accept contract."

Round-eyed, Sinit turned to Aelliana, sitting still and stricken over her shredded breakfast. "But the—the parties, and all the new clothes, and—"

"Good-morning, daughters!" Birin Caylon, Delm Mizel, swept into the dining room on the regal arm of her son Ran Eld, the nadelm. She allowed him to seat her and fetch her a cup of tea as she surveyed the table.

"Sinit, you have jam on your face. Aelliana, I wish you will either eat or not, and in anywise leave over torturing your food. Voni, my dear, Lady pel'Rula calls tomorrow midday. I shall wish to have you by me."

Voni simpered. "Yes, mother."

Mizel turned to her son, who had taken his accustomed place beside her. "You and I are to meet in an hour, are we not? Be on your mettle, sir: I expect to be shown the benefits of keeping the bulk of our capital in Yerlind Shares."

"There are none," Aelliana told her plate, very quietly.

Alas, not quietly enough. Ran Eld paused with a glass of morning-wine half-way to his lips, eyebrows high in disbelief.

"I beg your pardon?"

I've gone mad, Aelliana thought, staring at the crumbled ruin of her untasted breakfast. Only a madwoman would call Ran Eld's judgment thus into question, the nadelm being—disinclined—to support insolence from any of the long list of his inferiors. Woe for Aelliana that her name was written at the top of that list.

Beg his pardon, she told herself urgently, cold hands fisted on her lap. *Bend the neck, take the jibe, be meek, be too poor a thing to provoke attack.*

It was a strategy that had served a thousand times in the past. Yet this morning her head remained in its usual half-bowed attitude, face hidden by the silken shield of her hair, eyes fixed to her plate as if she intended to memorize the detail of each painted flower fading into the yellowing china.

"Aelliana." Ran Eld's voice was a purr of pure malice. Too late for begging pardons now, she thought, and clenched her hands the tighter.

"I believe you had an—opinion," Ran Eld murmured, "in the matter of the clan's investments. Come, I beg you not be backward in hinting us toward the proper mode. The good of the clan must carry all before it."

Yes, certainly. Excepting only that the good of the clan had long ago come to mean the enlargement of Ran Eld Caylon's hoard of power. Aelliana touched her tongue to her lips, unsurprised to find that she was trembling.

"Yerlind Shares," she said, quite calmly, and in the Mode of Instruction, as if he were a recalcitrant student she was bound to put right, "pay two percent, which must be acknowledged a paltry return, when the other Funds offer from three to four-point-one. Neither is its liquidity superior, since Yerlind requires three full days to forward cantra equal to shares. Several of the other, higher-yield options require as little as twenty-eight hours for conversion."

There was a small pause, then her mother's voice, shockingly matter-of-fact: "I wish you will raise your head when you speak, Aelliana, and show attention to the person with whom you are conversing. One would suppose you to have less *melant'i* than a Terran, the way you are forever hiding your face. I can't think how you came to be so rag-mannered."

Voni tittered, which was expectable. From Ran Eld came only stony silence, in which Aelliana heard her ruin. Nothing would save her now—neither meekness nor apology would buy Ran Eld's mercy when she had shamed him before his delm and his juniors.

Aelliana brought her head up with a smooth toss that cast her hair behind her shoulders and met her brother's eyes.

Brilliantly blue, bright as first-water sapphires, they considered her blandly from beneath arched golden brows. Ran Eld Caylon was a pretty man. Alas, he was also vain, and dressed more splendidly than his station, using a heavy hand in the matter of jewels.

Now, he set his wine glass aside and took a moment to adjust one of his many finger-rings.

"Naturally," he murmured to the room at large, "Aelliana's discourse holds me fascinated. I am astonished to find her so diligent a scholar of economics."

"And yet," Mizel Herself countered unexpectedly, "she makes a valid point. Why should we keep our capital at two percent when we might place it at four?"

"The Yerlind Shares are tested by time and found to be sound," Ran Eld replied. "These—other options—my honored sister displays have been less rigorously tested."

"Ormit is the youngest of the Funds I consider," Aelliana heard herself state, still in the Mode of Instruction. "Surely fifty years is time enough to prove a flaw, should it exist?"

"And what do I know of the Ormit Fund?" Ran

Eld actually frowned and there was a look at the back of his eyes that boded not so well for one Aelliana, once the delm was out of hearing.

She met his glare with a little thrill of terror, but answered calmly, nonetheless.

"A study of the Exchange for as little as a twelve-day will show you Ormit's mettle upon the trading floor," she replied, "Information on their investments and holdings can be had anytime through the data-net."

The frown deepened, but his voice remained dulcet, as ever. "Enlighten me, sister—do you aspire to become the clan's financial advisor?"

"She might do better," Mizel commented, sipping her tea, "than the present one."

Ran Eld turned his head so sharply his earrings jangled. "Mother—"

She held up a hand. "Peace. It seems Aelliana has given the subject thought. A test of her consideration against your own may be in order." She looked across the table.

"What say you, daughter, to taking charge of your own quarter-share and seeing what you can make of it?"

Take charge of her own quarter-share? Four entire cantra to invest as she would? Aelliana clenched her fists until the nails scored her palms.

"Turn Aelliana loose upon the world with four cantra in her hand?" Ran Eld lifted an elegant shoulder. "And when the quarter is done and she has lost it?"

"I scarcely think she will be so inept as to lose her seed," Mizel said with some asperity. "The worst that may happen, in my view, is that she will return us four cantra—at the end of a year."

"A year?" That was Voni, as ever Ran Eld's confederate. "To allow Aelliana such liberty for an entire year may not be to the best good, ma'am."

"Oh?" Mizel put her cup down with a clatter, eyes seeking the face of her middle daughter. "Well, girl? Have you an opinion regarding the length of time the experiment shall encompass?"

"A quarter is too short," Aelliana said composedly. "Two quarters might begin to show a significant deviation. However, it is my understanding that the delm desires proof of a trend to set against facts established and in-house. A year is not too long for such a proof."

"A year it is then," the delm announced and flicked a glance to her heir. "You will advance your sister her quarter-share no later than this evening. We shall see this tested on the floor of the Exchange itself."

Sinit laughed at that, and Ran Eld looked black. Voni poured herself a fresh cup of tea.

Aelliana pushed carefully back from the table, rose and bowed to the delm.

"If I may be excused," she murmured, scarcely attending what she said; "I must prepare for a class."

Mizel waved a careless hand and Aelliana made her escape.

"But this is precisely the manner in which Terrans handle affairs of investment!" Sinit said excitedly. "Each person is responsible for his or her own fortune. I think such a system is very exciting, don't you?"

"I think," Voni's clear voice followed Aelliana into the hallway, "that anthropology is not at all good for you, sister."

Chapter Two

*Each person shall provide his clan of origin with
a child of his blood, who will be raised by the
clan and belong to the clan, despite whatever
may later occur to place the parent beyond the
clan's authority. And this shall be Law for every
person of every clan.*

—From the Charter of the Council of Clans
Made in the Sixth Year After Planetfall
City of Solcintra, Liad

"LADY YOS'GALAN," THE BUTLER ANNOUNCED FROM THE
doorway.

The man at the desk looked up from his screen,
rose and came forward, hands outstretched in welcome.

"Anne. You're up early." His Terran bore a Liaden
accent, lighter than a year ago, and he smiled with
genuine pleasure. "Are you well? My brother, your
lifemate—and my most excellent nephew!—they enjoy
their usual robust health?"

Tall Anne Davis grinned down at him, squeezing
his hands affectionately before releasing him.

"You only saw us two days ago," she said. "What
could go wrong so quickly?"

"Any number of things!" he assured her, striking a tragic pose that won a ripple of her ready laughter. "Only see how it comes about: This morning I am a free man—this evening, I am affianced!"

Trouble crossed her mobile face, as well it might, she being Terran and holding little patience with contract-marriage. Intellectually, she allowed the efficiency of custom; emotionally, she turned her face aside and would far rather speak of other matters.

"Is it going to be very dreadful for you, Daav?" There was sisterly sympathy in her voice, acceptable from the lifemate of his foster-brother. And indeed, Daav thought wryly, rather more than he had received from his own sister, who, upon hearing the news of his impending contract, had allowed herself an ironic congratulation on duty embraced—at long last.

"Ah, well. One must obey the Law, after all." He moved his shoulders, dismissing the subject, and moved toward the wine table.

"What may I give you to drink?"

"Is there tea?"

"As a matter of fact, there is," he said, and drew a cup for each from the silver urn. He carried both to the desk and resumed his seat, waving her to the chair at the corner.

"Now, tell me what takes you abroad so early in the day."

Anne sipped and set her cup aside with a tiny click, leveling a pair of very serious brown eyes.

"I am in need of Delm's Instruction," she stated in the High Tongue, in the very proper mode of Respect to the Delm.

Daav blinked. "Dear me."

Anne's mouth twitched along one corner, but she otherwise preserved her countenance.

Sighing lightly, he glanced down at his hands—long, clever hands, blunt-nailed, calloused along palms and fingertips. He did not care overmuch for ornamentation and wore but a single ring: A band that covered the third finger of his left hand from knuckle to knuckle, the lush enamel work depicting a tree in full leaf over which a dragon hovered on half-furled wings. Clan Korval's Ring, which marked him delm.

"Daav?" Anne's voice was carefully neutral.

He shook himself and looked back to her face, one eyebrow quirking in self-mockery.

"Perhaps you had best make me acquainted with the details of your requirement," he said, in the blessed casualness of Terran. "The delm may not be necessary, tiresome fellow that he is."

Once again, the mere twitch of a smile.

"All right," she said, following him obligingly into her own tongue.

Daav relaxed. It was not entirely clear how much this very unLiaden member of his Clan understood of *melant'i*. He had never known her to make a blunder in society, but that might well be put to the account of her lifemate, who would certainly never allow her to place herself in a position of jeopardy. Whether now moved by understanding or intuition, she was willing to allow him to put off for the moment the burden of his delmhood, and that suited Daav very well.

"In obedience to the Delm's Word," Anne said, after another sip of tea, "I've been studying the diaries of the past delms of Korval, as well as the log books kept by Cantra yos'Phelium, the—inceptor—of the clan."

Daav inclined his head. It was necessary for every member of the Line Direct to master the knowledge contained in Diaries and Log. Terran though she was, Anne stood but two lives from the Ring herself—another subject of which she held shy. Much of the Diaries had to do with politics—doubtless she had come across the record of an ancient Balancing and found herself—understandably!—fuddled.

Daav smiled, for here was no case for Delm's Instruction, but only that teaching which elder kin might gladly offer junior.

"There is a passage in the Diaries which is not perfectly plain?" He grinned. "You amaze me."

She returned the grin full measure, then sobered, eyes darkening, though she did not speak.

"So tell me," Daav invited, since it became clear that such prompting was required, "what have you found in Korval's lamentable history to disturb you?"

"Hardly—entirely—lamentable," Anne said softly, then, firmer: "The Contract."

"So?" He allowed both brows to rise. "You doubt the authenticity of Cantra's Contract with the Houses of Solcintra?"

"Oh, no," she said, with the blitheness of the scholar-expert she was, "it's authentic enough. What I doubt is Korval's assumption of continuance."

"Assumption. And it seems to me so plain-written a document! Quite refreshingly stark, in fact. But I must ask why my *cha'leket* has not been able to resolve this difficulty for you. We have had much the same instruction in these matters, as he stands the delm's heir."

She looked at him solemnly. "I didn't ask him. He's got quite enough to explain about the Tree."

"You question Jelaza Kazone? That is bold." He waved toward the windowed wall behind him, where the Tree's monumental trunk could be glimpsed through a tangle of flowers and shrubbery. "I would have been tempted to begin with something a bit less definite, I confess."

Anne chuckled. "Pig-headed," she agreed and moved on immediately, leaving him no time to contemplate the startling picture conjured by this metaphor. "Er Thom says the Tree—talks."

Well, and it did, Daav acknowledged, though he would not perhaps have phrased it so—or even yet—to her. However, the Tree *did*—communicate—to those of the Line Direct. Er Thom, that most unfanciful of men, knew this for fact and had thus informed his lifemate, against whom his heart held no secret.

"I see that he has his work cut out for him," Daav said gravely. "Balance therefore dictates my defense of the Contract. It is fitting. I make a clean breast at once: The Contract does not speak, other than what sense the written words convey."

"Entirely sufficient to the discussion," Anne returned. "The written words convey, in paragraph eight, that—" She paused, flashing him a conscious look. "Maybe you'd like to call a copy up on the screen, so you can see what I'm talking about?"

"No need; the Contract is one of—several—documents my delm required I commit to memory during training." He sipped tea, set the cup aside and raised his eyes to hers. "I understand your trouble has root in the provision regarding the continuing duties of the Captain and her heirs. That seems the plainest-writ of all. Show me where I am wrong."

"It's very plainly written," Anne said calmly. "Of

course it would be—they were making such a desperate gamble. The Captain's responsibilities are very carefully delineated, as is the chain of command. In a situation where assumption might kill people, nothing is assumed. I have no problem with the *original* intent of the document. My problem stems from the assumption held by Clan Korval that the Contract is still in force."

Oh, dear. But how delightfully Terran, after all. Daav inclined his head.

"There is no period of expiration put forth," he pointed out calmly. "Nor has the Council of Clans yet relieved Korval of its contractual duty. The Delm of Korval is, by the precise wording of that eighth paragraph, acknowledged to be Captain and sworn to act for the best benefit of the passengers." He smiled.

"Which has come to mean all Liadens—and I do acknowledge the elasticity of that interpretation. However, one could hardly limit oneself to merely overlooking the well-being of the descendants of the original Houses of Solcintra. Entirely aside from the fact that Grandmother Cantra would never have accepted a contract that delineated a lower class of passenger and a higher, the Council of Clans has become the administering body. And the Council of Clans, so it states in the Charter, speaks for all clans." He moved his shoulders, offering another smile.

"Thus, the Captain's duty increases."

"Daav, that Contract is a thousand years old!"

"Near enough," he allowed, nodding in the Terran way.

She closed her eyes and took a deep breath, perhaps to calm herself. Eyes still closed, she said, flatly, "Paragraph eight makes you the king of the world."

"No, only recall those very painstaking lists of duty! I'm very little more than a tightly-channeled—what is the phrase?—feral trump?"

"Wild card." She opened her eyes. "You do acknowledge the—the Captain's *melant'i*? You consider yourself the overseer of the whole world—of all the passengers?"

"I must," he said quietly. "The Contract is in force."

She expelled air in a *pouf*, half laugh, half exasperation. "A completely Liaden point of view!"

Daav lifted a brow. "My dear child, I'm no more Liaden than you are."

Her eyes came swiftly up, face tensing—and relaxing into a smile. "You mean that you've been a Scout. I grant you have more experience of the universe than I ever will. Which is why I find it so particularly odd—the Council of Clans must have forgotten the Contract even exists! A thousand years? Surely you're putting yourself—the clan—at risk by taking on such a duty now?"

"Argued very like a Liaden," Daav said with a grin, and raised a hand to touch the rough twist of silver hanging in his right ear. "It does not fall within the scope of Korval's *melant'i* to suppose what the Council may or may not have forgotten. The second copy of the Contract was seen in open Council three hundred years ago—at the time of the last call upon Captain's Justice."

"Three hundred years?"

He nodded, offering her the slip of a smile. "Not a very arduous duty, you see. I oversee the passengers' well-being as I was taught by my delm, guided by Diaries and Log—and anticipate no opportunity to take on the *melant'i* of *king*."

Silence. Anne's eyes were fixed on a point somewhat beyond his shoulder. A frown marred the smoothness of her brow.

"I have not satisfied you," Daav said gently. "And the pity is, you know, that the delm can do no better."

She fixed on his face, mouth curving ruefully. "I'll work on it," she said, sounding somewhat wistful. "Though I'm not sure I'm cut out for talking Trees and thousand-year Captains."

"It's an odd clan," Daav conceded with mock gravity. "Mad as moonbeams. Anyone will say so."

"Misspeak the High House of Korval? I think not." Anne grinned and stood, holding out her hand. "Thank you for your time. I'm sorry to be such a poor student."

"Nothing poor at all, in the scholar who asks why." He rose and took her hand. "Allow me to walk you to your car. Your lifemate still intends to bear me company tonight, does he not? I won't know how to go on if he denies me his support."

"As if he would," Anne said with a shake of her head. "And you'd go on exactly as you always do, whether he's with you or not."

"Ah, no, you wrong me! Er Thom is my entree into the High Houses. His manners open all doors."

"Whereas Korval Himself finds all doors barred against him," she said ironically.

"That must be the case, if there were more students of history among us. But, there, scholarship is a dying art! No one memorizes the great events anymore—gossip and triviality is all."

Halfway across the sun-washed patio, Anne paused, looking down at him from abruptly serious brown eyes.

"How many is 'several'?"

He lifted a brow. "I beg your pardon?"

"You said you'd had to memorize 'several' documents, besides the Contract. I wondered—"

"Ah." He bowed slightly. "I once calculated—in an idle moment, you know!—that it would require three-point-three relumma to transcribe the material I have memorized. You must understand that I have committed to memory only the most vital information, in case the resources of Jelaza Kazone's library be—unavailable—to me."

"Three-point-three—" Anne shook her head sharply. "Are you—all right?"

"I am Korval," Daav said, with an austerity that surprised him quite as much as her. "Sanity is a secondary consideration."

"And Er Thom—Er Thom has had the same training."

So that was what distressed her of a sudden. Daav smiled. "Much of the same training, yes. But you must remember that Er Thom memorizes entire manifests for the pleasure of it."

She laughed. "Too true!" She bent in a swoop and kissed his cheek—a gesture of sisterly affection that warmed him profoundly. "Take care, Daav."

"Take care, Anne. Until soon."

She crossed the patio with her long stride and slipped into the waiting car. Daav watched until the car went 'round the first curve in the drive, then reluctantly went back into the house, to his desk and the delm's work.

Chapter Three

Those who enter Scout Academy emerge after rigorous training capable of treating equitably with societies unimaginably alien, some savage beyond belief.

Scouts are by definition courageous, brilliant, supremely adaptable and endlessly resourceful.

—Excerpted from "All About the Liaden Scouts"

"THE QUESTION WE ADDRESS IN THIS SCENARIO," AELLIANA replied sharply, "is not, 'am I able to perform this level of math without a computer lab to back me up?' but, 'shall I acknowledge the effort to be impossible, and give myself up to die?'"

The six students—five Scouts and a field engineer—exchanged glances, doubtless startled by her vehemence. So be it. If startlement bought them life, their instructor had served them well. She inclined her head and continued.

"I consider that any student still enrolled at this point in the course will possess sufficient memory and strength of will to win through to life, provided they also possess a ship with a functioning Jump unit."

Her students looked at her expectantly.

"Availability of the ven'Tura Tables is useful, but the full tables are not required if the following can be determined: Your initial mass within three percent. Your initial Jump charge to within twenty percent as long as it falls within the pel'Endra Ratio—which, as you know by now, may be derived using the local intrinsic electron counterspin and approximate mass-curve of the nearest large mass. If you are outside a major gravity well you may ignore the Ratio and proceed." She paused to consider six rapt faces, six pairs of avid eyes, before concluding the list of necessaries.

"You must, finally and most importantly, have lines one through twenty and one-ninety through one-ninety-nine of the basic table memorized."

Someone groaned. Aelliana suspected Var Mon, youngest and least repressible of the six, and fixed him with a stern eye.

"Recall the problem: You are stranded in an unexplored sector, coordinates lost, main comp and navigation computer destroyed or useless. Your goal must be to arrive within hailing distance of one or more space-going worlds. You will break many regulations by applying the approach I outline, but you will adhere to the highest regulation: Survive."

She paused.

"This approach requires thought before implementation: You must know the system-energy coordinates of the location you will be Jumping to before you arrive. There is opportunity for error here, as the Jump equation requires you to transform your current mass-energy ratio into one exactly equivalent to that of the rescue destination. Therefore, the initial definition, including the first Assumption, must be exact to within several decimal places, to assure a match of both magnetic and temporal magnitudes."

Once more Aelliana surveyed their faces; saw several pair of doubtful eyes. Well for them to doubt. The danger was real: A mismatched equation meant implosion, translation into a mass, explosion—death, in a word. It was hers to demonstrate that such a situation as the problem described—all too common in the duty the Scouts took for themselves—was survivable. She raised a hand.

"A demonstration," she said. "Please provide the following: Rema—an existing system equation."

It came, a shade too glib. Aelliana 'scribed it to the autoboard behind her via the desk-remote, sparing a mental smile for Scout mischief. Every class thought they would catch her out with a bit of clever foolery. Every class learned its error—eventually.

"Var Mon—a reasonable mass and charge for your ship—" He supplied it and she called on the others, bringing the portions of the equation together and transcribing them to the autoboard. Now.

"Overlooking for the present that one marooned in Solcintra Port might just as easily call a taxi—this is a survivable situation. One could indeed Jump from Solcintra to the outer fringe of Terra system by deriving the spin rates from the tables—note line fourteen and its match in line one-ninety-seven, part three for the proof."

There was sheepish titter from the class, which Aelliana affected not to hear. Really, to assume she would fail of knowing the coords for the largest spaceport on the planet! She raised her hand, demanding serious attention.

"To our next meeting you will bring the proof just mentioned, with an illustration of derived figures. Also, an explanation of the most dangerous assumption made by the student supplying the Terran system equations."

She looked around the half-circle. Several students were still 'scribing into their notetakers. Scout Corporal Rema ven'Deelin, who had an eidetic memory, was staring with haze-eyed intensity at the autoboard.

"Questions?" Aelliana murmured as the chittering of note-keys faded into silence.

"Scholar Caylon, will you partner with me?" That was Var Mon, irrepressible as always.

"I fear you would find me entirely craven in the matter of fighting off savage beasts or in conversing with primitive peoples," she said, bending her head in bogus scrutiny of the desk-remote.

"Never should I risk losing such a piloting resource to savage beasts! You should stay snug in the ship, on my honor!"

Rema laughed. "Don't let him cozen you, Scholar— he only wants someone to do the brain work while he sleeps. Though it is true," she added thoughtfully, "that Var Mon is uniquely suited to—ahh—*grunt-work*—eh, Baan?"

Scout Pilot Baan yo'Nelon moved his shoulders expressively as Var Mon slid down in his chair, the picture of mortification.

"Never, never, never shall I overlive the tale," he groaned. "Scholar Caylon, have pity! Rescue me from these brutes who call themselves comrades!"

But this was only more of Var Mon's foolery, entirely safe to ignore. Aelliana did so, rising to signal the end of the session.

Her class rose as one student and bowed respect.

"Thanks to you, Scholar, for an astonishing lesson," said Field Technician Qiarta tel'Ozan, who, as eldest, was often spokesperson for the class. "It is, as always, a delight to behold the process of your thought."

Prettily enough said, but inaccurate—deadly inaccurate for any of these, whose lives depended upon the precision of their calculations. Aelliana brought her hand up sharply, commanding the group's attention.

"Beholding the process of my thought may delight," she said, shaking her hair away from her face and looking at them as they stood before her, one by solemn one. "But you must never forget that mathematics is *reality*, describing relationships of space, time, distance, velocity. Mathematics can keep you alive, or it can kill you. It is not for the weak-willed, or—" she glanced at Var Mon, to Rema's not-so-secret delight—"for the lazy. The equations elucidate *what is*. Knowing what is, you must act, quickly and without hesitation." Her hand had begun to shake. She lowered it to her side, surreptitiously curling cold fingers into a fist.

"I do not wish to hear that one of my students has died stupidly, for want of the boldness to grasp and use what the calculations have clearly shown."

There was a moment's silence before the field tech bowed again: Honor to the Master. "We shall not shame you, Scholar."

Aelliana inclined her head; her hair slipped forward, curtaining her face. "I expect not. Good-day. We meet again Trilsday-noon."

"Good-day, Scholar," her students murmured respectfully and filed out, Rema and Var Mon already involved in some half-whispered debate.

Aelliana sank back into the instructor's slot, dawdling over the simple task of clearing the autoboard and forwarding copies of the lecture to her office comp and to Director Barq.

Chonselta Technical College employed Scholar of Subrational Mathematics Aelliana Caylon with pride, so the director often said. Certainly, it prided itself on her seminar in practical mathematics. What a coup for the college's *melant'i*, after all, that Scout Academy sent its most able cadets to Chonselta Tech for honing.

Such reputation for excellence earned her a bonus, most semesters, a fact she had never seen fit to mention to her brother. Ran Eld liked it best when she bowed low and gave him 'sir' as she surrendered her wages. Indeed, he had once struck her for her infernal chattering, which action had, remarkably, earned him the delm's frown. But Aelliana took good care never to chatter to her brother again.

The copies were made and sent, the auto-board was clear. The hall beyond the open door was empty; she sensed no patient, silent Scout awaiting her. They learned quickly enough that she was tongue-tied and graceless outside of class. This far into the semester no one was likely to disturb her uneasy peace with an offer of escort.

Yet she sat there, head bent, eyes on her hands, folded into quiet on the desk. She bore no rank within Mizel; her single ring was a death-gift from her grandmother. Aelliana stared at the ancient weavings and interlockings until the scarred silver blurred into a smear of gray.

How could she have been so foolish? Her mind, released from the discipline of instruction, returned to its earlier worries. Whatever was she thinking, to challenge Ran Eld's authority, to call his judgment into question and shame him before the delm? The last half year had seen a decrease in her brother's vigilance over herself. She had dared to believe—and now this. A slight that held no hope of passing unavenged, born of three words, whispered in a lapse of that essential wariness . . . Aelliana bit her lip.

Peace lay in meekness, safety in invisibility. To care—about anything!—to lift up her face and challenge the dreary, daily what-is—that was to become visible. And in exposure to Ran Eld's eye lay an end to both safety and peace.

In the warm classroom, Aelliana shivered. Resolutely, she unfolded her hands, placed the remote precisely into its place and rose, going down the hall silent and unnoticed, head bowed and eyes fixed on the floor directly before her.

Craven, she had tarried long in her office and returned home in the cool evening, ghosted across the dim foyer and up the front stairway, toward her rooms.

He burst from the shadows on the second floor landing, catching her hard around the wrist.

Aelliana froze, wordlessly enduring the touch. His fingers tightened, ring-bands cutting into her flesh.

"We missed you at Prime meal, sister," he murmured and she could not quite damp her shudder. Ran Eld laughed.

"How you hate me, Aelliana. Eh?" He shook her wrist, rings biting deeper. "You were bold enough at breakfast, were you not? Raised your head and stared me in the eye. I fancied I saw a bit of the old wildness there, but mayhap it was a trick of the light. Best to be certain, however, so one knows how to proceed."

That quickly he moved, knotting her hair in his free hand and wrenching her head up.

She gasped—a whispered scream—and closed her eyes against a surge of sick panic. Thus had her husband handled her, time and again, until her body grew to loathe the touch of any hand, kindly or severe.

"Look at me!" Ran Eld snapped. Precisely thus had *he* commanded her. Twice, perhaps, in the very beginning, she had willfully kept her eyes closed. He very soon broke her of such nonsense.

Half-strangled with fright, she forced her eyes open.

For an age she hung suspended in the malice of her brother's glare, the mauling of her wrist and the misuse of scalp and neck muscles reduced by terror to the veriest nothings.

"So." He twisted her knotted hair more tightly, perhaps hoping for another outcry. When none came forth, he brought his face close to hers, eyes glittering in the dimness of the landing.

"It occurs to me, *sister*," he purred, breath breaking hot against her cheek, "that you give very little toward the upkeep of this clan. Such paltry wages as you bring me from your teaching are hardly more than might be made by one or two well-considered contracts."

Her heart lurched. She forced herself to swallow, to hang limp in his grasp and keep her eyes open against the sear of his anger.

"The delm," she whispered, voice trembling, "the delm gave me her Word. I am acquitted of more marriages."

"So you are," Ran Eld murmured, eyes glinting.

"However, a new delm may very well hold a new understanding of the clan's necessities and the duty owed by—some." He smiled suddenly, eyes raking her face.

"Why, I do believe you had not thought of that! Poor Aelliana, did no one tell you that nadelms become delms?"

Her face must have shown the full measure of her dismay for he laughed then and released her with a shove that sent her reeling against the landing-rail.

"I am delighted we have had this opportunity for discussion," Ran Eld said, bowing with broad irony. "It would have been a dreadful thing, indeed, to allow you to continue on with no anticipation of the pleasant future to sustain you."

He laughed once more and shook his lace into order. Aelliana huddled where she had been flung, hands gripping the rail so tightly her fingers cramped.

Her brother turned to go; turned back.

"Ah, yes, there was something else," he said with studied negligence. One hand moved; four coins flashed in the dimness, falling. "Your quarter-share."

He smiled.

"Invest wisely, sister. And do remember to give me a written report on the progress of your portfolio every twelve-day. I would be behindhand in my duty if I did not closely oversee so chancy a venture." He bowed. "Good-night, Aelliana. Dream well."

He was gone. At last she shut her dry eyes, listening as his footsteps faded down the stairs and crossed the stone-floored foyer. A moment later she heard the door to the parlor creak on its ancient hinges, hesitate, and fall closed.

Aelliana sank to her knees on the thin carpet. Gods, how could she have been so stupid? How could she have forgotten, when from that single irrefutable fact came all that she was today: Nadelms became delms.

Of course they did.

And she, blind fool, to think Delm's Word would shield her forever; to believe that she had only to appease Ran Eld sufficiently, to show that she did not—had never—wanted it. To think that, eventually, matters would mend.

Ran Eld would be delm someday; gods willing, not soon.

But when he finally came into his rightful estate there was one task he would immediately set himself to accomplish: The annihilation of Aelliana Caylon, his old and bitter enemy.

He would kill her, she thought, shuddering. He would breed her until her body broke, choosing such husbands as would discover the first to be a paragon of gentle virtue. He would invite her to beg his mercy and glory in refusing it; he would slap her face in company and fling her into walls for the pleasure of hearing her cry.

Gods, why had she never seen that every time the current delm stayed Ran Eld's hand, two blows were banked for later delivery?

I must leave.

The thought was so shocking, so perfect, that she raised her head, shaking tangled hair away from her face, the better to stare into the dim air. Terrans lived clanless, did they not? And by all accounts prospered—or the clever ones did. One needed only be canny in one's investments, and—

Investments.

She flung forward, scrabbling among the frayed rug-loops. Her frantic fingers found them quickly; she cradled their coolness in her hot palm, breathing fast and hard.

Four cantra.

Not a fortune, certainly, though she approached seven, counting her hoarded bonuses. It might well be enough to buy her free of a future where Ran Eld was delm.

Clutching her meager treasure, she lurched to her feet. She would leave the clan, leave Liad, start anew among the free-living Terrans. She would go now. Tonight.

She stowed the four cantra in her right sleeve-pocket, sealing the opening with care.

Then she went, silent and breath-caught, down the stairs. She crossed the foyer like a waft of breeze and let herself out the front door and into the mist-laced night.

Chapter Four

As each individual strives to serve the clan, so shall the clan provide what is necessary for the best welfare of each. Within the clan shall be found truth, kinship, affection and care. Outside of the clan shall be found danger and despite.

Those whom the clan, in sorrow, rejects, shall be Accepted of no other clan. They shall neither seek to return to their former kin nor shall they demand quarter-share, food or succor.

To be outside of the clan is to be dead to the clan.

—Excerpted from the Liaden
Code of Proper Conduct

DAAV CAME INTO THE SMALL PARLOR, EYEBROWS UP.

"Good evening, brother. Am I late?"

"Not at all," Er Thom yos'Galan replied, turning from the window with a smile. "I came before time, so that we might talk, if you would."

"Why would I not? Wine?"

"Thank you."

Er Thom preferred the red. Daav splashed a portion into a crystal cup and handed it aside, surveying his *cha'leket*'s evening clothes with a smile.

"You look extremely, darling. Bindan shall have no hesitation in opening the door this evening."

"As they would certainly hesitate to admit Korval Himself," Er Thom said, in echo of his lifemate.

Daav grinned and poured himself a cup of pale blue *misravot*. "No, you are the beauty, after all. What could Bindan find for pleasure in such a fox-faced fellow as myself?" He sipped. "Discounting, of course, an alliance such as no one of sense will turn aside."

"So bitter, brother?" Er Thom's soft voice carried a note of sorrow.

Daav moved his shoulders. "Bitter? Say jaded, rather, and then pardon—as you always do!—my damnable moods." He raised his cup. "What had you wished to speak of?"

"We are on my subject," his brother said gently. "It had been in my mind that you did not—like—the match."

"Like the match," Daav repeated, staring in surprise. For Anne to question the validity of a contract-marriage was expectable. To hear such a query from Er Thom, who was Liaden to the core of him—that must give one pause.

"Have you information," he asked carefully, "which might—alter—the delm's decision in this?"

"I have nothing to bring before the delm. Indeed, lady and clan appear perfectly unexceptional, in terms of alliance and of genes. My concern is all for my *cha'leket*, who I—feel—may not be entirely reconciled to marriage."

"I am reconciled to necessity," Daav said, which did not answer his brother's concern, and held as its only virtue the fact that it was true.

Worry showed plain in Er Thom's eyes.

"Daav, if you do not like it, stand aside."

Plain speaking, indeed! Daav allowed astonishment to show.

"Darling, what would you have me do? The Law is clear. Necessity is clearer. I must provide the clan with the heir of my body. Indeed, full nurseries at Jelaza Kazone *and* Trealla Fantrol must be the delm's goal, for we are grown thin—dangerously so."

He saw that point strike home, for it was true that the Line Direct had suffered severe losses in recent years. And yet—

"If you cannot like the lady," Er Thom insisted, with all the tenacity a master trader might bring to bear, "stand aside. Bid Mr. dea'Gauss find another—"

"As to that," Daav interrupted, with some asperity, "I like her as well as any other lady who has been thrown at my head these past six years."

"You have grown bitter. I had feared it." He turned aside; put his glass away from him. "I shall not accompany you this evening, I think."

Shock sent a tingle of ice down Daav's spine. In the aftermath of disbelief, he heard his own voice, dangerously mild.

"You refuse to assist your delm in a matter of such import to the clan?"

Er Thom's shoulders stiffened, his face yet turned aside.

"Will the delm order me to accompany him?" he inquired softly.

Yes, very likely! Daav thought, with a wry twist of humor. Order Er Thom to any thing like and Daav would gain as his evening's companion an exquisitely mannered mannequin in place of a willing, intelligent ally. It was no more Balance than he would himself exact, were their places changed.

Er Thom being quite as much Korval as Daav, persuasion alone was left open. He extended a hand and lay it gently upon his brother's arm.

"Come, why shall we disagree over what cannot be escaped? If not this lady, it must be some other. I am of a mind to have the matter done with, and the best course toward finish lies through begun."

Er Thom turned his head, raised troubled violet eyes. "Yet it is not—meet, when you do not care for her, when any is the same as one—"

"No," Daav interrupted gently. "No, darling, you have lost sight of custom. The Code tells us that a contract-spouse is chosen for lineage and such benefits of alliance and funding as must be found desirable by one's delm. It notes that resolution may be brought about more speedily, if both spouses are of generally like mind and neither is entirely repulsed by the other. You know your Code, own that I am correct."

"You are correct," Er Thom acknowledged, with an inclination of the head. "However, I submit that the Code is not—"

"I submit," Daav interrupted again, even more gently, "that you have been taught by a Terran wife."

A flash of violet eyes. "And that is an ill, I understand?"

"Not at all. Scouts learn that all custom is equally compelling, upon its own world. I point out that Korval is based—however regretfully—upon Liad."

Er Thom's eyes widened slightly. "So we are," he

murmured after a moment. He grinned suddenly. "We might relocate."

"To New Dublin, I suppose," Daav said, naming Anne's homeworld with a smile. "The Contract is still in force."

"Alas." Er Thom recovered his wine glass and sipped, eyes roving the room.

The point was his, Daav considered with relief, and had recourse to his own glass.

"I do wish," Er Thom murmured, "that you might find one to care for—as Anne and I . . ."

Daav raised a brow. "I shall advertise in *The Gazette*," he said, meaning to offer an absurdity: "'Daav yos'Phelium seeks one who might love him for himself alone. Those qualified apply to Jelaza Kazone, Solcintra, Liad.'"

Er Thom frowned. "You do not believe such a one exists."

"I have met a great many people in the six years I have worn the Ring," Daav said with matching gravity. "If such a one exists, she has been—reticent."

Er Thom glanced away then, but not before Daav had seen the quick shine of tears in his eyes.

They finished their wine in a silence not so easy as usual.

"It is time, brother," Daav said at last. "Do you come with me?"

"Yes, certainly," Er Thom replied. "I had left my cloak in the hall."

"Mine is with it," Daav said, and arm-in-arm, they quit the room.

* * *

It was late.

Aelliana had no very clear notion of precisely how late; her thoughts, fears, and discoveries muddled time past counting.

Less hasty consideration showed that her initial plan—to leave Clan Mizel and Liad immediately—required modification. She walked the misty streets for unheeded hours, working and reworking the steps, weighing necessity against certitude, honor against fear.

Fact: In due time, and barring unfortunate accidents, nadelms did, indeed, become delms.

Fact: Learned Scholar of Subrational Mathematics Aelliana Caylon, lately resolved to flee her homeworld for the comforts of a Terran settlement, spoke not one word of Standard Terran, nor any of the numerous Terran dialects. She did, of course, speak Trade, and understand somewhat of the Scout's finger-talk, but she could not, upon sober reflection, suppose this knowledge to balance her ignorance.

She might take sleep-learning to remedy her deficiency of language. But even sleep-learning takes time; and the skills thus gained must be exercised in waking mind, or else be lost like any other dream.

There were, of course, luxury liners which made such things as Learning Modules available to their passengers, but to book such passage was—

Fact: Beyond her meager means.

A visit to the ticketing office in mid-city had revealed that seven cantra would indeed buy passage to a Terran world, via tramp trader. If she wished to crew as part of her fare—and if the captain of the vessel agreed—she might reduce her cost to four cantra.

In either wise, she arrived at her destination—one *Desolate*—clanless, bankrupt; ignorant of language, custom and local conditions.

A badly flawed equation, in any light. She leaned against a damp pillar and closed her eyes, sickened by the magnitude of the things she did not know.

Ran Eld was right, she thought drearily: She was a fool. How could she have considered leaving Liad? She was no Scout, trained in the ways of countless odd customs, able to learn foreign tongues simply by hearing them said...

"Scholar Caylon?" The voice was familiar, light and young, the mode, of all things, Comrade, though she took pains to be no one's friend.

"Scholar Caylon?" the voice persisted, somewhat more urgently. She had the sense that there was a body very close to her own, though her interlocutor did not venture a touch. "It is Rema, Scholar. Do you require aid?"

Rema, Scout Corporal ven'Deelin. She of the eidetic memory. Aelliana pried open her eyes.

"I beg your pardon," she whispered, answering the warmth of Comrade mode with the coolth of Nonkin. Her glance skated past the Scout's face.

"Indeed, it is nothing. I had only stopped to rest for a—" Her gaze wandered beyond the Scout's shoulder and for the first time in many hours Aelliana's brain attended to the information her eyes reported.

"What place is this?" she demanded, staring at a wholly unfamiliar plaza, at a double rainbow of lights that blazed and flashed along a sidewalk like a ribbon of gold. Folk were about in distressing number, most in cloaks and evening dress, small constellations of jewels glittering about their elegant persons. Others were dressed more plainly, with here and there a glimpse of Scout leather, such as the girl before her wore.

"Chonselta Port," Rema said patiently, yet insisting upon Comrade. "It is the new gaming hall—Quenpalt's Casino. We've all come down to see it—and half Solcintra, as well, by the look of the crowd!"

Chonselta Port. Gods, she had walked the long angle through the city, entirely through the warehouse district, passed all unknowing between the gates and then walked half her original distance again. It must be . . . must be . . .

"The time," she said, suddenly urgent. "What is the time?"

"Local midnight, or close enough," Rema replied. She swayed half-a-step closer. "Forgive me, Scholar. It is plain that you are not well. Allow me to call your kin."

"No!" Her hand snapped up, imperative. Rema's eyes followed the motion, snagged—and slid away.

Startled, Aelliana glanced down. The bracelet of bruises circling her wrist was green and yellow, distressingly obvious in the extravagant light.

"Perhaps," the Scout suggested softly, "there is a place where you would prefer to spend the night. Perhaps there is a—friend—in whose care you might rest easy. I am your willing escort, Scholar, only tell me your destination."

She felt tears prick the back of her eyes, who had long ago learned not to weep.

"You are kind," she murmured, and meant it, though she dared not allow herself the mode of comrades. "There is no need for you to trouble yourself on my behalf. I have only walked further than I had supposed and the hour escaped my notice."

"I see," Rema said gravely. She hesitated and seemed about to say more.

"Well, for space sake," commented an irritated voice only too plainly belonging to Var Mon, "if your object was to stand out in the damned mist all night—" He blinked, coming up short just beyond Rema's shoulder.

"Scholar Caylon! Good evening, ma'am. Have you come to beat the house?"

"Beat the house?" she repeated stupidly, wondering how she might explain her late homecoming, when Ran Eld was already watching, eager for a chance to pain her.

"Certainly! Have you not taught us that there is no such thing as a game of chance? For every mode of play there is a pattern which, once recognized, may be manipulated according to the rules of mathematics. You recall the lecture, Rema, I know you do!"

"I do," his friend said shortly, and without sparing him a glance. "Scholar, please. You are plainly far from well. Allow one who holds you in highest respect to offer aid."

"Not well?" Var Mon sent a brilliant glance into Aelliana's face, then tapped Rema's shoulder with an authoritative forefinger. "She's wet, is all. Anyone would be, standing around in this stupid mist. I'm getting wet myself, if it comes to that. Glass of brandy will set her right." He pointed down the length of golden sidewalk to a cascade of gem-lit stairs crowned by wide ebon doors.

"Nearest source of brandy's right there—not to mention shelter from the weather. There's room at our table for the Scholar. After she's warmed herself she can give us some advice on winning against the random and we'll see her into a cab before we start back to Academy. Everything's *binjali*, hey?"

Binjali—a not-Liaden word enjoying currency only among Scouts, so far as Aelliana knew—meant "excellent" or "high-grade." She forced her fuddled brain to work. Something must be done to disarm Rema's all-too-apparent concern. Scouts were observant, many were empathic, as well, though of a different skill level than an interactive empath, or Healer. Perhaps a glass or two of wine, and a lecture on practical math in relation to games of chance ...

"That sounds a good plan," she said, looking past Rema's grave eyes to Var Mon's mischievous face. "I am damp and would welcome a chance to dry."

"Good enough," the boy returned with a grin. Without more discussion, he spun on his heel and moved away down the crowded sidewalk, obviously expecting that they would follow.

"Scholar?" murmured Rema, but Aelliana pretended not to hear and pushed away from the friendly wall, following Var Mon's leather-clad back through the glittering crowd.

Chapter Five

Remember who we are.
We are not Solcintran.
We are not derived from the Old Houses.
We are Korval.

Keep the Contract, protect the Tree, gather ships, survive.
But never, never, never let them make you forget who you are.

—Val Con yos'Phelium,
Second Delm of Korval,
Entry in the Delm's Diary for
Jeelum Twelfthday in the Fourth
Relumma of the Year Named Qin

THE LADY HAD EXPECTED A MORE COSTLY JEWEL.

Not that she was so ill-bred as to actually say it, but Scouts are skilled in reading the language of muscle and posture: To Daav, her disappointment could scarcely have been plainer had she cried it aloud.

He was stung at first, for it was a pretty piece, and he had expended time and care in its choosing. However, his innate sense of the ridiculous soon laid salve upon injured feelings.

Come, Daav, he chided himself, *where is the profit in contracting Korval, if not in having extravagant jewelry to flaunt in the face of the world? Being so little fond of jewels yourself, this aspect of the case doubtless escaped you.*

He had a sip of tolerable red. *No matter,* he thought. *The marriage-jewels shall be more fitly chosen, now her preference is known.*

Beside him, Samiv tel'Izak gently replaced the troth-gift in its carved wooden box and set it on the table. Daav felt another twinge of regret. He had carved the little box himself—not, it must be admitted, with the lady at all in his thoughts, but rather as a means of calming mind and heart on a day some years past. Still, the feel of hand-carving must be unmistakable against her fingertips, odd enough to earn at least a second glance.

Samiv tel'Izak took up her glass and lifted grave eyes to his face.

"I thank Your Lordship for the grace of your gift."

It was said with complete propriety in the mode of Addressing a Delm Not One's Own. There were several other modes she might have chosen with equal propriety—and greater warmth: Addressing a Guest of the House, Adult-to-Adult, or even Pilot-to-Pilot, though that approached the Low Tongue, and might be considered forward-coming.

Samiv tel'Izak was not forward-coming. A solid daughter of a solid mid-level House, Daav suspected that her delm's instruction held her to a loftier mode than she might have chosen on her own: Addressing a Delm Not One's Own was taking the High Tongue high, indeed.

In balance, Daav should make answer in Addressing One Not of His Clan, which came uncomfortably close to Nonkin. He chose instead to set an example of good fellowship in this, their first meeting alone, and hope well-bred manners would force her to follow his lead.

"To give the gift is joy," he told her in Adult-to-Adult, then offered a branch of active friendship: "Joy would be made greater, did you consider yourself free of my personal name."

Long, mahogany-colored lashes swept coyly down, while shoulder muscles shrieked aloud of triumph and some daring.

"Your Lordship is gracious."

Daav's eyebrow twitched, which warning sign she did not see. He sipped his wine, blandly considering the studied curve of her neck.

So I'm to be smitten, am I? he thought sardonically— and then thought again. Perhaps, instead, he was punished for giving so paltry a gift? He wondered which would become annoying soonest, gloating or greed.

"One learns that your contract with *Luda Soldare* commences somewhat sooner than expected," he murmured, keeping stubbornly to Adult-to-Adult. "When do you lift?"

"The Master Trader was pleased to amend the route," she replied, keeping just as stubbornly to her own choice of mode. "We break orbit tomorrow, Solcintra dawn."

First Class Pilot tel'Izak had signed an employment contract with the captain of the newly commissioned trade ship *Luda Soldare* just prior to her delm's receiving notification of Korval's interest. This previous commitment was the reason that this evening

Samiv and Daav signed a letter of intent rather than a contract of marriage.

Once signed, they were bound to each other by the terms of the letter, which further stipulated that the actual marriage commence not more than three full days after *Luda Soldare* released Pilot tel'Izak from her duty. There were the usual buy-out clauses on the side of Bindan. As the clan seeking the marriage, Korval waived right of termination.

"And has the master trader also been pleased to alter the tour?" Daav wondered, watching his soon-to-be-betrothed closely.

Her face remained properly grave, though the breath on which she answered was slightly deeper than the one before it.

"On the contrary, the master trader counseled one to plan the signing of one's marriage lines on the third day of the coming Standard Year."

Three Standard Months—a very prudent time for a new vessel's shakedown voyage. Daav inclined his head and, obedient to the promptings of his lamentable sense of humor, offered the lady a sardonic compliment:

"I shall count each day as three, until you are returned."

"Your Lordship is gracious," she murmured, and he detected neither irony nor pleasure in her voice.

He was saved the necessity of forming a reply to this rather uncommunicative statement by the entrance of the butler, come to summon them to the signing room, where Delm Bindan and Er Thom had been arranging things this age.

Samiv tel'Izak rose immediately and bowed, allowing him to proceed her, which was the privilege of his rank. He stifled a sigh as he followed the butler down the hallway and decided that, before either greed or gloating did their work, propriety would drive him mad.

The table was large, crowded and boisterous. A place was made for Aelliana between Rema and Var Mon, the shortage of chairs being remedied by a bit of deft piracy from neighboring tables.

Brandy was called for—"A double for the Scholar!" Var Mon ordered—and arrived amid a chef's ransom of food platters. At once, Rema snatched up a filigreed plate and began loading it with exotic savories.

Aelliana had a cautious sip of brandy and watched the Scout in awe. Her own appetite was never robust and it seemed such an amount of food would serve her needs for a week. Yet Rema clearly intended this laden plate to be a mere snack or late-night luncheon.

She assayed another sip of brandy, relishing the resulting sensation of warmth. Brandy was not her usual beverage—indeed, she rarely drank even wine—but she found it pleasing. She had a third sip, somewhat deeper than the first two.

"Of your grace, Scholar." Rema again. Aelliana lowered her glass and regarded the plate the Scout set firmly before her with a mixture of astonishment and dismay.

"The house brandy is potent," Rema murmured. "You will wish to eat something, and minimize the effects."

Having thus issued her instruction, the Scout turned away and leapt willy-nilly into a spirited discussion taking place at the opposite end of the table. As less than half the comments were rendered in Liaden— and none in Trade—Aelliana was very soon adrift and perforce turned her attention to that dismayingly over-full plate.

Mizel laid a simple table and Aelliana was not such a pretender to elegance as her elder brother, to be always dining at the first restaurants. Of the foodstuffs chosen for her, she could reliably identify cheese, fresh vegetables and a thin slice of fruit-bread. All else was mystery.

Well, she thought, brief moments ago brandy had likewise been a mystery, and only see how pleasant that encounter had been.

Indeed, the brandy was displaying ever more beguiling charms. She not only felt warmed, but rather delightfully—unconnected, as if the terrors that had driven her from Mizel's Clanhouse only hours ago had someway ceased to exist. She sighed and reached for a flagrantly unfamiliar morsel, biting into it with a will.

It took very little time, really, to empty the plate of all its delightful mysteries. Sated, Aelliana leaned back in her chair, now and then sipping brandy, and drowsily watching her tablemates, paying no heed to their conversation, even when they happened to be speaking a language she understood.

It occurred to her that she felt *relaxed*, a state she dimly recalled from girlhood, when her grandmother had been alive, before Ran Eld Caylon had discovered the way to bring down the most dangerous of his siblings.

I believe, Aelliana thought, assaying another sip, *that I could come to be quite fond of brandy.*

"Warm now, Scholar?" That was Var Mon. She turned to look at him, shaking her hair back from her face and squarely meeting his eyes.

"Quite warm, I thank you," she said courteously, and saw his wide brown eyes go somewhat wider.

Before she had opportunity to wonder over that, he rose and stepped back with a light bow.

"Will you walk with me? A tour of a gaming house on your arm can only be instructive."

Well, and why not? Such opportunity to observe the laws of her study area operating under field conditions was not to be lightly set aside.

"Certainly."

Putting away her glass, she came easily to her feet, muscles moving sweetly, unencumbered by fear. Some unfamiliar, brandy-created sense told her that Rema had also risen, and she nearly smiled at the Scout's continuing concern.

She wondered if Rema knew about the healing effects of brandy. It seemed likely, Scouts being privy to just such odd knowledge. That being the case, Rema's continued vigilance suggested there was something in the nature of brandy-healing that was perhaps not entirely salubrious.

The thought should have disturbed, but Aelliana allowed it to flow away as she followed Var Mon through the restaurant and into the first of the playing rooms.

The moon was full, shedding more than enough silvery light for a Scout with excellent night vision to find his way through the familiar branches of the Tree.

A steady ten-minute climb brought him to a wooden platform firmly wedged between three great branches.

Daav sat with his back against one of the branchings, carefully folding his legs. Er Thom and he had built this sanctuary as children, a double-dozen years before—it had seemed a vast space indeed, then.

He leaned his head against the warm wood and sighed. As if in echo, a breeze stirred the branches around him. Something fell with a sharp thunk to the board by his hand. He picked it up: A seed-pod.

"Thank you," he said softly to the Tree and opened the pod, cracking the nuts in his fingers and solemnly eating the minty-sweet kernels.

"Oh, gods." He closed his eyes, allowing the tears to rise. Here, there was no one—no thing—save the Tree to know, if he wept.

His coming marriage—that was the smallest source of pain. If the lady were greedy and venial and held him no more than his rank, it was nothing other than he had expected. It was only required that she provide him a healthy child. Did she perform that one service, she might gladly have from him all the jewels and expensive gidgets her heart wished for.

His own child, held warm and safe in his arms—that image filled him with a longing so intense he felt nearly ill with wanting. His own child, upon whom he might lavish the love that threatened to sour, locked up as it was in the depth of his heart. His own child, who might replace the love Er Thom's lifemating had stolen away—

No.

Er Thom loved him no less, and to that mainstay of his life was added Anne's true affection, as well as the rambunctious regard of young Shan, Er Thom's heir. It was no drawing back on Er Thom's part—no slighting on the side of his lifemate—that fed Daav's loneliness. Truth was far more melancholy.

There, with his back against the Tree, Daav owned himself jealous of his brother's joy, and wept somewhat, that he should not be a better man and receive his beloved's joy as his own.

The tears soon spent themselves, for he was not a man who wept often, and he remained leaning against the Tree, his mind open and unfocused.

It was not meet that the new child bear the burden of all Daav's love. Did he discover himself so ill a parent, the child would be fostered into Er Thom's care immediately, there to be loved and disciplined in moderation.

Nor was it reasonable to expect Er Thom—with a lifemate, an heir, and the duties of master trader and thodelm to absorb him—to provide everything his more volatile *cha'leket* required of human contact. Another solution must be found, else Daav would grow bitter, indeed.

For the good of the clan, he thought, yawning suddenly in the cool, mint-tanged air.

He might have dozed—a few minutes, no more— and woke with the shape of an answer in his mind.

He smiled as he considered it, for, after all, it was an obvious step, and one he should have undertaken for himself ere this.

"Thank you," he said once more to the Tree and fancied the leaves moved in slight, ironic bow.

Then, he let himself over the platform's edge and began the climb down.

Chapter Six

Your ship is your life. Stake your air before you stake your ship—and your soul before you stake either.

—Excerpted from Cantra yos'Phelium's Log Book

PLAY WAS DEEP AND AS USUAL VIN SIN CHEL'MARA WAS in the deepest of it, pulling cantra from the pockets of the young fancies-about-town like a magnet pulling iron filings to itself.

He was a wizard with cards, was the chel'Mara, any of his cronies would say so. And it took either a god-kissed or an innocent to sit across from him at the pikit table and lay hand on deck to deal.

The universe being itself, there was no shortage of god-kissed for chel'Mara to fleece, innocents being something rare in the neighborhoods he frequented. Yet it seemed that tonight one had muddled into the depths of Quenpalt's Casino, and stood watching the play with wide, misty eyes.

She was utterly out of place in the jewel-glitter, silk-whisper crowd of players. Her quilted shirt was large and shapeless, fastened tight around her fragile throat. Her only adornment was an antique silver puzzle-ring.

Her hair, dark blonde or light brown, draggled too close around her face, and her eyes, thought yo'Vaade, who saw her first, were gray, or possibly a foggy green.

She stood quiet as a mouse at the side of the table, flanked by two halflings in Scout leather, foggy eyes intent in the thin, hair-shrouded face.

At first he thought it was chel'Mara she was after, so raptly did she watch his play. And why not? He was a well-looking man, and of good Line, though that would matter less to her than the cantra piled before him. The chel'Mara would never consider something so dowdy, yo'Vaade knew, but what harm to let the mouse dream?

Then he saw that it was the *cards* she was watching and frowned to himself. Fastidious as he was in bed-mates, chel'Mara would play against any who sat to table. But surely, thought yo'Vaade, a ragged girl, with scarcely a cantra for her quarter-share, if he was any judge—

"You find the game amusing?"

chel'Mara's query hovered on the edge of Superior to Inferior—proper enough for a High House lordling out of Solcintra when addressing a mouse of unexalted birth. It would have been more gentle to bespeak her otherwise, he being a guest in her city, but the chel'Mara was not a gentle man. He gathered in his latest winnings and stacked the coins before him in careful towers of twelve, hardly sparing a glance at the mouse's thin face.

"I find the game interesting," she returned in an unexpectedly strong voice, and in the mode of Adult-to-Adult. "And I cannot for the life of me, sir, understand why you continue to win."

chel'Mara raised his eyebrows in elegant amusement. "I continue to win because my line of play is superior."

"Not so," she returned with such surety that yo'Vaade

openly stared. "It is a badly flawed line, sir. Indeed, a solid loser, over time."

chel'Mara leaned back in his chair and gazed blandly up into her face.

"How very—interesting," he purred and moved a languid hand, showing table, cards and cantra. "We have before us the means to test your theory."

She hesitated not at all, but came forward and sat in the chair sig'Andir had just vacated. Her guardian Scouts came forward, as well, and stood, one behind each shoulder. "Certainly, sir."

"Certainly," chel'Mara repeated. "But it's a valiant mouse, to sit with the cats!" He bowed, seated as he was, the gesture full with mockery. "What shall you stake, Lady Mouse?"

"My quarter-share," she stated, and produced it—four cantra, which was better than yo'Vaade had thought, but nothing near chel'Mara's more usual stake.

"Four cantra it is," he agreed, plucking a matching amount from his treasury—

"Oh, yes, very handsome!" cried sig'Andir, who was a bitter loser. "The poor lady stakes her entire quarter-share and you match it with four from your hoard! Where's honor in that? Stake something that will pain you as much, should you lose it, and make the play worth her while!"

chel'Mara raised his eyebrows. "I cannot imagine," he drawled, "what could possibly mean as much to me as four cantra does to this—lady."

sig'Andir grinned tightly. "Why not your ship, then?"

"My ship?" chel'Mara turned wondering eyes upon him as a crowd began to gather, drawn by the ruckle.

"It would be done thus," the male Scout said

unexpectedly, "in Solcintra." He grinned, fresh-faced, and bowed to chel'Mara's rank. "My Lord need have no concern of pursuing a *melant'i* stake here. I am assured that Quenpalt's aspires to be the equal of any casino in Solcintra." He raised his voice. "The Stakes Book, if you please!"

There was a shifting of the crowd as the floor-master came panting up with Book and pens.

"A *melant'i* stake," someone of the crowding spectators whispered loudly. "Value for equal value, absolute. Ship against quarter-share."

"Ship against quarter-share!" The information ran the casino. Play stopped at other tables and in the main room, the Wheel was seen to pause. yo'Vaade held his breath.

For a long moment, chel'Mara stared at the Book the floor-master held ready. Then one elegant hand moved, fingers closing around the offered pen. He signed his name with a flourish.

The Book was presented to the mouse, who took the pen and wrote, briefly. The floor-master made the House's notation and stepped back, reverently closing the gilded covers.

Lazily, almost lovingly, chel'Mara replaced his four coins on the proper stack. Likewise, he produced a set of ship keys strung together on a short jeweled chain and lay it gently beside the mouse's quarter-share in the center of the table.

"Ship against quarter-share," he murmured and inclined his head. "Your deal, Lady Mouse."

It was a long game, and the mouse a better player than yo'Vaade would have guessed. Indeed, she won at first, made her four cantra into six—seven. Then chel'Mara found his stride and the mouse's cantra went back across the line, until only one remained her.

yo'Vaade thought it was ended then, but he had reckoned without the Scouts.

Indeed, he had quite forgotten about the Scouts, who had remained standing, silent and patient as leather-clad statues, behind the mouse's chair. It was doubly startling, then, to see the boy lean across the mouse's shoulder, ringless hand descending briefly to tabletop.

He straightened and yo'Vaade looked to the mouse's bank, richer now by three cantra.

chel'Mara frowned into the Scout's face.

"Do you buy in, sir? I had understood this a test of theory between the—lady—and myself."

"Payment of a long-standing debt, Your Lordship," the Scout returned blandly. A murmur ran the crowd.

There was no comment from the mouse. Indeed, there had been no comment from her since play began, she apparently being one who concentrated wholly upon her cards.

A moment longer the chel'Mara stared into the Scout's face.

"I have seen you," he remarked, in such a tone that said, *Having seen you twice, I shall remember you long.*

The Scout bowed. "Indeed. Your Lordship saw me but three nights ago, at the Stardust in Solcintra Port, where Your Lordship was pleased to win the quarter-share of Lyn Den Kochi and certain payments from three future quarter-shares."

chel'Mara lifted an ironic hand. "There are those who are not friends of the luck."

"As Your Lordship says." The Scout returned to stillness and chel'Mara went back to his cards.

"Are you mad?" Rema hissed into Var Mon's ear. "To set her against Vin Sin chel'Mara—"

"My dear comrade, *I* didn't set her against my lord, she set herself. Where's the harm?"

"You ask that, when you saw him ruin Lyn Den? What if she should lose, tipsy as she is?"

"She's winning and you know it. I can almost see where that line of play is going, and you're quicker than I am. Where is she going, Rema?"

"I—am not certain."

"But she's winning."

"Perhaps."

"No perhaps about it," Var Mon asserted, eyes on the fall of the cards. "You don't see it and I don't see it, but Scholar Caylon sees it—and it's her board." He paused as Aelliana took a trick, then continued, softly.

"As for being tipsy—look at her! She looks as she does when she lectures—I should be so cool when I sit to Jump!"

"If he should take exception . . ."

"The cameras are on it," Var Mon told her. "The Scholar's line is fair—she's got the pattern and she's got the break-key, even if her students are too stupid to see it. How can he take exception to a fair line? Stop fretting."

The tempo changed shortly after the Scout's three cantra entered the game.

It was as if, yo'Vaade thought, the mouse had at last found the path she had been seeking, though her previous play had in no way been marred by hesitation.

Now she played with a surety that was awesome to behold, calling the cards to her hand like kin. It took less than an hour for all the coins to cross back over the line, until it was seven on her side and the keys alone, and chel'Mara bidding a Clan Royale.

It was what all the rest had been building toward—this last hand, this locking of wills. The crowd held its breath, and yo'Vaade held his. chel'Mara's face was seen to be damp. The mouse sat cool as water ice, cards a smooth fan between quiet fingers, and called for her seconds.

"Scout's Progress," she announced in that surprisingly clear voice, which was esoteric enough, surely, but no match for a Clan Royale. One by one, she lay the cards out, face up for all to see, and looked over to chel'Mara.

"Ah." He sighed, and a great tension seemed to go out of him all at once, so that yo'Vaade began to feel sorry for the poor, valiant mouse.

chel'Mara's cards came down in a practiced sweep, face up for all to see: Delm, Nadelm, Thodelm, A'thodelm, Master Trader...

"Ship," the crowd whispered among itself. "He's missing the Ship. A broken run... The lady wins..."

"The lady wins," Vin Sin chel'Mara announced, loud enough to be heard in the far corners of the room. He snapped his fingers. "Bring a port-comm!"

"A port-comm!" the crowd babbled. "A port-comm for Lord chel'Mara!"

It came and he tapped in one sequence, then another, and looked over to his erstwhile opponent, who was staring down at her run as if she had never seen cards before.

"Your name?" he inquired neutrally and when she looked up with a start, explained with overdone patience:

"In order to change the registration of the ship, I will need to file your name as new owner."

"Oh," she said, and picked up the keys to frown at before replying. "Aelliana Caylon, Clan Mizel."

There was a flutter of something through the crowd at that, and yo'Vaade considered the taste of the name. It meant nothing to him: it obviously meant nothing to chel'Mara. Behind the mouse's chair, the Scouts preserved attitudes of silent attention.

chel'Mara had recourse to the port-comm's keyboard, finished his entry, tapped the send key and lay the comm aside. He came to his feet and stood gazing down at the mouse. The look in his eyes, thought yo'Vaade, was not good. Not at all good.

"The ship is called *Ride the Luck*," he said. "It is kept at Binjali Repair Shop, Solcintra Port. Ownership entire remits to you at Solcintra dawn. I shall require the hours between to remove my personal effects." He bowed, low and mocking. "I wish you joy of your winnings, Lady Mouse," he said softly.

He turned to go, his eye falling on sig'Andir, who was openly smiling. "Satisfied, sir?" he purred and waited until the smile died and all color drained from the boy's face before he swept away through the crowd, toward the lounge-room and the bar.

"Good evening, Jon."

The man at the desk finished writing out his line before glancing up. As it happened, he needed to glance up quite a way, he being seated and his visitor being somewhat above the average height, for a Liaden male.

He was also dressed in work leathers, his hands

innocent of rank ring, which meant High House gossip was not the purpose of this visit. The spirited dark hair was neatly confined in a tail that hung below his shoulders; from his right ear dangled the twisted silver loop he had earned from the headwoman of the Mun.

He bowed, Student to Master, and straightened; the glow off the desk lamp underlit his sharp-featured face, throwing the black eyes into shadow.

"I need work," he said, speaking in Comrade Mode, which was how they always spoke at Binjali's.

"Hah." Jon rubbed his nose. "Happens we have work." He jerked his head at the window and the repair bays beyond. "Go on out and call yourself to Trilla's attention."

"Thank you."

Another bow and he was gone, walking with a Scout's silent stride, melting out of the light as if he had never been. A moment later, Jon saw him crossing the bay, lifting a hand toward Trilla on the platform. The office noise-proofing was top-grade, so he missed the shout that must have accompanied the gesture. But he saw Trilla wave back and the flicker of hand talk: *Come on up.*

Needed work, did he? Jon thought, between a grin and a worry. He sighed and returned to his papers.

"May I work again tomorrow?"

Jon deliberately finished cleaning his hands, shook the rag and hung it back on its nail.

"We're open to casual labor. You know that."

"Yes. I only wanted to be certain I would not be—inconvenient."

"Inconvenient." Jon grinned, reached out and caught the younger man's elbow, turning him toward the so-called crew's lounge. "Let's have a cup of tea. I'll ask some nosy questions, you'll snatch what remains of my hair from over my ears and we'll part friends, eh?"

The other laughed, a rich, full sound that had pulled Jon dea'Cort's mouth into a grin from the very first time he'd heard it.

"A bargain," he cried and appeared to sober abruptly, glancing sideways from glinting black eyes. "How old is the tea, I wonder?"

"Must be six, seven hours old by now," Jon admitted without shame.

"Perfect."

A few moments later they were both seated on rickety stools. In addition to tea, Jon had helped himself to the last of the stale pastries and was busily dunking it into the depths of his mug.

"How is it, Master Jon, that the mugs never melt?"

"Had 'em made special out of blast glass," Jon returned and disposed of his soggy sweet in two bites. He took a scalding swallow of bad tea and threw his former student a stern look.

"They don't keep you busy enough out in Dragon's Valley, Captain?"

"Alas, they keep me out of reason busy," came the reply. "I swear to you, Master Jon, if I am required to speak to one more Liaden I shall either go mad or strangle him."

Jon laughed. "Spoken like a true Scout! But the fact of the matter is that you're too important a man to either go mad or take it upon yourself to strangle the bulk of the population. Not," he admitted around another gulp of tea, "that most of 'em wouldn't be better for a throttling. But it's out of Code, child: the natives are likely to take issue."

"Understood. And so I ask for work."

"I can give you work. But I'd like to know you're not turning your face from matters needing your attention. There are those things, as we all learn in Basic, that only you can do, Captain. Leave them aside and the world could be a lot worse."

"You terrify me."

"Some respect for your elder, if you please. I can give you work, but is work what you need?"

The other man sipped gingerly at his mug, screwing up his face in comic distaste. "Magnificent," he pronounced, and gave Jon dea'Cort all his black eyes.

"My brother," he murmured, "falls just short of suggesting we remove to New Dublin."

"It delights me to hear your honored kin has, however late in life, come into his heritage," Jon returned with a touch of acid. "Had he anything useful to suggest?"

"You are severe. Yes, something useful."

"But you'll see me damned before you tell me what it was," Jon said comfortably. He finished his tea and rose to transfer the dregs from the pot to his mug.

"All right," he said, resettling on his stool. "You need work, I've got work. Casual schedule; call if you're expected and something forestalls you. But if your self-healing hasn't earned out in a relumma, I will cease to have work, young Captain, and I would then strongly suggest—as a comrade—that you visit the Healers."

"A relumma should be more than sufficient to relocate center. I thank you." The younger man stood, poured his tea down the sink, washed out the mug and put it to drain.

"Until tomorrow, Master Jon."

"Until tomorrow, child. Be well."

Chapter Seven

The number of High Houses is precisely fifty. And then there is Korval.

—From the Annual Census of Clans

"WHAT LONG-STANDING DEBT?" AELLIANA DEMANDED OF a grinning Var Mon as they left the card room.

"Why, only the honor of being allowed to sit at the feet of Aelliana Caylon for an entire semester and catch the jewels as they fell from her lips!" He stopped to bow, coincidentally disrupting the flow of traffic between the card room and the music lounge.

Aelliana frowned. "You are absurd."

"Not to say impertinent," Rema put in, adding a rider to her comrade in a flutter of finger-talk. To Aelliana's eyes, it seemed a list: Twelve variations on the sign for *idiot*. Var Mon laughed.

"You will be very well served if Scholar Caylon pockets your three cantra and says no more," Rema scolded audibly. "How will you come about then?"

"Indeed, no," Aelliana said hastily; "I do not wish to keep Var Mon's money. But it is ill-done to say you are repaying a debt when it is no such thing!"

There was a moment of complete silence, her companions staring at her from rounded eyes.

"Chastised," Var Mon murmured.

"Justly," returned his partner. "Local custom."

"Exactly so." He bowed once more, taking care not to discommode others nearby. "I ask your forgiveness, Scholar," he said in the Mode of Lesser-to-Greater, which was the High Tongue and not a quiver of merriment to be heard. "You are gracious to illuminate my error."

Aelliana considered him, suspecting a joke. The boy's face showed nothing but serious courtesy, and perhaps a touch of anxiety. His three cantra were safe in her right hand, mingling with the jeweled chain and the keys to—the keys to *her* ship.

"You knew that lordship," she said abruptly.

Surprise showed at the corners of his face. "I know his name," he allowed, still in Lesser-to-Greater, "and his reputation."

"Vin Sin chel'Mara," Rema murmured, "Clan Aragon."

Aelliana sighed. She had learned, as any child, the rhymes for Clans and Sigils, Houses and Tasks. But childhood was many years gone and her general grasp of such matters fell far short of the knowledge held by one who moved in the world.

"High House?" was the best she could hazard now, looking at Rema.

The Scout blinked. "Not so high as Korval," she said slowly.

But this was merely a quibble. Who in all the world outranked the Dragon? Even Aelliana knew the answer was, none.

"I—see," she said, the keys hot in her hand.

"The play was clean." That was Var Mon. "We were surrounded by those who know their cards, and the house camera, beside." He grinned, irrepressible boy bursting free of the solemn gentleman he had been a moment before.

"Scholar Caylon, *you* don't say the game was false?"

"The game was entirely true," she said tartly. "Nor was it at all necessary for you to offer your cantra. His Lordship's line was irretrievably flawed." She held out the coins in question. "I thank you for your aid, though it was in no way required."

"Ouch," said Var Mon mildly, and took his money with a bow.

Aelliana shifted in the pulldown tucked between the pilots' stations and inner hatch, and considered her circumstances.

It would appear that she was, in unlikely truth, the owner of a spaceship, which she was even now on her way to inspect.

She closed her eyes, feeling how quick her heart beat. She owned a spaceship; possibilities proliferated.

If it was, as she suspected, a rich man's toy, she would contrive, discreetly, to sell, thus ensuring outpassage and a stake upon which to build her new life.

If, against all expectation, *Ride the Luck* was a working class ship, she would—

She would keep it.

A pilot-owner might find work anywhere, she was tied to no single world. A pilot-owner need owe none, was owned by no one.

A pilot-owner was—free. Alone, independent, autonomous, sovereign . . . Aelliana leaned back in the pulldown chair, stomach cramped with longing.

If *Ride the Luck* was a working ship . . .

Of course, pilot-owners held piloting licenses, which

Aelliana Caylon did not. The life she so avidly envisioned required she be nothing less than a Jump pilot.

"Asleep, Scholar?" Var Mon's voice broke in upon these rather lowering considerations.

"Not entirely," she replied, and heard Rema, at first board, chuckle.

"Good," Var Mon said, unruffled. "We set down in three minutes, unless Rema forgets her protocols. I'll conduct you to Binjali's, if you wish, and make you known to Master dea'Cort."

Aelliana opened her eyes. "Thank you," she said, as a flutter of her stomach reported the ship was losing altitude. "I would welcome the introduction."

"Master Jon! Joy to you, sir!" Var Mon strode into the center of the repair bay, head up and voice exuberant.

Aelliana, trailing by several steps, saw a stocky figure come to the edge of shadow cast by a work-lift, casually wiping its hands on a faded red rag.

"I'm not lending you another cantra, you scoundrel," the figure said sourly, for all the mode was Comrade. "What's more, you're due in Comparative Cultures in twenty minutes and I'll not have it said I was responsible for keeping you beyond time."

"Not a bit of it," Var Mon cried, apparently not at all put out by this rather surly welcome. He reached into his pouch and danced into the shadow. Grasping a newly-cleaned hand, he deposited two gleaming coins on the broad palm and closed the fingers tight.

"Debt paid!" he said gaily and spun, bowing with a flourish that called attention to Aelliana, hesitating yet between light and shadow.

"Master Jon, I bring you Aelliana Caylon, owner of

Ride the Luck. Scholar Caylon, Master Jon dea'Cort, owner of Binjali Repair Shop."

"Caylon?" Master dea'Cort at last stepped forward into the light, revealing a man well past middle years, sturdy rather than stout, his hair a close-clipped strip of rusty gray about four of her slender fingers wide. Eyes the color of old amber looked into her face with the directness of a Scout.

"Scholar Aelliana Caylon," he asked, big voice pitched gently, though he still spoke in Comrade mode, "revisor of the ven'Tura Tables?"

She inclined her head, and answered in Adult-to-Adult. "It is kind of you to recall."

"Recall! How might I—or any pilot!—forget?" He bowed then, distressingly low—the bow of Esteem for a Master—and straightened with his hand over his heart.

"Scholar, you honor my establishment. How I may be allowed to serve you?"

Aelliana raised her hand to ward the reverence in the old man's voice. To know her as the revisor of one of the most important of a pilot's many tools—that was grace, though not entirely unexpected. Jon dea'Cort had undoubtedly been a Scout in former years and Aelliana strongly suspected his "master" derived from "master pilot."

"Please, sir," she said, hearing how breathless her voice sounded. "You do me overmuch honor. Indeed, it is not at all—" Here she hesitated, uncertain how she might proceed with her disclaimer, without calling the master's *melant'i* into question.

"Var Mon, are you here, you young rakehell?" the old man snarled over his shoulder.

"Aye, Master Jon!"

"Then jet, damn you—and mind you're on time for class!"

"Aye, Master Jon! Good-day to you, Scholar. Until Trilsday-noon!"

Var Mon was gone, running silently past Aelliana's shoulder. She heard nothing, then a whine and sigh as the crew door cycled.

"So." Jon dea'Cort smiled, waking wrinkles at eye-corners and mouth. "You were about to tell me that I do you too much honor. How much honor should I lay at the feet of the scholar responsible for preserving the lives of half-a-thousand pilots?"

"Half-a—oh, but that's averaged over the years since publication, of course." Aelliana looked down, tongue-tied and graceless as ever when dealing outside the familiar role of teacher-to-student.

"You must understand," she told her boot-toes. She cleared her throat. "The tables were in need of revision and I was able to undertake the project. To recall my name as the one who did the work—that is kind. But, you must understand, to offer such honor to one who merely—" She faltered, hands twisting about each other.

"I teach math," she finished, lamely.

There was a short silence, before Jon dea'Cort spoke, voice matter-of-fact in Comrade Mode.

"Well, nothing wrong with that, is there? I taught piloting, myself, and to such a thankless pack of puppies as I hope you'll never see!"

Aelliana glanced up, hair swinging around her face. "You are a master pilot."

"Right enough. Most of us are, hereabout." He tipped his balding head to one side, offering another smile. "What might I do for you, math teacher?"

She lowered her eyes, refusing the smile as she refused Comrade Mode.

"I had come to inspect *Ride the Luck*, of which I am owner."

"So my problem-child said," Jon dea'Cort said placidly. "I hadn't known *Ride the Luck* was for sale."

"I—it wasn't." She moved her shoulders. "I won it last evening from Lord Vin Sin chel'Mara—in a round of pikit."

"Beat him at his own game!" Jubilation was plain in Master dea'Cort's voice, from which Aelliana deduced that His Lordship was not a favored patron. "Well done, math teacher! Here, let me fetch the jitney and I'll take you out myself. Beat the chel'Mara at pikit, by gods! I won't be a moment..."

"She's a sweet ship," Jon dea'Cort was saying some minutes later, sending the jitney full-speed down the yard's central avenue. "She's seen some hard times of late, but she's sound. Show her kindness and she'll do very well... Here we are."

The jitney shivered to a stop; Master dea'Cort slid out of the driver's slot and walked toward the ramp.

In the passenger's seat, Aelliana sat and stared, her hands cold and slick with sweat.

"Scholar Caylon?" There was worry in the big voice.

With an effort, Aelliana moved her eyes from the ship—hers, *hers*—to the face of the man standing beside her.

"It's a Jump-ship," she told him, as if such a vital point of information could have someway escaped a master pilot's expert notice.

He glanced over his shoulder and up the ramp, then

returned his amber gaze to her face. "Class A," he agreed gravely, and held out a companionable hand. "Care to see inside?"

She could remember wanting nothing else so much.

"Yes," she said hungrily and slipped out of the jitney, deftly avoiding Jon dea'Cort's touch.

Aelliana brought the board up and watched, rapt, as the ship ran its self-check. Each green go-light added to her wracking store of joy until she found herself clutching the back of the pilot's chair, wet fingers smearing the ivory leather.

The check ended on three chimed notes and she reluctantly touched the off-switch before allowing Jon dea'Cort to lead her further into the ship.

There was a dining alcove containing a gourmet automat, as well as a tiny dispensary housing a premium autodoc.

"Likes everything binjali, the chel'Mara," Master dea'Cort murmured and led her down a short companionway.

Aelliana followed him over the threshold of what should have been the pilot's quarters and stopped short, blinking at mountains of silks, sleeping furs, pillows of every hue and size. The floor was covered in a rug so fine she felt a pang of sorrow for having set her boots upon it. Tapestry gardens burgeoning with ripe fruits made the walls an oasis.

The illumination in the chamber was unusually firm and Aelliana glanced up, expecting to see a light fixture in keeping with the rest.

Instead, she looked up into the room she was standing in, Jon dea'Cort at the door, lined face carefully bland, while her own, reflected without distortion, showed slightly pale, with lips half-parted.

She glanced down, not quite able to stifle the sigh, and spoke over her shoulder.

"Everything binjali?"

"Understand," Master dea'Cort said earnestly, "the chel'Mara's no pilot. Happens he had other uses for a ship. And yon mirrors are top-grade."

"I see." She walked past him and into the room across the hall, which would have been the co-pilot's quarters in any other ship. In this ship, it was the twin of the orgy room. Aelliana sighed again and turned down the light.

"Guess you're ready to see the hold," Master dea'Cort said then, and showed her the way to the access door and how to punch in her code.

The door slid back and the lights came up and the first things she saw again were the damned mirrors. She had just enough time to wonder how anyone could be such a popinjay, when she saw the rest.

Some items she could name—silken cords and leather lashes, a few of the less arcane articles laid neatly in their cases, the swing suspended from the ceiling, the post with its built-in manacles.

Most, however, were unfamiliar: What, for instance, was the purpose of that oddly-shaped table, or the counterbalanced bench or—

Aelliana took a deep breath, turned carefully and lifted her face. Resolutely, she met Jon dea'Cort's eyes, and saw sympathy there.

"Master dea'Cort, I need your advice," she said, yet keeping to Adult-to-Adult.

"Math teacher, ask me."

With an effort, she kept her face up, her eyes steady; her hands were behind her back, twisting themselves into sweat-slicked knots.

"I had—thought," she said, "that I had acquired a working ship. It seems instead that I have acquired a—a bordello. What is your estimate of the time and expense required to restore this ship to its—original specifications?"

"Not a cantra," he said promptly, "and about a three-day—maybe four, depending on the crew I get." He grinned.

"No need to look like I'm pulling teeth," he told her. "I told you the chel'Mara liked everything binjali, eh? The toys are worth something, sold to the right party, and the mirrors—Math teacher, you could refit to spec on the profit from the mirrors alone! Had 'em set on gimbals, so they'd always be oriented, whatever G or spin the ship took on—made out of scanner-glass to withstand take-off stress and not flow—a rare wonder, these mirrors, and there are those who appreciate wonder."

Aelliana closed her eyes, trying to think, to work the steps.

"Do you know the proper—the proper buyers? I confess that I am not—"

"I can act as broker," he said easily. "My fee's ten percent off the top. We'll bring her back up to working weight, deduct labor and parts from what remains and put the profit into your ship's account. Deal?"

She opened her eyes. "Profit?"

"Bound to be a cantra or two left over," he said, looking around the gleaming playground. "Some of the toys are speciality items, and those mirrors haven't gotten any cheaper."

"Oh," Aelliana said, feeling rather adrift. She inclined her head formally. "Thank you, sir. I accept your deal."

"Well enough, then." He waved her out ahead of him.

"Will you be starting to work her at once?" he asked as they went back down the companionway.

"At once? I—I must take the piloting exam," Aelliana said, slowly. "And—flight time..."

There was a slight sound from behind her, as if Master dea'Cort had sneezed.

"You haven't—forgive me. I understand you to say that you have no piloting license."

"Not at the moment," she said, "but I shall be taking the exam—I have classes tomorrow...I shall take the exam on Banim. Second class is required to lift Class A locally, sir, is that correct?"

"Correct."

They had reached the dispensary. Aelliana paused, staring down into the 'doc's opaque hood.

"I shall acquire a second class, then," she said, feeling necessity like a stone in her gut. "I *will* work this ship."

"I don't doubt it," Jon dea'Cort said from beside her. "If you wish, I can test you, or one of my crew. We're all of us master class, as I said. Or call ahead to the Pilot's Guild in Chonselta and be sure they can accommodate you on Banim."

"I believe that will be best," she said, still staring down into the darkness.

"I'll call them now," he said, "while you use the unit here."

She turned sharply. "Use the unit?"

"No sense leaving that untreated when you've the means to mend it," he said, tapping his own wrist. "It's a rare wonder how those little things can eat away at your concentration." He moved down the hall. "I'll just get Chonselta Guild on the line..."

He was gone. Aelliana looked down at the bruises circling her wrist. They seemed more vivid now than they had, hours earlier, outside of Quenpalt's Casino. And, now that she was reminded of them, they did ache.

Well, she thought, with a flash of amused irritation, she was here and the autodoc was here. At the very least, mending the hurt would put a stop to all this rather embarrassing solicitude.

So thinking, she tapped the proper code into the 'doc, rolled back her sleeve and slid the wrist through the open hood.

Chapter Eight

What's in a name? That which we call a rose
By any other name would smell as sweet.
—From Romeo and Juliet, Act ii, Scene 2
William Shakespeare

VIN SIN CHEL'MARA WAS NOT A MAN ACCUSTOMED TO HIS delm's close attention. Most especially, he was unaccustomed to the felicity of receiving such attention during his rather belated breakfast.

"How pleasant it must be," Aragon murmured politely, as tea was poured and set before him, "to sleep so far into the day that one may dispose of noon meal and waking meal in one repast. I quite admire the efficiency of such an arrangement."

Since this particular arrangement had been in force for a number of years without awaking the delm's displeasure, his comment now was doubtless prologue to some other, less amiable, subject. chel'Mara inclined his head, as one acknowledging a pleasantry, and poured himself a second glass of wine.

"The single difficulty I detect in such a system," Aragon pursued, "is that it opens one to disadvantage in the matter of collecting rumor and anecdote—vital

71

work, as I am certain you will agree. For an instance, I had today from Delm Guayar an entirely amusing anecdote out of Chonselta, of all places. Had I adopted your strategy of late sleeping, rather than rising early to attend Lady yo'Lanna's breakfast gather, I should have failed of harvesting this amusing—and instructive—tit-bit."

The chel'Mara schooled his face to calmness; deliberately raised his glass and sipped.

"You are behindhand, Vin Sin," his delm chided softly. "Good manners dictate you allow me the pleasure of imparting my news."

Vin Sin chel'Mara did not reign over Solcintra's deepest tables because he was a fool. Still, there was nothing for it but to allow this trick to fall to Aragon and accept whatever chastisement became his due. He was not in the habit of falling under his delm's displeasure, and he considered the odds favorable for a quick recover.

He inclined his head. "Forgive me, sir. I fear I am dreadfully stupid so early in the day. Whatever came out of Chonselta to amuse you?"

"Why, the drollest tale I've heard in many a breakfast gather," Aragon said composedly. "It seems a certain Quenpalt's Casino has opened in Chonselta Port and it is rumored to stand with the best Solcintra has to offer. Last evening, indeed, much of Solcintra undertook the journey to the far side of the world in order to see this wonder for themselves."

"And was reality as pleasing as rumor?"

Aragon pursed his lips in consideration.

"Rumor and reality appear to have agreed splendidly," he said after a moment. "Quenpalt's is, by all accounts, a casino in which one such as yourself, let us say, may be perfectly at ease."

He paused to sip tea. chel'Mara refrained from his wine.

"To make a long tale short," Aragon resumed gently, "it transpires that—again—one such as yourself was present at Quenpalt's last evening, and, having availed himself of certain monies thrown in his direction by a gentleman who has regrettably never mastered the art of pikit, set himself to contend against a walk-in." Aragon gazed pensively into chel'Mara's face.

"There were some oddities attending this walk-in. She was shabby-dressed, according to report, and plain-spoken, when she spoke at all; she did not offer her name, nor was she asked to give it. She was accompanied by two Scouts—one male, one female, both young.

"The shabby lady declared she would stake her quarter-share, some four cantra, according to my information. The gentleman so like yourself plucked four cantra from his bank—and was forestalled by the person he had just bested, who called to mind—quite properly!—certain delicate points of *melant'i*, in which he was seconded by the male Scout. The Stakes Book was called for and the wager recorded thus: Quarter-share against ship. It was the very first entry, you will be interested to learn, in Quenpalt's Stakes Book." He had recourse to his tea once more. chel'Mara sat like a stone, his hands quite cold.

"So. The shabby lady won her venture—aided once more by the male Scout, who chose, I am a told, an interesting point in the play to settle a debt he had long owed her. The ship of the gentleman so very like yourself changed hands. In the course of recording the win, the shabby lady at last gave her name: Aelliana Caylon."

It was time to have done with this charade. chel'Mara inclined his head with exquisite courtesy.

"So she did."

"So she did," his delm echoed gently. "And, having now heard it twice, the name yet awakes no interest. I fear, Vin Sin, that you have not been as close a student of the world as I had always supposed."

chel'Mara swallowed a sharp return, preserving a courteous countenance with—some—effort.

"Aelliana Caylon," Aragon continued, after a moment spent savoring the last of his tea, "is the third child of the four borne by Birin Caylon, who has the honor to be Mizel." He moved his shoulders. "Mizel totters on the edge of mid-House. It is my notion that it will tumble into Low House, when the present nadelm comes to his own. But that is not the card we must trump."

"Aelliana Caylon," the chel'Mara suggested, with delicate irony, "supports the tottering fortunes of her clan by performing—card tricks, shall we say?"

Aragon raised a considering brow. "It might do," he allowed gently, "although I believe the lady's range to be somewhat wider than mere—card tricks." His eyes sharpened. "Do the ven'Tura Tables wake recollection, Vin Sin?"

"Certainly."

"Ah, delightful. You will then be able to tell me the name of the author of the revision, dated, I believe, eight years ago?"

chel'Mara frowned. "The name? Truly, sir, it was merely this scholar or that. No one I've met."

"Until last evening. How unfortunate, that you were not able to give Honored Scholar of Subrational Mathematics Aelliana Caylon her full bow, upon introduction." Aragon leaned forward, hands flat on the pale cloth.

"The foremost mathematical mind on the planet," he said, very softly, indeed, "who makes the study of random event her *speciality*. Her thesis—a classic in the field, so Guayar assures me—was entitled, *Chaotic Patterning in Pseudorandom Events*. In it, the scholar demonstrates the manner in which one may predict card-fall, based upon an ordered diminishment of pooled possibility, as one might find when playing pikit." He leaned back, with a soft sigh.

"By happenstance—I place it no higher!—the pattern which gains the final prize in Scholar Caylon's illustration is *Scout's Progress*. This is the woman you thought to best at pikit, Vin Sin. Are you not diverted? I assure you that Guayar, who made it his business to be at my side throughout the gather, found the tale amusing in the extreme. Indeed, he repeated it to everyone."

The chel'Mara grit his teeth and met his delm's eye steadily.

"But you do not smile!" Aragon said, sitting back in sudden ease. "My tit-bit has not amused. Never mind, I have an addendum calculated to please. You recall the Scouts?"

"Indeed, sir, I recall them—specifically."

"Ah, then you will certainly know their names."

chel'Mara raised a brow. "Whatever for?"

His delm lifted an admonitory finger. "Now that was careless. One should always know the names of those with whom one is engaged in an affair of Balance. How fortunate it is that I am able to supply you with this vital information. The name of the female Scout is Rema ven'Deelin, Clan Ixin—High House, you perceive. The male is Var Mon pin'Aker, Clan Midys—solidly mid-House. He and Corporal ven'Deelin are partnered. He likewise has the honor of standing *cha'leket* to one Lyn Den Kochi, whose quarter-share was tragically left behind at Sunrise House three—possibly four—nights ago."

There was silence. chel'Mara stared down into the dark depths of his wine, considering the trap and the skill with which it had been sprung.

Certainly, a *cha'leket* might undertake Balance on behalf of his foster-kin. That the trap had been set with skill and something of wit made it no easier to bear.

"A nameless lady attended by Scouts approaches your table and calls your play into question before all the world," Aragon said pensively. "Did it not occur to you, Vin Sin, that you might—just possibly—have been set up?"

"Alas, sir, it did not. An error, I admit."

"Do you? But how gracious you are!" The bite of irony in his delm's voice brought chel'Mara's eyes up.

Aragon held his gaze, allowing him to see anger.

"I shall say no more of your carelessness in this matter of last evening," Aragon said in clipped tones, "except that I find you well-rewarded in the loss of your vessel—and that I see no necessity for Aragon to Balance the Caylon's most valuable lesson to yourself. Of this other, however—you will tell me, Vin Sin, if you habitually prey upon halflings and innocents."

chel'Mara felt a flicker of his own anger and lowered his eyes, lest it be seen.

"As you say, sir, the lady was no innocent. For

Master Kochi—I fear he forced the matter and then did not know when to bow away."

"And you, most naturally, gave him no hint, but continued to play until he had lost not merely this quarter's share but significant amounts from future shares. You waited, in fact, for his *cha'leket* to comprehend the situation and act to end it. After all, Master Kochi has the accumulated wisdom of seventeen entire Standards to support him. His *cha'leket*, I believe, is every day of eighteen."

"He was cleared to play," chel'Mara said flatly. "Am I to be held as nanny for every babe with the means to buy a deck?"

"I see. You consider that fleecing children adds to your *melant'i*. I am desolate to inform you that your delm considers otherwise. You will restore Master Kochi to his quarter-share and relieve him of the burden of future debt. You will accomplish these things before Prime meal this evening. I do expect you to dine at home this evening, Vin Sin."

chel'Mara allowed surprise to show. "Certainly I shall undertake your orders regarding Master Kochi, sir. However, I am engaged to dine with—"

"Cancel it." Aragon held out his empty cup and chel'Mara, perforce, poured tea. His delm sipped. "Excellent. Yes." He set the cup aside and met chel'Mara's eyes with a cool smile.

"You think me harsh, but indeed my concern is solely for yourself, that you have opportunity to take proper leave of your close-kin."

"Leave-taking?" The chel'Mara fairly gaped. "I have no plans to travel, sir."

"Ah, I have been maladroit! Your delm, Vin Sin,

requires you to travel on business of the clan. A bunk has been reserved in your name aboard *Randall's Renegade*, which breaks orbit an hour before Solcintra midnight. Prime has been set up an hour, to accommodate the necessity of your early departure."

chel'Mara sat still, the chill having moved from his hands to his belly.

"If I have indeed purchased so large a share of my delm's displeasure in the matters of Master Kochi and Scholar Caylon, I am of course desolate," he said, speaking gently, indeed. "But—sent off-world on a Terran trampship? Surely, sir—"

Aragon held up a hand. "You are about to say that such a measure is over-Balance, are you not? I repeat that the Caylon's instruction on her own behalf surpasses anything I might undertake for her. As for Master Kochi, I believe a return of his losses and relief from the specter of indebtedness shall settle his account fairly, with additional benefit accruing him through the vehicle of a very stern fright." He sipped tea. "Yes, I think we emerge a little to the good from your encounter with Master Kochi."

"Then this travel, this—ship . . ."

"Ah, yes." He leaned back in his chair, hands cradling his cup. "Guayar and I are well-known to each other," he said, at what one who did not know him might consider a tangent. "We are not *comrades*, you understand—the interests of our Houses but rarely intersect. And yet, I have known Guayar many years, since before ever the Ring was set upon his finger. His is a stringent *melant'i*, I do allow you that. But I have never known him *spiteful*, Vin Sin, nor inclined to go beyond verifiable certainties in discussion."

chel'Mara reached for his glass, downed the half of it in one swallow. It met the roil in his belly like oil poured on live flame.

"So," Aragon said softly. "I offered Guayar a ride to his next appointment as we left yo'Lanna's, which he was gracious enough to accept. His grace extended to a recitation of some of your past activities, and a candid avowal of concern."

chel'Mara cleared his throat. "Surely, sir, rumor and—"

"I spent the remainder of my morning verifying Guayar's information," Aragon continued, "which was—illuminating." He raised his eyes and chel'Mara could not look away.

"You may not be aware of certain inclinations of Aragon's fortunes—indeed, you concern yourself so little with the business of the House, that I am persuaded you cannot know!—but for the past several years we have been in a state of—mild, but worrisome—disadvantage. Interest rates rise by a point. Warranty periods are made shorter. Surcharges are added to the most commonplace of orders. Contract renewals are written so tightly one might almost suppose dea'Gauss himself had put his hand upon each. And I wondered, Vin Sin. I wondered, why. Guayar has shown me the answer, and I count myself in his debt."

"Sir—"

"No less than *three* delms of clans with which we do business regularly lost—catastrophically lost—to you at play—two of them when they were no older than Master Kochi. Four thodelms, an equal number of nadelms—and this does not begin to account for the favored youngers and *cha'lekets* who have been dealt public humiliation at your table since you reached your majority." He sighed, abruptly.

"I had known you were expensive. It is my error, that I failed to know *how* expensive. Now that I am informed, my duty is plain. It may be that the clan can yet recover something of value from you. The attempt must be made, else I am remiss in my duty to those others I hold in care."

The chel'Mara sat with his hands in his lap, thinking, *this cannot be happening.* And yet, incredibly, his delm continued, as if he were in verymost earnest.

"You will be aboard *Randall's Renegade* this evening, Vin Sin. My own car will bear you to the shuttle. In due time, you will be set down upon Aedryr, where you will be met by your aunt my sister Sofi pel'Tegin, who will conduct you to the family holding and instruct you in your responsibilities. I will tell you that I believe those responsibilities will at first have to do with mastering the recipes of various soil mixtures required to sustain the plants grown at the holding. The major portion of the holding's income derives from these same plants, so you will readily understand that a thorough knowledge of soil is of utmost importance."

chel'Mara licked his lips. "Uncle . . ."

Aragon reached into his sleeve and produced a card.

"Your identification card. I council you to guard it closely, as it is necessary to present it whenever you wish to travel beyond the land to which you are registered."

The card was extended toward him. chel'Mara raised an arm grown heavy with dread and forced nerveless fingers to grip the slick plastic. He took a rather ragged breath and looked into his delm's face.

"How long?"

Aragon sipped the last of his tea and put the cup down. "Your aunt appears confident that you will be able to master the intricacies of the House's business on Aedryr in five Standard years. I leave it to her judgment, if you require a longer curriculum."

"Five Standards." On a *farm*? Mastering the mixtures of *soils*? It was a jest. It must be a—

Aragon rose. chel'Mara rose as well and made his bow, barely attending what he did.

"Until Prime, then," Aragon said, and turned. Halfway down the room, he checked, as if he had bethought himself of something else. chel'Mara sighed, feeling his heart lift, for now, surely, his delm would reveal the jest and—

"I had almost forgot, Vin Sin, the most diverting thing imaginable! Do you care to hear?"

He forced his lips into a smile and bowed lightly. "Why, certainly, sir."

"Ah, good. This planet—Aedryr. Gaming is unlawful by order of the planetary government. Anyone found with so little as a deck of cards in his possession is favored with a Standard of government labor, no appeal. Is it not amusing? Good day to you."

Aragon was gone.

chel'Mara sank down into his chair and closed his eyes, the thin plastic card gripped tight between his fingers.

He had never felt less like laughing.

It was early afternoon in Chonselta.

Aelliana began the walk from the train station to Mizel's Clanhouse with an absurdly light heart. The

keys to her ship hung about her neck on a chain
provided by Jon dea'Cort.

Using Binjali's comm, she had verified the transfer
of ownership, opened a ship's account with the Port
Master's Office and transferred her hoarded bonus
money from Chonselta Tech's in-house bank.

She had perused *Ride the Luck's* regular maintenance records, finding also that the ship's berthing
at Binjali Repair Shop was paid a full year ahead.

"Shall I refund that amount to Lord chel'Mara?"
she had asked Jon dea'Cort doubtfully.

The old Scout snorted. "Ship paid the berthing fee
out of its former account. The chel'Mara's arrangement was that he paid in advance without benefit of
refund, should he decide to berth elsewhere. Your
luck, math teacher."

"I suppose..."

She had been introduced to Master dea'Cort's
apprentice, a compact and cheerful person who spoke
with a marked Outworld accent.

"Trilla, give greeting to Aelliana Caylon, math
teacher and owner of *Ride the Luck.*"

"Aelliana Caylon." The bow was crisp and matter-
of-fact, augmented by a smile and a flash of bright
eyes. "Good lifting."

"Thank you," Aelliana said, returning the bow with
relief. No embarrassing respect from Trilla, thank
gods; merely a very Scout-like acceptance of what was.

Departing Binjali's, she had not forgotten to stop at
the Ormit Fund's Office and make disposition of her
quarter-share before catching the ferry to Chonselta.

Now, heading home lighthearted and not a bit
weary, she re-assessed her position.

By her reckoning, she had one year to achieve a first class piloting license, learn Terran and garner what money she might. The delm had given her a year, after all, to prove her point regarding the investment of funds. Ran Eld would be held in check for precisely that long, saving Aelliana did nothing to provoke him or to arouse his suspicions.

So be it. She had ten years' practice of appeasing Ran Eld. For *Ride the Luck*—for freedom—she could endure one year more.

She walked up Raingleam Street, rapt and unseeing, so that her sister's voice gave her a severe start.

"Aelliana!" Sinit caught her sleeve and tugged her hurriedly up-street. "Come in the back way, do. Ran Eld's got his eye on the front door." She giggled. "Primed to ring down a terrifying scold!"

She turned stricken eyes to her sister's face. "What have I done now?"

"Well, you didn't come down to breakfast," Sinit said, turning into the back courtway, Aelliana firmly in tow. "That annoyed him. He sent Voni up to rouse you, but you weren't in your room. That annoyed him even more—you know what Ran Eld is. Then it transpired you weren't in the house at all!" She grinned and paused to work the latch on Mizel's gateway.

"Voni says your bed hadn't been slept in. *She* says you have a lover." She looked up, eyes brimming laughter. "Ran Eld's not about to stand for that!"

"A lover?" Aelliana stared, stone-still. "Voni thinks I have a lover?"

"Why not?" Sinit asked matter-of-factly. "Go in— quickly! Up the serving stairs and into your room—and mind you remember to come down to Prime!" She gave Aelliana a firm push and turned back to latch the gate.

For one long moment, Aelliana hesitated, heart pounding.

Then she turned and flew into the house, taking the thin back stairs two at a time.

Silent as a Scout, she negotiated the short hallway leading to her rooms, slipped inside and—futile gesture!—locked the door behind her.

She affected not to see the house comm's blinking message-waiting light, opaqued the windows and crossed to the narrow bed.

Fully clothed, she lay upon the coverlet, closed her eyes—and slept.

Chapter Nine

...by this note convey said land and building to the Liaden Scouts for the purpose of establishing an academy and training center for future Scouts and those whom the Scouts deem it wise to train...
—Excerpted from a Contract of Gift
signed by Jeni yos'Phelium,
Ninth Delm of Korval

"WE MISSED YOU AT BREAKFAST, SISTER." RAN ELD'S VOICE was sweet and mild—a bad sign.

Aelliana set her teacup down and kept her eyes on her plate. They were four at table, the delm having sent word that she would join them later.

"Such an unusual happenstance," Ran Eld pursued. "Our sister was concerned for your health. Imagine her surprise when she entered your room and found you absent, the coverlet smooth atop the bed."

"I am grateful to my sister for her care," Aelliana told her plate, though the words felt like to choke her.

"Very proper, I am sure," Voni snapped from her place up-table. "But that does not address where you were all the night, Aelliana."

"Where would I be?" Aelliana wondered softly.

85

"Exactly what I wish to know!" her sister said sharply. "Really, Aelliana, I suppose you will deny that your bed had not been slept in!"

"Not at all. I—" she focused on a grayish square of vegetable pudding. "I was up much of the night, considering the wisest investment of my quarter-share. This morning I placed the funds as seemed best." She cleared her throat and reached for the teacup. "I did not wish to be behindhand in obeying the Delm's Word."

There was a charged pause, before Ran Eld's voice, very dry: "Commendable."

"Well, I think it is commendable," Sinit announced from her seat at the foot of the board. "Truly, Ran Eld, you make it seem a crime to heed the delm's wishes! The Code tells us plainly—"

"Thank you, little sister. I believe my comprehension of Code may be—somewhat—superior to your own."

"Oh, then you know you're making a stupid twitter over none of your concern," Sinit cried in a tone of broad enlightenment. "I, for one, am greatly relieved. You mustn't mind them, Aelliana—Ran Eld's in a temper and Voni's snipe-ish because Lady pel'Rula found fault with her dress."

"You were listening at the door!" Voni's voice shook in outrage. "I shall tell mother. Of all—"

Through the shield of her hair, Aelliana saw Sinit smile.

"Lady pel'Rula said Voni's dress was immodest, and not at all what one looked for in a lady of impeccable manner." The smile broadened to a grin. "It was, too."

"What do you know of the matter?" Voni snarled. "That design was copied from a gown created for yos'Galan! If Lady pel'Rula is so provincial that she turns her face from a look sanctioned by Korval—"

"Then she's well-rid of," Sinit suggested, eyes wide.

Voni frowned and extended a graceful hand for her wine glass. "Naturally not. Mother and I are to call upon Her Ladyship tomorrow after luncheon."

"And you'll wear a less dashing dress, won't you, Voni?"

Aelliana saw Voni's fingers tighten on the stem of her glass, knuckles paling. She answered in a voice rigid with fury.

"You need not concern yourself with my wardrobe, Sinit. I shall consider it an impertinence if you continue."

"Sinit, let be," Aelliana whispered urgently.

"Excellent advice." Ran Eld said, voice cloying as sugared tea. "How good of you to overwatch your sister, Aelliana, and drop these little hints in her ear. Allow me to perform the same service on behalf of yourself."

Aelliana reached for her teacup. It was empty. She swallowed hard in a dry throat and folded her hands onto her lap, eyes on her untasted dinner.

"Certainly," she said, hearing her voice tremble. "I welcome instruction from one so much my elder, and who is accustomed to going about in the world."

"Yes, you're not much used to the world, are you?" Ran Eld murmured, swirling his wine. "One tends to forget just how ill-suited you are to caring for even so small a portion of the clan's *melant'i*. But, there. If those who are wiser do not pause to instruct their inferiors, the wiser must share in the fault, when the inevitable disgrace occurs." He sipped, waiting.

Aelliana clenched her hands about each other. "As you say," she whispered.

Voni giggled and helped herself to another spoonful of baked melon.

"Precisely," Ran Eld said, lazily. "No, Sinit, *don't* speak, I pray you. Aelliana and I have quite agreed that she welcomes my tuition." He finished off his wine and set the glass aside, pushed plates, bowls and sauce-thimbles back and folded his arms atop the cloth.

"Look at me," he murmured, leaning forward.

Teeth-grit, she raised her head, met his eyes with a flinch.

"So." He smiled, not pleasantly. "Scouts, Aelliana."

She stared at him, speechless, saw his mouth tighten with impatience and blurted, "I teach Scouts."

"Precisely," he purred, mouth easing with satisfaction. "You teach Scouts, for which you receive a wage. A regrettable necessity. However, necessity ends with the ending of the school-day. There is no need for—and, indeed, very good reason to refrain from—association—with Scouts."

"Scouts are not our kind," Voni elucidated, perhaps for Sinit's benefit. "Scouts, pilots, mechanics—it all comes down to bad manners, oily fingers and dirty faces. I hope no one of Mizel is so foolish as to credit such disreputable persons with heroism and vast knowledge. Heroism is a great piece of nonsense. I infinitely prefer good manners."

A flicker of mind pictures: Jon dea'Cort tidily wiping his broad hands on a red rag; Rema's spotless leathers and courteous concern; Var Mon's scrubbed-til-it-shone, mischievous boy-face . . .

"I—"

Ran Eld raised a hand and leaned closer across the table, eyes leveled like lasers.

"Scouts are not fit companions for one of Mizel. For *anyone* of Mizel," he said, spacing his words as if her ears were defective—or her wits. "Do you understand me, Aelliana?"

Bow the head, she told herself, desperately. *Be meek. Remember. Remember your ship.*

"I understand you," she whispered, heartbeat pounding in her temples.

"Well, what have we here, a tableau?" Birin Caylon stood in the doorway. She raised a hand on which Mizel's Clan Ring gleamed and stabbed a finger toward her son.

"Ran Eld is the insatiable cat about to eat the unfortunate mouse, portrayed by Aelliana—so!" She dropped her hand and came into the room. "Did I guess correctly?"

Ran Eld laughed and eased back into his chair. "Correct as always, Mother!"

"Indeed, ma'am," Voni ventured, rising to hold the delm's chair, "we were merely striving to show Aelliana and Sinit the unsuitability of associating with Scouts and other such persons."

"A cup of wine, Ran Eld, if you please—and a saucer of soup, if any remains."

Provided with these, she tasted her wine before turning her attention to her middle daughter, who sat yet in her pose of mouse-about-to-be-devoured. Birin Caylon felt a stir of compassion. The child looked unwell, her thin face was pinched and there were great bruised circles under her misty eyes.

Abruptly, Birin wondered if a particular Scout might be the subject of this lesson in appropriate behavior. She had a spoonful of soup. *Really*, she thought, *Ran Eld is too hard on the girl.*

"No doubt but that Scouts are odd-tempered," she said, after another spoon of soup. "I recall your father, Aelliana. What that man was for questions! He would babble on concerning a certain mix of tea, or the practice of drinking morning-wine only in the morning, or whether cats told jokes. He found the most mundane affairs cause for high amusement. Very nearly he drove me to distraction—and he merely trained at Academy and not a true Scout at all!" She sighed.

"Your grandmother, who was of course delm at that time, found him unexceptional. For his part, he showed her great deference and spoke highly in her praise, so he was not lost to proper feeling at all, as some claim of Scouts."

"And yet you do not deny that he, as all Scouts, was odd in his manner," Ran Eld said.

"No," said Birin, frowning after her thoughts. "No, my son, I cannot deny that he was considerably out of the common way. At the time, I suspected him of laughing at me. However, I have come to see that much of his oddness must be laid to his training." She paused.

"It is necessary for those who would take up the chancy duties Scouts claim for themselves to undergo rigorous and specialized education, the better to survive in the wide universe. It is to be regretted that an effect of attaining excellence in this curriculum must also make one—different.

"I have heard it said that Scouts are other than Liaden—that of course is nonsense. What I believe is that Scouts are burdened with an understanding that takes into account not only Liad, but the universe entire." She reached for her wine. "I believe such understanding sets them apart forever from those who look no further than Liad."

"Then you credit Scouts with heroism, do you, ma'am?" Sinit's voice carried clear amusement and Birin turned to frown at her.

"I credit Scouts with other-ness," she said sternly, "and perhaps with loneliness. It is possible that there is something to be learned from them, should one have the ability to grasp it. Not all do—which is no shame. Nor is there shame in finding that one has that certain ability." She moved her gaze to Ran Eld, sitting attentive beside her.

"I find no disgrace in the companionship of Scouts."

He inclined his head politely. Satisfied, Birin returned to her soup.

The silence was broken by the scrape of a chair. Aelliana rose and made her bow.

"If you please, ma'am. I have student work to review."

Birin waved a hand. "Certainly. Good evening, daughter."

"Good evening," the girl whispered and pushed her chair to, leaving a full plate of food and an empty teacup behind.

At the door of the dining hall, she paused and spun, one hand outflung. The silver ring that had belonged to her grandmother caught the light; lost it.

"Please, ma'am," she said breathlessly. "What came of him?"

Birin glanced up with a frown. "Of whom?"

"My—my father."

"Child, however should I know what came of him? I last saw him twenty-seven years ago, when we signed the completion of contract."

"Oh." Her shoulders drooped inside the cocoon of her shirt. "Of course. Good evening, ma'am."

"Good evening, Aelliana," Ran Eld called dulcetly, but the doorway was empty.

"He did what?" Var Mon stared at his *cha'leket* in patent disbelief. "Have you gone mad?"

"No, but my Lord chel'Mara doubtless has!" Lyn Den crowed. He flung himself into his *cha'leket's* arms and kissed his cheek. "Come and rejoice, darling, I needn't join the Terran mercenaries, after all!"

"As if they'd have you," Var Mon retorted grumpily, "or as if you'd live a day in battle, if they did. And the office of informing your father doubtless falling to myself. Lyn Den, are you certain it was Vin Sin chel'Mara?"

"Am I likely to forget his face?" the other asked, spinning about in sheer exuberance. "Hello, Rema."

"Lyn Den." She inclined her head and came to stand at Var Mon's side, her face serious. "How do you go on?"

"Delightfully. Deliriously. I have had the best fortune imaginable, could I but convince this brute of a *cha'leket* that my mind is firm."

"Or as firm as ever it has been," Var Mon muttered. Rema smiled, briefly.

"What's come about? Has your father redeemed your debt?"

"Better—a dozen times better! Vin Sin chel'Mara himself met me after my early class—only imagine His Lordship cooling his heels in a university hallway! He met me, I say, and returned my entire loss, with a paper stating I owed him nothing in the future; that anything I might have come to owe him in the past is forgiven. Here—" He pulled a much-folded piece of vellum from his sleeve—"read it for yourself."

Var Mon snatched the paper free and unfolded it. Rema put her head against his and together they scanned the brief document.

"His signature, certain enough," she murmured, fingering the drop of orange wax and pendant silver ribbon. "Sealed up proper as you please."

"Well." Var Mon re-folded the page and thrust it back to his foster-brother, setting his face into a most un-Var Mon-like frown.

"I judge you've encountered an unreasonable bit of good luck. One only hopes that the fright you've had will be sufficient to keep you out of gaming-houses for the rest of your days."

"Oh, indeed. I intend to live retired and entertain but rarely, and that at home."

"Laugh, do," Var Mon said, severely. "Rema and I are a twelve-day away from our solo examinations. Have the grace to grant me ease of mind where you are concerned. Or must I leave Academy and appoint myself your keeper?"

"There, old thing, don't take on!" Once more, Lyn Den flung into Var Mon's arms. He lay his cheek against the leather-clad shoulder. "I'll be good, darling, never fear it. Truly, I've learnt my lesson—if I never see a deck of cards again it will be some days too soon for my taste!"

"Well." Var Mon allowed himself a tender smile as he set his *cha'leket* back. "Mind you stay wary. You'd best get on, now. We're bound for piloting practice— and you have your afternoon classes to consider."

"Monster." Lyn Den grinned, sobered. "Shall I see you again, before you leave for your solo?"

"Of course," Var Mon said. "You know I daren't leave planet without making my bow to my mother your aunt."

"True enough," Lyn Den laughed and swept a bow. "Pilots. Good lifting."

"Take care, Lyn Den," Rema called, as he ran lightly down the Academy's front ramp. She glanced aside and met Var Mon's puzzled eyes.

"A peculiar course for His Lordship to plot," she commented.

Var Mon sighed. "Do you know, I was only just now thinking that exact thought."

Chapter Ten

There shall be four levels of pilot acknowledged by the Guild. The base level, or Third Class, shall be qualified for work within system and orbit, operating ships not above Class B.

Mid-level, or Second Class, shall be qualified to lift any ship to Class AA within system and orbit.

A pilot holding a First-Class license shall be competent in accomplishing the Jump into and out of hyperspace.

Master Pilot is one able to perform all aspects of piloting with excellence. This grade may undertake to train and test any of the lower three levels.

For the purposes of these by-laws, Scout-trained pilots shall be understood to hold a license equal to Master Pilot.

—Excerpted from the By-laws of the Pilots Guild

THE TESTING CHAMBER WAS FAMILIAR, EVEN COMFORTING. In just such a cubicle had she taken her university placement tests, winning a full mathematics scholarship to the University of Liad.

Even the problems that flashed so quickly across the screen were comforting. There were no mysteries here; no danger. No doubt.

Aelliana's fingers flew across the keyboard, structuring and restructuring the piloting equations as required. She hesitated when the focus of testing shifted from practical application to law and regulation, blinked, shifted thought-mode and went on, speed building toward a crescendo.

The screen went blank. A chime sounded, startling in the sudden absence of key-clicks.

"Part One of your examination is completed," a mechanical voice announced from the general area of the cubicle's ceiling. "Please await your examiner with the results."

Aelliana sat back in the squeaky chair, hands folded sternly in her lap, head slightly bent, eyes on the quiet keys.

She felt no anxiety regarding this initial phase of testing. The piloting problems had been quite ordinary, almost bland. The abrupt change from math systems to regulatory language had startled her, but the questions themselves had been entirely straightforward.

She was less sanguine regarding her ability to perform satisfactorily at a live board. It was true that she had lifted and landed a Jump-ship. It was equally true that she had done so exactly thrice, each time monitored closely by Scout Lieutenant Lys Fidin, one of her most brilliant—and outrageous—students.

Within the shelter of her hair, Aelliana smiled. Lys had taken advanced training, gaining for herself the ultimate prize. When she left Liad it had been as a First-In, among the best the Scouts possessed, trained to go alone into uncharted space, to make initial contact with unknown cultures, to map unexplored worlds and star systems.

It had been Lys who attempted to convince her teacher to "go for Scout," and would hear nothing like "no" when it came to Aelliana's lifting a live ship.

"Theory's all very well," the Scout insisted. "But, damn it, Aelli, you can't teach pilots survival math without ever having a ship in your hands!"

Lys won that effort, and lift a ship Aelliana did.

The next campaign had been for Aelliana's enlistment in a piloting course, which came to a draw: Ran Eld would certainly have denied such an expenditure from his sister's wages and might well have felt moved to make a retaliatory strike to remind her of his authority.

So, Aelliana audited Primary Piloting at Chonselta Tech, read the manuals from basic to expert, worked with the sim-boards in the piloting lab—and with that Lys had to be satisfied.

"Scholar Caylon." The door to the cubicle slid back with a rush, revealing Examination Officer Jarl. He bowed.

"I am pleased to report that you have flawlessly completed the initial testing. If you will accompany me to the simulation room, you may commence the second segment of the examination."

Once again scene and task were familiar, clear and comforting. Indeed, Aelliana found the sim sluggish, less sprightly than the board she still worked from time to time in the piloting lab.

The slow response threw her off-balance during the systems check and clearance operations. By the time it became necessary to engage the gyros and lift, she had largely adjusted to the slower pace, though the sluggard navcomp irritated. In the end, she simply ran the equations herself, feeding the numbers into the board and executing required maneuvers without bothering to wait for the comp's tardy verification.

She attained the prescribed orbit and, as before, the screen went abruptly blank. A chime sounded, the webbing retracted and the hood lifted. Aelliana stepped out into the larger room.

Examination Officer Jarl, who had been monitoring her progress in the master-sim, cleared his throat.

"Very quick—ah—Scholar. I note you were routinely ahead of the navcomp."

"The comp was slow," Aelliana said, hanging her head. "It was much more efficient to simply do the calculations myself and feed them in manually." She paused, gnawing her lip. "Shall I be penalized, sir?"

"Eh?" He coughed. "Oh, no. No, I don't believe so, Scholar. Though I must remind you that Port regs insist a ship's navcomp be engaged and online during lift and orbiting."

"Yes, sir," Aelliana whispered. "I will remember."

"Good," he said, rising and rubbing his hands together. He looked at her askance, as if she had suddenly grown a second head, then made his bow.

"As before, Scholar, a flawless—if slightly irregular—performance. I believe it is time for you and I to walk out to the field and see what you might make of the test-ship."

"Yes," Aelliana said and followed him out of the sim-room, head down and stomach churning.

Aelliana initiated the system checks and webbed into the pilot's chair, nervously double-checking the calibrations in her head. She brought the navcomp online and ran a test sequence, comparing the computer's results against her own.

Satisfied to six decimal places, and relieved to find this board more lightsome than the sim, she glanced over to the examination officer, who was webbed into the co-pilot's station.

"I am here as an observer, Scholar," he said, folding his hands deliberately onto his knee. "If difficulties ensue, or if it becomes obvious that ship's control is not firm, I shall override your board. If that should occur, it will be understood that you have failed the third phase of testing and may retest in twelve days. In the meanwhile, I am barred from answering any questions you may ask, or from offering any aid save override and return to berth. Is this clear?"

"Sir, it is."

"Good. Then I will tell you that I expect to arrive in Protocol Orbit Thirteen within the next local hour. Once stable orbit has been achieved, you will receive instruction for return to planet surface. You are cleared to proceed."

Aelliana took a deep breath, shook her hair back and opened a line to Chonselta Tower.

Stable P-13 orbit was achieved in just under one local hour. The lift was without incident. Aelliana paid scrupulous attention to her navcomp and charted a course remarkable for its dignity.

It must be said that several times during this stately and undemanding progress Aelliana found herself computing quicker, less grandmotherly approaches. Once, indeed, her hand crept several finger-lengths in the direction of the communications toggle, while her mind was busy formulating the change of course she would file with the Tower.

She pulled back with a gasp and continued the course as filed.

"Protocol Orbit Thirteen achieved, Master Pilot," she murmured, tapping in the last sequence and relaxing against the webbing. "Locked and stable."

"So I see." Examination Officer Jarl spun his chair to face her. "You disappoint me, Scholar. After such a run at the simulation, I had expected a lift like no other."

She swallowed, forcing herself to meet his eyes. "This navcomp is more able, sir."

"That would account for it, naturally," he said with a certain dryness. He glanced at his board, then sent a sharp gaze into her face. "Tell me, Scholar, how much time could have been saved, had you filed that change of course mid-lift?"

"I—As much as five-point-five minutes, sir. Perhaps six, depending upon precise orientation with regard to orbit approach."

"I see," he said again. "Yet you chose to continue the course first filed, despite significant time variation. I wonder why."

Aelliana inclined her head. "The safety factor was slightly higher," she murmured, "as well as the chance of absolute success. It is—important—that I gain my license, sir. I dared risk nothing that might endanger a positive outcome."

"Dared not put your license on the line, eh? Forgive me, Scholar, but this is not promising news. Surely you know that a pilot's first concern is for passengers and for ship. If he loses his license preserving either, that is regrettable, but necessary."

Aelliana bit her lip, feeling sweat between her breasts, where *The Luck's* keys hung. Surely—surely he would not fail her because she had chosen a less-chancy approach. The regulations—

"I shall give you an opportunity to redeem yourself, Scholar, and to show me your mettle."

She caught her breath, hardly believing she heard the words.

"Sir?"

He inclined his head, lips curved slightly upward.

"I wish you to return us to our original location. I expect you to halve your lift time—or better."

It was frightening, exhilarating. It demanded every bit of her attention, so that she forgot to sweat or worry or take precious seconds to calculate some alternate, less rambunctious descent.

She abandoned the navcomp early on, letting it babble gently to itself while she ran and modified the necessary equations and plugged them into the board.

Local traffic presented no difficulty, though she caught an edge of chatter from a slow-moving barge: At least one pilot thought she was pushing the luck. She forgot it as soon as she heard it.

Numbers flickered, equations balanced, altered, formed and re-balanced; Aelliana dropped the test-ship through eleven protocols, skimmed along the twelfth and fell like a stone into atmosphere.

Lys had taught her to extend the wings and wait on the jets. It was a Scout trick, designed to conserve fuel in circumstances where fuel might very well be scarce.

"Fly her as long as you can," the Scout had told her. "You don't have to kick in those retros until you can see the street where you live."

Flying was somewhat more difficult than mere lifting or jet-aided descent. Flying meant manual defeat of local weather conditions. Local weather conditions had been milk-mild on Aelliana's three previous ventures.

They were not so today.

The ship bucked and twisted, nose going down despite her efforts at stabilization. Scan reported precipitation, turbulent winds. Maincomp reported hazard.

Aelliana hit the jets.

One short blast, as Lys would have done it—just enough to get the nose up and calm the bucking. They flew smoothly for a minute, two.

Aelliana hit the jets again.

And again.

And one more time, as she took up the approach to the Guild's field. This time she kept them on, letting them eat the remaining velocity, until the ship hesitated and touched down, light as a mote of dust, on the designated pad.

The jets killed themselves. Aelliana drew in the wings, ran the mandated systems check, reported her safe condition to Tower and began the shutdown. Beside her, Examination Officer Jarl was silent.

Check completed, Aelliana shut down the board, retracted the webbing and spun her chair, lifting her head and meeting the man's eyes.

"Arrived, sir. I believe the time is somewhat less than half the ascent time."

"Yes." He closed his eyes, sighed deeply, opened his eyes and retracted the webbing. "I apprehend you have trained with a Scout." He stood and looked down at her, his face damp with sweat.

"Such an approach is very effective—and entirely acceptable, should you be carrying Scouts or—inanimate cargo. For your general run of passenger, however, you will wish to go more gently."

Aelliana inclined her head. "Yes, Master Pilot."

Once again, he closed his eyes and sighed, somewhat less deeply. Apparently recovered by this exercise, he bowed as to a fellow Guild-member.

"If you will accompany me to the registry office, Pilot, I shall be pleased to issue a provisional second class license in your name."

Aelliana stared at him, gulped air and managed to stand on legs suddenly gone to rubber. She returned the bow, augmenting it with a hand-gesture conveying gratitude to the instructor.

"Yes, well." He cleared his throat. "You are required to complete certain hours of flight-time in order to gain regular status. Flight-time requirements must be met within a relumma of this date and certified by a master pilot. I note you are acquainted with Jon dea'Cort. He or any of his crew are qualified—I would say, peculiarly qualified—to assist you and in providing any further training you may wish to undertake."

Aelliana bowed her head. "Yes, Master Pilot. Thank you, sir."

"I believe there are no thanks due, Pilot. You have earned this prize with your own hands. Follow me, if you please."

Shivering with reaction, heart pounding in terror—or jubilation—Aelliana followed.

Chapter Eleven

I have today received Korval's Ring from the hand of Petrella, Thodelm yos'Galan, who had it from the hand of Korval Herself as she lay dying.

My first duty as Korval must be Balance with those who have deprived the clan of Chi yos'Phelium, beloved parent and delm; as well as Sae Zar yos'Galan, gentle cousin, a'thodelm, master trader. There is also Petrella yos'Galan, who I fear has taken her death-wound.

Sae Zar fell defending his delm. All honor to him.

Chi yos'Phelium died of a second treachery and in dying gave nourishment to her sister, my aunt, who alone of the three was able to win back to home.

The name of the world which has fashioned these losses for Korval is Ganjir, RP-7026-541-773, Tipra Sector, First Quadrant.

This shall be Korval's Balance: As of this hour, the ships of Korval and of Korval's allies do not stop at Ganjir. Korval goods do not go there; Korval cantra finds no investment there. And these conditions shall remain in force, though Ganjir starves for want of us.

. . . I note that my mother is still dead.

—Daav yos'Phelium
Eighty-Fifth Delm of Korval
Entry in the Delm's Diary for
Finyal Eighthday in the First Relumma
of the Year Named Saro

DAAV FINGER-TIGHTENED THE LAST SCREW, REACHED
over and swung the powertorque into position.

The repair had been tedious, badly located and
generally ill-wished. His back ached from bending,
his wrists tingled from the torque's vibration, his left
leg had gone numb some minutes ago and sensation
was now returning in a flood tide of needles.

He aligned the torque with the first screw, steadied it with his left hand and hit the go-stud with his
right. Vibration rattled his hands, screamed through
his head. He welcomed these minor pains as he had
welcomed the others.

He hit the second, third and fourth screws, killed
the power and allowed the torque to rise to the height
of its tether. Cautiously, he straightened.

Abused back muscles sued urgently for their guild rep.
Daav raised his arms shoulder-high, then over his head,
stretching high on his toes, pulling his entire body taut.

At the height of the stretch, muscles quivering and
tense, he closed his eyes and ran a mental sequence
he'd been taught as a Scout cadet. Colors whirled
before his mind's eye, there was an abrupt *click*, loud
in the inner ears. Daav brought his arms down to
shoulder-height, then the rest of the way, tension and
minor aches receding in a wave of delicious warmth.

By the time he had settled flat on his feet, he felt as if he'd had, if not quite an entire night's sleep, a very substantial nap.

"Well," he said to himself, or possibly to Patch, Binjali's resident cat, who had watched the repair from atop the tool cart. "That would seem to be that."

Patch yawned.

"Yes, very good. Denigrate my efforts. It won't do for me to go above myself. I do remind you, however, that I am merely casual labor, which must account for my clumsiness and ill-use of time. I make no doubt that Master dea'Cort—or, indeed, yourself!—would have managed the thing in high style and half the time. Perhaps someday very soon now I shall be privileged to see Master dea'Cort work."

That he had not lately been so privileged was not Jon's fault, but Daav's, as he would have been first to admit. Indeed, after pleading so urgently for access to Binjali's particular grace, he found the necessities of Clan Korval conspired to keep him away for four days together. He had returned only this morning, to be greeted with precious off-handedness by Jon, who had set him to the repair of the back-up jitney.

An hour or so later, Jon called that he was going over to Apel's for a glass, which Daav knew to be an undertaking of some hours. Trilla was due in the afternoon, Clonak, Syri, Al Bred and perhaps a few others would appear when they were seen. If trouble arose which Daav couldn't handle, Jon desired to be called from his wine so that he might marvel at it.

Now, the repair at last done, there was no sign of Trilla, Clonak or the other possibles. Daav moved Patch from the cart to his shoulder and stowed the tools. The cat arranged himself, stole-like, about the man's shoulders and stuck his nose into a vulnerable ear, purring.

"I suppose it's nothing to you that your nose is cold and damp? I thought not. Contrive to leave my hair rooted to my head, if you please. And if I detect so much as a paw-flick toward that earring, you, my fine sir, are mouse meat."

Tools neatly hung away, Daav closed the cart and moved silently toward the front of the garage, stripping off his work gloves as he walked. The sight of his naked hands gave him a momentary shock, and he lifted a finger to touch the chain about his neck. Korval's Ring hung, secret and safe, hidden below the lacing of his shirt.

"Do you know," he said to the cat riding his shoulders, "I believe I shall see if I can repair the tea-maker. It's my belief Jon has recalibrated the brewing sensor in order to save money on leaf."

Patch yawned. This was an old line of chat, after all. Dozens of Scout fingers had been inside the tea-maker over the years, seeking to correct its tragic fault—all, thus far, in vain.

"I might just buy a new unit," Daav mused, rounding the ladder that led to the cat-walk. "And install it one day while he's out courting Mistress Apel."

That idea appealed. Daav ducked under a guy-rope and came out into the minor open space of the crew's lounge. Sitting before the tea-maker on the scarred counter—indeed, entirely concealing that rather bulky object—was a box. Attached to the box was a paper, 'scribed in garish orange ink. Daav plucked the paper free.

"Leave my teapot alone, you assassin." Jon dea'Cort's perpendicular hand was unmistakable. "When you've done with that minor five-minute repair job up-bay, lift this to Outyard Eight. Gat expects delivery before Solcintra midnight."

Daav grinned. "Horrid old man," he said affectionately, reaching up to rub Patch's ear. The purring intensified, setting up a very pleasant vibration across his shoulders.

"So, my friend, shall you watch the shop until Trilla arrives? Or shall we go back to the office and see what sense can be made from the roster-sheet? There's a—" Patch shifted abruptly on his shoulder, claws skritching across the leather vest.

Daav turned as the crew door cycled, admitting a wedge of mid-morning sun and a bulky, hesitant shadow.

The shadow came two steps into the garage, walking with something near Scout silence, then paused, head moving from side to side while the door cycled closed behind.

Patch twisted to his feet and jumped from Daav's shoulder, landing noisily atop one of the ancient stools.

"Hello?" The voice was strong and even, an odd partner for that uncertain manner. She came forward, soft-footed on the hard floor.

"Master—oh." A tensing of her entire body, as if for a blow, and a jerky inclination of the head. "I— beg your pardon," she stammered in Adult-to-Adult. "I was—Is Master dea'Cort about?"

"Not just at the moment," Daav said, deliberately relaxing his muscles and letting his mouth curl slightly upward. "May I assist you? I am Daav—one of the crew here, you see." He used his chin to point at the black-and-white cat now perched, erect and dignified, atop a stool cushioned in dull green leather.

"Patch will vouch for me."

She turned her head, furtively, as if expecting a reprimand, and drifted forward another few steps, pausing with her hip against the farthest of the disordered semi-circle of stools.

"Patch?"

"Half-owner and resident cat," Daav returned, pitching his voice for foolery. "We've been known to each other any time these eight years. His word is quite as good as Jon's."

She turned back, head lifting sharply, giving him sight of a tense, fine-featured face dominated by a pair of shadowed green eyes.

"You—are—a Scout."

"Retired, alas," he replied, hoping serious gentleness might fare better than comradely joking. "Is there some way in which I might serve you?"

"I had come," she began, and then cut off with a gasp, not recoiling so much as freezing in place, head bent to stare—

At Patch, who was twisting this way and that, stropping himself against her hip and purring outrageously.

"What—" Her voice died as if breath had failed her. Daav stepped gently forward.

"He wants his chin rubbed, spoiled creature. Like this." He reached down, carefully unthreatening, and demonstrated. The purring reached an alarming level. "I—see." She extended a thin hand adorned by an antique puzzle-ring and used two tentative fingers on the black-splotched chin.

"A bit more forcefully," Daav coached gently. "It's a hedonist, I fear."

Once again, that quick lift of the head and startled flash of eyes. Then her attention was back on the cat, her face hidden by a rippling fall of tawny hair.

Daav made himself restful, as Rockflower had labored to teach him, cleared his mind of judging thoughts and allowed the woman before him to elucidate herself.

Observed thus, she was not bulky, but desperately thin, disguised and armored in layers of overlarge clothing. Likewise, the feral tension and the quiet, uncertain movements were two wedges of the same shield, meant to hold the world away.

Look away, her tense shoulders seem to say. *Look at anyone—at anything—else, but at me.*

She was misused, whoever she was—a person urgently in need of the benediction of friendship.

One of Jon's stray kittens, Daav thought, but the notion sat not entirely balanced. He watched her fingers on the cat, more certain now, having moved from chin to ear in response to Patch's explicit direction.

Comrades she might need, and someone to ensure she was fed, yet he felt she was not entirely a stray. About the rigid shoulders sat a mantle of purpose and from beneath the imperfect, ill-confining armor roiled such a potent brew of energy that Daav shivered.

The woman's thin body registered his movement, countered it with an abrupt cessation of her own motion. He received the impression that green eyes had read his face through the curtain of her hair.

"I had come," she said, and the burr of a Chonselta accent tickled his ear, "to find if my ship was ready to lift. Master dea'Cort had said—perhaps it might be—today. Depending upon the crew."

"Ah. I am able to assist you, then. If you will walk with me to the office, we may check the roster."

"I am grateful," she said formally, and kept a wary step behind him down to Jon's office at the back of the bay, Patch walking, high-tailed, at her side.

Daav tipped the screen up and tapped the on-switch.

"May I know the name of your ship?" he murmured as she came forward, stopping with the solid mass of the desk between them. Patch jumped nimbly to the cluttered surface and leaned companionably against her side.

"*Ride the Luck.*"

In the act of calling up the roster, he froze, and shot a glance at her shrouded face. Daav knew Vin Sin chel'Mara, as well as mutual dislike allowed, and knew somewhat of His Lordship's habits. He cleared his throat.

"Ma'am..."

"It is not complete," she interrupted, shoulders sagging within her large, shabby shirt. "I had hoped—but of course there was a great deal of work to be done. Might—might the roster indicate, sir, when she will be ready to lift?"

"Well," Daav murmured, "let us see." He tapped in the required information, then stood, blinking like an idiot, reading the name on the work order, over and over.

"Up to spec and ready to lift," he said after a moment, eyes yet stuck to the screen. A moment more and he managed to move, transferring his stare to the person before him.

"Forgive me. You are Aelliana Caylon?"

Green eyes met his amid a silken ripple of hair. "Yes, I—Of course, you will want identification! I do beg—" Her head was bent once more. She produced a thin metal card from a sleeve pocket and held it out, face averted.

He took it, automatically, noting the blurry likeness, and the date—two days gone. Provisional Second Class.

"Thank you," he murmured and gave himself a sharp mental shake, trying to align this tentative individual with the extraordinary mind that had reconstructed the ven'Tura Piloting Tables, the brilliant scholar who taught Practical Mathematics, or, as it was called in Scout Academy, Math for Survival.

"You are the revisor of the—"

"Of the ven'Tura Tables," she said breathlessly, all but snatching her license back from his hand. "I am. Please do not bow. I—I have explained to Master dea'Cort."

"Which is certainly enough for both of us," Daav said, grabbing for equilibrium. He smiled. "Your ship is ready and able to lift. You have, as I see, the skills necessary to the task. Good lift, pilot."

"I—That is." She floundered to a halt, took a shuddering breath and raised her head to squarely meet his eyes. "The fact is, I am in need of flight time. I've never lifted—you understand, I've never actually *gone* anywhere. And the regs—I had thought Master dea'Cort . . ."

"I see." Daav tipped his head, considering. "It happens there is a small errand left me by Jon. If you like it, I can serve as your second, and you may actually go somewhere. Outyard Eight to be precise."

The misty eyes took fire. "I would like that—extremely, sir."

"Then that is what we shall do. However, I must insist upon a condition."

Wariness cooled the fire, leaching color from her eyes. "Condition?"

"It is relatively painless," he said, offering her a smile. "The custom at Binjali's is to speak in Comrade. No one demands it, it is merely custom. In no case, however, am I 'sir.' I prefer to be addressed as Daav. If you find that too intimate, then 'pilot' is acceptable." He tipped his head. "Are you able to meet this condition?"

She inclined her head, very solemn. "I am—pilot."

"Good," he said, and shut down Jon's computer. "Let us see if Trilla has come on-shift."

Chapter Twelve

The delm must be a smuggler-class pilot—take from yos'Galan if yos'Phelium fails, as it likely will. I'm a sport, child of a long line of random elements, and Jela—

Young Tor An's folk have been pilots since the first ships lifted beyond atmosphere, back among the dead Ringstars. yos'Galan will breed true.

The best pilot the clan possesses must be delm, regardless of bloodline. This will be taken as a clan law.

The delm's heir must be a pilot—of like class to the delm—and as many others of the clan as genes and the luck allow.

There must be ships, spaceworthy and ready to fly: As many ships as it is possible to acquire. Such a number will necessarily require funds for maintenance—whole yards devoted to their readiness. Therefore, Clan Korval must become wealthy as Jela and me only dreamed of wealth.

Serve the contract, as long as it's in force. The boy don't hold with oath-breaking.

—Excerpted from Cantra yos'Phelium's Log Book

"LIFTING TO OUTEIGHT?" TRILLA GRINNED. "CONVEY MY undying affection to Gat."

"Yes, very likely," Pilot Daav returned, shrugging into a worn leather jacket.

Aelliana looked at that battered item hungrily. "Pilot's jacket" most would say, because of the cut, and as if any third-class barge runner might have one. In truth, only those who mastered Jump held the right to wear a pilot's jacket.

Trilla laughed and winked at Aelliana. "Scholar, good day to you. What luck at Chonselta Guild Hall?"

"Second class provisional," she said, pulling her eyes away from Pilot Daav's jacket, and warily meeting the other woman's merry glance.

"Everything fulfilled but the flight time! *Ge'shada*, pilot." Surprisingly, the Outworlder swept a bow of congratulation. When she straightened, her face was somewhat more serious.

"Daav's among the best you can have next to you at board, don't fret yourself there. Very good with ships—eh, Master Daav?"

"It humbles me to hear you say it, Master Trilla."

She laughed again, fingers shaping the sign for *rogue*. "Get your box, then, and haul out. I've work to do. Where's the Master?"

"Apel's."

"Think they'd just set up house—be cheaper, which ought to compel Jon."

"Yes, but Apel's not such a fool," the man said earnestly. "Besides, I expect she likes drinkable tea."

"Much more compelling, I allow. Heard news of crew?"

"Clonak, perhaps, and Syri. Al Bred this evening, if at all. The back-up jitney's on-line."

"Put you on that, did he?" She grinned and lifted a hand, turning toward the office with Patch at her heels. "Good lift, pilots."

"Thank you," Aelliana whispered, watching the man raise the bulky cargo box easily to his shoulder.

"After you, pilot," he said courteously, black eyes level and calm. Scout's eyes, that saw everything, gave back little, and judged nothing.

"Of course," she stammered, and turned to lead the way to the crew door, feeling him, silent and solid, behind her.

Outside, he stowed the box in the jitney's boot, straightened and stood looking down at her from his height, head tipped to one side.

"Shall you drive, or shall I?"

Aelliana swallowed, trying without success to calm nerves set all a-jangle by the last few harrowing days. The acquisition of the precious piloting license had not eased her position within Mizel, but rather increased the necessity for Ran Eld's unquestioning acceptance of her subservience. It had been necessary to placate her brother not once but several times, each time bowing lower, until she could taste carpet dust on her tongue, mixed with the bile of impotent fury.

It had been a risk to steal away today, she thought with a heart-wrench of panic. In general her days off were spent in the tiny office at Chonselta Tech. Ran Eld knew that. What if he were to seek her there and find the door bearing her name locked? He would want to know where she had been—would demand to know—and what might she tell him, that would buy his belief, while preserving her limited independence? She had been mad—she *was* mad, gods help her. How could she have thought—

"Scholar Caylon." Calm, deep voice, warm sense of a body near—too near!—something, feather-light, against her sleeve—

She gasped, cringing back, shoulders jamming up around her ears. Through her hair, she saw alarm cross the tall Scout's face, replaced instantly with careful neutrality. His hand, for it was his hand, dropped from her sleeve and he stepped back, beyond the boundaries of isolation she had woven for herself.

If he had simply turned and gone, she would certainly have fled to the ferry, and spent the return trip to Chonselta pleading with a pantheon of uncaring godlings for the grace of undiscovery.

He did not leave. He spoke, in Adult-to-Adult mode, very precisely, so the accent of Solcintra rang sharp against her ear.

"I regret that my presence troubles you, Scholar. Allow me to bring Trilla, so that she may sit second board for you."

His presence *did* trouble her: Tall, slim and graceful, with his odd, twisty earring and neat, overlong hair, the black eyes bold in a sharp, compelling face—He troubled her as the cat had troubled her, and for the same reason.

The cat—so soft, so *comforting*. Once she had started to stroke it, she could not stop; the joy the creature received from her caresses had awakened some dangerous nameless need—

The cat had *seen* her.

Tall Daav, with his bright black eyes, had *seen* her as well and knew her to be—real.

"Scholar?"

"I—" She shook her hair away from her face, forcing herself to meet those sightful eyes. "I beg your pardon yet again, sir—pilot. The last few days have been—uneasy. It would be best, I think, not to lift today."

"Hah." His mouth curved slightly—a gentle smile—though his eyes remained neutral. "Sky-nerves, we had used to call it at Academy," he said, in Comrade once again. "The best cure is to lift as planned."

Lift as planned. Aelliana felt the words strike somewhere at the nearly-forgotten core of her.

She took a deep, trembling breath and inclined her head.

"That is doubtless excellent advice," she said evenly and saw something move in the depths of the Scout's dark eyes. "I will ask that you pilot the jitney, however. It seems the surest course for arrival."

The smile became more pronounced. "I drive with delight," he said, and moved 'round the jitney to the driver's slot.

Aelliana filed a course on the challenging side of the equation, scrupulously remembering to bring the navcomp on-line, and took the opportunity of the quarter-hour wait to tour *Ride the Luck*.

The refurbished hold was eminently satisfying, though the pilots' quarters remained in their previous state of lavish comfort, lacking only the ceiling mirrors.

Aelliana looked about the chamber, feeling the slight vibration of the ship's gyros, hearing the hum of the support system, the muted clamor of Port chatter feeding in over the mandatory open line, and sagged against the wall, the room blurring through a rush of unaccustomed tears.

Hers.

The fierceness of possession warmed her, terrified her. It was dangerous to want something this much. So many things might go wrong—and the clan . . . Until the day she cleared Liad orbit, heading for her Jump-point, she was an asset of Clan Mizel; her possessions no more her own than the clan's. Mizel could as easily dispose of Aelliana Caylon's ship as it was legally able to dispose of Aelliana.

"Pilot?" Daav's voice came quietly from the wall speaker at her shoulder. "We are cleared to lift in two minutes."

"Thank you," she said, pushing shakily away from the wall. *Sky-nerves . . .* "I am on my way."

The lift to Outyard Eight was almost—restful. Master pilot that he was, Daav kept a serene second board. He took communications to his side with a murmured, "By your leave, pilot," and offered neither chatter nor any other assault upon her privacy.

Not so Yardkeeper Gat.

"What ship?" It was not so much query as demand, loud enough to pierce Aelliana's concentration on the approach path, so she shot a glance full of startlement to her co-pilot.

A wiry golden hand moved to flick the proper toggle. There was a band of lighter gold about the third finger, Aelliana noted, and a faint indentation, as if Pilot Daav had left off an accustomed ring.

"*Ride the Luck,*" he answered the abrupt query.

"Pilot Aelliana Caylon at first board. Daav from Binjali's on second. Yard comp downloaded ship's particulars two-point-four minutes gone, Keeper, and cleared us for Bay Thirty-Two."

"I don't care what her name is or how good she can add! I've got a second class provisional on a non-standard approach to my Yard. What does she know about docking? How do I know she won't hole the ring?"

Daav grinned, which did unexpectedly pleasant things to his foxy face. "Ah, the sweet anticipation!" he said gaily. "Never fear, sir, all shall be resolved in a very few minutes. Unless you would rather we simply jettison the cargo and leave?"

"All a good joke, is it?" the Yardkeeper snarled. "Bay Thirty-Two ready to accept *Ride the Luck*. You've got eight minutes to get in, unload that cargo and dump out."

"Unless, of course, we hole the ring," Daav murmured politely.

The in-line hummed empty.

Daav laughed, sending a bright glance toward Aelliana. She ducked her head, but did not entirely turn away.

"Non-standard approach?" she asked, voice breathless in her own ears.

"Dear Gat. He only means to say that, measured against other first approaches to ring-docking by provisional second class pilots he has seen in the past, this one is a bit too quick, a bit too flat—very nearly Scout-like, in fact." His fingers moved, swift and certain among the instruments. "Two-thirds local velocity must be dumped within forty-three seconds, pilot, else we buy a bumpy docking and Gat's disapprobation."

"Good gods." Aelliana spun back to her board.

✳ ✳ ✳

Seven-point-nine minutes later, *Ride the Luck* tumbled out of Bay Thirty-Two, oriented, and commenced descent.

The boards worked sweetly under Daav's fingers; he was agreeably surprised in *Ride the Luck*, which seemed to sing with joy around them.

He was likewise surprised in Aelliana Caylon, who, for all her skittish, wary ways, knew what to do with a ship in her hands. From power-up to dump-out, there had been not one false move. The minor flutter of hesitation upon approach he assigned to Gat's account, for breaking the web of her concentration and recalling her to the chancy world of human interaction.

The course she had chosen to OutEight had been ambitious for a second class provisional, though well within her abilities. Daav had several times noted her pushing the navcomp, as if she found its entirely respectable response time almost too slow to bear. The filed descent was worthy of a Scout and Daav had no doubt she would execute it with aplomb.

Aelliana Caylon, he thought, watching her fragile hands flickering over prime board, might very well be that rarest of precious things: a natural pilot.

Guild law required a master pilot engaged in evaluating a junior to judge and implement appropriate training. Aelliana Caylon, in the judgment of Scout pilot/Master Daav yos'Phelium, was easily capable of achieving first class. It was likely that master pilot was within her grasp, did she care to leave her own work for a relumma or two and devote herself to study.

Thus, a variation from the simple meeting of second class flight-time requirements was mandated. Daav ran an experienced eye over his scans, double-checked the filed approach and addressed the pilot, pitching his voice soft out of care for her concentration.

"I wonder," he murmured, keeping his eyes scrupulously on his board, "if you might wish to attempt a sling landing."

"Now?" she asked, voice sharp with surprise.

"You will have to master the skill, soon or late," he said, all gentle reason. "Why not begin today?"

"To refile the course, to tie up the Port's emergency sling..."

"The most minor readjustment of course," Daav soothed, "and no need to discommode Port at all. Binjali's has a sling."

Hesitation. Daav consulted his scans and dared push his point a bit, before time became too short.

"I can call Jon, if you like it, and see if we have clearance. We will come in on automatic first time, of course." He paused. "Unless you have already trained on sling-shots?"

"No..."

"I'll call now," Daav said, flicking the line open.

"Good-noon, Captain darling!" Clonak ter'Meulen's voice filled the tiny cabin a moment later. "What service shall my humble self be delighted to perform for you?"

Daav's lips twitched. "Where's Jon?"

"Up to his neck in a gyro-fix. Service?"

"Sling-shot, automatics, current coords—" he reeled them off, confident of Clonak's abilities as of his own. "Flight plan downloaded—*now*. Cleared?"

"Cleared, oh Captain. You and the pilot can take a nap. Until soon."

"Until soon, Clonak." He cut the connection and turned his head to glance at Aelliana Caylon.

She was looking directly at him, green eyes wide, less misty than he recalled, and holding something akin to—amusement.

"It seems a sling-shot is mandated," she observed, and there was the barest thread of laughter, too, in the weave of the fine, strong voice. Daav grinned.

"Your pardon, pilot. Of all people, you must know what Scouts are!"

"Bent on mischief," she agreed, astonishingly tranquil, "and decided entirely upon their own course." She turned back to her board and her hair shifted to conceal her. "I shall file an amended descent."

They were well into the amended descent when a certain subtle lack called Daav's attention to the upper left quadrant of his board. Apparently the navcomp's inefficiencies had become too burdensome to tolerate, for it was shut entirely down. He reached for the reset.

"That's wrong," Aelliana Caylon told him sharply.

"Wrong?"

"Off by two places." Her fingers were flying over the board, as well they should, he thought abruptly, with her running such a course on manual. He punched navcomp up.

Wrong, indeed, and off by nearly three places. Swearing silently, he called for the back-up. It came on-line with a suspicious stutter, accepted its office— and failed.

Chapter Thirteen

In the absence of clan, a partner, comrade or co-pilot may be permitted the burdens and joys of kin-duty. In the presence of kin, duty to partner, comrade or co-pilot must stand an honorable second.

—From the Liaden Code of Proper Conduct

"COMP TWO DOWN," DAAV SAID, EYES RAKING THE SCANS. It was too late by several minutes to change course now.

"We're committed to the sling. I'll call Jon and file the change. Begin sending your numbers to me for verification."

"Yes," she said, never looking away from her board. Daav hit the comm.

"Navcomp suspect," he told Clonak a heartbeat later, "back-up's dead."

"How lovely for you, darling."

Daav grinned. "Pilot Caylon will be bringing her to the sling on manual."

A short pause, then a cheery, "Right-o!" in what Clonak fondly considered an Aus accent.

"Ride the Luck out."

"Ta-ta."

Daav slapped the line off, dumped his holding bank and leapt into a river of numbers.

Ordered and swift, the equations flowed, through his bank, into the board and out, a continuous perfect stream of checkpoint and balance. He forgot about the navcomp, which should have been tested and cleared as standard procedure. He forgot the oddities of the woman beside him. He forgot Delm Korval.

There were the equations flowing to him, cold and pure, to be verified and fed in. There were the scans. There was the sense of the ship around him. There was the background chatter along the open line.

"When you feel the sling lock," he said, hardly hearing his own voice through the wall of his concentration, "you will cut the gyros. Immediately."

The small portion of his mind not urgently concerned with equations, scan and ship expected an outcry, for to cut the gyros was to be immediately and irrefutably within the talons of gravity. Cutting the gyros meant the ship would *fall* . . .

"Yes," said Aelliana Caylon and said no more.

He picked up the next sequence, noting that it was the set-up—the final equation. He scrutinized, verified and locked it, leaning back slightly in the web of safety straps.

"Twelve seconds. Mind the sling-lock, pilot . . ."

It came, a distinct sensation of ship's progress halted, of plate metal and blast glass grasped tightly in the jaws of an inconceivable monster . . .

Aelliana cut the gyros.

The stomach twisted, the inner ear protested, the heart clutched as for an instant it seemed that the monster's jaw had slackened, and the ship sliding free to—

"Caught," Daav announced quietly. "And retained. A difficult task, executed well. Ge'shada, pilot."

"No need for congratulation," she said. "You were correct, after all. I shall need this skill." She threw him a glance, eyes brilliantly green in a pale golden face. "What is the procedure for clearing the sling?"

"Jon sends a workhorse and hauls the ship to its berthing—heading out now, your two-screen."

"I see. And the pilots?"

"In this case, I believe the pilots should make haste to Master dea'Cort. The luck was in it, you caught that error in time."

Once again, that brilliant green glance. "I know regs demand the navcomp be running—but I find it distracting. Doubtless it is my inexperience and I do expect to learn better, s—" She paused, lips tightening. "I cannot help but keep checking the equations, and when it started giving me bad numbers..."

"It was even more distracting," Daav concluded amiably. "Perfectly understandable. Point of information: Normal procedure in such circumstance includes engaging the secondary comp."

She looked abashed, the brilliancy of her eyes dimming a fraction. "I had no notion there was a back-up navcomp, sir."

"Daav. Ships of this class carry a primary navcomp and one back-up as standard. Most pilots will install a second back-up. Some prefer more. It is wise to check before dropping to manual, especially if you are running solo."

She bowed her head. "I will remember."

"Good," he said and retracted the webbing. "Lessons being done for the moment, I suggest we wait upon Jon."

* * *

"A beautiful landing!" Jon dea'Cort announced, raising a large, heavy-looking tea mug. "Not at all like some I've seen, where the ship comes in upside down and backward, eh, Daav?"

Clonak, the pudgy Scout with hair on his face—"A *mustache*," Pilot Daav had murmured in Aelliana's ear, at her initial start of surprise—laughed aloud and made an ironic, seated bow. "You shall never outlive it, Captain."

"So it seems," Pilot Daav returned placidly and looked back to Master dea'Cort. "What about that navcomp, Jon?"

The older man took a hearty swig from his mug. "I'd say replace it."

"Replace—Oh. Oh, no." Aelliana slid off the stool Jon had insisted she take and stood, hands knotted before her. "Navcomps are—Master dea'Cort, *Ride the Luck* is not a wealthy ship. I intend to work her, but until work can be found, expenses must be held to a minimum. You have been very helpful—indeed, generous, in the refitting, but I—" She stumbled to a halt.

A pair of humorous amber eyes considered her. "Spit it out, math teacher. We're all comrades here."

She drew in a breath, trembling as she met that gaze. "I cannot afford to replace the navcomp."

"Well." Master dea'Cort took counsel of the ceiling. "Regs are pretty clear," he said eventually. "Navcomp's got to be online while the ship is in use within Port-controlled space. Unless you can afford fines and temporary suspension easier than a replacement comp?"

"It—it needn't be off-line for an instant!" Aelliana cried, the plan taking shape even as she spoke. She leaned forward, cold hands twisted into a cramped knot, eyes on Jon dea'Cort's face.

"I'll engage the navcomp, sir, I swear it! It will be—I can learn to ignore it, use override and merely run manual, as I did today. Then, when there has been sufficient work—" Something moved in the man's face and she stopped, gulping.

Clonak broke the small silence, voice hushed.

"Daav, I'm in love."

"What, again?"

The sound of his calm, deep voice recalled her to a sense of duty left undone and she spun, not quite meeting his eyes.

"I am remiss. You did very well, pilot, to keep the pace. I am—I am grateful for your assistance and the gift of your expertise."

Trilla, seated beside Clonak, gave a shout of laughter. Jon grinned. Clonak popped off his stool and bowed full honor.

"We shall make a pilot of you yet, oh Captain!"

Aelliana gasped in dismay. She had not meant to hold him up to ridicule before his comrades, but to thank him sincerely for his aid. She felt her cheeks heat.

"No, I—"

But Daav was already making an answering bow toward Clonak.

It was a pure marvel, this bow, swept as if the work leathers were the most costly of High House evening dress. One long arm curved aside and up, holding the imaginary cloak gracefully away as the sleek dark head brushed one elegant, out-thrust leg.

"You do me too much honor."

"Well, that's certainly likely," Jon declared, and

shot a glance aside. "Clonak, sit down or go away. In either case, be quiet. Daav, descend from the high branches, if you please. Math teacher, pay attention."

She turned to face him, hands clasped tightly before her.

"Yes, sir," she said humbly.

"Huh." He glanced to the ceiling once more, then back, eyes and face serious.

"Nobody here says you can't run the board by hand forever without a mistake. But there's nobody here who hasn't at least once made a mistake, and been glad there was a double-check to save 'em. We're master class, each one of us." He used his chin to point: Trilla, Clonak, Daav, and tapped himself on the chest with a broad forefinger.

"Master class. The ship don't fly us, which is the case with the chel'Mara. We fly the ship. But blood and bone gets tired, math teacher—even Scouts have to sleep. Say you were hurt and needed time in the 'doc—do you leave the ship to a glitched comp, or do you sit that board and hope you don't pass out?"

She licked her lips. "Surely, in Solcintra. In local space—"

"The luck is everywhere—for good or for ill—and it's best not to spit in its face." Jon leaned forward on his stool, one arm across a powerful thigh.

"We're not talking regs, child. We all agree the regs are expendable—given sufficient cause. What we're talking is common sense. Survival. You understand survival."

"Yes," she whispered and swallowed hard in a tight throat. "Master dea'Cort, I cannot afford a replacement navcomp. I cannot afford to be grounded. *Ride the*

Luck is a working ship and I intend that we—that we earn our way."

"That being the case," Daav said from behind her, "commission Binjali Repair Shop to replace the navcomp and drop in two back-ups. Jon holds the note and you pay as work becomes profit."

Jon looked at her seriously. "That's sound advice, math teacher."

"Daav has very sound judgment," Clonak chimed in, irrepressible as Var Mon, "though I grant you wouldn't think so, to look at him."

"I—I can't ask—hold a note for a replacement—for *three* replacements? Master—"

"No choice in the matter," Trilla said in her blunt, Outworld way. "Need a working comp to lift. Need work to finance the comp." She grinned. "You might take a loan against the ship, of—"

"No!"

"Huh." Jon again. "Sounds settled to me. I'll hold the note for my cost, plus labor. You'll pay me as able. In the meantime, if I have something to lift, you take it at your cost and we'll call that the interest. Agreed?"

There was, as Trilla said, no choice. Still, Aelliana struggled with necessity a moment longer. A debt of such magnitude would surely increase the time she must stay upon Liad, thus increasing the chance of discovery. And yet, it was required that the ship be able, if work was to be gained.

She inclined her head, vowing to pay this debt as quickly as she might.

"Agreed, Master dea'Cort."

"Good enough. When's your shift end, Daav?"

"Midnight."

"Glutton. Take Clonak and go pull that comp. I'll find the replacements." He smiled at Aelliana. "We'll have you up to spec by tomorrow mid-day, math teacher. I'll leave a complete accounting in your ship's in-bank."

"Thank you," she said, feeling tears prick her eyes. She ducked her head. "I am grateful."

Jon slid off his stool and stretched. "Same as we'd do for any of our own—no gratitude demanded."

"Clonak, old friend, your skills are in demand!" Daav had a tool belt over one shoulder and was holding out another.

"And I with a thought to dinner," the pudgy Scout sighed. He turned as he passed Aelliana and performed an absurdly ornate bow.

"For you, goddess, I forgo even food!"

"Nor like to starve of it," Daav commented.

"Cruel, Captain."

"Merely honest. Come along, dear." Black eyes found hers, though she made an effort to avoid the glance. "Pilot Caylon, it was a rare lift. I hope to sit second for you again."

"Thank you," she stammered and felt she should say more.

But Daav was gone.

"Navcomp pulled, sealed and dispatched to the Port Master via Pilot ter'Meulen, who swears he's for a sup and a glass, lest he die of starvation."

"Well enough," Jon allowed, pouring the dregs from the pot to his mug. He glanced over his shoulder at the slender man perched on the green stool, Patch sitting tall on his knee.

"Pastry?"

"Thank you, no."

"Not stale enough for you?" Jon speared a iced dough-ring for himself and carried tea and snack over to his accustomed stool.

"Too stale, alas. My *cha'leket* insists upon fresh pastries for his table, and you see how his decadence affects me."

Jon snorted and had a bite, followed by a swallow of tea.

"I wonder," Daav said pensively, rubbing the cat's ears. "Who certified that navcomp at refitting?"

"Checked it myself," Jon said, somewhat indistinctly. "Sang sweet and true." He paused for more tea, and pointed a finger.

"Occur to you to wonder how it is the chel'Mara, who never piloted anything other than a groundcar on manual in all his life, isn't splattered from here to the inland sea, running automatic with an insane navcomp?"

"It did." Daav sighed. "I spent an hour looking for a meddle, but if it was there, it was very cleverly tucked away."

"Don't have to be there now," Jon pointed out. "I checked the log—suspicious old man that I am—and you looking to become another such, if I may say so." He finished off the dough-ring in two bites.

"Log says that on the night he played pikit with our math teacher and lost his ship by way of it, Vin Sin chel'Mara—that's *Lord* chel'Mara to you—stopped by the shop and entered his once-was ship, to clear out his personal effects. Didn't take him long. In fact, turns out he left quite a number of very expensive— and portable—items behind."

Daav said something impolite in a language native to a certain savage tribe some fourteen zig-zagged light-years out from Liad. Jon grinned.

"No proof. Not that I don't favor it myself, for personal reasons. The chel'Mara's very careful of his *melant'i*. Doesn't do a man's *melant'i* any good to lose his ship, true enough. But you might be able to recoup something from the debacle, if she were straightaway seen to crash it."

"Which she might have done," Daav said, so heatedly Patch jumped to the floor. "If she had been *any* second class provisional, making her first sling-shot when that comp went bad—" He took a hard breath. "Your pardon."

"Nothing to it." Jon grinned. "A rare wonder, our math teacher, eh?"

Daav moved his shoulders. "I'd like to know who beats her."

"I'd welcome news of that, myself. At least they didn't send her here battered and bruised-up today, small grace." He finished his tea and looked up into the younger man's eyes.

"Good idea of yours, me holding the note."

"I can guarantee the loan, if you like it," Daav returned quietly. "Or tell me the account and the price and I'll make the transfer now."

"Don't be an idiot. She intends to work that ship, and I'll tell you what I think. I think what our math teacher puts her mind to do is good as done. I'll hold her note."

"If it becomes a burden, old friend, only tell me. There's the Pilots Fund, after all."

"So there is. Well." He bounced to his feet and

stretched with a mighty groan. Daav slid lightly from the stool and stood looking down at him, affection plain in his sharp, clever face.

"Hah." Jon smiled up at him. "You coming in tomorrow?"

"Perhaps the day after."

"All right, then. Glad you were to hand today. Matters could have gone ill, even if she is a wizard at the board."

"She wouldn't have attempted the sling if I hadn't suggested—demanded—it." He hesitated. "She's a natural, Jon."

"Is she?" the older man said, with vast unsurprise.

Daav laughed and bowed. "Good-night, Master."

"Good-night, lad. Convey my highest regards to your *cha'leket*."

Chapter Fourteen

A Dragon does not forget. Nor does it remember wrongly.

—From the Liaden Book of Dragons

"MASTER DEA'CORT SENDS YOU HIS BEST REGARDS, BROTHER." Daav and his *cha'leket* were strolling arm-in-arm across Trealla Fantrol's wide lawn, angling more-or-less toward the wild garden and the river.

Er Thom sighed sharply. "Whatever have I done, to earn Jon dea'Cort's notice? We have scarcely exchanged a greeting in twelve years, so seldom do our paths cross, yet I cannot be abroad these last few relumma without hearing news of his regard! Only yesterday, Clonak ter'Meulen crossed Exchange Street at the Port's busiest hour to bring me Master dea'Cort's wish for my good health!"

Daav laughed. "Why, I suppose you've won his admiration, darling. Is it burdensome?"

"Merely bewildering, since I go on quite as usual, with the exception of succeeding to yos'Galan's ring, and I cannot for my life see what that should have to do with Jon dea'Cort!"

"Nothing at all—and you are correct in supposing a man's coming into his intended estate would utterly fail to win Jon's interest, much less his admiration. No," Daav murmured, "I believe it is your lifemating which has bought his heart."

Er Thom stiffened and shot a brilliant violet glance into Daav's face. "My lifemating, is it? A subject which falls well outside his reasonable area of concern."

"You are severe," Daav said, stroking the stiff arm soothingly. "Recall that Jon is a Scout. He expresses the greatest admiration for Anne's work. For yourself, he admires your—*moxie*, as he would have it."

"*Moxie*?" Er Thom frowned after the Terran word.

"Courage," Daav translated, rather freely. "It is not every Liaden, after all, who might lifemate a Terran, flying in the face of custom and—some would say— good sense."

Er Thom laughed softly. "Indeed, there was hardly a choice!"

"Yes, but you mustn't let Jon know that!" Daav said earnestly. "Allow him, I beg, to continue believing you and Anne lifemated because love was stronger than custom!"

"Of course—" He caught himself with another slight laugh. "Let Jon dea'Cort believe what he likes, then! I only wish he will give over such lavish regard."

"You might send him a token in Balance, if you find his esteem a burden." Daav grinned. "In fact, I believe I know just the thing! Have you a tin of that particular morning tea Anne favors?"

"'Joyful Sunrise'? Certainly. I can easily part with a dozen, if you feel it might answer."

"One tin should suffice, I think, and a card inscribed by your lady, desiring Master dea'Cort to enjoy the beverage as she does."

"Hah. It shall be done this evening!" Er Thom smiled, then sobered. "What word from Pilot tel'Izak?"

Daav lifted an eyebrow. "Word? No, no, darling—you mistake the matter entirely! It is I who ought to be about sending word. The lady believes me at her feet." He sighed lightly as they passed through the gap in the hedge. "And means, I fear, to have me remain there."

On the other side of the hedge, Er Thom stopped, rounding with such a look of outrage that it was all Daav could do not to laugh aloud.

"*You* at Samiv tel'Izak's feet? She has audacity, I see."

"Merely self-consequence." He slanted a glance into Er Thom's indignant eyes and fetched up a doleful sigh. "You have taken her in dislike."

"Indeed, how might I take her in anything at all, when she kept High Mode the evening through and refused to give one sight into—" Er Thom's mouth tightened. "This is a joke."

"Ah." Daav caught the other's arm and turned him gently toward the wild garden. "Alas, it is not a joke, but plain observation. The pilot considers that Korval's solicitation of herself exposes vulnerability." He paused. Er Thom's eyes were still stormy; he stood on the knife's edge of taking the lady in extreme dislike, on Daav's account.

And that, Daav thought suddenly, was neither seemly nor kind. For a time Samiv tel'Izak would be his wife, bound by the terms of the contract to live apart from the comforts of clan and kin, surrounded by strangers upon whom she must depend for what day-to-day gentleness one human being might have from another. To enter thus unprotected into a House where so substantial a person as her husband's *cha'leket* held her in despite—no, it would not do.

"The assumption is doubtless original with the lady's delm, and is not altogether shatterbrained," he said, looking gravely into Er Thom's eyes. "Only think: All the world wishes to marry Korval—and Korval chooses Samiv tel'Izak. Those of Korval wed pilots—and she is a pilot. But there are other pilots, who are not Samiv tel'Izak, and who remain unchosen."

Er Thom's eyes were somewhat less stormy. "True enough," he allowed, though brusquely.

"True enough," Daav murmured and shaped his lips into a gentle smile. "Think again, brother. It was you urged me stand away, if I did not like the match. We are Scouts and traders—odd folk by any count. We might think of turning our face from custom—even at the risk of our delm's displeasure, eh?"

Er Thom laughed quietly.

"Yes." Daav allowed his smile to grow to a grin. "But consider one who is without our resources—to whom custom bears the weight of law—desired by her delm to come forth and take up duty. She must accept her delm's elucidation of circumstance: The Dragon offers for Samiv tel'Izak because none but herself will do." He moved his shoulders. "Shall we deny such a small comfort to one who will be so short a time among us?"

There was a pause.

"Certainly the lady is welcome to what comfort she may make for herself," Er Thom said softly. "I had been angered because it seemed she held you cheap."

"My lamentable sense of humor," Daav said ruefully and offered his arm. Er Thom took it and they continued their walk along the artful wilderness, talking of this and that, until Daav turned them, regretfully, back toward the house.

"The Council of Clans devours the remainder of my day," he said.

"Another meeting?" Er Thom frowned. "They proliferate."

"Geometrically," Daav agreed. "A land dispute has arisen between Mandor and Pyx. I think it a matter requiring the skills of two or three *qe'andra*, rather than a full Council."

"Why not offer Mr. dea'Gauss as arbiter?" Er Thom murmured, naming Korval's own man of business.

"Pyx has already taken up the *melant'i* of victim," Daav said, "and chose the Council as offering the widest scope for spite." He sighed sharply as they passed through the hedge.

"Had you heard that Vin Sin chel'Mara lost his ship in a game of pikit?"

"The Port speaks of nothing else," Er Thom replied. "The detail that remains unclear in the reports I have heard is the name of the winner. Some say a pair of Scoutlings, some others say a professional sharp-player from Chonselta City."

"Ah? I had heard Aelliana Caylon."

Er Thom's winged brows pulled together. "The mathematician? Who had that tale?"

"Clonak. His father was present during the play."

"Well, then, there can hardly be doubt," Er Thom said, who knew Delm Guayar for a person of quite savage accuracy. "Good lift and safe landing to the scholar." He paused, his fingers exerting a mild pressure on Daav's arm.

"Do you know," he said softly, "I had heard something else. Talk is that the chel'Mara is sent off-world by his delm, in Balance for losing his ship." He flicked a quick violet glance to his brother's face. "Which is no more than he bargained for, no matter the winner. What fool stakes his ship at chance?"

"The chel'Mara's sort of fool, apparently," said Daav. "Well, and if Aragon is at last moved to apply discipline, then the world is twice indebted to Scholar Caylon."

Er Thom laughed lightly. "Thrice, you must mean, brother, else you cannot have ever seen the chel'Mara fly."

"Well," said Daav with a smile, "perhaps I do." And the talk turned to other things.

"That was a binjali sling-shot, Scholar Caylon!" Var Mon hit his seat with a grin. "We scanned the tape, then rode the sims 'til dawn, but no one came close to your run—not even Rema."

"Hardly until dawn," Rema said, entering the room with rather less energy and giving Aelliana a proper bow of greeting. "Good-day, Scholar Caylon."

"Good-day, Rema." Aelliana returned the bow with an inclination of the head, then shook her hair back to consider Var Mon.

"I thank you for your praise. However, it must be remembered that my co-pilot was most able. I doubt the landing would have been so adroit, had I made the attempt solo."

Var Mon's face went abruptly and entirely blank. He lowered his eyes and bustled noisily with his notetaker.

"No doubt but your co-pilot was exemplary," Rema murmured, over her comrade's sudden clatter. "However, the tape clearly shows it was your hand brought the ship in, Scholar. An astonishing run, our piloting instructor declared it."

"And you never saw one so tightfisted of praise!" Var Mon finished, returning to his usual mode as abruptly as he had departed. "Scholar Caylon, you must go for Scout!"

"Indeed, I must not," she replied firmly as Baan, Qiarta and Nerin arrived, made their bows and took their seats.

"Good-day. This is, as you all know, our last session together. I have given you everything that I know how to give, to insure you each hold the best possibility for survival. In spite of my best effort, it is conceivable that I have failed of being as clear as I might have been upon this point or that. This last session is yours. What is less than glass-clear and utterly certain in your minds? Review now what we have covered throughout the semester. No point is too insignificant to ask upon. I shall take the first question in six minutes."

That quick, notetakers were out and fingers were flying. Rema leaned back in her chair, eyes unfocused on a corner of the ceiling.

Aelliana bent her head over her console and felt her lips curve in the rarity of her smile.

A beautiful landing! Jon dea'Cort applauded from memory, while Daav's deep voice gave quieter praise: *A difficult task, executed well.* And now: *A binjali sling-shot, Scholar! ... An astonishing run ...*

Aelliana closed her eyes and felt something loosen, down close in her chest, so the next breath she took was a shade deeper, a fraction less hurried, as if she had taken one single sip of brandy.

The timer rang, and Aelliana raised her head, smiled at her class and lifted a hand, inviting the first question.

The dispute between Pyx and Mandor was resolved with gratifying speediness. No more than six additional delms had found it necessary to rise and speak of matters in tenuous relationship to the subject and the vote, when taken, showed a clear majority in favor of Mandor's claim.

Daav shut down his tally screen, almost smiling with a surge of sheer exuberance. An entire afternoon open to his own expenditure, with no meetings and no duty pressing upon him. He considered going down to Binjali's, but that would mean returning home, to exchange his delm's finery for the comfort of his leathers. Perhaps—

"Hedrede is seen. Rise and state your business." Speaker for Council's voice contained a note of dryness that Daav registered as out of place even as he re-activated his tally screen.

Hedrede was old: The name was to be found on the passenger list of *Quick Passage*, 'scribed in Cantra yos'Phelium's strong, sharp hand. Indeed, one Vel Ter jo'Bern of House Hedrede had been co-signer of the contract between Cantra and the Solcintran Houses.

For all of these years and past glories, however, Hedrede was not High House. It stood for centuries within the top five percent of Mid-Houses, and there it seemed content to remain, neither speaking out in Council nor concerning itself with matters outside of Liad's orbit.

There was a faint shuffle, then a figure rose along

the tables of the fifth hub and made a perfunctory bow toward the Speaker.

"Hedrede calls upon Korval." The voice was strong, not young, female.

Swallowing surprise, Daav came to his feet, bowing toward the fifth hub. "Korval is here."

There was a slight pause to accommodate the rustling of amaze from among those gathered. Hedrede calls upon Korval before full Council? Two clans less likely to have aught to do with each other could scarce be found.

What could it be? the rustling delms asked each other, by eye and by whisper. Indeed, conjecture stretched so wide that Speaker for Council was moved to touch her chime and command them all to silence.

"Korval rises at Hedrede's word. Hedrede may speak."

"No one here," Hedrede announced to a chamber grown suddenly still, "need be reminded of the place Korval holds in history. More, perhaps, than any clan here-gathered may it be said of Korval, 'This clan is kin to Liad.'"

This, thought Daav, standing in the formal attitude of attention which custom demanded of him, *is going to be bad*.

"Having so illustrious an history," Hedrede continued, "and standing so close to Liad and Liadens, it must surely be mere—oversight—that a certain item which wrongs both homeworld and history has been lately published by Korval." She bowed, with lavish respect. "I call upon Korval to riddle this paradox."

Oh, thought Daav, as the chamber again erupted into murmuring speculation. *Oh, damn*.

Speaker for Council touched her chime, forcefully, and raised her voice to ride the hub-bub.

"Korval may reply to Hedrede's query."

He bowed—to Speaker for Council, and to Hedrede. He turned slightly in his place, opening his hands in a gesture of gentle astonishment.

"It is assumed that honored Hedrede refers to a certain scholarly work compiled by one of Korval and recently published through University Press." He paused and bowed again, careful to avoid irony. "One wonders in what way this work is found to wrong the homeworld."

"The work in question," Hedrede replied, for the benefit of those observing this unexpected and delightful diversion, "purports to establish a link between Terra and Liad by demonstrating an ancient, common tongue." She bowed. "Korval will, naturally, correct any error in this summation."

"The summation is entirely accurate. One is yet unenlightened as to the wrong thus visited upon Liad."

There was a short pause, which carried the vinegar bite of irritation to Daav's sensitivities.

"The work," Hedrede continued, after a moment, "has been written by one of Korval who is by birth, Terran. To the untutored eye, this combination of fact would seem to spell one who has seen the value of a wide and varied *melant'i* and has determined to spend that value, for the betterment of her own kind."

Anger rocked him. *How dare—*

He closed his eyes, ran the calming sequence of the Scout's Rainbow; remembered to breathe. This was a direct attack upon Korval. To answer in anger would be to answer in error. Anne's *melant'i* was

staked here—and Er Thom's—and his own. Kin to
Liad, was he? He'd bloody well—

He snatched the thought, turned, searched—found
the face he wished to find, high up in the ninth tier,
and bowed.

"Korval calls upon Yedon."

She rose with an alacrity that led him to think she
had been expecting the call.

"Yedon is here."

"Verification is sought of the initial scholarship of
the work under discussion," Daav said, forcing his voice
to calmness, though he could feel anger shivering in
elbows and knees. "One recalls that the first discovery
of a common tongue from which proceeded both Terran and Liaden was made by Learned Scholar Jin Del
yo'Kera, Clan Yedon."

"Korval's memory," said Yedon solemnly, "is accurate—
and long."

A slight murmur stirred the chamber at that. Daav
bowed.

"One also recalls that before his death Scholar
yo'Kera had completed much of the work toward eventual publication."

"Correct," Yedon replied and turned to Hedrede in
explanation. "Jin Del had considered this work to be
the crown of his life. It was his intention to publish
the results. That Scholar Davis was available to com-
pile his notes and see them published in accordance
with his express wish could only give joy to kin and
colleagues."

Hedrede inclined her head. "You tell me that a
Liaden had formulated this theory and had intended
to publish it abroad?" She raised a hand. "But perhaps

the theory which is published is not that which the Learned Scholar had at first put forth?"

The anger was less jarring this time; colder, more dangerous. Daav allowed himself a small sigh as Yedon made answer.

"Indeed, I had seen the work directly before publication, as had several of Jin Del's colleagues. It matches his intention in every particular. Scholar Davis was generous with the gift of her genius."

There was silence in the chamber. Eventually, Speaker for Council touched her chime.

"Has Hedrede further call upon Korval in this matter?"

Hedrede started, visibly collected herself, and bowed.

"Hedrede has no further call upon Korval within Council," she said formally and resumed her seat.

Daav bowed, in his turn releasing Yedon, and sat with exquisite care.

Soon after, Speaker for Council ended the session and touched the chime to release them. Daav fussed over gathering and regathering papers and by such schoolboy stratagems eventually left the chamber alone, and last.

Chapter Fifteen

"Liaden Scout" must now be seen as a misnomer, for to become a Scout is to become other than Liaden. It is to turn one's face from the home-world and enter a state of philosophy where all custom, however alien, is accepted as equally just and fitting.

We are told by certain instructors that not everyone may aspire to—nor all who aspire, attain—that particular degree of philosophical contrariness required of those who are said to have "Scout's eyes."

For this we must rejoice, and allow the Scouts full honor for having in the past provided refuge for the disenfranchised, the adventurous, and the odd.

—Excerpted from remarks made
before the Council of Clans
by the chairperson of the Coalition
to Abolish the Liaden Scouts

THE WOMAN BEHIND THE COUNTER WORE AN EMBROI-
dered badge on the shoulder of her leather jacket: A bronze-winged, green-eyed dragon hovering protectively over a tree in full, luxuriant leaf. Beneath the

graphic was written, not the "I Dare" which would have completed the seal and identified the wearer as one of Clan Korval's Line Direct, but "Jazla pen'Edrik, Dispatcher."

She heard Aelliana out with grave courtesy, hands folded upon the counter.

"As it happens, we do from time to time require the services of freelance pilots," she said at the conclusion of Aelliana's rather breathless presentation. "May I see your license, please?"

She held it out, wishing bitterly that her hand did not tremble so, then folded both hands before her as the dispatcher turned and fed the card into the reader.

Korval was ships, everyone knew that. No clan owned so many; no other clan or company employed so many pilots. It had always been so—stretching back to the very ship, the very pilots, who had brought Liadens safely out of the horror of the Migration.

Clan Korval took pilots and piloting very seriously, indeed. Thus Aelliana had gone first to Korval's Solcintra Dispatch Office to request that her name be added to the list of pilots available to fly.

"Aelliana Caylon," the dispatcher said, eyes intent on the reader's screen. "Provisional second class—quite recent. One assignment completed on behalf of Binjali Repair Shop. Master Pilot dea'Cort lists himself as reference. So." She tapped a sequence into her keyboard, retrieved Aelliana's card and held it out with a grave smile.

"I shall be very pleased to add your name to our roster, Pilot Caylon. May I know the best means of contacting you?"

"Chonselta Technical College," Aelliana recited

the number of her private office line, "or a message might be left at Binjali's—" She repeated the code Jon dea'Cort had given her. "You may wish to note that I am owner of a Class A single-hold."

"So," the dispatcher said again, fingers dancing briefly across the keys. "Please contact this office immediately your certification changes, pilot." She glanced up. "I advise that the possibility of a second-class provisional attaining work from this office is not high. That you own a ship is of value; that you have already successfully completed one assignment is likewise of value," she smiled. "As is, of course, Master dea'Cort's word."

Aelliana swallowed, face stiff.

The dispatcher inclined her head. "If it is not amiss, pilot, I offer advice."

"I should be grateful for advice," Aelliana returned sincerely, clutching her license in cold fingers.

"Register with the Guild Office on Navigation Street. Tell them that you fly your own ship and are willing to carry a hold-full or a courier pack. Ask to be placed on the Port Master's Roster." She tipped her head, birdlike. "They may not wish to do so until you have achieved solid second-class. But ask. And when you lose provisional, go back and ask again."

Aelliana bowed. "That seems sound advice. I thank you."

"No thanks due," the dispatcher assured her. "Good lift, pilot."

"Safe landing," Aelliana returned, which proper response tasted oddly sweet along her tongue. She made her bow and exited Korval's office, making for the next dispatching station on her carefully-researched list.

* * *

"Is this your idea of a joke?" Jon demanded, holding a gaily-painted tin high on one broad palm.

Daav gave the tin a moment of earnest perusal before turning a grave face to the older man.

"Alas, Master Jon, try as I will, I find nothing amusing within the object. It seems quite an ordinary tea-tin."

"Ordinary!" Jon roared, at such volume that Trilla leaned over the edge of the catwalk and Syri came out from behind the toolbox, head cocked inquisitively.

Jon thrust the tin in her direction. "Identify this."

"Joyful Sunrise morning blend," she returned promptly.

"In a stasis-sealed tin," Jon amended, and fixed Daav in an awful glare. "Do you know the price of this tin on the Port?"

Daav opened his black eyes wide. "No, how could I?"

"Puppy. A cantra on a glut-day, for your interest."

"Ah, then I appreciate your concern!" Daav cried, much enlightened. "Such a leaf will do no justice to your teapot, Master! Best return it to the merchant who sold it you, and ask for less of something more noble."

High on the catwalk, Trilla laughed. Syri raised a hand to hide her smile and Patch the cat wandered over to strop against Daav's legs.

Jon's lips were seen to twitch. "I suppose it's nothing to do with you, that the yos'Galan chooses to send this particular gift?"

"The yos'Galan?" Daav repeated, with a fine show of bewilderment.

"Oho, you wish me to believe that the yos'Galan's *lady* conceived this, do you? It may be her hand, young Captain, but I know better than to suppose it her thought." Jon raised his face to shout.

"Trilla, bring your hammer!"

"Aye, Master Jon!" She snagged a guy-rope and rode it briskly down, alighting with a snappy salute.

"Come along," Jon directed, and turned toward the crew lounge, Trilla at his heels.

Syri sent Daav a wide stare. "He never means to break the seal with a hammer!"

"Perhaps he merely intends to deliver the coup to the teapot," Daav said, bending to scoop Patch to his shoulder before moving off in Jon's wake.

"Never," Syri returned, falling in beside him. "That teapot's like a child to him. He'd sooner use a hammer on Patch."

"Hah. In that wise, we had best put speculation aside, and consider the evidence of our senses."

She laughed, that being one of the basic precepts of Scouthood, and they continued like two shadows down the bay, Patch riding tall on the man's leather-clad shoulder.

"We'll have a shelf here," Jon was telling Trilla, tapping his finger on the wall next to the teapot. "Good, sturdy work, mind. We'll need a locking case, and a place to display the lady's card. You," he turned to glare at Daav. "Get 'round to Min Del's and tell him I need a case, so—" he shaped it roughly in the air, one hand still holding the tin—"quicktime. Mind you tell him it's to lock to my print and none other! I'm damned if I'll have you bunch of hooligans breaking into my tin and replacing this leaf with sage!"

"But, Master Jon," Syri protested, "don't you mean to drink it?"

"Drink it?" Jon stared. "Have you run mad? Drink Joyful Sunrise? Why, I'd as soon—"

The crew door cycled noisily and Patch leapt from Daav's shoulder, running tail-high and spring-footed to greet the new entry.

Aelliana Caylon bent and stroked the cat's back where it curved against her knee in exuberant hello. Straightening, she tried to walk on, but found herself forthwith entangled in cat. She paused once more, bent and stroked; straightened—and nearly fell as her feline admirer wove joyfully between her legs.

She hesitated a heartbeat—two—before bending again and inexpertly gathering the cat into her arms. Patch settled against her shapeless chest, eyes slitted in ecstasy, front paws kneading the sleeve of the thick shirt. Aelliana came forward.

"Afternoon, math teacher!" Jon called, raising the tin in salutation.

"Good afternoon, Master dea'Cort," she replied solemnly. She paused, Patch purring like a cat besotted in the basket of her arms. One-by-one she surveyed Trilla, busy with her measurements, Syri's open-faced concern, Jon's hand and the tea-tin. The question, when it came, was addressed to Daav.

"Forgive me. I wonder if there is something—gone awry."

"Not a bit of it," he returned cheerfully. "Jon is only building a shelf to house a newly-acquired treasure."

Aelliana's head turned back toward Jon, hair shimmering. "A tea-tin?" she asked, bemusement sounding clearly. Daav grinned.

"Damn me if you're not as bad as he is!" Jon cried, sweeping his unencumbered hand toward the taller man. "This isn't just any tea-tin, math teacher, this is a gift from Master Trader Er Thom yos'Galan, honored son of the exalted House of Korval! What've you to say now, eh?"

Aelliana cuddled Patch absently against her. "It's a very pretty tea-tin," she offered after a moment.

Trilla choked and nearly dropped her measuring-wand. Syri gulped and walked rather unsteadily over to inspect the contents of the pastry-carton.

"Pretty," Jon repeated tonelessly. He reached into his vest pocket and reverently produced a folded card of the sort used to write notes of invitation. Gravely, he showed the front of the card—the Tree-and-Dragon, complete with the boldly embossed "Flaran Cha'men-thi"—and thrust it at Aelliana.

"Read it, then."

Smoothly, she readjusted Patch's weight, took the card and opened it, one-handed. She frowned for a moment at the message within, then raised her head, hair falling away from her face as she offered the card back to Jon.

"I am ashamed to admit that I neither read nor speak Terran," she said quietly. "It is a deficiency I intend soon to remedy. For today, however, I am ignorant."

"Hah." Jon fingered the card open. "It says—this is from Lady yos'Galan, understand, Learned Scholar of Language Anne Davis, out of the Terran Community. It says: 'To Master Pilot Jon dea'Cort. Please accept this token of . . . regard . . . from myself and my—' lord, would you say that rendered, Daav?"

Daav lifted an eyebrow. "How can I know?"

"Uncommonly awake," Jon commented and went

back to his note. "'... lord. It is our ... wish that you will ... delight in ... the gift, as we delight in the giving.' Then it is signed, you see, 'Anne Davis, Lady yos'Galan.'"

Aelliana's head was bent above Patch, her hair obscuring all of the cat but the blissfully kneading toes. "She sounds a—most gracious lady," she said after a moment. "Though I cannot help but wonder, sir, if she might have wished you to drink the tea."

"Truly, Jon," Syri said, turning from her study of petrifying pastries, "Lady yos'Galan cannot have meant you to imprison the gift in a lock-box. Where is joy in that?"

"Joy a-plenty," he returned promptly. "How many other garages have a gift from Korval to display, eh, Daav?"

"I have no notion, Master Jon. Shall I mount a survey?"

Jon grinned. "I thought you were sent to Min Del's on an errand."

"I can take that one," Syri offered. "My shift is done and it is a simple matter to chart a course past Min Del's on my way down-port."

"Simple enough," Jon agreed. "Are you here tomorrow?"

"Dawn to luncheon," Syri returned, "then I'm wanted back with my team." She bowed. "Pilot Caylon. Good health and fair flying."

"Fair flying." Aelliana tried to return the courtesy, but Patch took exception and the bow turned into a scramble to set him safely down. When she looked up again, Syri was gone and Trilla was walking toward the back of the bay.

"What've you been up to today, math teacher?"

Aelliana sighed and looked to Jon dea'Cort, who was carefully returning Korval's note to his vest pocket.

"I've been to the dispatch offices, and to the guild hall, requesting my name be added to the freelance rosters," she said. "The dispatcher at Korval's office advised me to put my name on the Port Master's list, but the guild rep ruled I must lose provisional status first."

"So you did go to Korval's offices." That was Daav, moving silently over to perch on a stool.

"Of course," she said, with a flicker of green eyes. "Korval is ships, after all."

"So it is," he agreed gravely. "Were you accepted for the roster there?"

"Readily—and asked to update my information, when I came full second-class." She turned to Jon dea'Cort.

"Your word of reference was in my favor, sir. I—am grateful—for your kindness."

"No kindness about it," he said gruffly. "If you'd done a bad job, there would have been no reference. Happens you did a binjali job and earned every word. How are you going about learning Terran?"

She sagged onto the edge of a stool, blinking at him. "I—hardly know," she said, somewhat abashed. "I had—thought—sleep tapes, you know. Chonselta Tech's library is not so well supplied..."

"Hah. No surprise. You might be able to get tapes copied from Scout Academy—your name's cantra there. Problem with tapes is you need to practice or the data just fades out again."

"Most of us are fluent," Daav said, offering her a smile. "What sort of Terran do you wish to learn?"

She blinked. "What—sort?"

"Indeed. You teach practical mathematics, do you not? So—do you wish to learn practical Terran, or theoretical?"

"Oh. Of course. I—I wish to understand and be understood under—under field conditions."

"Easy enough," Jon said, moving over to the teapot and pouring himself a mug full. "You get around all right in Trade?"

"I am comfortable conversing in Trade," Aelliana assured him in the mode-less monotone of that language.

"Even easier, then. We teach you from Trade, eh, Daav?"

"It would seem best," he replied. "Shall you arrange for the tapes?"

"Might be better for her to learn it in waking mind." Jon chose a pastry and ambled back to the stools. "You have a timetable?"

She swallowed, took a breath, and raised her eyes to his. "As soon as possible," she said, voice gone raspy and tight. "It would be—good—if I were—fluent—within the year."

The amber eyes held hers for a long moment, then Jon looked away and hoisted himself atop the green stool. "All right. We'll lay the basics, then supplement with tape as necessary. Daav's most fluent among the current crew. Trilla's good. Clonak's good, if he can be prevailed upon to speak something other than Aus-dialect. My ear is better than my accent, I fear, though I read well enough. Syri's about at my level—no, Syri's back to her team tomorrow..." He paused for a sip of tea. "This course of study suit you?"

"I—" She cleared her throat, looking from the old man to the young one. "Thank you—extremely. Balance must be—owing, however. I cannot—"

Jon sighed gustily. "First lesson in Terran, math teacher—pay attention."

She swallowed. "Yes, sir."

"Stop thinking like a Liaden." He grinned. "Thought it was going to be easy, did you? I told you we're all comrades here, eh? Happens that's true. What's owing is what's received: Comfort, safety and succor. Balance, right?"

The words vibrated in the air. She sat on the edge of the stool, listening to them, feeling them strike, one by one, at the core of her. What they offered was—clan. What they asked in return was that she strive for her most perfect self—to the betterment of them all.

And I tell you, Birin Caylon, it's Aelliana should be set upon the delm's road, and none of that vain, precious boy of yours! Hanelur Caylon's voice was as strong in memory as it had been a dozen Standards ago, when carelessness had left a study door ajar and two pair of ears heard what had far better been left unsaid.

Aelliana raised her head and met Jon dea'Cort's knowing amber gaze. "Balance," she said, solemnly. "I shall do my best."

Chapter Sixteen

The thing to recall about Dragons is that it takes a special person to deal with them at all. If you lie to them, they will steal from you. If you attack them without cause, they will dismember you. If you run from them, they will laugh at you.

It is thus best to deal calmly, openly and fairly with Dragons: Give them all they buy and no more or less, and they will do the same by you. Stand at their back and they will stand at yours. Always remember that a Dragon is first a Dragon and only then a friend, a partner, a lover.

Never assume that you have discovered a Dragon's weak point until it is dead and forgotten, for joy is fleeting and a Dragon's revenge is forever.

—From the Liaden Book of Dragons

IT WAS WARM IN THIS CORNER OF THE GARDEN—WARM and blessedly quiet. So quiet, indeed, that orange-and-white Relchin had given over birding to lounge in the shade of the old stone wall and watch Daav grub about in the dirt.

Korval employed several very able gardeners, whose task it was to tend the formal gardens and lawns. The most senior of these formidable individuals walked the Inner Court once each relumma, offering suggestions and advice—only that. The care of the Inner Court, from the moss garden to the Tree itself, was Daav's self-appointed and jealously-held privilege.

This morning, he was engaged in digging and dividing gladoli bulbs. Much of this bounty would be ceded to his gardeners, but he wished to hold out a dozen to present to Lady yo'Lanna, who had been his mother's stalwart friend, and would know how to value a gift of Chi yos'Phelium's favorite flowers.

He was roused from this agreeable work by the step, and then the person, of his butler.

"Delm Bindan is come, sir, on the matter of Your Lordship's pending nuptials."

Daav sat back on his heels, bulb in one hand, trowel in the other.

"Bindan is here?" he repeated stupidly.

Mr. pel'Kana inclined his head. "I have put her in the Small Parlor, sir."

Daav closed his eyes, swallowing a regrettable reply.

"Provide Delm Bindan with refreshment," he said instead. "I shall be with her, say, before the next hour strikes."

Mr. pel'Kana bowed and departed, leaving Daav to stare down at his crusted gloves and grubby coveralls. For one mad instant he considered rising and going directly to the Small Parlor in all his dirt, which was surely no more than she had purchased by appearing thus, dispatching neither card nor call to warn him.

The instant passed. He sighed and lay aside his trowel, made certain the bulbs were damp in their nest of moss, and rose, stripping off his gloves.

"On the matter of Your Lordship's pending nuptials," he told Relchin, in wickedly accurate imitation of Mr. pel'Kana's stately tones. The big cat smiled up at him through slitted green eyes. Daav dropped his gloves beside the trowel and went, reluctantly, away.

It lacked a few minutes of the new hour when he arrived in the Small Parlor, freshly showered and dressed in a comfortable white shirt and soft blue trousers.

He bowed, Delm to Delm, and Bindan rose to do likewise, muscles stiff with outrage.

"I regret you were obliged to wait," he said, in response to that outrage. "Had word been sent ahead, I should have been immediately accessible."

Her eyes narrowed, though she otherwise preserved her countenance. "I shall bear the lesson in mind," she said, inclining her head. "In the meanwhile, Korval, there is a matter touching upon our contract which must be discussed."

"Ah. Then you must allow me first to refresh your wine, and provide myself with a glass."

She did allow it, though he had the impression she would have rather not, and took a single ritual sip before setting the cup aside.

In his turn, Daav drank and set aside, then leaned back in his chair.

"How may Korval serve Bindan?"

She considered him for a long moment before inclining her head. "It is known," she said, very carefully, "that Korval charts its own course and cares little for scandal. It is perhaps lesser known that Bindan holds itself aside from such matters as may lead to the shouting of its name in open council."

Daav lifted an eyebrow. "And yet the matter upon which Korval was called in yesterday's council was found to be no scandal at all."

"It was found," Bindan said tartly, "that Korval had sidestepped the question in favor of showing that initial discovery was made by a Liaden scholar from a clan of scholars, all of whom are quite mad enough to wish such a thing introduced to the world." She inclined her head, ironically. "Korval's greatness is no matter of luck."

He grit his teeth against irritation and inclined his head in calm acceptance of the jibe.

"I ask you plain, my Lord: Will you keep your Terran within propriety?"

There was a charged silence, long enough for Bindan to feel the full force of her error.

"Thodelmae yos'Galan," Daav said deliberately, "is an honored member of Korval. She has done nothing to incur her delm's censure and much to excite his pride. I remind you that a contract of alliance does not in any way surrender Korval's authority to Bindan."

Her mouth tightened, but, to her credit, her gaze did not falter. "I say again, we are a House unused to scandal. Korval shall soon have the care of one of Bindan's dearest treasures. If Korval cannot hold itself aloof from scandal for the duration of its alignment with Bindan, Korval might best seek contract elsewhere."

For a heartbeat, he thought he would accept the trade she offered and count himself well-rid of Clan Bindan and Samiv tel'Izak.

Then he recalled the weary round of searching to be undertaken once again—the grids to be scanned, the gene-maps to weigh, and there were none of them different at core from Samiv tel'Izak, and none of them less respectable and solid than Bindan. Korval was trouble and scandal and oddity. It had always been so: Descendants of a pirate, a soldier and a Houseless schoolboy, had could it be otherwise?

Gods, he thought, *only let me soon hold my child.* He inclined his head into Bindan's glare.

"Korval shall make every effort to avoid scandal from this hour and until the conclusion of our association with Bindan," he said formally, and glanced up.

"Bindan must understand that Korval's necessities are—unique."

"Necessity does not trouble me," she replied. "Scandal is my concern."

She rose and made her bow, and Daav likewise. He touched the bell and Mr. pel'Kana came and escorted Delm Bindan out.

"Correct to five places," Aelliana announced, leaning back in the pilot's chair with a sigh.

"At least while we're sitting safe and cold," Daav amended, concluding his own checks and releasing the second backup comp to slumber.

Aelliana turned to look at him, hair a silken shimmer in the glow of the board lights.

"You suspect a main system error?"

"Ah, no, nothing on that line!" He raised a quick hand, smile tinged with irony. "It is merely that Jon certified the former comp while the ship was quiet— and see what nearly came of us while we flew!" He moved his shoulders, sending a bright black glance sideways into her face.

"Jon predicts I shall grow into a suspicious old man."

"Better than to die a naive young man," she replied, tawny brows drawn above frowning green eyes. "You are correct. In light of previous failure, a prudent check must include lift and land."

"Hah." He grinned. "Shall you request clearance, pilot?"

She hesitated on the edge of an eager affirmative, looking away from his face to scan the board. The clock's message killed the *yes* before it passed her lips, and she glanced back to him with a sigh.

"I haven't time left me today for a proper test. What is your shift tomorrow?" She bit her lip, then, the darker gold of a blush kissing her cheeks as she looked aside. "Forgive me," she said, voice tight. "I meant no offense, pilot."

"Nor was offense taken," Daav answered, still in the warmth of Comrade mode. "I had said it was an honor to sit board with you and wished to do so again. Gods know, it's an ill enough face, but does it seem to you deceitful?"

Her eyes flew up, startle-wide and brilliantly green. And then was Daav forced to sit quite still, face and eyes plain as for any comrade or clanmate, while she subjected each feature to minute study.

"Indeed," she said, eventually and quite seriously, "I find it neither ill nor dishonest. As for the other matter—It is my understanding that you are a master pilot employed by Master dea'Cort. Surely it is out of my place to order you?"

"But you had not ordered me," he pointed out. "You had merely asked my shift. To which the answer must be, as I am casual labor and Jon allows me woeful license—When shall you be ready to lift?"

"I—" Her eyes moved, taking in the board, lit and waiting to receive its office. Hunger, and a dizzying desire to spin her chair now, open the line to Solcintra Tower and file a course up—out and away...

"Tomorrow," she said to the man at her side and looked into his calm eyes. "I can be here in the first hour after Solcintra dawn." Better—much better—to be gone from Mizel's clanhouse before anyone was about to ask questions, or to forbid her going at all.

Daav inclined his head. "I shall meet you at the foot of the ramp," he said, "in the first hour after dawn, tomorrow." He grinned. "And then we shall give her a proper testing, eh?"

In the depths of her chest it seemed as if another knot loosened and relaxed toward uncoiling. Aelliana felt her lips curve upward as she met the sparkling black gaze.

"Indeed we will."

"Hah." Daav tipped his head slightly to one side. "I wonder, must you leave at once?"

She flicked another glance at the clock, wariness awake once more. "There are nearly three hours," she said slowly, "before the twilight ferry leaves."

"Plenty of time to inventory your emergency equipment," he returned briskly, "and to be certain your suits are functional."

She looked at him in patent dismay. "I—forgive me. I am afraid I don't even know where the suits are."

"I thought as much," Daav said, with an odd side-to-side movement of his head. He rose and beckoned with one long-fingered hand. "Come along, pilot."

Master Daav pronounced the emergency equipment adequate, though he frowned a long moment over the neat rack of four oxy-tanks, forefinger tapping the status dials.

"Keep close watch on these," he said, and Aelliana heard a tremor of something chill down near the root of his warm deep voice. "You don't want to run out of air. It might be wise to add another can or two, in case of malfunction."

"Is it likely," Aelliana wondered, "that life support will malfunction?"

"I had been on a ship that lost life support," he said, frowning down at the canisters. "While such a failure does not often occur, I submit that once is more than sufficient, should you carry inadequate air, an inferior emergency kit or a defective suit." He took a deep breath then and seemed to shake himself—flashed her a brief smile.

"There, I don't mean to alarm you. Merely be vigilant and watchful of your equipment, as any good captain must be. Extra cans will become a necessity, should you add a co-pilot. For the moment—" He turned a hand palm up. "Pilot's choice."

She blinked, inclined her head. "Thank you. I shall recall your advice."

"Well enough," he said briskly and turned to lay a hand on the suit rack. "Tell me, have you ever worn one of these?"

"Good evening, Captain, darling!" Clonak moved his arm sharply as Daav walked by, releasing a red ball about the size of Aelliana's two fists together.

The ball zagged a crazy course, dipping and wobbling until the eyes ached trying to track it.

Daav extended a negligent hand, barely checking

his stride, snagged the ball and skated it back in one smooth, unhurried motion.

"Hello, Clonak."

The pudgy Scout skipped one step forward and two aside, captured the ball and threw again.

"Your servant, goddess."

Aelliana blinked, panic rising—and saw her hand flick and snatch, felt the weird weight of the thing and threw, instinctively calculating a trajectory that would take it—

Clonak leapt up with a laugh, cradling the ball against his chest. His boot-toes barely brushed the floor before he threw again.

"Well tossed! I hereby issue challenge, the loser to drink a mug of Jon's tea!"

"Challenge?" Aelliana choked. "I can't—" But there was the ball hurtling not exactly toward her and before she had properly attended her body's doings she had danced into the place where it *would be*, scooped it out of the air and hurled it back with a will.

"Aha, she means to hurt me, Daav!" Clonak dove, rolled and tossed from the floor.

"No more than you've asked for," Daav returned, hoisting himself atop a tool-chest and crossing his long legs under him.

The ball's erratic course took it floorward and into an unlikely arc. Aelliana spun to catch it as it swerved behind her, reached—and stumbled, blinded by the swirl of hair across her eyes.

"A clear miss!" Clonak cried, bounding down-bay after the escaped toy. "I claim the win!"

On one knee, half-blinded by hair, Aelliana felt a bite of fury at her own incompetence, an acid wash of failure in the base of her gut. Slowly, she climbed to her feet, shoulders sagging even as she scraped the clinging strands out of her eyes.

"A win by default," Daav was saying in his deep voice; "Pilot Caylon was disadvantaged."

"A win, nonetheless," Clonak argued, coming back, tossing the ball from hand to hand.

"Always the lazy course," Daav said, then, slightly sharper. "Pilot."

Aelliana glanced up, eyes pulled by his tone. He smiled and reached behind his head, twisted—and threw.

"Don't let him win," he said. "Make him fight for it."

Aelliana's hand flashed out, snatching a plain silver hair-ring out of the air. She glanced back at Daav, sitting crosslegged atop the tool cart, his hair falling loose along his shoulder, one eyebrow up and his smile with an edge of—challenge?

Once again, her hands moved of their own will, sweeping her mass of hair back, twisting and clipping it tight. She turned to face Clonak and inclined her head. "I am ready to accept your challenge, sir."

"Right-o," he said. And threw.

It was more difficult this time. The universe narrowed to the ball and its antics, to the absolute necessity of catching and throwing and catching and—

There was no ball.

Disoriented, Aelliana spun, found Clonak, his hands hanging empty and a sheepish look on his round, mustached face. To the right Daav still sat atop the tool cart, his hair neatly braided. To the left was Jon dea'Cort, red ball held high in a hand.

"*I* win," Jon announced, fixing Clonak in his eye. "How long has this been going on?"

"About half-an-hour," Daav spoke up. "Indeed, Master Jon, I was about to call time, as Pilot Caylon must make the twilight ferry."

Jon moved his glare to Aelliana, who became aware that her heart was pumping hurriedly and she was warm and rather damp.

"If you have to catch the ferry, math teacher, now's the time to jet. Good evening."

She bowed, trying to bring her rapid breathing under control. "Good evening, Master dea'Cort. Clonak—"

"I'll deal with Clonak," Jon said awfully. "Move."

Aelliana blinked and flicked a glance to Daav. His fingers moved atop one knee, shaping a word in Scout finger-talk: *Jet.*

In the back of the bay, the clock that kept official Port time sang the quarter hour.

Aelliana ran.

It wasn't until she left the ferry in Chonselta Port and was walking quickly toward the train station that she recalled the hair-ring and reached up to pull it free.

Her hair flowed forward, shielding her from the world. Slowly, almost reluctantly, she slipped the ring into her pocket.

Tomorrow, in the first hour after dawn, she thought and smiled within the fortress of her hair. Whatever pain Ran Eld might mete this evening, tomorrow she would fly.

Chapter Seventeen

Preserve your life, preserve your folk, preserve the Tree, no matter what the means. Grovel, if your enemy demands it; beg; swallow any insult. Stay alive, preserve you and yours.

Watch close, stay alert. And when your enemy turns his back, kill him and run free.

—Excerpted from Cantra yos'Phelium's Log Book

THE CREW DOOR CLOSED AND JON SPUN BACK TO CLONAK, red ball held out like a judgment.

"I shall be very interested to hear," he stated in a height of tone one very rarely had from Jon, "your reasons for engaging in a round of bowli ball with Pilot Caylon."

Clonak very nearly gaped. He did shoot a glance over his shoulder at Daav, but gained nothing from that quarter save a grave inclination of the head.

"Why not?" he asked, returning his full attention to Jon. "She gave good game."

"Good game!" Jon's glare grew blacker. He took a step forward, shaking the bowli ball until its internal gyro squealed. "Good game! Do you have any notion how long I stood there, watching you?"

169

"Well," Clonak allowed, leaning slightly back from the older man's approach, "there was the game to be concerned with, Master Jon, and my goddess out to knock my head off, if she could but manage it." He grinned. "I'm fond of my head, after all, so it seemed prudent to keep both eyes on the ball."

"You never had a prudent thought in your life, you heedless—" Jon cut himself off abruptly. "Fifteen minutes I stood there, watching as you—you, who visit the gym every day and follow a full exercise routine!— barely held your own against a desk-bound, half-starved scholar with her second-class license shiny-new in her hand! I've a good notion to tell your trainer that—"

"Second class!" Clonak yelped, going back a step and flinging a look of wild amazement over his shoulder. "Daav!"

"Second class provisional," that gentleman said calmly, "awarded barely ten days gone."

"What meat-brain granted her a provisional? She's as fast as any first class I've ever seen—faster than most!"

"Flight time, Master Clonak," Daav chided gently. "The regs are quite clear."

Clonak said something rude regarding the regs.

"Yes, dear. I showed her where her suits were stowed today, and helped her inventory the emergency kit."

"She's never so green as that!"

"She's every bit as green as that!" Jon shouted. "And if she had succeeded in knocking your useless block into the center of next twelve-day—which I swear is no more than she should have!—she'd have stuttered and stammered and blamed herself and we'd have never seen Aelliana Caylon at this yard again!" He took a mighty breath, and released it in a roar.

"Gods abound, I *will* tell your trainer!"

"It never happened!" Clonak cried. "Jon, for pity's—"

"And you!" Jon hurled the ball forcefully to the right and down. It twisted, hummed, skated and charted a rising course for the tool chest, speed increasing. Daav put out a long arm, captured the thing in a swoop and set it upon his knee, stroking it with firm fingers, as if it were a particularly frolicsome kitten.

"I?" He lifted an elegant eyebrow.

"Don't you come all High House with me! What the devil did you mean by letting that go on? Timing it, were you? I suppose it never occurred to you to interfere? It was easier to sit up there like a *melant'i*-choked dirt-scruffer—"

"Certainly not," Daav said, his calm voice cutting effortlessly across the other's tirade. "I hope I know my obligations, as trainer, as comrade and as co-pilot. In any of those faces I'd be blind not to see she needs to learn how to fight—quickly."

It could not be said that Jon's mouth actually hung open. However, there was a long moment of silence before a grudging, "Well, that's the first sensible thing I've heard said in the last ten minutes, all considered. Still, lad, she might have took damage. Clonak's got the edge."

"It's what I've been telling you!" Clonak cried plaintively. "My so-called edge was enough to keep the pace." He moved his shoulders. "I don't say I couldn't have worn her down, if it came to an endurance test. But the unvarnished truth is, Master Jon, she might very well have pegged me before it came to stamina—and I'd be in the 'doc even now, growing me a new head!" He set his hands on his hips and gave Jon back his glare. "Tell my trainer, then!"

"Hah." Jon flicked his glance aside. "Daav?"

"Not entirely unlike my own judgment, though I believe Clonak over-tender in regard to his head. I rather thought she was homing in on his nose."

"Smashed to a purple pulp," Clonak mourned. "Blood all sticky in my mustache."

"Brace up, darling, the 'doc would have put everything right."

"Yes, but you know," Clonak said earnestly, "it still hurts."

"One of life's inequities," Jon said, and sighed. "Why I ever let the pair of you pass piloting is a puzzle for my old age. How came you to be our math teacher's co-pilot, young Captain?"

"She asked me to accompany her on a thorough testing of the new navcomp and backups," Daav said, sliding silently to his feet. He tossed the bowli ball lightly to Clonak, who scooped it up in the instant before it touched his belt buckle.

"We're to lift in the first hour after dawn, tomorrow."

"If she keeps this pace, she'll lose provisional well ahead of spec," Jon said. "Good lift to you, then." He turned back toward his office.

"Fair flying, Master Jon," Daav returned softly, and cocked a meaningful eyebrow at Clonak.

"End of shift, old friend?"

The pudgy Scout sighed and used the tips of three fingers to smooth his mustache. "I suppose you're right," he said, walking at Daav's side toward the crew door. "Why are you always right, Captain?"

"Now, do you know, my perspective is that I'm often wrong."

"A terrifying statement! Do not, I pray, say it to

anyone else! As for myself, consider my lips sealed—I shall carry your secret to the grave."

The crew door cycled and they stepped out into the twilight. Clonak drew in a noisy lungful of free air and grinned up at Daav. "Come 'round to Apel's and let me buy you a glass of wine."

A glass of wine with Clonak had a woeful tendency to become many glasses of wine, and a night so late it might just as easily be called tomorrow. Daav moved his shoulders and returned his friend's grin.

"Another time. I've an early lift."

"So you do! I'm reminded that I'm jealous." Clonak lifted a hand and moved away. "Until soon, darling."

"Take good care, Clonak." Daav stretched, drinking in the evening air, then turned toward Mechanic Street and his landcar. *An early lift*, he thought, and smiled.

Ran Eld strolled into her room without the courtesy of a ring to announce his presence. He had long ago possessed himself of an override to Aelliana's door-code and used it as his right. She suspected that he also kept an ear on her so-called private comm-line, and thus routed all calls to her office at the college.

Aelliana blanked the reader and spun, coming quickly to her feet. She had as little desire for Ran Eld to discover her perusing a volume on Terran culture as she had for being trapped in her chair against the desk, her brother looming close above her.

As it was, her position was less than perfect, with her back to the L-shaped desk and a bookshelf cutting off escape to the right. Still, she was on her feet and that was something, she told herself as her brother

came close—and then closer—a sheaf of printout in
his ring-heavy hand.

"Good evening, Aelliana, how delightful to find
you yet awake." His voice held its usual note of sweet
malice, though with a certain undertone that said he
would have been better pleased, if it been necessary
for him to roust her from bed.

He moved the sheaf of papers carelessly, fanning
her face with a cold, tiny breeze. Aelliana shivered.

Ran Eld smiled. "I have the report on the progress
of your investment, sister. Allow me to congratulate
you on the timeliness of your delivery. Alas, I find I
am not entirely convinced of the superiority of your
Fund; it seemed to run neck-and-neck with my own."

"A twelve-day is not sufficient time to test out,"
Aelliana said, hating the quaver in her voice. "You
know that."

"Do I? But perhaps I had forgotten. Stupid of me."
He moved the papers closer, laying the sharp edges
against her cheek. Aelliana shrank back, the papers
followed, edges beginning to bite. She froze.

"I hear," Ran Eld said conversationally, "that you
have taken to frequenting gaming places. That you
tend—after receiving tuition on the subject from
your elders—toward the company of Scouts. Is what
I hear true, sister?"

The paper edges burned against her skin. One quick
move of her brother's hand and her cheek would be
sliced, eye-edge to jaw. Aelliana took a deep breath
and forced herself to meet his eyes.

"How could I frequent gaming houses?" she asked,
keeping her voice humble, welcoming now the despicable, cowardly quaver. It sometimes happened that

Ran Eld gave over punishment, if her groveling proved sufficiently amusing. "My wages are given entirely to yourself, brother—and you even now hold the proof of what befell my quarter-share."

There was a long pause, long enough for Aelliana to feel the breath begin to thicken in her throat.

"So I do." He lifted the papers away, glanced at them—and glanced up.

"I note a copy forwarded to the delm. Why is that?"

"I—Merely I had thought it proper," she gasped. "It was the Delm's Word began the venture and I—I meant no offense, only right action."

Another pause, excruciating to her quivering nerves.

"Better to err on the part of right action than to fail of giving full honor," Ran Eld allowed at last, though not as if this judgment pleased him. "I advise that there is no need to send future reports to the delm. Do you understand me?"

She bowed her head cravenly, blessing the forward-falling shroud of hair. "I understand you, brother."

"Good. Of this other matter—you will look at me, Aelliana."

Swallowing against terror, she raised her head. Gods, what if one of Ran Eld's cronies had seen her in Quenpalt's Casino? What if the tale of her win had come after all to his ears? Her ship—Ran Eld must not, *must* not, be allowed—

"I ask you again, sister, if you have not been gambling in casinos. If perhaps you had not acquired—a spaceship—through playing a game of chance with a High House lord out of Solcintra?"

"A spaceship?" She stared at him, striving for a look of rankest stupidity. "What should I do with a spaceship?"

Ran Eld's eyes bored into hers. Somehow, she endured it, feeling the weight of *Ride the Luck's* keys, hanging cold between sweat-slicked breasts.

"I thought it a wine-tale," he said at last, moving his eyes from hers. It took every erg of will not to sag against the desk and sob aloud with relief, though she did dare bow her head, and draw the curtain of her hair once again across her face.

Above her, Ran Eld sighed. "Do you recall, Aelliana, your instruction regarding Scouts?"

"I am—am only to teach those Scouts registered to my courses," she said hoarsely, "and shun their company at all other times."

"Precisely. I warn you now, sister, that it will go extremely ill with you, do I find you have disregarded this instruction. Scouts are not fit company for one of Mizel—even if that one is only yourself. Do you understand?"

"I understand," she whispered around a sudden surging desire to behold at this moment any of Binjali's crew, with a special thanks to the gods if that any should chance to be Daav or burly Jon dea'Cort.

"Very good," Ran Eld said, out of the real and dismal present. "I give you good-night, sister. Sleep well."

She raised her head sufficiently to watch him cross the room and pass through the door. The closing of that portal was like a knife against the wires of fright that held her upright.

With a dry sob, she crashed to her knees, hands flying up to cover her face as she huddled against the desk-legs and shivered.

Chapter Eighteen

We signed the final draft of the contract tonight.
Thought they'd choke on Captain's Justice. Stu-
pid groundlings. How do we know the length of
voyage, assuming we even break out? How do we
know there's any worlds left to run to? Situation
like this, there has to be one voice that's law, not
some damn committee. And that law has got to
be in favor of the ship, and the greatest good.
There can only be one captain. One voice. One
law. For the best survival of the ship.

—Excerpted from Cantra yos'Phelium's Log Book

IT WAS RAINING IN SOLCINTRA PORT.

Aelliana ran through the downpour, less conscious
of the wet than the joy that heated her blood, reduc-
ing Clan Mizel to a speck and Ran Eld Caylon to an
infelicity born of a bad night's dreaming.

Here in the wakeful world, she would soon meet
her co-pilot at the foot of her ship's ramp, and Liad
itself would be left behind, reduced to a mathematical
necessity, one of many factors supporting an equation
of flight.

She reached *The Luck's* pad, raced 'round the curve

to the end of the ramp—and all but cried aloud, her run shattered by dismay.

There was no tall graceful figure awaiting her at the base of the ramp, rain-jewels glittering along leathered shoulders. The gantry was empty, from tarmac to hatch. Aelliana swallowed, shivering in the dismal downpour, and walked the rest of the way forward on joy-dead feet.

To the left, a flicker of noiseless movement. Aelliana spun as Daav ducked out from beneath the ramp, leather collar turned up against the wet, long fingers dancing cheerfully.

Relief hit in a giddy wave, rocking her into laughter as she shook sodden hair away from her face.

"A very fine morning, to be sure!" She answered the silent greeting aloud. "I thought you had forgotten me!"

"No, but I have an excellent memory," he said earnestly. "Even Jon allows me that much." He sighed heavily, shoulders slumping in an attitude of exaggerated remorse. "My woeful decadence is to blame for your distress and I humbly ask pardon."

Giddy yet with the return of joy, Aelliana smiled and tipped her head, trying to read beyond the mischief in the black eyes and into the heart of the joke.

In a moment she had given it up, glancing away from a gaze that seemed to read her all too easily, while remaining a cipher to her closest study.

"Decadence?" she asked.

"Well, you see," he said, slipping past her and ghosting up the ramp, "I would much rather be dry than wet."

She choked on another laugh and followed him, pulling the keys up on their neck-chain and slipping it over her head. "I wonder that Master dea'Cort allows one so in love with comfort to work for him."

"How could you not, when Master dea'Cort wonders as much himself? Often. And loudly."

Almost she laughed again, but lost it in a tiny shiver of alarm. The landing was very thin and Daav, slim as he was, filled a significant percentage of the available space. She would need to practically lean against his chest to access the hatch panel.

As if he felt her hesitation in his own muscles, Daav pivoted sideways on the ramp, arms outstretched, one hand gripping the rail, the other resting against the hull. He grinned and inclined his head.

"Your shelter from the storm, pilot. Be quick, I beg you, else I will be wet!"

She slid by, feeling his nearness like sunlight on her back, raised the shield and fingered the first key into place. The ID board came alive. She fed in her code and seated the second key. There was a muted click and the hatch began to rise.

Aelliana pulled the keys free and turned carefully on the landing, inclining her head with a forced smile. "Quickly, before you are soaked."

"Pilot first." Daav stayed where he was, one eyebrow askance. "I've been well drilled in protocol."

Pilot first. Aelliana blinked as the words found home, then drew a deep breath and stepped into her ship, deliberately squaring her shoulders as she did.

Daav entered the ship; the outer hatch cycled and locked behind him.

Before him, Aelliana hesitated on the edge of the inner hatch. He read in the set of her body an awareness that had nothing to do with wariness and saw, in one of the flashes of instinctive understanding characteristic of him, that Aelliana was poised on a precipice of change. Here and now, she was engaged in letting go of something past and potent and simultaneously reaching forth to grasp something other and infinitely precious.

He took a careful breath, and remanded himself to utter stillness, that he not distract her in the midst of this chanciest of undertakings.

That she reached toward claiming her own skills, her ship, her comrades, seemed likely. That his taking shelter beneath the ramp had precipitated this moment of change also seemed likely. Her dismay at discovering an empty ramp, and the giddy relief she showed at his appearance told the tale plainly. He wondered if she yet realized that she was speaking to him in Comrade.

Within the frame of the inner hatchway, Aelliana shifted—turned.

"Will you check the board while I go and dry myself?" she asked, as a comrade might well ask. She held out the ship keys on a link of short chain and long. Daav stepped forward and received them with a smile.

"Indeed I will."

"Thank you." She crossed the threshold into the pilot's chamber, moving left toward the companionway, wet garments clinging heavily, hinting at the shape they were meant to conceal. Daav went right, sorting the keys for the board—

"Daav?"

For the first time, his name: Intuition had not failed him. He turned, taking care to move gentle, and smiled.

"Aelliana?"

She came forward a few steps, hand outstretched, a silver gleam between the fingers.

"I had—taken your hair-ring—last evening..."

"Ah." He lifted a hand to touch his queue. "I have another, you see, and it seems you might put that one to good use. Keep it, of your kindness." He offered a grin. "Clonak may demand a rematch, you know."

Her eyes took fire and her mouth curved, fingers closing tight around the paltry gift.

"Thank you," she said again, and hesitated, head tipped to one side. "Clonak. Did Jon—"

"No mortal wounds," he said cheerfully. "Clonak has a gift for irritation against which even Jon is not immune."

Laughter sparkled across her face, gone in the next instant. She turned without another word and went down the companionway. After a moment, Daav went to the board and slid into the co-pilot's chair.

The thick overshirt refused to give up its moisture.

Aelliana, who had been simultaneously warmed and dried by the 'fresher in the pilot's cabin, fingered the sodden beige item uncertainly.

The valet had done admirably by the rest of her clothing, depositing them in the out-bin pressed and smelling softly of jazmin.

Liked everything binjali, the chel'Mara, she thought with a grudge of admiration as she pulled on black trousers, plain singlet and a white silk day-shirt trimmed with faded green ribbon. None of these garments was new, nor did they fit her well. Indeed, in the absence of the overshirt, the trousers required severe belt-pleating to keep them even indifferently moored by her waist. The shirt—a gift from Sinit on a name day long past—had wide sleeves pulled tight into green-trimmed cuffs, and a loose cut, though the silk would cling, here and there.

But the overshirt, that was the thing. It was her custom always to wear this article of clothing; it was her armor, her huddling place, her quilted coat of invisibility.

And it hung, like a dozen or so freshly caught fish, chilling her fingertips.

Aelliana bit her lip. Even her boots had dried under the valet's persuasion, and been returned to her gleaming with polish, worn heels evened. That the one most necessary item should—

"Tower gives us grace to lift, pilot." Daav's voice flowed out of the wallspeaker. "Pending receipt of course."

Aelliana gasped and spun toward the speaker, her eye catching a flash of movement to her right.

"I shall be—another moment," she managed and barely waited to hear his "Right" before spinning back to the valet, snatching open the hatch and stuffing the soggy shirt within.

She chose "ultra-dry" from the option list, slammed the hatch, and turned again, confronting the mirror.

No lift-proof wonder, this, but a simple rectangle of polished metal, showing, at the moment, a painfully thin woman in baggy trousers and a shabby silk shirt, blast-dried hair snarled across her face.

Aelliana snatched at her pocket, finger-combed the static-charged mass back from her face and clipped it firmly with Daav's hair-ring.

The woman in the mirror hesitated a heartbeat longer, poised on the balls of her feet, thin body quivering, eyes wide and green in a gaunt, pale face.

She inclined her head. "Pilot," she said quietly, and was gone.

A mug of tea steamed gently on the arm of her chair, keeping company with a cheese muffin. Daav, reclining in the co-pilot's place with his long legs thrust out before him, glanced up from finishing his own muffin, earring swinging.

"I hope you don't mind cheese," he said apologetically. "I meant only to order my own, you know, and what must my fingers do but stutter on the key and the automat give out two!"

Aelliana considered him thoughtfully.

"I should like to see your fingers stutter," she decided after a moment.

Daav grinned. "Alas, it happens all too often. Dreadfully clumsy."

"No doubt even Jon will say so," she agreed gravely, slipping into her place. She picked up the cup and frowned into the reddish depths.

"What is it about Scouts," she wondered, "that makes them so eager to feed one?"

"Well, you see, we're trained to respect efficiency and to mend those things which hinder efficient work. Observation has shown that a person carrying significantly less than optimum body-weight functions at lowered efficiency. Such persons are subject to exhaustion, muddled thinking, and bouts of terror, which are not merely inefficient, but active threats to survival."

Startled, she looked up and met a pair of sober black eyes.

"A pilot keeps herself fit," she said, quoting from the guild-book.

Daav inclined his head. "That," he agreed quietly. "Also it is the duty of the co-pilot to ensure the pilot's health—and the care of a comrade to answer need with aid."

"I see." She put the teacup back on the broad arm of the chair and reached for the muffin. "I have been—long aside—from the world," she said, breaking the cake open and breathing in the cheesy aroma. "While I eat, will you tell me if you have formed any notion of how best to test the navcomp?"

"Several," he said readily, "but you must tell me how much time you may spend."

Aelliana glanced at the board clock and back to her co-pilot. "Twelve hours."

"Ah," he said with a smile, "in that wise..."

Chapter Nineteen

A statistically significant number of Scouts are reported eklykt'i—unreturned—every Standard Year. While some undoubtedly fall prey to the omnipresent dangers of their duty, there is reason to believe that most have simply found a world that suits them better than the homeworld and have decided to stay.

There are those who argue that Scouts who are eklykt'i are the most successful Scouts of all.

—Excerpted from "All About the Liaden Scouts"

LIAD HUNG IN HER THIRD SCREEN, A GLOWING WIZARD'S-ball caught fast in a thick net of traffic. Outyards Four, Five and Three, moored to the edge of the net, also showed, gratifyingly distant. All that remained between *Ride the Luck* and the beginning of Jump space was the hailing beacon—and Scout Station.

Aelliana sighed.

"Tired, pilot?"

"Not at all," she returned, spinning in her chair to meet her co-pilot's smile. "I was merely thinking how—satisfying—it would be to continue our route out."

"Eminently satisfying," Daav said, his smile going

a little crooked, "and very tempting. Liad does grate upon one, from time to time." He extended the hand which bore the mark of the ring he did not wear and locked his board.

Aelliana bit her lip, leaning over to lock her own board. "Have you been—retired—very long?" she asked, which was none of her concern at all.

"Six years," Daav answered, as if it had been an entirely appropriate question. "I had been active for ten."

"Clonak—Clonak calls you captain," she told him, as if this might have someway escaped his notice.

Daav laughed. "Well, and Clonak's an odd creature, as even those who love him must own. It happens I had been his team leader, though I barely had such courtesy from him then. And," he added kindly, "before you sprain your tongue in an attempt not to ask the next perfectly logical question: Scout Captain, with a specialty in Cultural Genetics."

Swiftly, she lifted her eyes to his. "I beg your pardon," she said, feeling heat wash along her cheeks. "I had been taught it impolite to inquire of—of—" She staggered to a halt, for "stranger," the word she had been about to utter, did not fit the cipher; nor did "non-kin," her other choice, strike closer. Indeed, she was more likely to receive care and accurate data from stranger-Daav than ever she might of Ran Eld.

"All by the Code and very proper in its place," Daav said, coming smoothly to his feet. "The so-called polite world being its place. You have every right to ask of me, Aelliana. I am your co-pilot and your comrade. It is imperative that you trust me, as I might well be required to make a decision in your name. If you cannot trust me to act as you would, you had best know it quickly."

She stared up at him for a long moment before rising with a sigh. "I venture to say that you would not in any case act as I would," she said slowly. "I would far rather trust your judgment than my own."

"Then you are no pilot."

She flinched, snapped straight, hands fisted at her sides. "I am a pilot!" she cried, as if it were wrenched from the core of her. "I will master Jump within the year!"

Daav lifted an eyebrow. "If you will," he said with a cool and distant courtesy that put her forcefully in mind of Lady pel'Rula. "I must allow, however, that I have never known a Jump pilot who would place another's judgment above her own in any matter of her ship."

She glared, her own voice echoing in memory's ear: *I do not wish to hear that any of my students has died stupidly* . . .

She drew a careful breath.

"Master pilot," she said. Daav inclined his head.

"Pilot?"

"I strive to be an apt pupil," Aelliana said formally, and bowed as one of her students might bow to her: Respect and honor to the instructor. "I have been many years aside the world. This information is not offered to excuse ineptitude, but to aid the instructor's judgment. It may be I am unworthy of the instructor's notice. Certainly, I have much to learn."

"Though nothing to learn at all in the science of delivering a devastating setdown!" Both of Daav's eyebrows were up. He flung out that curiously unringed hand, fingers slightly curled. "Cry friends, Aelliana, do! I swear not to come the lordling."

She blinked at him, baffled. "But—you are entirely correct," she stammered. "I must learn all a pilot's *melant'i*, and that quickly. Else how shall it be when I am beyond Liaden space and none but myself to consult? I read of all manner of strange custom in out-space. When my ship and myself are ranged against such and the decision must always be first to preserve the ship—" She slammed to a stop, heart pounding.

"Your ship is your life," Daav said softly, and with the air of quoting someone.

"Yes." She let out a shaky breath. "Yes, exactly so."

"Which is why the chel'Mara is a fool." He smiled, tipping his head so the silver earring spun sparkling in the cabin's light. "Shall you cry friends, Aelliana, or am I in blackest disgrace?" The long fingers beckoned gently.

She hesitated, feeling the familiar clutch of fear in the pit of her belly. A test . . . And once again, she thought, clammy fingers twisting together as she stared at that beckoning hand, Daav was right. Who was she to claim for herself the courage necessary to leave clan, kin and homeworld—the boldness to survive among strange custom—when she dared not even reach out her hand to touch the hand of her comrade?

It was difficult. To her screaming, hard-won instincts, it required an entire day to step closer, a twelveday to raise her hand, another to hold it forth, a entire relumma to close her fingers around his and feel the warm, answering pressure, by the end of which quarter-year she was trembling in every muscle and her legs barely firm enough to hold her.

"Reprieved!" Daav's voice sounded gaily. He pivoted smoothly, drawing her with him as he moved across the chamber. "I expect you'd like some lunch before we proceed."

"Lunch?" Aelliana repeated. She shook herself and drew a ragged breath, noting with something like panic that she was clutching Daav's hand with a force that hurt her own. "Thank you, but I—don't believe I am hungry."

"Yes," he said placidly, "I know."

It was not until he had seated her in the tiny canteen and gently reclaimed his hand in order to ply the menuboard that a certain ominous thought struck her.

"Daav?"

He turned his head. "Yes."

"I—" she stared down at her tightly-folded hands, her eyes following the intricacies of the puzzle ring, round and round. She bit her lip. "Are you a Healer?"

"Ah." He left the board and leaned across the little table, laying one hand over both of hers. He smiled as her eyes leapt to meet his.

"My empathy rating is—high," he said softly, "but I am not a Healer." He looked closely into her eyes, his own serious. "Shall I fetch you a Healer, Aelliana?"

It was an appropriate offer, from a comrade. Aelliana blinked against tears, tore her gaze away.

"Thank you, no. It is—I believe it is—too late—by many—years. I had only wondered—it seemed you are so—"

"Meddlesome," Daav said lightly, standing away with a smile. "It's a sad case, but—Scouts, you know. Shall you have soup with your salad or merely a roll?"

She stared at his back, torn between frustration and laughter. "Only a roll, of your goodness."

There was, of course, no hope that she would merely receive a roll and a cup of tea, and it was with no real surprise that Aelliana sat some moments later considering a rather large salad, augmented by cheese and breadstick.

Daav, who was having soup with his own salad, dug in with a will. Aelliana picked up her tongs.

"How did you learn the silent tongue?"

Aelliana glanced up from her all-but-empty plate with a blink.

"I teach Scouts," she said, with a slight smile, "and Scout minds—as you must know!—are very often bent on mischief. I learned it for survival, through observation." She moved her shoulders, denying his look of admiration. "When I finally came to realize that the finger-flickers among the class must be a language of some kind, it was only a short step to reading it—which is the extent of my skill."

"You've never tried to speak so yourself?"

"Oh, no," she said, glancing down at her plate and fingering her tongs. "I would be hopelessly clumsy, you know."

"Having observed you at a piloting board, not to mention deep in a game of bowli ball," Daav said somewhat dryly, "I know nothing of the kind. It's a useful language—and staggeringly simple to learn. Much easier than Terran."

"Which I must also master." Aelliana sighed, shoulders slumping. To capture first class, to become proficient in Terran, to acquire tolerance of exotic custom, to earn both funds and recommendations, all the while keeping ship and comrades hidden safe from Ran Eld's eye—

"Have you only a year?" Daav asked and she started, so closely did he echo her thoughts, then relaxed, lips curving upward.

"Very high," she commented, and moved her shoulders. "A year it must be. It may be necessary to give over the seminar."

"Ah, no, that would be cruelty. If Liad is to lose you altogether, at least allow another class of Scouts the benefit of your knowledge."

Extremely high in the empathy range, Aelliana thought, with sudden understanding. *And augmented by all a Scout's observational skills. Small wonder he finds the polite world grates on him.* She raised her eyes.

"Do you know anything of a world called Desolate?"

"Yes, and none of it good," Daav said bluntly. "If that is your destination, and the hope of your study, you would do far better to remain on Liad."

"I had thought—some time ago—that I might go there," she said. "Before *Ride the Luck*. Plans have—altered. But I had wondered."

"Hah." Daav finished off his tea and set the cup aside. "The World Room at Scout Academy is what you want. Apply to the commander for use-time."

She hesitated. "Do you think—"

"Your name is cantra at Academy, Aelliana," Daav said, pushing back his chair and gathering up the remains of his meal. "Jon had told you so."

"So he had." She rose, gathered up her leavings and fed them to the disposer before turning back to her tall co-pilot.

"I wonder," that gentleman said with the easy air she was beginning to recognize with trepidation, "if you might wish to have a taste of Jump."

Her heart leaped, the calculations running, quicksilver, in her head. "The gravity well..."

"A serious problem, were we to attempt full Jump. I'm suggesting Little Jump, or Smuggler's Ace, as my piloting instructor was used to call it. We barely phase out, skim atop hyperspace and return. In such a venture, the gravity well—"

"The gravity well acts as anchor and catalyst—I see!" Aelliana interrupted, the figures flowing, bright and perfect, before her mind's eye. She looked hungrily into Daav's face.

"Can we..."

"Let us call Scout Station and clear it with them. However—no disgrace of your skill!—I will run first board."

"Yes, of course," said Aelliana, and almost ran back to the pilot's chamber.

Scout Station gave its aye with cheery unsurprise, recommending them to "enjoy the bounce." Daav grinned and closed the out-line—and then the mandatory open line.

"No open lines in Jump," he murmured, fingers dancing along his instruments. "Your board to me, if you please."

She assigned it with a pang, sighing as her screens went dark.

"Patience, child," he chided, and before Aelliana could protest such address, her screens were live again, board-lights winking bright.

"Your board is slaved to mine. Every toggle I trip, every bit of data I feed in—everything will be reflected there, for your interest. Well enough?"

For her most intense interest! "Well enough," she agreed, eyes hungry on the tell-tales.

Daav laughed. Across Aelliana's board lights brightened, darkened, flared, flicked; data strings like a river at thaw stormed across the pilot's net; navcomp held steady, steady, perfect to five digits. Scout Station passed from screen three to four to five, outline stretched by velocity, until it shot off the edge of screen seven and vanished as the warning beacon flowed into screen one, heading for two—

The ship flinched, the screens went gray. Navcomp beeped and took itself off-line.

"Jump achieved." Daav's voice was calm as always, but Aelliana thought she detected a thread of sheer, savage joy in that smooth weaving.

At the bottom right corner of prime screen, red digits ticked time. One-minute-six, one-minute-nine, one-minute-twelve—The lights jigged manic across the board, data hurtled—one-minute-fifteen—

Navcomp sang and came alive; ship's eyes opened, showing the diminished, ensnared globe of the homeworld. Aelliana bit back something woefully near a curse, hand moving to demand elucidation from maincomp. Nothing happened, of course, she was still slaved to the master board.

"But—"

"Smuggler's Ace, recall it?" He wasn't even trying to hide his exuberance. He grinned like a boy and opened the mandatory line with a flourish, letting in all the babble of the workaday universe.

"How can we be—be—" She slammed to a halt, aware that she was not entirely certain where they were, excepting beyond range of Port and Tower, beyond Scout Station, beyond the beacon—

"Ah, hyperspace!" Daav said gaily. "We don't go through, we go between. The gravity well gives a pretty boost, though brief."

She glared at him, suspicion gathering, now that it was too late. "Where are we?" she demanded awfully.

"My dreadful manners." His hands moved across his board, reassigning control to her.

She blinked, snatched at the board, read the numbers and found herself not much enlightened. Irritably, she slapped maincomp up, demanding the filed record of their outward course—

"I fear that won't be there," Daav said apologetically. "My cursed clumsiness."

"You wiped the comp?" She stared at him in patent disbelief, while she recalled his fingers moving across the board. So swift, so—very—certain.

He sighed dolefully. "Alas."

"Another lesson, master pilot?"

"You had," he pointed out, "indicated a need for accelerated study. Only consider, Aelliana, how rich this situation is in practical application."

"Is it indeed?"

"Oh, amazingly," he assured her, ignoring irony. "Why, by the time you've discovered where we are, calculated a return, and taken us home, you will be well on the way to losing provisional entirely."

She eyed him, suspicion flowering into dread—or perhaps, anticipation. "I'm to take us home? Unaided?"

Daav folded his arms elaborately across his chest.

"Well, you don't think I'm taking us home, do you? I did my part. I got us here." He closed his eyes.

Aelliana took a breath. "You are—" Words deserted her.

"Despicable," Daav offered obligingly, not bothering to open his eyes.

She let her breath out in a puff that might have been exasperation or laughter. Sharply, she cycled her chair, opened the board and set about the task of discovering just where, precisely, they were.

Chapter Twenty

*It must be the ambition of every person of melant'i
to mold individual character to the clan's necessity. The person of impeccable melant'i will have
no goal, nor undertake any task, upon which the
clan might have reason to frown.*

—Excerpted from the Liaden
Code of Proper Conduct

"YOUR LORDSHIP IS ALL GRACE, TO BESTIR YOURSELF TO
meet me at this hour." The red-haired man bowed
profoundly.

Ran Eld Caylon inclined his head haughtily and sat
first, as befitted his rank. The red-haired man took
the chair across.

"Wine, Your Lordship?"

"I thank you," Ran Eld said and took the glass of
canary as it was poured, tasted it and sighed.

Ran Eld Caylon was fond of fine things: Fine wine,
fine jewelry, fine comrades. The man across the table
was one of the latter class—or had been. Recently,
however, San bel'Fasin had become a dead bore.

"I trust Your Lordship enjoys his usual robust
health?"

Once again, Ran Eld inclined his head. "I am quite fit."

"And Your Lordship's delightful sisters are likewise well?"

The red-haired man had never met Ran Eld's sisters, though it had been his policy from the first to find them delightful.

"My sisters are well," Ran Eld admitted, and assayed another sip.

"And your honored mother, the delm—she is—of course!—in the best of good health?"

"My mother blooms, I thank you."

"Excellent, excellent! Then there will be no difficulty in calling upon her with my little matter."

Ran Eld froze, wine glass halfway to his lips.

"I beg your pardon."

bel'Fasin moved his hands in gently. "Why, the insignificant matter of twenty cantra forwarded to Your Lordship last relumma. Certainly you recall it?"

"*Twenty* cantra?" Ran Eld treated the red-haired man to his coldest stare. "You are mistaken. The amount owed is four."

"Four cantra were originally lent," San bel'Fasin agreed urbanely. "At interest of twenty percent per twelve-day, plus penalties."

"Penalties? What penalties?"

"One hundred percent rolled over at the conclusion of each twelve-day unpaid," bel'Fasin said promptly, and met Ran Eld's glare with a glance so deathly chill the nadelm shivered. "Your Lordship signed a paper."

So he had, and Aelliana's quarter-share had been destined to retire this particular debt of honor. But what must occur, Ran Eld thought furiously, except the Delm's Own Word had forced him to hand the sum to *Aelliana* and no way to loose another four cantra from the House's meager funds . . .

"When might it be convenient for me to call upon your delm?" bel'Fasin asked courteously.

Ran Eld set aside his glass, of a sudden sick of wine. *Twenty cantra, gods* . . .

"There is no reason for you to call upon Mizel, friend bel'Fasin."

"Alas, Your Lordship, there is every reason. Unless . . ."

Ran Eld looked up, hope a painful crush of heart and lungs.

"Unless?"

"Perhaps Your Lordship would be willing to represent another case to your honored delm?"

"What case?"

bel'Fasin smiled and sipped his wine. Ran Eld grit his teeth and let the moment stretch, though it was torture to his screaming nerves.

"Mizel owns a certain—leather manufactory, I believe?"

Sood'ae Leather Works was the most profitable of Mizel's three manufactories. Alas, it was also the eldest of the clan's holdings and certain updates were sorely needed.

Ran Eld inclined his head. "True."

"Ah. Then I wonder if you might not be able to—bring your delm to see the—benefit—of a partner in that business."

Sood'ae was freeheld, Ran Eld thought. The delm would never . . . He caught San bel'Fasin's cold eyes on him and took a deep breath.

Twenty cantra, at twenty percent and one hundred percent penalty every . . .

"I shall speak to Mizel," Ran Eld told the red-haired man with formal coolness. He picked up his glass and threw the rest of his wine down his throat.

They were in mid-port, between Virtual Arcade and the zoological museum. It was mid-evening and the byways were crowded with jostling strangers—Liadens, mostly, but with a mixing of Terrans, tall and loud in their clusters of comrades. Aelliana and Daav were holding hands, that they should not lose each other in the press.

The problem set her up-space had, indeed, been rife with opportunity. Aelliana bested the problem, eventually, and earned not only her tutor's quiet praise, but a warm glow of pride in her own accomplishment. They were in mid-Port by way of celebration.

To Aelliana, whose knowledge of Solcintra Port encompassed the ferry station, the monorail and Mechanic Street to the door of Binjali's, mid-Port was an unrelieved marvel. She craned into shop windows, marveled at street-corner playlets, and stared at passersby, the jangle of a dozen languages like wine for her ears.

"Here." Daav tugged on her hand, charting a slantwise course from the edge of the walk inward, toward the shops lining the right. Perforce, Aelliana followed, trusting him to bring them to safe docking, then paused on the threshold of the shop he chose, her nose telling tales of exotic spices, hot bread and other delights.

"More food?" she cried, hauling back on his hand.

"Food!" His eyes sparkled like black diamonds, in-lit with delight. "You wrong me, pilot, and so I swear. As if I would guide you here for mere food!"

It was so easy to laugh. Laughing, she let him tug her inside, to stand beside him in a long line until it was at last their turn at the counter.

Daav saluted the grizzled counterman with a grin. "Pecha, of your goodness, old friend—and a pitcher of the house's best! This my comrade has never partaken of your specialty."

The counterman grinned and rang in the order, though Aelliana saw no coin change hands.

"Enjoy!" he recommended in badly-accented Liaden and waved a big hand, giving Aelliana a wink before he turned to the customer behind.

"He's—" Aelliana began, as Daav guided across the crowded floor to a table against the rear wall.

"Paol Goyemon," Daav said. He slid onto the bench seat at her right and gave her a lifted eyebrow. "You find him repulsive?"

"Not at all. I hadn't known Terrans held shop in Port."

"A cantra is a cantra, no matter who makes it—or pays it." He grinned. "A principle of economics that does much to sustain my faith in humankind."

She chuckled, then sobered, slanting a look into his face. "Is it burdensome, being—world-bound?"

Something flickered across his face, touched his eyes.

"It is," he said slowly, "somewhat of a burden. It is the training, you understand. In making us fit for the universe, we are made unfit for Liad." He smiled, wryly. "It does not help, of course, that the polite world labels Scouts odd and holds us in mingled trepidation and dismay. 'scout's eyes' they say, as if it were something of magic, rather than merely learning to see what stands before one."

She frowned, groping after a certain thought . . .

"There is Clonak, growing hair on his face—like a Terran. Liadens don't grow beards. Surely those who have never left Liad cannot be expected—"

"Liadens," Daav broke in, "live in danger of losing the game to complacency. They think themselves the ultimate in civilization and scorn what is not written in the Code. The Code is all very well, but courtesy to difference has not been named a virtue. If—" He caught himself on a half-laugh and raised his hand, gesturing apology.

"There, I promise not to rant."

Before she could assure him that he was not even approaching one of Ran Eld's lectures, let alone a rant, the pecha and pitcher arrived.

Pecha was flat round dough, spiced red sauce, vegetables, and cheese, baked until cheese and sauce bubbled, served on a hot stone. The dough was cut into six fat slices. One detached a slice from the circle of its fellows, balanced the treacherous wedge atop one's fingers—and ate.

Aelliana followed Daav's example, imperfectly at first, gaining confidence with each bite. The flavor was strong, spicy enough to raise tears—delicious. The wine—sweet, red, glacier-cold, with citrus smiles floating in it—cooled the mouth and sharpened the appetite.

"This is wonderful," Aelliana said, liberating her second slice. Daav smiled and raised his glass in silent salute.

Too quickly, it was done. They lingered over the wine, side by side and backs comfortably braced against the wall, watching the crowd of diners ebb and change.

"How did Clonak come to have a—*mustache*?" Aelliana wondered lazily.

"We all have our souvenirs." Daav's voice was

equally lazy. He lifted a hand and touched his earring. "The tale of how Clonak came by his mustache is—alas!—not to be told for forty years, by order of the Scout Commander. What I can tell you is that he very badly wished to speak to someone who would not treat with a 'beardless boy,' as the phrase went. Clonak thus sought permission of his team-leader and then commended himself to the autodoc, rising much as you see him today." He paused, considering.

"Slightly more demented," he said at last, sipping his wine. "I do believe age has mellowed him."

"And yourself?" Aelliana wondered softly. Daav looked up, one brow askance.

"Ah, but I have always been precisely as demented as you see me today!"

She laughed and moved her head in the Terran negative he had taught her. "But I meant your earring," she said. "Surely that is a—a *souvenir*?"

"So it is." He touched it once again, smile going slightly askew.

"This certifies my place as a son in the tent of the Grandmother of the Tribe of Mun, whose name, we would say, is 'Rains-in-the-Desert,' though I rather think 'Rockflower' a closer fit." He paused for a sip of wine; reached 'round to finger his tail of hair.

"This signifies that I am unmarried."

Aelliana stirred, looking up into black eyes gone misty with remembering.

"And when you marry?" she asked, meaning it for lighthearted, though it sounded utterly serious to her own ears.

Daav smiled, wistfully, she thought. "A married hunter will wear his hair clipped close to his skull, of course. And he will have a second earring, that names his wife's tent. But until one has been chosen from among those who stand around the marriage fire and enters the tent of one's wife, the hair is worn thus."

"Marriage fire . . ." Aelliana sighed and sipped at the last of her wine. "Did you—But you said you were unmarried."

"Rockflower had determined I should stand around the fire at the next gathering of the tribes," he said, very softly. "My team came back for me before then."

She looked up into his face. "You're—sorry?" she asked, tentatively, because it did seem there was sorrow shadowing his bright eyes.

"Sorry?" He moved his shoulders. "I should have been a poor choice, for a woman of the Mun. Undergrown—and not—terribly—skilled with my spear. To choose such a one to provide for a new-made tent, where there likely would soon be children—" He shook his head, Terranwise, drank off his wine and turned a full grin upon her.

"But, who can say? I might have been chosen by a woman of an established tent, secure enough to please herself, and then I might have had a life of ease!"

His grin was infectious. Aelliana smiled back and thought she had never felt so happy.

"Shall we walk?" Daav asked, and Aelliana put her hand unhesitatingly into his and allowed him to lead her once more into the bustling, exhilarating, magical evening.

The virtual arcade was full of bodies and light in motion, and sound that ranged from racket to roar.

Aelliana and Daav waded through the uproar, stopping here and again to watch the play at the games.

Aelliana, Daav noted, seemed particularly interested in the more sophisticated games of chance, and as they went further into the Arcade, her tendency was to stop for longer intervals, lips moving silently, as if forming the boundaries of an equation.

Another might have felt pique at this apparent desertion. But Daav neither hurried nor chivied her, finding himself well-content with watching the changes in her eyes and face as this thought or that caught at her. He did keep a firm hold on her hand, for in her present tranced state he considered it possible that she might wander away and lose herself, and used his body to shield her from the worst of the crowd's jostlings.

So it was, traveling in this stop-and-go, eventual way, that they came to *Pilot to Prince*. Aelliana watched the computer replay a space battle of epic proportions from memory: Battle gave way to an emergency docking, which evaporated into a trading session, which segued into—

Daav smiled at the attention she gave the game. It was popular among the shuttle-toughs and Port-crawlers and usually, he thought, had lively play. This evening, it stood empty.

Not quite empty, he amended, as two figures stirred in the dimness of the back corner and walked toward them: A girl and a boy—halflings, no more—identically dressed in tight clothing a parody of genuine space-leathers, faces hard, hungry—desperate.

Daav tightened his hold on Aelliana, meaning to draw her away, but before he could do so, the boy raised his hand and the girl called out:

"Game, gentles? Sed Ric and me will stand the fee, if you care to play for something more tangible than fun."

Aelliana frowned. "You mean play for money?" she demanded, with very real sternness. "That would be terribly foolish of you, ma'am."

The girl smiled humorlessly. "Ah, the challenge is too heady for the lady! Let us play three-way with your partner, then—he looks a man game for—"

"Wait," said Aelliana, looking about her for the 12-sided die in a wheel that was the symbol of a sanctioned betting station. "This game doesn't pay off," she told the girl seriously. "You would be risking your funds against strangers. That hardly seems fair."

The boy—Sed Ric—laughed this time. "So what is fair, ma'am? We all risk our money with every purchase. We'll pay the game fee—dex a player at hazard—if you care to see what kind of pilot you might be."

Aelliana glanced at the replay in progress beyond the boy's shoulder: A holed ship careered about the screen until a barrage of rockets sent it slamming into a nearby asteroid.

"You will lose your money," she said flatly. The boy jerked a shoulder.

"Maybe so," the girl said. "*We're* not afraid to bet."

Aelliana hesitated, her hand tightening—indeed, Daav thought she would turn and walk off . . .

Her eyes wandered back to the screen, flicked to the posted game-regs.

"We can win," she murmured, perhaps to herself.

"Can we?" Daav asked, just as softly, and with one eye on the halflings. Tension whined off the pair of them; Daav's teeth ached with the intensity of their desperation.

They bore themselves as if they knew kin and clan—not ordinary Port rats. Though marred by fear,

there was a certain smooth efficiency in their movements which spoke of potential pilots—*If they don't
skid off the edge of mid-Port*, Daav amended silently,
and land themselves in a Low Port bordello.

"Daav?" Aelliana murmured. He glanced down
into shadowed green eyes. "Tell me what is wrong,"
she whispered.

"Wrong..." He sent one more glance at the halflings:
Hungry, afraid and too proud to ask aid. Too young
to be here, hustling strangers for two dex the game...
He sighed sharply and smiled into Aelliana's eyes.

"I think we should play," he said softly, "since these
young gentles ask so nicely."

She hesitated, her eyes scanning his. He saw the
decision cross her face, then she turned away, fingers
dipping into a pocket. Two coins flashed toward two
halflings.

"Done," she said with professorial sternness. "We
shall take the merchanter."

The start of joy from their opponents was regrettably obvious.

"After you, pilot," Daav said, and followed her to
their station.

Chapter Twenty-One

After the safety of the ship, the well-being of the passengers is the captain's greatest care.
—Excerpted from Cantra yos'Phelium's Log Book

THE SITUATION WAS NOT QUITE UNTENABLE, BUT IT WAS far from good. They were down on fuel, having chosen to run from the last attack rather than pit the merchanter's light weapons against the pirates' superior firepower.

The pirates had followed, of course, and were now lurking just off-station, waiting for the hapless merchanter to set forth.

Daav's suggestion—faking a refuel and coming around the planet to attack—was refuted by Aelliana: "Suppose they go for a LaGrange Point rather than a simple orbit? They'd have all the advantage and we would be in a difficult orbit."

Her suggestion of dropping all cargo pods but one in favor of a high-value freight and top acceleration had merit, though it relied heavily on the skill of the pilots in eluding the pirates and gaining the Jump point first. Meanwhile, the longer they sat at station, the more points they lost.

Instinctively, Daav glanced over the instruments, checking ship's stats. The board was authentic, the image surrounding them utterly convincing. The bits of station-chatter filtering across the open line had apparently been lifted from tapes of the real thing.

The station master's messages had been rather too courteous to a ship which had come in trailing pirates and debris, but there were limitations, Daav thought wryly, to even the best of games. He sighed and put his attention back on the cargo board.

"How if we drop five pods," he suggested softly. "We trade in the cargo with known destinations for cargo the pirates can't suspect."

"It would give us an edge in gaining a Jump point," Aelliana agreed, fingers flying across the board. "Carador," she said, echoing his thought as if they were partners of many years. "We'd have close to a stern chase to Jump. If the timing favors us, and if we buy all the Greenable listed, we should turn a profit."

"Agreed. What of the synthfish—high intrinsic value and rare on Carador, according to the chart."

"But badly affected by high acceleration. We'd need an eighty-nine percent survival rate to make our margin and we could hit—" She paused, briefly. "Six gee is not out of reach—"

Not quite out of reach, Daav thought with a mixture of amusement and respect. Aelliana Caylon expected a great deal of her ship—and of herself.

"All right," he said, watching her fingers work the keypad to prove the results her head had already produced. "We load Greenable. But I want to buy pod-lot 47—distress merchandise listing. It won't slow us too much and it's cheap."

"Surplus material from Losiar's Survey? But—"

"Trust me," he murmured, and her fingers danced,

approving the purchase while she sang out orbit and range figures for him to check.

Daav felt better now, though the run was still risky. The creator of this game had a wonderful mind for trivia, and with a very small corner of luck he hadn't just bought fifteen thousand Terran tons of survey rods. The density levels on that pod were extremely close to something his lamentable pack-rat of a memory thought it recalled . . .

The ship readied: He pulled in the fuel figures, calculating times in his head and running trajectories as if they really were about to launch.

"They'll fire to capture, won't they, Daav?" Aelliana's voice was serious.

"Or at least to get the goods. Likely a capture, though, since they score extra for that."

"Yes. I'm arming the long-range weapons as soon as we break seal, and hit the meteor shield to full—"

Her face was earnest, snared in the seeming reality of the game. Daav lifted an eyebrow. "Station will scream—not to mention the fine."

"Only if we come back," she returned and Daav nearly laughed with joy of her, speaking as bold as if she broke a dozen rules every morning, and he—what was he but the grandchild of a pirate, himself?

The sequence ran down to *go*. The ship tumbled away from its dock and Aelliana slapped up weapons and shield.

In the real universe, taking arms off safety so close to a station would cost the pilot her license. In this universe, station, as predicted, screamed, though with nothing approaching the verve of any actual station master of Daav's acquaintance.

"They see us," Daav said as the pirate ship hove

into view around the curve of the nearer moon. "I'll take the guns, you fly her."

The virtual ship shuddered and acceleration pressed him into his seat as the couches tilted to simulate motion. He watched the cross-hairs converge, his hands moving toward the fire button—

"*Fancy-Freight* we've got a fine on you unless you cut those weapons now! You have your warning—cut those weapons—" The simulated station master blared his accusations.

"Trap!" Aelliana cried. "They broadcast everything we do to the pirates!"

"Hah. So that's why the children think they have a fixed game."

His hands moved, slapping fire buttons. Virtual rockets crossed virtual space, arcing away toward the suddenly retreating pirates.

The explosion was a bright flare across his screen. It drew howls of protest from the station master and unsubtle curses from the pirates, who immediately returned fire.

A waste of energy, Daav thought, holding his own meager weapons in reserve: *Fancy Freight* was still in the shadow of the station, protected by its defenses.

That situation changed as Aelliana kicked the ship into a lurching high-gee skid toward the proper Jump point. Even on game time they'd need all of the luck to make the distance and score.

Daav watched his boards carefully, saw the pirate ship taking a leisurely tumble toward—

"They're targeting the wrong Jump point," he said quietly. "They thought we were heading out with the flegetets on board for Terra."

Aelliana sighed. "I regret those—But the math didn't work. Four hundred percent profit and three hundred percent dead . . ." Her eyes narrowed.

"They aren't coming on with as much acceleration as they did before, Daav."

He looked to his screens, touched a knob to increase magnification.

"Took some damage, poor children—running on eight tubes instead of ten. Pegged to the intercept course, though—you have that stern chase you wanted—"

"I didn't *want* a stern—Ah, *no* . . ."

The distress in her voice caught him. He looked up sharply, saw real pain in her face.

"Aelliana! What has happened?"

"I—" She looked over to him, eyes wide and stunned. "I—miscalculated. The fuel reserves on the pirate ship—they have the edge. I forgot—Forgot! They'll catch us before Jump."

Daav blinked, recalled the reserves the pirates had taken on from a peripheral kill early in the game. Something moved in the corner of his eye; he turned to track it—and saw six missiles drop out and leave the pirate's ship.

"Recalculate," he said, automatically calling up interceptors, slapping dead plastic where the defense beam toggle would be on a real ship—"based on losing the lot of non-Greenable."

The screen flared as one of Daav's interceptors took out a missile; half a second later another did the same.

"Aelliana?" he asked gravely, glancing up at her again.

"Yes. I had forgotten that you are a Scout. That was a difficult interception there . . ." She lapsed into silence, flying and calculating at once, then shook herself. "We may win, but the margin is small—one percent, perhaps one-point-five, depending on when and how we lose that pod." Her voice was somber.

"Shall we surrender, then?" Daav asked quietly.

There was a moment's hesitation, too short for him to be certain that the struggle he sensed was anything other than his imagination. Her eyes lifted to his, green and wide.

"No."

"Good," he said, letting her see the pride he felt in her, and turned back to his board.

The play got tighter as the pirate ship's greater power-to-mass ratio began to tell. The pattern of attack changed though: Now the goal was interception. No fancy flying for extra points, no capture option, just interception.

"Daav. We have one hundred seventy-six seconds until Jump. They'll intercept in one hundred forty."

"I see. When they're 30 seconds behind, jettison Lot 47. That should give us—"

"The added acceleration will help, but they'll still catch us by fourteen seconds—"

"But we'll be throwing things at them. They'll have to avoid."

"That's random—I can't calculate—"

"No surrender," Daav said earnestly.

"No surrender."

They were quiet then, each watching their screens. Daav fended off several more missile attacks. The pirates were being more careful with their weapons now, and so was Daav. By his count they had thirteen to launch and he had three . . .

"On my mark," Aelliana said calmly, "it's five. Mark. Four, three, two, one . . ."

The ship lurched as the pod fell away, looming

huge in the simulated view screen. It tumbled behind them, directly into the path of the oncoming pirates.

Daav counted to three and launched his last missiles.

"Oh," said Aelliana, "that's more mass away... I still don't think it's going to be—Daav, a bad trajectory. You've targeted the—"

Two missiles skimmed the edge of the tumbling pod, dodged by and went on toward the pirate ship, which was beginning evasion. The missiles followed, and the pirate launched four interceptors.

Daav's third missile hit the tumbling pod full center. The flare of explosion grew, brightened, grew still more, expanding into a glowing rainbow cloud.

The Jump warning went off: 12 seconds.

"What was it?" cried Aelliana.

"In a moment. They'll be firing the last of their—yes. Avoidance pattern, please."

Through the glowing cloud came two missiles, though only one was on course for them. Aelliana used the maneuvering rockets to spin the ship, hit acceleration, kept accelerating until the red warning light came on.

They saw the simulated explosion fade into green nothingness behind them in the instant before the virtual ship Jumped away.

Aelliana cheered.

The piloting chamber melted, the shock webbing retracted. Daav rose, looked about—and sighed.

The pirates were gone.

* * *

"This way, Sed Ric," Yolan hissed, groping ahead in the thick darkness of the service corridor.

There! Her questing hand found the emptiness that meant the cross-hall. Another few minutes in

this stifling darkness and they would be free of the
Virtual Arcade and the two undoubtedly angry marks
they had deserted at *Pilot to Prince.*

Yolan sighed. She hated the service corridors; the
hot dark gave her horrors, calling forth ghosts and
hobgoblins from childhood stories. There were no ghosts
or goblins, of course. She knew that. The world held
far more terrible things than mere monsters. Cops,
for instance. Port proctors, for another. Not to mention angry marks who had won a game they had no
business to win and were now cheated of their cash.

"Here." Sed Ric's voice rasped in her ear.

"Right. Stay close." She found his hand and held
it—to lead him, she told herself fiercely—and groped
her way toward the cross-hall.

Slowly, she moved forward, free hand extended,
fingers touching the wall. The wall ended, her fingers
stroked emptiness—

Something grabbed her hand.

Yolan screamed.

"Well," an amused masculine voice said. "What a
noise." Light snapped on and Yolan blinked, gasping
into silence.

Before them stood the very marks she and Sed Ric
had just rooked of their rightful winnings. The man,
with his sharp, foxy face and his worn leathers, looked
infuriatingly amused, though his fingers, now around
Yolan's arm, were surprisingly strong.

The pale-haired woman held a portable light, and
she looked angry, her eyes cat-green in the sudden
brightness.

"What clans own you?" she demanded as Sed Ric
stepped up to Yolan's side.

Yolan moved her shoulders. "We own ourselves."

The green eyes widened. *Shocked her*, Yolan thought, with a twist of bitter satisfaction.

"You're clanless?" the woman asked, casting a look at her tall friend.

"More profit to ourselves," Sed Ric said, "than the clan ever showed."

"Playing tourists for two dex a round?" the man drawled, dark eyes showing something Yolan thought uneasily was not amusement. "And running when it's time to pay?"

"We usually play for higher stakes," Sed Ric said, as Yolan snapped, "We don't often lose!"

"Hah." The man looked from one to the other, moved his shoulders and glanced at his partner. "Well, pilot? You had wanted them."

"If you want your four dex," Sed Ric, with a calm Yolan knew he was a long way from feeling, "we'll pay now."

"After we've chased you and shaken it out of you," the pale-haired woman said ironically. "How kind." Her bright eyes moved from Yolan's face to Sed Ric's. "In truth, you are clanless?"

"*Yes*," Yolan hissed, and felt the man's fingers tighten around her arm.

"Grace to the pilot, Clanless," he said softly, and Yolan swallowed, abruptly cold.

"Where do you live, then?" the pale-haired pilot demanded.

Yolan clenched her jaw.

"I expect that they had been sleeping in a way-room," the fox-faced man said. "I also expect the rent on the cot came due today, and that the money they

stole from you, pilot, was meant to buy it tonight."
He sounded bored.

"Is that true?" the woman asked.

It was Sed Ric who answered. "True," he said, trying
to sound as bored as the man. He didn't quite succeed.

There was silence, stretching long. Yolan tensed
against the man's hand; froze at his lifted brow.

"What shall you do, if we let you go?" the woman
asked quietly.

Yolan looked away. *On the Port tonight*, she thought
dismally, clenching her jaw tight. No place to sleep
and nothing to eat, unless the luck smiled. They
could always walk a bit further south, slip over the
line into the Low Port. There might be something to
gain there. But Low Port was dangerous . . .

"Low Port, is it, Clanless?" If anything, the man
sounded more bored than previously. He looked at Sed
Ric. "Will you sell your lady here to the first bidder,
or were you planning to sell yourself and leave her
without a partner?"

Sed Ric's jaw tightened. "We don't have to cross
the line."

"No? Well, it's your life, free as you are of the
restrictions of House and, apparently, honor." He
said carelessly, though his grip on Yolan's arm never
slackened.

The pilot stirred. "Will you play an honest game?"
she demanded, her eyes wide and half-wild in the
glow of her torch. "Or are you thieves, and craven?"

"We'll play," Yolan snarled and Sed Ric said, "What's
the game?"

"Take the four dex and buy a bed," the pilot said
sharply. "Tomorrow dawn show yourselves to Master

dea'Cort at Binjali Repair Shop in Mechanic Street, Upper Port. Tell him that Aelliana Caylon thought you might be of use. You tell him, too, to keep four dex out of whatever wages he might care to grant you and put it aside, to repay a debt of honor." She fixed them both with a stern eye. "You're still game?"

Yolan hesitated, looking for the trap; it was Sed Ric who said, "Still game."

"Good." The pilot stepped back, dimming the torch. Her mate released Yolan's arm and likewise went back, clearing the way to the exit hatch.

"That's it?" demanded Sed Ric. "That's the whole game?"

"Something more," the man said, taking the pilot's hand and flicking a quick smile down into her thin face. "Over on Scorn Street there's a grab-a-bite called Varl's. You know it?"

"Yes," said Yolan.

"Go over now and order yourselves a meal—high-quality protein, and solid carbohydrate, mind me! Tell the counter help to add it to Daav's chit."

"But, why?" demanded Yolan, horrified to find herself close to tears. She hadn't cried in—in—Sed Ric's hand came up to grip her shoulder; she bit her lip and blinked.

"Why not?" returned the man, amusement back in the foxy face.

"At least work long enough to pay back what you owe," the woman said. "If you've no delm to look to, how much more closely must you mind your own *melant'i*?"

Yolan stared at her, torn between a desire to laugh and to fling herself into the thin arms and wail.

In the end, she did neither, merely took Sed Ric's hand and inclined her head gravely.

"Good evening, gentles."

"Good evening," the man returned, and "Take good care," said the woman.

They walked away, scarcely comprehending what had happened, triggered the hatch at the end of the hallway and slipped out into the night.

After a moment, Daav and Aelliana followed.

She shivered as they came out into the street and Daav looked at her in concern. "You're cold."

"A little," she admitted, handing him the torch and watching him stow it in his belt pouch. She shivered again. "I left my overshirt on the—Dear gods."

He turned, following the direction of her eyes, seeing the crowd, the clutter of kiosks, the ship-board, the clock—

"The time," she whispered urgently. "Daav, I *must* go home."

He flicked another look at the clock and did a rapid calculation. "We can make the next ferry. Can you run?"

"Yes!" she answered and they wasted no more words. Hand in hand they crossed the plaza, running quick and pilot smooth, and hurtled down a side street.

Chapter Twenty-Two

Each clan is independent and each delm law within his House. Thus, one goes gently into the House of another clan. One speaks soft and bows low. It is not amiss to bear a gift.

—Excerpted from the Liaden
Code of Proper Conduct

"DAAV, THERE IS NOT THE SLIGHTEST NECESSITY FOR YOU to escort me. I am quite accustomed to riding the ferry."

"Ah," he said, neither perturbed nor persuaded by this argument. He maintained his position at her side, fingers laced in hers, waiting for the gate to slide away and admit them into the Chonselta Ferry.

The holding platform was crowded, nor were all who waited perfectly sober. Daav had detected at least two pickpockets, discreetly working the edge of the crowd. He nudged Aelliana closer to the gate, deliberately adopting the stance of a man prepared to argue right of place with his fists. The crowd shifted, grumbled—and let them by.

Beside him, she shivered. He glanced down, frowning at the thin silk shirt.

"Let me give you my jacket, Aelliana, you're cold."

He moved—stopped in something very near awe when she lay a quick hand against his chest, looking up at him with a laugh, her eyes outdazzling the platform's spotlight.

"I'll soon be in the ferry, and warm. My friend, you cannot have considered. To give me escort to Chonselta means four hours gone from a night already far advanced. I shall be perfectly fine."

Behind them, a mutter of conversation, the ugly edge of drunkenness clear to a trained ear.

"My company wearies you?" he asked, meaning it for a joke. Aelliana-like, however, she chose to hear it as serious and honor him with an answer.

"Your company is—a joy," she said, with her nearly Scout-like frankness. "I—Daav, I—cannot—offer you hospitality of the house. To have you journey so far in my behalf and be constrained to return without even a cup of tea—It shows poorly on the clan, yet I dare not—"

She was beginning to tense, the foggy misery moving into the edges of her eyes. *Damn them,* he thought, with concise, futile fury. Aelliana shrank back as if she had heard the thought, hand falling from his chest, eyes widening in alarm.

Gods, he must be sliding into idiot ineptitude, that his anger at her clan showed plain enough to frighten her! He conjured a smile, quirked an eyebrow.

"And an ill-mannered fellow I'd look, indeed, rousing the house to do the pretty at this hour of the day! My desire to escort you is utterly selfish, Aelliana—I could not sleep a moment, without knowing you were safe at home." He let the smile widen to a grin. "Indulge me."

Her alarm faded in a sigh that was also a laugh; her fingers tightening, unconsciously, he thought, about his.

"Indeed, I am—glad—of your escort," she said, tipping her head toward the rising discussion behind.

"Then the matter is settled," he said, at which moment the gate slid wide and all his thought went to shielding her from rude jostlings and locating well-placed seats.

"Do you think they're really clanless?"

Daav retracted the shock webbing and turned in his seat. Aelliana looked up at him from her place against the bulkhead, worry plain in her face.

"Something is certainly—wrong," he said carefully, wishing neither to influence her to a chancy course, now she had time for cooler reflection, nor lose the children her friendship, was she yet disposed to grant it. "Possibly something is very wrong. Whether they are in fact clanless..." He moved his shoulders. "I had been trying to recall. It seems to me that there have not been any casting-outs listed in *The Gazette* this relumma, and I don't think they can have been on the Port longer—even granting them extraordinary luck."

She sighed, settling her shoulders against the metal wall. "They're no older than Sinit," she murmured. "And to be without kin on Liad, and no hope of going elsewhere..." Her mouth tightened. "Will Jon be angry? I hardly know how I dared, except that Binjali's is so—safe—and I had thought... But to put Jon's *melant'i* at peril—that was ill-done."

"If Jon considers you've put his *melant'i* at peril, he shall not be shy of explaining the matter to you. In the meanwhile, if they go to him and present you as their patron, he's certain to keep them by until you can explain the matter to him."

"If they go," she repeated. "You think they will not?"

"They may," Daav said gently. "Or they may not. That rides upon *their melant'i.*"

She was silent for a moment, her eyes on his, before reaching out and taking his hand.

"It is the custom," she said, as much perhaps for her own benefit as for his, "to shun the clanless and withhold any aid."

"Merely custom and not law," he returned calmly. "The Code, not the Council."

"Ah," she smiled, very slightly. "Yet another concept to master." She squeezed his fingers. "It was kind in you to feed them."

He returned both her smile and the pressure of her fingers. "Little enough to do—and not the first time Varl has had the feeding of my stray puppies. Scouts, you know . . ."

Aelliana chuckled; raised her free hand to cover a sudden yawn.

"Your pardon," she murmured, and then, more strongly: "Now, tell me what was in that pod, if you please!"

He laughed softly and settled back in his seat. "Why, only a comet."

"A comet!"

He smiled at her disbelief. "You've heard of Losiar's Survey? Not many have—it's ancient history, and Terran history, at that." He shook his head.

"Mr. Losiar, you see, was wealthy, of scientific bent, and quite, quite mad. Over time, he became convinced that the—how did he have it?—that the 'building blocks of the universe' might be discovered in the hearts of comets. Convinced, he acted, and outfitted hundreds of drone ships to go forth and capture all the comets in the galaxy, or near enough, and bring them back for study." He sighed.

"Alas, Mr. Losiar died testing an anti-gravity machine he had invented soon after the last drone left Terran space. His ships full of comets are still found, now and again. Most use them for target practice."

"So there was ice and particles in that pod," Aelliana said slowly, "and when you blew it open—"

"The children found themselves flying through the center of a comet. Disconcerting."

Her laugh turned into a second yawn, and that yawn became a third, belatedly covered with a languid hand.

"I do beg your pardon. I cannot think why I should be so tired."

"After all," Daav said ironically, "you have only been flying since Solcintra dawn, not to mention a Port walk and an engagement with pirates."

She grinned, eyelids heavy. "True. I had—" another yawn interrupted her.

"Sleep, if you like," Daav said, knowing it was scandalous and out-of-Code. Yet why should she struggle to stay awake when she was so tired and there was her co-pilot at hand to guard her?

"I think I shall," said Aelliana, rather muzzily, and without further ado released his hand and settled herself closer into the chair.

Snug against the bulkhead, with himself between her and the aisle, Aelliana slept.

Seen thus, without the great green eyes sparking

fire, she seemed astonishingly frail—a mere bundle of bone shrouded in the golden velvet of her skin, carelessly wrapped in rusty black and shabby silk. Daav knew a desire to gather her up and hold her against him, head tucked under his chin, as if she were one of his small nephews. He shook the feeling aside: Aelliana was no child, but a woman grown, and none of Korval, beside.

He wondered anew at her clan, who seemingly placed her value so low it cared nothing if she ate or starved, went clothed or naked.

Not permitted to grant a comrade courtesy of the house, is it? he thought with a recurrence of anger, and sighed. Well, and perhaps her kin misliked Scouts. There were those, in sufficient plenitude, though his darker side noted sardonically that Delm Korval would likely command slavish welcome, whatever hour he might call.

In her sleep, Aelliana stirred, shivered, nestled deeper into the cool plastic seat.

Daav sat up, moving with exquisite care. He slipped off his jacket and tucked it around her, turning the soft leather collar up to shield her face from the eyes of the curious.

Settling back, he thrust his legs out before him and folded his hands over his belt buckle. Eyes half-closed, he reviewed a linked series of exercises, assigning one segment of his mind to keep watch while the most of him dozed.

She tried to leave him in Chonselta Port, arguing that there was no call for him to endure a train ride halfway across the city only to be obliged to return immediately to the Port.

"No, but I shan't be returning *immediately* to Port," Daav said, sliding his coin into the box and requesting two tickets. "Unless you live in the station?" He handed her a ticket.

Aelliana stared up into his face, trying valiantly for a glare. "You are quite stubborn enough!"

He sighed, taking her elbow and guiding her toward the platform. "My *cha'leket* tells me exactly the same. It's a burdensome nature, I agree, and far too late to correct it. I am on my knees before the gift of your forbearance."

"Yes, very likely. Daav, nothing ill is going to befall me between here and Raingleam Street."

He looked down at her, eyes wide. "A foretelling, *dramliza?*"

"I am not a wizard! You, however, are entirely ridiculous!"

"Yes, yes, as much as you like," he assured her over the hiss of the train's stopping. "Is this our shuttle?"

She gave it over then with a laugh and marched before him into the compartment.

That was the last laugh he had from her—and very nearly the last word. The closer the train brought them to her clanhouse, the quieter she became, sitting stiffly beside him on the bench, steadfastly staring at nothing.

The train stopped four times to discharge and admit passengers. As it slowed for the fifth time, Aelliana raised her face. Daav bit back a cry of protest: The bright green eyes were shrouded in fog, wary and chill in a face etched with tension.

"Aelliana—"

She raised a hand, forestalling he hardly knew what mad speech.

"This is my stop," she said, and the warmth was at least still in her voice. "I suppose it's useless to ask that you spare yourself a walk and a return alone through an unknown city?"

He smiled for her, keeping his voice light. "I'm a Scout, my friend. Unknown cities are something of a specialty with me."

Her lips quirked a smile. "I suppose they are," she said and stood, moving toward the door.

She made no protest when he took her hand, though the station was hardly crowded. Indeed, her fingers tightened about his as she guided him out to the street.

As urgently as she had cried her need to go home, it seemed that now, with home near to hand, her urgency had deserted her. She led him sedately down thin streets lined with yard-enclosed houses. The further they walked, the smaller the yards became, the more closely the houses crouched, shoulders all but rubbing their neighbors.

Raingleam Street was meager, the public walk crumbling and weed-pocked, the houses brooding over scanty squares of grass held captive by rusting, lance-tipped fences.

"Here." Aelliana stopped before a fence near the top of the way. The grass beyond the lances looked unkempt in the light from the street lamp, a flowering vine softened the brooding facade of the house.

In the puddle of lamplight, Aelliana spun to face him, catching up his other hand in hers.

"Daav—thank you, my friend. For the escort, for the lessons, for—for your care. I cannot—I don't believe I recall when last I spent a pleasanter day."

"Well, as to that," he said gently, feeling her hands

trembling in his, "the pleasure has been mutual." He hesitated, glanced over her head to the forbidding house, looked down into a face from which all joy had retreated.

"Aelliana?"

"Yes?"

"I—may I give you my comm number, Aelliana? Call me, if there is need."

She did not laugh, nor ask what need she could possibly have of him, now she was delivered safe back to her kin.

She sighed, seemed to sag—and caught herself, looking up.

"Thank you. You're very kind."

"Not at all." He recited the code for his private line, saw her memorize the digits as she heard them. "There is an answering machine," he told her softly, "if I am not—immediately—to hand."

"Thank you," she said again and stepped back, her hands slipping away with a reluctance he could taste.

"Good lift, pilot," she said from the shadow aside the lamplight. "Have a care, going home."

"Safe docking, Aelliana."

He tarried in the light-splash, watched her cross the walk and open the sagging gate. Her footsteps were light on the flagstones, her figure no more than a thin shadow. The footsteps changed, climbed three wooden stairs; he lost her shape in the larger shadow of the vine.

The porch creaked, a door opened on faintly whining hinges, hesitated, soundless—and shut with a clatter of tumblers falling home.

Abruptly, Daav shivered, though the night was

barely cool and his jacket very warm. Almost, he went forward, through the gate and down the path—*Some pretext—some bit of piloting lore you forgot 'til now to tell her...*

"Do be sensible, Daav," he chided himself, voice loud in the still street. He turned his back on his inner urgings, on the gate to Mizel's Clanhouse, and retraced the route to the station, walking with determined speed.

"Good morning, Aelliana, how pleasant to have you thus returned to us."

Two steps into the foyer, Aelliana froze, staring into her brother's eyes, recalling all at once the overshirt left behind on *The Luck*, and her hair, drawn back and caught with the ring Daav had given her. Voni erupted from the parlor to her right—where the large window enjoyed an unimpaired view of the street.

"I saw him!" she squealed. "Great, lank-limbed creature flaunting his leather in a respectable street! A Scout or a grease-ape, brother, and Aelliana with no more shame than to be clutching his filthy hands!"

"Gently, sister." Ran Eld was gliding closer, savoring his moment. "I feel certain Aelliana will tell us everything we wish to know about the fellow." He raised a hand heavy with rings and smiled lazily at her. "Won't you Aelliana?"

She swallowed, mind gone to putty. He meant to strike her, she read that plain in his eyes: He meant to hurt her...

"Whatever is the reason for so early a racket?" Birin Caylon peered over the rail, blinking sleepily down at the three in the foyer.

"Ran Eld? Voni? Aelliana, then! *Some*one explain this untimely commotion!"

It was Voni who recovered her wits first. She bowed and flirted her eyes as their mother came stubbornly down the stairs.

"Aelliana was so late coming home, ma'am, we had quite despaired of her!"

"I see," the delm said in a dry tone that indicated she found this explanation wanting. She reached the foyer floor and paused, subjecting first her son and then her eldest daughter to an uncharacteristically penetrating stare. This done, she continued forward and took Aelliana's arm.

"Just come home, have you?" she said pleasantly, turning back toward the stairs, middle daughter in tow. "How delightful it is to be young and able to roister with friends until dawn! I recall my own youth—why, there were twelve-days together when I was scarcely home at all! I was a sad scamp in those days, though I daresay you would hardly credit it—" Talking thus, she mounted the stairs, and Aelliana with her, barely able to believe in her rescue.

At the top of the stairs, Mizel changed her subject, lowering her voice to a level not meant to reach the two left below.

"So, had you a fine, bold day, daughter?"

"In—Indeed I did, ma'am," Aelliana took a hard breath. "I had meant to be home for Prime, but the time—the time quite got away from us."

"And your friend, I apprehend, was good enough to escort you to our gate. Could you not have offered the house's hospitality, child?"

"Ran Eld—" she swallowed. "Ran Eld has no liking

for Scouts, ma'am. And, indeed, my—friend said himself he would seem a rag-mannered fellow, rousing the house at such an hour."

"Very nice of him," Birin Caylon said approvingly. "You must, however, invite him to tea soon so that I may thank him for his care of you." She frowned at Aelliana's start. "It need not trouble you—or your friend—what private opinion Ran Eld chooses to hold of Scouts."

Oh, gods, and if Mizel rebukes Ran Eld for this evening's work—She swallowed and inclined her head. "Thank you, ma'am."

They had reached Aelliana's door. Birin Caylon smiled and patted her daughter's arm before relinquishing it. "Never mind, child. What is your friend's name, I wonder?"

"Daav," Aelliana whispered, voice catching. She cleared her throat and looked straight into her mother's eyes. "His name is Daav."

If Mizel found anything odd in the lack of surname or clan, she chose not to mention it.

"I see. A well-enough name. Gentle dreams, daughter." She turned and went back up the hall, toward her own apartments.

Trembling in every muscle, Aelliana escaped into her room.

Chapter Twenty-Three

Feed a cat, gain a cat.

—Proverb

"WELL, AND WHERE HAVE YOU BEEN?" JON'S VOICE CAR-
ried an edge of amused irritation.

Daav continued to the counter and poured himself
a cup of pitiless black tea.

"Chonselta," he said and threw the murderous brew
down his throat with a shudder.

"Chonselta, is it? I suppose that answers for the
whereabouts of Pilot Caylon." Jon came forward to
perch on the green stool. "I reviewed that tape."

Daav manfully swallowed the rest of his tea and set
the mug in the sink. "Did you? And your recommendation?"

"She pilots solid second class—which we'd all known.
On the basis of yesterday's adventure—setting aside that I
believe the Master in charge to be moving matters along
rather swiftly—I'd be tempted to write a provisional first."

"If it were board-skill alone, I would agree with
you," Daav said, sitting down and bracing a heel on a
stool-rung. "However, there are those things of which
she knows very little."

"And of which she ought to know much, bound as

she is for the wide universe." Jon sighed. "All too true. Second class it is, then. Will you sign it?"

"Yourself, if you will."

"Hah. She know who you are yet?"

Daav lifted an eyebrow. "She does not know my surname, or my clan."

"Quibbled like a Liaden! I'll play that game to the extent it does her no harm."

"And how shall I harm her, I wonder?" Dangerously soft, that question.

"Gently." Jon raised both hands in the age-old gesture of surrender. "Gently, child—I meant no disrespect. Forgive an old man his meddlesome ways."

Abruptly, Daav became aware of tense muscles, of a hand curled closed along his thigh. He shut his eyes, ran the Scout's Rainbow, and felt the tension flow away. Opening his eyes, he offered Jon a smile.

"It is you, rather, who must forgive a young man his equally meddlesome ways—and his weariness." He showed an empty palm. "I mean her only well. If she learns the workings of comradeship through Daav, who flies out of Binjali's, where's harm in that?"

"Well enough," Jon said, lowering his hands. "Seek your bed and we'll say no more about it."

"In a moment." Daav shifted on the stool, sent a quick glance into Jon's face. "Dawn-time brings you rare joy, Master."

Jon sighed. "Now what?"

"A brace of halflings, boy and girl. They claim to be clanless."

"Sending me your lame kittens, Captain?"

"Not at all," Daav said austerely. "They belong to Pilot Caylon."

"Oh, do they? And what does Pilot Caylon want me to do with them?"

"Put them to work, if you think they might be useful."

Jon considered him blandly. "Are they likely to be useful?"

"Possibly. I believe them to be pilot-grade; the girl at least has had some training. They're able-bodied and quick, though not as quick as they think themselves. Cocky, but well-spoken enough when forced to the point."

"A pair of delightful children, I see. All right. I'll hold them, pending Pilot Caylon's pleasure."

"Thank you," said Daav and came to his feet. He tipped his head, looking down into Jon's seamed face. "Find out who they are, if you can manage it."

Grizzled brows rose over amused amber eyes. "I thought they belonged to Pilot Caylon."

"My lamentable curiosity," Daav murmured, moving a languid hand.

Jon laughed. "Sleep well, lad."

"Good evening, Master. I have no shift this three-day."

"All right," Jon said and watched him walk, graceful and tall, across the bay and out the door.

She woke from a dream of rich, easy safety, her mouth still curved with pleasure.

Sunlight bleached the thin blue curtains to gray; the clock on her desk told of an hour approaching mid-day.

The first thought that occurred was tinged with wonder: Ran Eld had allowed her to sleep through breakfast.

Her second thought was that it was late, and she would be wanted in Solcintra.

She flung the blanket back with energy, came to her feet and slipped on her ragged robe. The house beyond her door was quiet, the hall empty; there was no Voni barricaded in the bathroom they shared. More and more curious. Aelliana locked the door behind her and took a rapid shower.

Back in her own room, she stared into her tiny closet with dismay, seeing the meager rack of shabby shirts and shapeless trousers as if for the first time. Exploration did uncover an orange day shirt laced with black cord, of a slightly more recent vintage than the rest, and a pair of tough indigo trousers that required only minimal pleating with a wide black belt. In the very back of the closet, she found the blue jacket her grandmother had given her on the occasion of her fifteenth name day.

The bold blue had faded somewhat, but the lining was whole, the outer shell water-resistant. She shrugged it on.

That she not outgrow so expensive an item before she had used it fully, the jacket had been bought too large. It settled over her shoulders now as if it had been made for her. Aelliana smiled.

Then it was time to leave.

Cautiously, she stepped out into the empty hall. From below, she heard the sound of a door opening, and the waspish echo of Ran Eld's voice.

There was no time to be lost. Heart in mouth, she ghosted down the hall to the back stairs, thence out into the world.

✷ ✷ ✷

"Morning, math teacher."

"Good morning, Jon," Aelliana said, stopping to stroke Patch. She straightened and looked around her. The garage was unusually quiet; neither Trilla nor any other of Binjali's changeable crew in sight. She turned back to Jon.

"I wonder—did—did the pirates come to you?"

He raised his eyebrows. "Pirates? I wouldn't rate 'em much higher than Port rats, myself." He used his chin to point at the crew door. "They're here. Trilla's got them doing clean-up on Number Six Pad."

"Oh." Tension eased out of her, though a wrinkle of worry remained around the bright green eyes.

She was in looks today, Jon thought with approval, and dressed like she'd paid some attention to the matter instead just draping herself in whatever outsized bits of clothing came to hand. The tawny hair was combed neatly back over her ears and caught into a tail, showing the world a face at once ethereal and intelligent.

Some fitting clothes and a sprinkle of jewels and no one in the room would deny her a beauty, Jon thought, and said aloud, "Well?"

The worry intensified. "I was afraid you would care, though Daav—" She cleared her throat. "I meant no assault upon your *melant'i*, Jon."

"Take more than a gaggle of halflings to do that," he said gruffly. "You sent them to work off a debt, according to their tale. I've enough unskilled labor to keep them a day or two, and welcome they are to all of it. But what will you do with them after that? Turn them back onto the Port?"

She stared at him, eyes wide. "They're clanless."

"So they said."

"To turn them back onto the Port, after having taught them to hope—" She caught herself, teeth indenting her lower lip.

"I do not consider," she began anew, after a moment. "I do not consider that they are stupid, or even without honor. They were frightened and in despair, which condition might make a thief of anyone. They are very quick, and—and pilot-like. Surely, they can be trained—"

"Might be," Jon agreed, "if they had clan. Them claiming no one, that gets tricky. Though," he amended, seeing she was disposed to take it hard, "if they're real good, or found a patron, they might gain the Academy. The Scouts don't care who's clanless."

Hope showed in her thin face, tempered with wariness. "Are they—real good?"

"Too soon to tell. They're sharp enough—and quick, as you say. Whether they're quick enough, or sharp—that wants testing. Also—" he eyed her consideringly. "Might be only one will make it. I think the girl's some faster."

"And the boy seems somewhat sharper," Aelliana returned, chewing on her lower lip. "And the Scouts do train others, who are never meant to be fully Scouts." She raised her eyes. "My name was cantra, you said, at Academy."

"That's right."

"Then there may be a way, though I doubt two days is long enough to find who they are themselves. Perhaps—"

"I'll find work," Jon interrupted. "We'll keep them by long enough to test them fairly."

She smiled, and there was no need for jewels or fine clothes to make her beautiful, Jon thought.

"Thank you," she said. "You are very kind."

"I'm an interfering old man," he corrected her, and swept a hand toward the back and his office. "Daav left you a thing, if you'd care to claim it."

Eagerness made the bright eyes brighter. "Yes."

They went side-by-side, Aelliana carrying Patch.

"You'll spoil him so he'll always want a ride," Jon grumbled and almost gasped to hear her laugh.

"I must carry him or I cannot walk," she said. "Which is worse: To stand for hours stroking him, or to carry him where I wish to go?"

"I'll put a team on it," he said and bowed her into the office ahead of him.

She paused at the near side of his desk to put Patch down; Jon went 'round to the terminal side and fingered a stack of hardcopy.

"Here we are." He held it out; watched her take the thin metal card, disbelief warring with joy across her face.

"Second class." Wonder gleamed along her voice.

"Daav left me a tape of yesterday's little adventure, along with his recommendation that you be relieved of provisional. Asked me to get the card to you, if I agreed." He grinned then, in simple pride of her. "If I agreed! How I could do other than agree is what I'd like to know!" He held out his hand. "Binjali flying, pilot."

She blinked at the outstretched hand, extended her own and met his firmly.

Jon grinned again, gave her fingers a little squeeze and released her.

"I'll have to speak to Master Daav about his methods," he said. "To expose a new pilot to that level of stress—"

"Indeed," Aelliana said earnestly, clutching the precious card tightly. "Indeed, I had asked him to—to try me fully. My need is for working first class in no more than a year."

"If he keeps you at this pace, you'll be working master in two relumma," Jon told her, with very little exaggeration.

She smiled briefly. "I shall need to update my registration with the guild," she said. "And with Korval." She looked up, suddenly hesitant.

"Is Daav working today? Or—possibly—tomorrow?"

"Left word not to expect him for a day or three," Jon said, and marked how her shoulders drooped inside the blue jacket.

"I—see." Another hesitation, then a deliberate squaring of those thin shoulders. "I wonder—is there someone willing to sit second for me tomorrow? I wish to lift—early."

A second class pilot lifting in local space did not require a co-pilot, according to regs. However, Daav, damn him for a pirate, had shown her Little Jump and Jon dea'Cort was too wily an old piloting instructor to think that one brief taste of hyperspace would suffice her. Indeed, it was to her honor, that she asked for second board.

"Clonak's due early tomorrow," he said. "Or I could spare Trilla, if you'd rather. You'd best chose who, otherwise you'll have them fighting for the honor."

She smiled and moved her shoulders, disbelieving him. "Is Clonak never serious?"

"Clonak's a damn' fine pilot," Jon said soberly. "Daav came up drinking coil fluid instead of tea—they haven't built the ship he can't fly. Got the master's easy as breathing. It wasn't that way with Clonak. He sweated for every equation, bled for every coord. He learned his piloting piece by piece and he earned that license. You can learn from him, if you care to."

Aelliana inclined her head. "I care to learn all I can about piloting," she said. "If Clonak will fly with me, I will have him with joy."

"I'll tell him," Jon said. "When do you lift?"

Something flickered over her face: Jon read it as mingled exhilaration and terror.

"An hour after Solcintra dawn," she said firmly.

"I'll tell him," Jon repeated and she inclined her head.

From the main garage came the sound of exuberant voices.

"Trilla's back," Jon said, moving around the desk. "Care to have a word with your rescues?"

Aelliana hung back a instant after Jon left, looking quickly down at the card in her hand: Second class, dated this very day. Fingers none too steady, she turned it over, found the name of the master pilot certifying grade...

Jon dea'Cort.

She sighed, then, and put the card safely into her pocket before going to make the re-acquaintance of the pirates.

"Pardon us, Pilot, but are you Aelliana-Caylon-who-rewrote-the-ven'Tura Tables?" The boy's face was earnest.

She inclined her head. "I am."

"I told you so!" he rounded on his mate, who had the grace to look abashed. He turned back to Aelliana.

"Yolan thought you weren't old enough. In fact," he added, flicking another glance at the girl, "she thought the tables had been revised fifty or sixty years ago!"

"Well, what does it matter when they were revised," the girl snapped, "as long as they're correct?"

"Very true," Aelliana said gravely and Yolan sent her a quick glance before ducking her head.

"Indeed, pilot, Sed Ric and me are grateful for your—patronage—to Master dea'Cort. We'd looked for work, but no one would have us . . ." She looked to her partner, who promptly took up his part.

"We're also grateful to the fox-face—to your partner— for putting us in the way of a meal. We don't intend that he be out of pocket for . . ."

Aelliana frowned and the boy stumbled to a halt, stricken. She sighed, releasing the irritation she felt on Daav's account—fox-face, indeed!—and moved her hands in the gesture for peace.

"You may give him his rank, which is captain," she said, with a measure of austerity she had not intended.

Yolan flicked a mischievous look aside. "*Captain* Fox," she told her partner, soto voce.

Aelliana turned toward her, but before she could deliver the blistering set-down rising to her tongue, Jon dea'Cort spoke up.

"In point of fact," he said, considering the pirates impartially over the rim of his mug, "Scout Captain Fox."

"Scout!" The boy sagged—laughed, short and sharp. "Of all the marks to pick up—a Scout and the Caylon! Our luck, Yolan!"

"Seems exactly like," she agreed wryly and looked back to Aelliana.

"We meant no disrespect to the captain, pilot. It's only we didn't know what to call him, isn't it Sed Ric?"

"That's right," he said eagerly. "We'll speak him fair, pilot—you needn't blush that you know us!"

"Very well," Aelliana said, after a short silence. "Master dea'Cort has said that you may work for him until—until such work as he has is complete. I expect you will comport yourselves honorably and give honest work for honest wages. If Master dea'Cort should find it necessary to turn you off, you needn't look for grace a second time."

"No, pilot," the boy said, bowing low; and: "Yes, pilot," said the girl, bowing equally low.

Aelliana looked over their bent heads to where Jon leaned against the counter, sipping his tea. He grinned at her and one hand came up to shape the word, *binjali*.

Chapter Twenty-Four

FOUR HOURS' SLEEP AND A SHOWER DID MUCH TOWARD restoring one's perspective. Robed, damp hair loose along his shoulders, Daav poured himself a glass of morning wine and padded out to his private study.

He had barely crossed the threshold into this rather cluttered chamber when the comm chimed.

Six people had the number to Daav's private line: Er Thom; Clonak ter'Meulen; Scout Lieutenant Olwen sel'Iprith, former lover, former team-mate, currently off-planet; Frad Jinmaer, another team-mate; Fer Gun pen'Uldra, his father, also off-planet—and Aelliana Caylon.

The chime sounded again; Daav had crossed the room and struck the connect key before the note was done.

"Yes."

Er Thom's image was serious, even for Er Thom; the inclination of the head stiffly formal.

"The delm is hereby made aware of yos'Galan's Balance to an insult received of Clan Sykun."

Balance . . . Daav sank to the arm of his desk chair, staring into Er Thom's eyes. He read anger; he read resolution; worry—and an utter absence of grief. Anne and the child were safe, then.

"The delm hears," he said, the High Tongue chill along his tongue. He moved a hand in query and dropped into the Low Tongue.

"What's amiss, darling?"

Er Thom took a hard breath. "Delm Sykun found it fitting to turn her back upon Thodelmae yos'Galan at a public gather this morning." He paused. "You haven't heard?"

"I've just risen," Daav said, reaching for the keypad. "You know how slugabed I am." Three keystrokes accessed the house computer and his mail.

"My, my. A letter of apology from Ixin. An apology from Asta. A letter from Lady yo'Lanna, promising to strike Sykun from her guest list—" He glanced over to Er Thom, still and solemn in the comm screen.

"There's a good come out of whatever it is. Lady yo'Lanna does so love to strike people from her guest list."

Er Thom did not smile. "As you say. Mr. dea'Gauss has been instructed to sell any stock yos'Galan may hold in Sykun's concerns—at a loss, if necessary, and noisily. Letters of cancellation have been issued on all contracts yos'Galan holds with Sykun. Mr. dea'Gauss has advised that he will also be selling his private holdings of Sykun business."

"Hah." Daav tapped more keys, mind racing. A public cut was a serious matter, demanding swift and unhesitant answer. Such a cut to Anne Davis, Lady yos'Galan, author of a text which linked Terra to Liad in a manner not likely to find acceptance among many Liadens—It could not be said that Er Thom's answer was too harsh.

That Korval's man of business also chose to enter Balance was eloquent of the magnitude of the insult. In Mr. dea'Gauss were mated pure *melant'i* and an exacting sense of honor.

"Aha. I have Mr. dea'Gauss' analysis," he said to Er Thom. "The Pilots Fund holds four hundred of Sykun's shares." He touched a key, scanning the file rapidly, and grinned.

"Mr. dea'Gauss indicates that the Fund shall realize sufficient cash from the sale of these four hundred shares to buy a block of stock in Vonlet's instrumentation venture." He flicked another glance to Er Thom's face, finding it marginally less angry.

"In fact, Mr. dea'Gauss is in a fair way to considering the incident fortuitous."

A smile showed unwillingly at the corner of Er Thom's mouth. "Hardly that, though one readily comprehends Mr. dea'Gauss' thoughts upon the subject."

"Just so," Daav agreed, keying in instructions for his man of business to sell any and all Sykun shares held by Korval or, privately, by Daav yos'Phelium.

"Shall the delm take further action?" Er Thom asked, very softly.

Daav shook his head. "Korval takes no public action, other than divesting itself entirely of Sykun stocks. Of course, the delm shall not find it possible to attend any function where Sykun is also a guest, but I rather think the world will have decided that already. I fancy I hear the match programs running as we speak."

Still Er Thom would not be tempted to a laugh, nor even to the fullness of his smile.

"I wish you will come to us," he said suddenly. "Anne—She is not in agreement with Balance. She feels—she says that it is—a joy—to have found Sykun so rude, for now she is relieved of the necessity of courtesy when they meet."

"Which is true enough," Daav pointed out. "Excepting that they shall—very likely!—not meet again."

"Yes, but—" Er Thom bit his lip, looked away. "She says," he continued, very low, "that to answer insult with Balance is to bring all eyes upon it—upon her—us. She—I feel she—is angry." He looked up. "She is gone to play the 'chora."

"Hah." Daav stood, shaking his hair back. He smiled into his *cha'leket*'s worried face. "I'll come. Until very soon."

"Until soon, Daav."

"What do you think of these oxy tanks?"

Clonak gave them consideration, fingering his mustache with absent affection.

"They're very nice oxy tanks," he offered after a minute's critical study. "Symmetrical—and of a pleasing color. Full, too. I like that in an oxy tank."

Aelliana sighed. "Forgive me. I had meant to ask if you thought four sufficient, or if these four should be replaced with four of larger capacity."

"Four's the regulation number, beautiful goddess, but no one's going to howl if you want to carry more. If the hold's empty you can indulge your whim to the limit."

"Yes, but it's not my whim," she said with a fair

semblance of patience. "Daav had seemed to think that four was not enough, and I—"

Clonak's face changed, and she suddenly knew she had his serious and entire attention.

"What precisely did Daav say, goddess?" Very careful, that tone, with the taffy eyes gone solemn as stone.

Aelliana blinked. "Why, that he had been on a ship which had lost life support, and that one need only be in such a situation once, with a too-short supply."

"So-ho. I shouldn't have thought he remembered that." His voice was quiet, as if he spoke to himself. He made no other comment.

"Why shouldn't he remember?" Aelliana demanded and almost flinched at the sharpness of her own voice.

"Because he had the Healers," Clonak said, and grinned his crazy grin. "And the Healers had the devil's own time, as I heard it. They swore he'd forgot. Gods know, he wanted to forget."

"He—ran out of air?" *But that's absurd*, she thought distractedly. People who ran out of air were far beyond giving advice of any kind . . .

"Not quite," Clonak assured her. "Not—entirely—quite." He shifted, opened the suit closet, slid the rack free.

"You understand, his ship was holed—comps blown to bits, shielding in rags. He kept patching the hole, the patching kept cracking—an outside job, but he'd had the bad luck to Jump into the middle of a rock storm—a matter of a place error in the unrevised Tables, as it happens.

"However that was, it was certainly suicide to go out. Daav's no suicide—he stayed in. Loosed his beacons. Blew what was left of the coils trying to send Mayday along the pinbeam. Did what he could, you see? Then all there was to do was wait—and use up oxy."

"But you came—" Aelliana said, without knowing how she knew it.

"I came," the pudgy Scout agreed, bending to check the seams on suit number one. "I came in thirty-six Standard Days." He looked up, showing her eyes bleak as rain.

"I Jumped in, caught the beacons, hit the comm—" He took a hard breath. "He didn't answer—for a—a long time." He moved his shoulders.

"Took some talk before he'd believe I was there—he's always been stubborn. I finally latched on and crossed. He was on his last canister—three-quarters down, I guess. Maybe more. He was building a gadget—planned to separate the hydrogen atom and the oxy atoms in the reservoir—make his own air. Last I heard, they were still studying that one, down Academy lab . . ." He glanced aside, mouth twisting.

"Convinced him to come over to my ship. Convinced him to leave the gadget behind. Even convinced him to crack the suit—to conserve the air in the canister, you see. But damn me if he didn't sit there in the co-pilot's slot and keep turning the air down from the board! Had to threaten to sprain his head for him and stuff him in the 'doc before he stopped." He fingered his mustache. "Wouldn't have liked to try that. Daav's strong—and scary quick. Even then. Especially then." He shook his head, Terran-wise.

"He started to shake when we hit Headquarters. Olwen and Frad got their arms around him and just hung on 'til the Healers came through."

"And the Healers made him forget," Aelliana whispered.

"That's what I've always thought." Clonak frowned.

"I'll tell you what," he burst out suddenly. "I was ready for the Healers myself. Daav—Daav's the best pilot you're going to find—and one idiot math error left him hanging in a holed tin can, waiting to die! I thought I was too late, when it took him so long to open his line. Then I knew he was alive and I thought everything was binjali—until I saw him sitting his board calm as you like, turning the air down and talking in that reasonable way of his—And if that could happen to Daav, who's the best there is, then what might happen to clumsy Clonak? It scared me. I thought about quitting Academy. I talked to Jon. I talked to the Commander—to Olwen—Frad. The more I talked, the more I determined to quit. Had my kit packed, in fact." He shook his head, hard.

Aelliana licked her lips, forced herself to extend a hand. "But you didn't quit."

Clonak stared, stepped forward and took her hand gently between his palms.

"I didn't quit," he said, "because I stopped to say good-bye to Daav. He asked why I was leaving and I told him, 'Because it's dangerous. Because people die, doing what we're trained to do.' And he said . . ." He grinned, lopsided.

"He said, 'That's life, you know.'" Clonak moved his shoulders. "So, I stayed."

"Are you glad?" Aelliana asked. Clonak snorted.

"Glad? I'm doing the only work worth doing. Does that make me glad? Or mad as any other Scout?" He stepped back, releasing her hand, and gestured toward the suits. "Have you done any practice with these?"

"I've had one on and tested the circuits."

"Well, I see we've got our work cut out for us! Why don't you file for something upper-level and out of the way? Outyard One has a nice quiet little lagoon where we can park us and do a bit of walkabout outside."

"All right," Aelliana said, pushing away from the wall and heading for the companionway. She paused. "What is *walkabout*?" she asked, pronouncing the non-Liaden word with care.

"Aha!" Clonak said with a laugh. "Odd that you should ask . . ."

"It's that damn book!" Anne snapped. "Of all the foolishness I never heard—it was meant for scholars! Who else minds about the dead, dusty past?"

The dialect was the one she had spoken in her childhood, which was, Daav thought, indication enough of her upset. He perched on the arm of a parlor chair and lifted an eyebrow.

"Very true," he said, calm in Standard Terran. "What would you have had us do instead of what has been done?"

"Ignore it," Anne cried, rounding on him swiftly. "Let it go. Turn the other cheek. Act as if the great House of Korval were above children's games and found such goings-ons just—faintly—ridiculous."

"Ah. And what would that accomplish, I wonder?"

She glared as if she suspected him of laughing at her. He showed her his palms, fingers spread wide and empty.

"Anne, I ask because I don't know. You say there is a better way to answer Sykun's insolence. Teach it to me."

"You're not a fool."

A complimentary manner, indeed, in which to address one's delm. Daav grinned. "I have my moments. As do we all. What is gained by allowing Sykun license to abuse you?"

She sank to the edge of the chair opposite his, fingers tightly gripped together. "Forgetfulness."

He waited, head tipped and face attentive.

"She—cut me—because she wanted to show that the book—the proof of the common back-tongue—was a lie. She wanted to make a stir, don't you see? And by rising to the bait, you've given force to her argument. You've said, in effect, that Korval has something to apologize for. People will notice. People will talk. Instead of the whole thing dying down, like an eight-day wonder..." She shook her head.

"If you had just ignored it, then people would have shrugged and said that Sykun was making a mountain out of a molehill—She would have looked ridiculous—and people would have talked about something else."

"Ah." He closed his eyes, weighing it, tasting it, feeling the shape of it and the outline of the culture which would make such action sensible.

"I see," he said eventually, "that this might, indeed, be the appropriate response." He opened his eyes to Anne's hopeful face. "Elsewhere."

Hope died. "Daav—"

He raised a hand. "Given a society based upon the communal effort of unallied individuals, each of whom cooperates with the others solely for individual gain, this response has obvious merit. To shake off an insult is to conserve energy for the more important work of individual advancement. However, such a society does not exist upon Liad and the answer you suggest will not work. Worse," he said, deliberately softening his voice, "it may do active harm."

"I don't—"

"Recall that we are predators, enclosed in kin-groups, held in check by the laws of Clan and Council. Precedence is guarded as jealously as children. *Melant'i* opens more doors than cantra, as a rich man who has sullied his name may tell you. Insult must be Balanced, immediately and stringently, else the other predators see that you are weak."

"But—"

"Hear me out. I do not say that your answer is wrong. I merely say that Er Thom's is better. On Liad. To preserve our *melant'i*, our precedence—and our right to peace—Sykun must be lessoned. Did we ignore this morning's insult, the world would talk, and wonder—and plan. The next insult must in such a case be more daring—and we reach a point very soon where we play with lives."

Anne stared.

"This way," Daav said gently, "Sykun looses a few cantra and the pleasure of a few parties. Korval must make some adaptation of trade and contract. It is done. The world is satisfied and the matter falls away, as you wish it to do, in a twelve-day or so. To follow your plan—" He leaned forward and took her hands in his.

"We are too few. I cannot risk one life on the chance of a Balance done badly. It is Korval's duty to protect its own. Which duty I take most seriously."

She was silent a moment or two, eyes searching his face.

"What are the odds," she asked then, "of this getting—dangerous?"

Dangerous. He paused a moment, considering what that might mean to her. Surely, he decided, in this case her danger and his were the same—physical harm befalling lifemate, child, herself, or other kin.

"Less this afternoon than this morning," he told her, with the utter truth one owed to kin. "Two moves have so far been made upon the theme and we have answered appropriately. It may be some shall try a third time. Vigilant response to that must establish our position without doubt."

She sighed, and took her hands away, though pensively, and not in anger.

"Your lifemate," he said softly, "will protect you with all of his skill. And your delm shall protect you, with all of his."

"Yes." She sighed, then, and rose, tall and graceful and Terran. "Thank you," she said, which—Liaden—kin should have no cause to say, one to another. "I'll speak to Er Thom."

He smiled and rose also. "Rest easy," he told her. "All will be well."

Chapter Twenty-Five

*In an ally, considerations of house, clan, planet,
race are insignificant beside two prime questions,
which are:*
*   *1. Can he shoot?*
*   *2. Will he aim at your enemy?*
        —From Cantra yos'Phelium's Log Book

"YOUR ANALYSIS IS ELOQUENT, MY SON. ALLOW ME TO
hold it for a day or three, that I may give it the
study it merits."

Ran Eld bowed, fighting to conceal his dismay. He
had sweated over that analysis, striving to illuminate
every benefit to be gained by adopting San bel'Fasin as a
partner in Sood'ae Leather Works. Indeed, he had written so compellingly of the advantages of upgraded facil-
ities and increased production he had quite convinced
himself that selling bel'Fasin as much as half the enterprise would be all Mizel's gain. Surely even cursory study
must make these advantages plain to the delm's eye?

And the twelve-day was winding to a close.

"The gentleman who makes the offer of partnership,"
he said, careful to keep his voice even, his face calm,
"did seem desirous of a speedy resolution."

"Ah, did he?" Mizel glanced up. "It is well to recall that the gentleman approached us, we did not seek him. If he cannot wait upon rational consideration, he is free to offer his partnership elsewhere."

Ran Eld went cold. "Mother, perhaps—"

She raised a hand. "My son, I see that you are convinced of the benefits of the scheme. You are perhaps too young to understand that no scheme brings unalloyed profit. I must consider what it is this San bel'Fasin thinks he will gain in the venture, and whether Mizel can afford to indulge him." She smiled. "We learn something of value, should it transpire that San bel'Fasin cannot afford to wait. Nor do I think a man who is unable to adopt a temperate course will be a suitable partner for Mizel. Slow, steady and careful are the cards to play, when we decide for the clan's future. I shall give your analysis due thought, never doubt it."

There was finality in her voice and, perforce, Ran Eld bowed.

"Good-day, mother."

"Go in joy, my child."

He gained the safety of his rooms and shut the door firmly behind him. Gods, what should he do, if the Delm refused the scheme? Twenty cantra—soon to be doubled! But there, he assured himself, splashing brandy into a cup, she would not refuse. Further study could only show the plan's excellencies to fuller advantage. His mother was not stupid, merely conservative. Caution must bow to good sense.

Soon.

It was a small, neat house on a small, neat street handy to Solcintra's business district. Daav worked the gate-latch and followed the stone path through the meticulously-kept front-garden, mounted six shallow stairs to the porch and pulled the bell.

He had not sent ahead, nor was he dressed in the formal style mandated by the Code, when a delm went calling upon a delm. Indeed, he might almost be a solicitor who had wandered a few blocks north of his usual preserve, excepting, of course, that not many solicitors were adopted of the Mun.

The plain blue door opened wide and Daav found himself looking down into the serious face of a boy no older than eight Standards.

"Good-day," the child said, eyeing the leather jacket with interest even as he lisped the doorman's traditional challenge. "Who calls and upon what business?"

"Daav yos'Phelium calls," he returned, in Visitor-to-Child-of-the-House, "upon business of the House."

The child frowned. Line yos'Phelium belonged to Korval, as he assuredly knew. The precise place held by Daav of Line yos'Phelium was likely at the root of the frown, as the personal names of delms tended to become lost outside the circle of their own kin.

"Line yos'Phelium does not belong to Reptor," the boy said, with certainty. "I shall need to know your business, sir."

"Very proper," Daav murmured, bringing his hand slightly forward, so that Korval's Ring glinted in the afternoon sun. "My business is with Delm Reptor."

The boy's eyes moved, tracking the glint—widened and came up.

"Sir," he said and stepped back from the door, bowing as Child of the House to Honored Guest. "Be welcome in our House."

"Thank you," Daav said gently and stepped into the dim entrance hall.

He stood aside while the child shoved the door to and engaged the lock, then followed him down a short hall to a room overlooking the back garden.

"Refreshment will be brought," the boy said, with all the gravity due his House's honor. "I go to fetch the delm, sir."

"Thank you," Daav said again, and the boy ducked back into the hall, leaving the door open.

Daav glanced around at the book-lined walls and comfortably shabby chairs. This was no state chamber, as called for by the Code, preserved in soulless perfection for the edification of formal visitors. This was a room lived in, enjoyed and enjoyable. Daav moved toward those temptingly overfull shelves.

A step in the hall beyond brought him around in time to see a girl perhaps a year the doorman's senior cross the threshold, bearing a tray.

This she carried to the stone table before the window; rapidly set out a sweat-studded carafe, two plain crystal cups and a painted plate piled high with cookies. Turning, she made a hasty bow, "Sir," and was gone, all but running out into the hall. The door swung gently on its hinges as she passed.

Refreshment, as promised, and which courtesy required that he sample. Daav poured clear liquid from the carafe to the cup and sipped: Simmin wine, icy cold and tart enough to take one's breath. He looked wryly at the hopeful plate of sweet things and carried his cup with him to the shelves.

He had barely grazed the contents of the first shelf when a new tread was heard down the hall. Daav turned and moved to the center of the room, wine cup in one hand, Korval's Ring in plain view.

The man who stepped firmly into the chamber was soft-bodied and sandy-haired, not old, though some years older, Daav thought, than himself. He was dressed in rumpled day-clothes and scuffed houseboots and had extraordinarily quick brown eyes, set wide in a weary, clever face.

Those quick eyes flicked to Daav's hand and back to his face, betraying puzzlement without alarm. He raised his own hand to show Reptor's Ring and bowed, Delm-to-Delm.

"How may Reptor serve Korval?"

"By forgiving this disruption of your peace," Daav said in Adult-to-Adult. "And by granting Daav yos'Phelium the gift of a few minutes of your time."

"Well." Reptor took a moment to consider Daav's face, eyes bright with intelligence. He moved a hand, as if he threw dice, and inclined his head.

"Daav yos'Phelium is welcome to my time," he said at last, and in Adult-to-Adult. He went to the stone table, poured wine into the remaining cup, sighed lightly at the plate of cookies and turned back to Daav.

"I am Zan Der pel'Kirmin." He waved at the two comfortable chairs. "Sit, do."

"I thank you." Daav sank into the nearer of the two, sipped his wine and set the cup on the elbow table. Zan Der pel'Kirmin followed suit and sat back, eyes showing curiosity, now, and somewhat of speculation.

"What brings Daav yos'Phelium to my house?"

"A rumor," Daav said gently. "I am fairly confident of my information, but I ask, for certainty's sake: Has Reptor lately—mislain—two of its own?"

The clever face went still, brown eyes glancing aside. "Mislain," he murmured, as if to himself. "Gently phrased." He looked back to Daav's face.

"Their names are Yolan pel'Kirmin and Sed Ric bin'Ala," he said, and his voice was not entirely steady. Pain and hope warred in the quick eyes. "Have you— you do have—news?"

"They are safe," Daav told him, and saw relief leach some of the pain. "Just now, they are under the protection of Pilot Aelliana Caylon, who flies out of Binjali's Yard in Upper Port." He paused, looked square into the other man's eyes. "They claim to be clanless."

Color drained from the round face; the brown eyes shone tears.

"Clanless." He might have said *dead* with the same inflection. "I—" He turned his head away, biting his lip. "Forgive me," he managed after a moment. He groped for his cup, lifted it, drank.

"I had inquired," he said, low and rapid, eyes yet averted. "I made certain they would seek the Port, ship-mad as they both are—" He glanced to Daav, pale lips tight. "Your pardon."

"No need. I believe many halflings are so."

"As you say. Be it so, my inquiries came to dust. They—I recruited myself to wait, but they did not return home, and I began to fear—offworld . . ." He sighed. "Clanless. Gods." He sagged back into his chair, showing Daav a face at once bewildered and relieved. "They are not clanless."

"And yet they have said that they are. Several times."

"A word, spoken in anger and no more meant than—" He closed his eyes, took a deep breath and opened his eyes.

"Their—patron. Aelliana Caylon, I believe you had said. That is the same Caylon? Of the ven'Tura Revision?"

"It is."

"I am in her debt. To extend her *melant'i* in such a wise, and care for those who claim no kin—that is—extraordinary. I am in her debt," he repeated and moved a hand. "And in your own."

Daav smiled, deliberately rueful. "No debt on my account, if you please. I am meddling, if you will have the truth, and must ask you to fail of mentioning this visit to Pilot Caylon, should you speak to her."

"Of course I shall speak to her!" Zan Der pel'Kirmin cried, eyes opening wide. "I must speak to her—and at once! They cannot be left a burden upon her grace, when they have kin eager to welcome them home . . ." He paused, brows drawing together.

"What had the pilot—I mean no disrespect!—I only wonder what Pilot Caylon had thought she might do for them, crying clanless and so little trained . . ."

"Ah." Daav reached to his glass and sipped the cool, tart wine. "I believe she had meant to sponsor them into Scout Academy."

"Scout Academy," the other repeated blankly.

"Pilot Caylon's name is cantra, among Scouts," Daav explained gently. "As she has very little, herself, in the way of other currency, and as your pair seemed quick enough, and clever . . ."

"Gods smile upon her, a great and wide-hearted lady," Reptor said reverently. "They—Yolan and Sed Ric have had some small training on the boards; their piloting instructors do not despair of first class. If it had not been for this other matter—but I shall go to her, to Pilot Caylon, immediately, and relieve her of Reptor's troubles."

"Immediately," Daav said delicately, "may not be possible, as Pilot Caylon resides in Chonselta. She does, however, fly—"

"Out of Binjali's Yard," the other interrupted, with a pale smile. "I understand. You are very good."

"No, only meddlesome, as I've said." Daav stood and made his bow to the host. "Having meddled sufficiently for one day, I shall restore you to your peace. Be well, and thank you for the gift of your time."

"The gift was well-given." Zan Der pel'Kirmin said, standing and bowing in reply. "My name is yours, to use in need."

Daav smiled, profoundly warmed, for it was no light thing given, but a man's whole *melant'i*, for Daav to use as he would.

"You do me too much honor," he said, and meant it.

"Not at all," the other man said firmly and offered his arm. "Allow me to guide you to our door."

"Fight?" Aelliana looked from Jon to Trilla to Clonak. "Why shall I need to know how to fight?"

"Because ports and docks and Outworlds in general are chancy places, beautiful goddess."

"Because a captain must protect herself, her ship, her cargo," said Jon, "and her partner, should she take one."

"All true," Trilla finished in her casual, Outworld way. "Ability to frame a clear 'no' never stood a pilot ill."

Aelliana stared at the three of them and hoisted herself to stool. Patch immediately jumped from the floor to her lap.

"I don't know the first thing about fighting," she said, as the cat rammed his head into her shoulder, rumbling like an infant earthquake.

"That's why you have to learn," Clonak said patiently. "If you already knew, it would be a waste of our time to teach you."

"We learned self-defense as part of pilot training," Yolan observed, looking up from the parts bin she and her mate were sorting.

"It wasn't enough, though," Sed Ric added. "We had to make adjustments." He stood and Yolan with him, and they stepped toward the stools in their usual formation: Yolan on Sed Ric's right.

"See?" the boy said and his right hand moved, jerking something bright and lethal from his belt. It jingled, hissed and fell still as Clonak came forward, hand outstretched.

"Jang-wire," he said, holding it up for the rest to see. Aelliana blinked.

It looked like nothing more than a length of thin chain, looped and hooked into a leather grip.

"Illegal, of course," Clonak finished and tossed the loop back to Sed Ric, who snagged it out of mid-air and hung back on his belt.

"Works," he said, and Yolan added. "We keep it on the right because I'm left-handed. I walk at Sed Ric's right. If he goes down—"

"There's one of you still weaponed and able," Jon concluded. "Partner-work, right enough." He turned to Aelliana. "Those who don't fight die, math teacher."

She met his eyes squarely. "I am craven, Master Jon. Only raise a hand and see me cringe."

"All the more reason to learn, fast and well," Trilla said. "If you get real good, no one'll touch you." She slid off her stool, shaking a shower of finger-talk at Clonak.

"Couple different styles of fighting," she said, pointing

out a spot for him to stand. "Clonak here likes Port rules, which is to say, no rules."

"See a head," Clonak said gleefully, "punch it."

"This way," said Trilla and moved.

Aelliana leapt from her stool, dumping Patch floorward. Jon caught her wrist and she cried out sharply, then stood, aghast and enthralled, watching as Clonak countered Trilla's attack with a kick toward the Outworld woman's midsection, except Trilla had sidestepped and aimed her own kick at Clonak's knee and he went down, rolling, and she jumped forward, kicking at his head, except Clonak had jackknifed and it was Trilla down, one arm bent high behind her back and her cheek against the concrete floor.

"Yield!"

Clonak was up before the word's echo died, bending and offering a hand for her to rise.

"Well played, old friend."

She grinned and moved her shoulders, looking over to Aelliana. "So, I'm not real good."

"Trilla likes the dance," Clonak said, reaching into his belt and withdrawing a wickedly curved finger.

"Pretend a knife!" he shouted, and lunged.

Trilla melted away from the attack, spun, kicked, wove. The knife followed, desperate for a hit, growing increasingly heedless—and Trilla swept forward with no more force than a dance move, her hand connected sharply with Clonak's wrist, his hand snapped upward—

"Disarmed!" he cried, and collapsed cross-legged to the floor, grinning up at Aelliana. "Bow to necessity, divine. The universe is dangerous."

"First lesson tomorrow," Jon decreed, at last loosing her wrist. "Trilla will teach you to dance."

Chapter Twenty-Six

Jela spent his whole off-shift rigging guy-wires and safety nets to hold his tree in what it thinks is proper position. He was going to run an orientation plate off the main engine, but I canceled that project.

If that tree's got to be in the pilot's tower, it can damn well take the same risks the pilots take.

—Excerpted from Cantra yos'Phelium's Log Book

DAAV KNOTTED THE SILVER RIBBON AND LET THE BEADED ends fall. Glancing into the mirror, he straightened his lace and pulled his collar into more perfect order. The beaded ribbon trailed an elegant tendril across a shoulder, counterpoint to the rough twist swinging in his ear.

He paused in his toilette, hand rising to touch the earring, seeing again the morning Rockflower had led him out of the tent; dew soaking his boots, on the edge of the plain, on the edge of the dawn.

She faced him to the rising sun and shouted his name—Estrelin—Starchild—which was not the most fortunate the Mun might bestow, who considered the stars brought madness—and bade him stand fearless. He saw the knife flash in the corner of his eye, felt it bite his earlobe, heard Rockflower grunt with approval.

"Blood and blade, Estrelin, child of the grand-mother's tent."

It was back to the autumn camp then, and the silver worker's tent. Rockflower herself twisted the heated metal into the proper design, the hot wire went through the gash in his ear, cauterizing the minor wound, and the ends sealed into a continuous loop. As nothing could break the silver loop, she told him, so nothing would break his bond to her tent.

At Jelaza Kazone, in the hour before a formal meal, Daav smiled wryly at his own reflection. The silver loop could, of course, be broken all too easily: A snip of wire cutters, a careful withdrawal, a minute or two in the aut-odoc to erase the tiny scar . . . He had not done it. He would not do it. Captive among Liadens, there yet remained a fragment of Estrelin, child of the grandmother's tent.

He broke his own reflected gaze, looked down and opened his ornament case. Among the guests tonight would be his betrothed, home between test-Jumps, and who would expect to see him jeweled as befit his station. He chose a sapphire-headed pin and seated it carefully in the lace at his throat, wondering idly if Estrelin of the grandmother's tent would follow custom and cut his hair when he was wed.

Actually, he thought, slipping a sapphire ring onto the first finger of his right hand, Mun custom dictated that one's wife perform this service on the morning following the consummation of their vow. He tried to imagine dainty Samiv tel'Izak bowing to such a custom, but very soon abandoned the effort. A Mun marriage was a lifemating, within its peculiar laws; and, come to consideration, it was much easier to picture Anne cutting Er Thom's hair. Not, he assured himself, with an amused glance at his reflection, that one's *cha'leket* was ever less than impeccably barbered.

"Very fine, Your Lordship," he told himself, gesturing fluidly with a hand that glittered silver-and-blue. He moved his head, sending the earring swinging and felt the weight of his hair slide across his shoulder.

"I don't think I shall cut it," he said, giving his reflection serious attention. He shook the lace cuffs out, brushed a possibly imaginary speck of dust from the soft black trousers and stepped back, making his bow with a bite of irony.

"Have a pleasant evening, sir. And do try to value Pilot tel'Izak as you ought."

Master dea'Cort had said they might sleep in the pilot's dorm off the aux supply room. Accordingly, they had pushed two cots together, arranged blankets and pillows—and discovered that they were neither sleepy nor in the mood for sport.

"Walk?" Yolan asked, running her hands through her hair and standing it all on end, so she looked like a Yolan-sized dandyweed. "I'm all over twitches."

"Me, too," Sed Ric admitted. He dug around in his pouch and brought out their carefully hoarded wages. Master dea'Cort paid generous for grunt-work, though not quite enough to make a four-dex loss into a nothing. Sed Ric counted the ready and looked up with a sidewise grin.

"Buy us an ice?"

Yolan laughed. "Why not?"

They went out through the main garage, cutting past Master dea'Cort's office.

The old Scout was sitting at his desk, head bent over

a bound book, seemingly oblivious to his surroundings. Sed Ric looked at Yolan. Yolan cleared her throat.

"Out Port-running, is it?" Jon asked, without bothering to lift his head. "Give Pilot Caylon joy, to find the two of you turned up dead."

Yolan bit her lip. "We're only gone for an ice, Master. If you think the pilot won't like it—"

He did lift his head, then, and considered them out of bland amber eyes. "Young things," he said after a moment, and waved a broad hand. "Go on and have your sweet. Watch yourselves, that's all. I don't want to be the one to explain a tragedy to the pilot."

"No, Master," Sed Ric said, jerking his head at Yolan. "We just thought to step around to the East Selling."

"We'll be careful," Yolan put in. "Of course we will."

"All right," said Jon, and went back to his book.

Yolan and Sed Ric faded back out of the office and made their way across the garage, through the crew door. Outside, they went left, aiming to cut a diagonal course across Binjali's Yard and use the utility gate at the eastern corner. From the gate to the East Selling was a matter of two short blocks, and an ice vendor was among the first of the kiosks encountered.

"Think the pilot will be needing crew, when she takes herself off-world?" Yolan voice was too casual, as it was when she wanted to pretend that a burning question was of no moment.

Sed Ric sighed. "Not much crew room on a Class A Jump," he commented. "Her and the captain'll run things snug between 'em."

"Likely," Yolan allowed and they walked silent awhile, down the long corridor of ships asleep on their cold-pads in the Port's early evening.

"Maybe they'll take us," Yolan said and it was desperation in her voice.

Sed Ric stopped and looked at her. "Take us where?"

"Offworld," she said and reached for his hand. "Someplace where they don't mind what's our family—or how close we stand cousins. They might take us—the pilot would, I'll wager."

"Yes, and her partner's cut from whip-leather."

"Maybe not," she said, clutching his hand feverishly. "Maybe not—so much. Who fed us, after all? And the counter help never blinked, did they, Sed Ric? Runs a chit there, does Captain Daav—for all we know, he feeds the Port."

"All of which argues him stupid enough to lift dead weight when cargo is what keeps his ship able. Air dreams, Yolan. You know it."

Her shoulders sagged. "What will we do, then? Master dea'Cort won't keep us forever—he paid us for make-work today! Who else will have us? Walking the dim side, that's not—you heard him: Who will we sell first, you or me? If it comes to that—"

"It won't," Sed Ric said firmly. He chewed his lip, looking into her face. "I've been thinking," he said, slow and careful, because he had been thinking—and because she wasn't going to like hearing what his thoughts had taught him.

"I've been thinking," he said again, "that we might go and—talk—to Uncle Zan Der."

"Talk to father? We talked to father—and more use talking to hullplate! We showed him the chart and how the genes scanned—did he even look? Did he even *care* that it's only been us for each other since we were in nursery together? Did he even—"

She was working herself into a state, which he might have known she would. He gathered her close, pushing her head down to his shoulder and rubbing his cheek against her hair. "Easy. Easy. I was just thinking, that's all."

And thought still showed that Port-running was increasingly risky. Yolan was in peril, whether she would face it or no. Uncle Zan Der would see she got the rest of her training—went for Jump-pilot. He thought—he thought he could make a case for himself being 'prenticed to Cousin Peri, who kept warehouse on Mordra. They would be separated and the reason they had left the clan was that they *would not* be separated.

But he couldn't keep her safe.

"Let's get that ice," he said, husky into her hair.

She stirred, lifted her head and stepped back. "Sure."

Hand-in-hand they walked on, down the row and across, nearing *Ride the Luck*, snug on her ready-pad.

Yolan froze, her hand tensing in his. "What's that?"

"What's—" He saw it, a shadow, moving stealthy near the bottom of *The Luck's* ramp.

"Maybe Captain Fox?" Yolan sounded uncertain.

"Why would he sneak around in the dark?" The figure moved and he frowned. "Not tall enough."

The figure set foot on the ramp, boot heel hitting metal with a sharp clang.

"Let's go!" Yolan urged and was gone, running full tilt toward the ramp.

Heart in mouth, Sed Ric ran after.

Daav had exerted some care in the matter of the guest list. It would not, on one hand, be considerate of Bindan's rank among the mid-level clans to invite

exclusively from the Fifty, however much it might gratify
Delm Bindan's ambition. And to have only Er Thom,
Anne and cousin Luken bel'Tarda in addition to his
affianced wife and her delm—the scheme he favored
most—would surely be seen as an insult by Bindan,
and justly so. Such intimate gatherings belonged to
the days preceding a formal offer of contract.

The number of guests for a gathering such as this,
falling between offer and final signing, might with
perfect propriety be kept to a dozen, but very few
of those dozen had best be Korval's kin or Bindan's.

Korval's allies, that was something else.

In the end, he had Er Thom and Anne, for his own
comfort; Guayar and Lady yo'Lanna, for the comfort
of Bindan's ambition. To leaven the loaf, he called
upon Thodelms Hae Den pen'Evrit Clan Yron and
Dema Wespail Clan Chad, pilots both, and keepers
of secondary lines in mid-level Houses long tied to
Korval with the threads of trade and ships.

Dutiful Passage being at the moment in port, he
invited sensible Kayzin ne'Zame—Er Thom's First
Mate, and another with long ties to Korval—finishing
the list with two representatives of Port merchant
families—Gus Tav bel'Urik and Len Sar Anaba, clans
Shelart and Gabrian, respectively.

The gather had begun well. The guests had arrived
and been made known to each other. Wine had been
served, conversations had begun and then Guayar had
prettily—not to say, audibly—complimented Anne on
the process of her thought and begged that she do
him the favor of endorsing his copy of her book.

"I should certainly be delighted to do so, sir," Anne
said properly, and Guayar bowed, hand over heart.

"I am in your debt." He turned to Bindan. "Have you yet had the opportunity to read Lady yos'Galan's work?" he inquired, which was, Daav thought, really too bad of him. He had put his coin on Lady yo'Lanna, Guayar's sister, that she would be equal to stemming just such a start, but she was across the room, speaking with Kayzin ne'Zame and Merchant bel'Urik.

Bindan bowed with only a trace of stiffness. "Alas, sir, circumstance has not yet permitted me this pleasure."

"It is an excellent work," Guayar said. "I cannot praise it too highly. You must assuredly obtain a copy and read it."

"Indeed, ma'am, you must not encourage him to prate on about books!" Lady yo'Lanna reproved with mock severity, swooping into the conversation amid an aggression of scented draperies. "He will have you here all night and well past tomorrow morning's meal if you give him the least excuse! Do you admire flowers at all? I confess to a passion. Walk with me to the window, do. There is the most exquisite bank of gloan-roses! I was only just now saying to Master pel'Urik..."

Chattering, she bore Bindan off. Er Thom moved over to engage Guayar's attention and Daav allowed himself an internal sigh of relief before returning his attention to the discussion nearer at hand.

The topic was the most efficient coil-to-mass configuration in Class C Jump-ships and his conversational partners—pilots tel'Izak and pen'Evrit—were so absorbed by it that neither had noted his momentary lapse of attention, or, he fervently hoped, Guayar's bit of mischief.

"And I tell you, sirs," Samiv tel'Izak was saying,

with rather more spirit than Daav had heretofore observed in her, "had we not had that autonomous tertiary system, we might yet be in Jump this evening. The matter ran that near the edge of irrecoverable."

"Yes, but, ma'am, you speak only to one case," pen'Evrit objected. "How often, in truth, is the third— never say the fourth!—system called into use? Certainly, in the case of a liner, where the mass to be translated is already vast, dropping a redundant and statistically underused system can only—"

"Endanger the passengers," Daav said, re-entering the lists with a vengeance.

"Precisely!" Samiv tel'Izak flashed him a look of approval. pen'Evrit raised his eyebrows.

"Yes, but it is Korval, ma'am, and he is bound to say so. Are you not, pilot?"

"Not at all," Daav said courteously. "I would merely point out that a line which is forever losing passengers and ships will likely be ruined in a very short time. How much better to err on the side of a tertiary safeguard—the translation mass of which is already figured into the cost of the voyage—and continue to reap profit?"

pen'Evrit inclined his head. "Indeed, who among us can argue against profit?"

"And cantra is so much more compelling than lives," Daav returned, smoothly deflecting what was surely a thrust devised to test the strength of Samiv tel'Izak's armor.

pen'Evrit's mouth quirked and he inclined his head just slightly, conceding the point, and was prevented from making another foray by the chime of the hour bell.

Er Thom offered his arm to his lifemate and flicked

a quick violet glance over one shoulder. Daav lifted an eyebrow and his *cha'leket*, thus instructed, led the company from the formal parlor, down the hall to the dining room. From the edge of his eye, Daav saw Guayar accept Kayzin ne'Zame's arm, a meal-pairing that would, he thought, serve very well indeed.

pen'Evrit made his bow, "Your pardons, Korval—ma'am," and escaped precisely three steps before his right arm was commandeered by Lady yo'Lanna on behalf of Delm Bindan, the Lady herself having appropriated the corresponding limb attached to Len Sar Anaba, who was one of her particular favorites.

Daav turned to his betrothed—and paused in the midst of his bow, arrested by the tension of the muscles around her eyes.

"Have I offended you?" He asked impulsively, before weighing the question's propriety, which was certainly wanting. Worse, he asked in the mode between pilots, which they had been speaking with pen'Evrit, which was as close to Comrade as the High Tongue allowed, when she had not given him use of her name . . .

She drew a breath and it was puzzlement he saw in her face, more than anger.

"No offense," she answered, at least allowing him Pilot-to-Pilot. "Surely you knew that stroke was meant for me. I wonder why you took it to yourself."

Daav lifted an eyebrow. "Should I allow my proposed wife to be abused?"

Her face cleared, as if, disturbingly, his answer had verified some opinion about himself that she held close. "I am instructed," she murmured, still in the mode between pilots. "One currently holds place among the Dragon's possessions."

He had thought himself as well-armored as any other player on the fields of Liaden society, but the cut was cunning and actually struck flesh. Daav drew a breath, and saw Samiv tel'Izak raise a quick hand, her eyes wide with something very like fear.

"Forgive me. I meant no disrespect, merely an understanding of motive and what shall be required of me, beyond the lines of contract."

They were alone in the parlor. If they did not gain the dining room soon, the timing of the evening would be cast into disarray and the guests would be supping scandal stew.

"My motive," he said, speaking as gently as he was able, "was to keep you from distress. You are a guest in my house and it was in my power to shield you from pen'Evrit's boorishness. As for what may be required of you—only the contract lines, if you will, Lady. But I should be honored, if we were to be friends."

"Friends." He might have been speaking the tongue of the Grandmother's tent for all the comprehension he saw in her eyes. She glanced about her, apparently only just now aware that they were alone. "We are behind."

"So we are." He drew a careful breath. "Samiv."

She looked up at him, startled.

"My name is Daav," he told her, and offered his arm. After a moment, head slightly bent, she lay her hand on his sleeve.

"One is not—accustomed," she murmured, "to considering *friendship* a factor of marriage. Friendship is for—crewmates, pilot. You understand me, I am certain."

"Indeed I do," he assured her, moving them toward

the door. "But perhaps we might consider ourselves crewmates, even—co-pilots."

She was silent as they went down the hall. On the edge of the dining room, she raised her head and gave him a straight glance.

"It seems the sort of thing a Scout might perfectly well consider," she said slowly, "but which comes—uneasy—into less—encompassing—minds."

She did not say she would attempt it, which of course she would not, having survived thus long in a society where the slightest weakness invited attack.

Still, she sat next to him at table and conversed easily during the meal, with much less than her previous restraint, and Daav was encouraged to believe that she might, after all, try to consider him more pilot and less Dragon.

There remained one more tradition to satisfy, and Samiv had not been adverse to a suggestion of a walk in Korval's famous Garden.

So, while the other guests retired to the card tables in the parlor, Daav led his betrothed down a side hall and let them both through a door, into the Inner Court.

The path grew dim as they strolled away from the house, and he offered an arm. She lay her hand atop his sleeve, allowing him to guide her down the old stone path.

"What a delightful spot, to be sure," she murmured. "Our gardens are not a half so—full."

The Inner Court did tend toward profusion, as even Daav would admit. He loved the wild, half-magical feel of the place, with its riots of flowers and congregations of shrubs, its unexpected glades and secret pools. The hours he spent caring for it were among the happiest of his present wing-clipped life.

"I would like to show you to Jelaza Kazone, if you will walk just a bit further," he murmured.

It was Korval's custom to present proposed spouses to the Tree—a courtesy, so Daav considered it, though his mother had taught such presentation was made to gain the Tree's approval.

"I shall be honored to see Korval's tree," Samiv tel'Izak said courteously.

"I warn you that it is rather large," he said, negotiating the path's penultimate and largely overgrown twist. "And somewhat—unexpected."

The path twisted once more, and ended in a smooth carpet of silvery grass.

The Tree gleamed in the clearing, casting the pale blue phosphorescence of moonvines into banks of fog. Daav paused at the edge of the glade and looked down into Samiv's face.

"Of your kindness—it is our custom to ask spouses-to-be to come forth and lay a hand against the Tree and speak their name. It would gladden my heart, if you consented to do this."

She hesitated a heartbeat, but what, after all, was the harm in touching a plant, no matter how large, and speaking one's name in the moonlit quiet of a garden?

"I am honored," she said once more and walked by his side across the grass to the Tree. A low wind rustled the moonvines and Samiv shivered in the sudden chill.

"A moment only," Daav said, slipping his arm free. "In this manner, you see, pilot." He placed his hand, palm flat against the massive trunk, feeling it warm immediately with the Tree's accustomed greeting. "Daav yos'Phelium."

Samiv stepped forward, placed her right hand against the trunk and said, very plain, "Samiv tel'Izak."

It happened in a heartbeat. Daav's hand went ice-cold. The wind, which had been playing among the moonvines, roared, rushed across the clearing and hurtled into to the branches above their heads, showering them with leaves, twiglets and bark.

Samiv tel'Izak cried out, wordless and high, and raised both arms to shield her head. Daav flung forward, caught her up amid a hail of twigs and urged her toward the entrance of the clearing.

The wind stopped the moment Samiv's feet touched the pathway.

"How can you abide it?" she demanded, whirling to face him in the dimness, left hand cradling right. "Cold, horrid, *looming* thing—how can you live here, knowing it might fall at any time and crush the house entire!"

He stared at her, his own hand just beginning to warm into flesh.

"The Tree is Korval's charge," he managed, keeping his voice level in the mode between pilots, while his mind replayed the wind, the chill, the rain of arboreal trash. "As best we know, it is in the prime of its life, pilot, and not likely to fall for many, many years."

Samiv tel'Izak drew herself up, face stiff.

"If that is all which is *required*, my Lord," she said, and it was all the way back to Addressing a Delm Not One's Own, "I wish to be returned indoors."

"Certainly," Daav said, and offered his arm, hardly

noticing that the touch of her fingers on his sleeve was slight and shrinking. He guided her down the pathway absently, remembering the hail of Tree-bits shaken loose by that puppyish wind—leaves, wood bits, twists of ancient birds nests.

But not one seedpod.

They reached an overgrown portion of the path and he stood back to allow Samiv tel'Izak to precede him. That she did so without demur, though his rank gave him precedence, spoke eloquently of her distress. Daav shook himself, for it was no more than his duty to soothe her fear.

"Samiv," he began and felt her fingers twitch.

"Please," she said, her voice tight, "I do not wish to speak."

"Very well," he said and guided her silently back down the Inner Court, all the while wracking his memory to recall if the Diaries told of any previous time when a spouse was spurned by the Tree.

Chapter Twenty-Seven

*Pen vel'Kazik comes into the Pilot's Tower only
when forced by her fellow Counselors, and stands
as near the ladder as she may, sweating and
wringing her foolish hands until the others declare
their business done. The boy swears it's Jela's tree
that frightens her. I say, if it is, may the gods
soon afflict them all likewise.*

—Excerpted from Cantra yos'Phelium's Log Book

"MORNING, MATH TEACHER." JON WAS LEANING AGAINST
the counter, tea mug in one hand, attention centered
on a bound book held precariously open in the other.

"Good morning, Jon. Is Trilla on-shift?"

"Haven't seen her yet," he answered, trying to turn
a page with his thumb. The book wavered and slipped,
leaves fluttering helplessly.

Aelliana swept forward, captured the slim volume
in the instant before it hit cement and straightened,
holding it out.

Amused amber eyes met hers. "Quick," Jon commented and turned to set his mug aside.

A test, Aelliana thought, feeling the weight of the
book in her hand. Of course it had been a test. Master

Pilot Jon dea'Cort would never be so clumsy as to drop—She glanced down, frowning at the silver-gilt lettering.

In Support of the Commonality of Language, the glittery title read. *The Lifework of Learned Scholar Jin Del yo'Kera, Clan Yedon, Compiled by Learned Scholar Anne Davis, Clan Korval.*

"Book worthy of study," Jon said as Aelliana glanced up. "You can have the loan of it when I'm done, if you like."

"Thank you, I would like it, very much," she said, surrendering the book. "The last issue of *Scholarship Review* was given to discussion of this work."

"Ah? And what did the host of learned Liadens think of the proof of a common back-tongue linking Terra and Liad?"

"That I cannot tell you," she answered seriously. "Most wished only to say that such a notion was entirely ridiculous, without addressing the proofs at all. The single reviewer attempting to face the work on its own merit was Scout Linguist pel'Odyare. In her estimation the scholarship had been impeccable throughout and the conclusion logically drawn. She wrote that she would implement a search of certain Scout records, to find if independent corroboration of the conclusion could be established."

"Master pel'Odyare does binjali work," Jon said, smoothing the gilt letters with absent fingers. "If proof is there, she'll find it." He sighed, and slid the book away next to the tea-tin trophy box. "Bold heart, Scholar," he said softly.

He looked back to Aelliana with a wry smile.

"Your pirates came in last evening with a tale of

someone hanging about your ship," he said. "Gave chase, but lost the quarry—which is a smile from the luck, though they won't see it. Seem to think they're quick enough to dodge a pellet, if the sneaker had held a gun. Anywise, I did a check and nothing seemed amiss. You might want to do the same, for certainty's sake."

"Yes, of course . . ." She blinked. Someone had been hanging about *The Luck*? Her heart stuttered, animal instinct shrieking that it had been Ran Eld, that she was discovered, hovering on the brink of lost . . . She took a hard breath and met Jon's eyes.

"I shall do an inspection immediately. Are the pirates—Sed Ric and Yolan—available to attend me?"

"Hah." Jon grinned. "They're here." He raised his voice to a bellow. "Pirates!"

There was a clatter and two rapid shadows flung into the lounge.

"Aye, Master Jon!"

They spied Aelliana then and made their bows, low and respectful.

"Pilot."

"I am told that you surprised a lurker about my ship last evening. Your assistance is required now on a cold-inspection, during which you will give me the round tale."

"Yes, pilot." More bows, and attentive waiting, Yolan at Sed Ric's right hand.

Aelliana inclined her head and looked to Jon. "If Trilla should arrive, sir, will you assure her that I am eager to learn the dance and shall engage to do so, directly I return?"

Jon grinned. "I'll do that, never fear."

Her lips twitched, but she otherwise preserved her countenance. "I thank you."

She gathered the pirates with a gesture, turned and marched them out. Jon watched until the crew door cycled, then reached up and pulled down his book.

"She is afraid of the Tree?" Er Thom sank to the stone wall enclosing Trealla Fantrol's patio and stared at Daav out of wide purple eyes.

"Worse," Daav said ruefully. "I apprehend that the Tree holds her in severe dislike."

Er Thom digested this in silence as Daav paced from the wall to the ornamental falls and stood looking down into the tiny, frothing torrent.

His search through Korval's Diaries had been fruitless. None of the delms before him had discovered the Tree in disliking anyone, much less an all-but-signed spouse. The single hint toward the possibility of such a thing came from Grandmother Cantra's log, and even there it was writ so vague...

"What will you do?" Er Thom asked quietly from the wall.

Daav sighed.

"I thought," he said, coming back to sit next his brother on the warm stones. "I thought perhaps—my wife—and I—might live at the ocean house. If the ocean pales before the matter is done, there is the chalet, or even—"

"Daav."

He stopped. It took an active application of will to raise his eyes to Er Thom's.

"Hear yourself," his brother said. "Will you actually get a child upon a woman whom the Tree dislikes?

What then? Shall you live at the ocean house for the rest of your days? Or only until the child is of an age to be sent off-world? How can you—"

"How can you assume that the Tree will likewise disdain the child?" Daav demanded, voice rising above Er Thom's arguments—true, just and sane, gods—"The child will be yos'Phelium, and yos'Phelium guards the Tree! There is no proof—" His voice squeezed out and he remembered, all too vividly, his hand, held there against the Tree, and how cold, how inhumanly cold...

"You chart a chancy course, darling," he said, sounding sullen as a halfling in his own ears. "Whenever did you ask the Tree's aye of Anne?"

"And yet we both know," Er Thom said after a moment, "that the Tree approves Anne. Your point is moot."

Daav closed his eyes; opened them and held out a hand. "It is, and ill-natured, besides. I—"

"What's wrong?" Anne was halfway across the patio, and moving fast, her face etched in worry, her eyes on Er Thom.

Her lifemate came to his feet in a fluid rush, went forward and caught her hands in his. "Anne—"

She allowed herself to be stopped, though the look she threw Daav was anything but calm.

"What's *wrong*?" she demanded once more, staring down into Er Thom's face.

"It is—" But here Er Thom faltered and flung a helpless glance to Daav, who slid to his feet, showing empty palms.

"It is nothing," he said, pitching his voice for gentleness. "My brother and I have had one of our rare disagreements. There is no cause—"

"Don't lie to me." Standard Terran, her voice absolutely flat.

He drew a deep breath and bowed, very slightly. "And yet there is nothing you can do, should I tell you the truth."

"Then there's no harm in my hearing it," she returned, "and knowing what frightens Er Thom."

Frightens. Daav looked to his brother. Purple eyes met his unflinchingly, showing all.

"Hah." He resumed his seat upon the wall and in a moment Er Thom did likewise, leaving Anne standing alone, hands on hips and her face filled with waiting.

"Well?"

"Well," Daav replied, looking up. He sighed. "Are you able to believe that the Tree can—make its wishes known—to those of the Line Direct?"

She stood quiet for a long moment, then went to sit beside her lifemate and placed her hand upon his knee.

"For the purposes of this discussion," she said, like the scholar she was, "it is stipulated that Jelaza Kazone the Tree is able to communicate with those of Korval's Line Direct."

"Then you may know that my brother's trouble springs from the knowledge that Jelaza Kazone the Tree has expressed a—distaste—for Samiv tel'Izak. A distaste of which she is—alas—very aware."

"Oh." She blinked, turned her head to gaze across the valley, where Jelaza Kazone could be plainly seen, stretching high into the morning sky. "That wouldn't be good, would it?"

"Not—very—good," murmured Er Thom. "No."

"Well," she said, turning back to Daav. "You have other houses. There's no need to make her uncom—"

"There must not be a child born unsanctioned by the Tree!" Er Thom cried.

"Yes, but, love, Shan wasn't sanctioned by the Tree," Anne pointed out with shocking calm. "I don't—" She stopped abruptly, staring from one pair of serious eyes to the other.

"I think," she said finally, and a bit breath-short, "that I have to draw the line at a galaxy-wide telepathy."

Daav inclined his head. "Say then that Er Thom, who as a child was used to climb all over the Tree, had been far too well-trained to choose other than one who would meet approval."

"Then," Anne asked reasonably, "what happened to you?"

Daav lifted a brow. "I beg your pardon?"

"What happened to you?" She repeated, and used a long forefinger to point, one to the other. "You were raised side-by-side, learned the same things, ate the same things, *memorized* the same things. Interchangeable parts, made by the delm's wisdom, so Korval could go on, if one of you happened to die!" Her voice was keying upward. Er Thom stirred, raising a hand toward her cheek.

"Interchangeable," Daav said. "Not exact."

She glared, though it seemed to him her eyes were not—precisely—focussed. "Call it off."

So simple. It struck at the core of him and he came upright before he knew what he did, shaking with—with—"I must have a child!" He heard raw anguish in his voice and swallowed, closing his eyes and seeking after the Rainbow.

"But not *this* child," Anne pursued relentlessly. "You and Er Thom are the sons of identical twins, so close there's no choosing between you. Er Thom and I are lifemates, hooked by the soul, so I can feel his touch halfway across the house—and more!" She paused and Daav opened his eyes, meeting her fey gaze with fascination.

"Where is your lifemate, Daav yos'Phelium?"

"Anne!" Er Thom snapped to his feet, his hands on her shoulders, his body between her and his delm. "Have done."

"I repeat." He was breathless, voice squeezed out of a chest gone achy and cramped. "We may be interchangeable. We are certainly not identical. And even if what you suggest is true—that we were both formed for lifematings—there is yet no guarantee that—my—lifemate has been born." He took a hard breath. "Or that she has survived."

"Oh," she said, and of a sudden sighed, reaching up to rub at her eyes like a child. "Well," she murmured, almost too softly for him to hear, "I guess you'd better ask the Tree."

"I guess I had better," he returned, just as softly, and smiled sadly into Er Thom's eyes.

Ride the Luck tested clean.

Aelliana heard Sed Ric and Yolan's account of their adventure and read them a stern lecture on the stupidity of charging unknown and potentially deadly lurkers. They both looked rather sheepish and assured her most earnestly that they would never again undertake so shatterbrained an enterprise.

All thus in accord, they exited *The Luck* and walked back toward the garage, Yolan speculating on this ship and that, with Sed Ric occasionally amending her IDs.

They turned out of the avenue of sleeping ships just as a landcar pulled up before Binjali's and a light-haired man got out, heading for the crew door.

"Father!" Yolan hissed, braking hard and flinging an arm across her partner's chest.

"Uncle Zan Der!" Sed Ric gulped at the same moment—and in the next, they were gone, flying back down the row of cold pads, heading for the eastern gate.

Aelliana had gone three steps after them before common sense reasserted itself. It was useless for her to chase them, Port-wise as they were. They knew the way back—and the odds were they would return, once they reckoned "Uncle Zan Der" gone.

So thinking, Aelliana turned back to discover what it was about a mere light-haired man that sent two Port-runners to flight.

"... Pilot Caylon?" the stranger was asking as Aelliana stepped through the door.

Jon used his chin to point over the man's shoulder. "There she comes now."

He turned, brown eyes flicking across her face in the moment before he bowed respect.

"Pilot Caylon, I am Zan Der pel'Kirmin, Clan Reptor," he said, as if he were but a clansman, and the delm's Ring he wore merely an ornament. "I ask pardon for this disruption of your peace. My excuse can only be that I have had news of two over whom you have spread your protection."

She considered him, and he bore it, patient as if he treated with Scouts every hour. Besides patience, she saw worry, and weariness and a wary sort of hope. Behind

those cares, she saw also humor and a glimmer of inde-
finable something that reminded her, forcibly, of Yolan.

"I have recently—commended—two halflings to
Master dea'Cort's attention," Aelliana said carefully,
watching the man's weary, wary eyes. "He is kind
enough to provide them day-work. But I must tell you,
sir, that this pair of children claim—most strongly—to
have no kin."

Hope flared beyond wariness for an instant; the
mouth bent into a tired smile. "I had heard that they
claimed themselves clanless. To you, I take oath that
this is not so, though they may themselves believe
otherwise. If I might be granted an opportunity to
speak with them—" He raised a quick hand, Ring
glinting. "They are under your protection. I honor
that. There is nothing I wish to say to them that I
would be ashamed to have you hear as well."

And that, Aelliana thought, was extraordinarily
courageous, for a man who had all but lost two of his
clan through what he represented as a misunderstand-
ing. She had thought Yolan and Sed Ric might have
had reason, such as she had, to embrace the clanless
state. Indeed, it might be that their reasons were just.
Yet this man here seemed no one like Ran Eld, only
exhausted with worry and eager to amend a wrong.

"If you might—produce them...?" he said, delicately.

Aelliana smiled wryly, thinking of two swift figures, racing down the row of cold pads. "I think
it unlikely—" she began—and heard the crew door
cycle behind her.

Daav set his hands along the trunk, took a breath
and swung up into the branches. At the first major

cross-branch, he ended his climb, sitting astride the big limb, feet swinging in air, leaves rustling and whispering around him.

"If you have anything to say," he stated, rather crossly, "you might as well say it to me."

There was neither a cessation nor an increase of leaf-rustle. Not, Daav thought, that he had expected it.

"I hope you're proud of yourself," he continued aloud. "Terrifying a guest of the House—and one's wife-elect. I should think an ancient hulking brute like yourself might find more seemly amusements. Forgive me if I speak too plainly."

The leaves directly above him flittered. Daav frowned.

"Laugh, by all means. I suppose it's nothing to you if yos'Phelium dies with me? No, I do an injustice. yos'Phelium shall die with Pat Rin—but before that, young Shan will be delm."

A breeze kissed his cheek, and the smaller branches nearby danced. Daav closed his eyes, feeling the warm bark beneath his fingers, the age-old solidity of wood between his thighs. "I shall marry Samiv tel'Izak," he said, forming each word with precision, "and the child of that union shall come to Korval."

The wood beneath his hands cooled. Perceptibly. Daav sighed.

"May I then solicit your further guidance? Or do we return to placing an advertisement in *The Gazette*? Notice, I do not ask how I shall extricate Korval solvent from a contract most binding. I am fully alive to the fact that details do not interest you."

The leaves had stilled all about. The branch he straddled became neither warmer or cooler. Deliberately, Daav emptied his mind of all conscious thoughts, treading a path Rockflower had once shown him, past need and want and everyday busy-ness to a place where there was only—peace.

He sat there, tranced, until the late noon sun lanced a ray through the leaves and dazzled him awake. Jelaza Kazone had not spoken and he wished, with everything in him, to be at Binjali's.

"Uncle Zan Der." He came forward, alone, which made him seem half, for Aelliana had never yet seen one pirate without the other—and made his bow to his elder.

"Sed Ric." The man put out his hands, eyes afire with longing. "Are you well, child?"

"Well..." He went another jerky step forward, and stopped, face twisting. "I think—we should come—home, Uncle..." His voice choked out and he threw a glance to Aelliana, eloquent of she knew not what.

"Where is Yolan?" she asked him, thinking, of a sudden, of lurkers, and guns and the girl's bright, brash courage.

"Here." The single word was flat with despair. Stiff-legged, Yolan came forward, to her place at Sed Ric's right. The look she gave him might have frozen iron.

"Now what?" she rasped—and began, quite suddenly, to cry.

Chapter Twenty-Eight

Delm's Discretionary Account Three, The Pilots Fund. Established for the aid and succor of pilots and former pilots, regardless of clan, race or lineage. Profit margin of funding stocks no less than forty percent.

—From Korval's Account Ledgers,
Discretionary Monies

THIS TIME SHE WOULD NOT ELUDE HIM.

Ran Eld waited in the shadow of the main staircase, ears straining for the sound of stealthy footsteps.

He had determined to follow her yesterday and the day before yesterday, only to find upon arising that she had quit the house hours before, leaving behind insolent messages about engagements to dine elsewhere. Very well.

Today, she would not elude him.

He would follow her to the Scout and deal with that. Then, he would escort her home, and deal with *that*.

In the shadow of the staircase, Ran Eld smiled.

It was plain that Aelliana wanted disciplining—oh, badly. She so far forgot herself as to disobey a direct order from one who was both her elder and her superior—then flaunted her disobedience, daring him to do what was no more than his duty. For the good of the clan.

The fact that disciplining this most dangerous of siblings would give him positive delight was to Ran Eld's way of thinking no more than just. Aelliana should not be delm. It was a sad pity that the old delm, their grandmother, had put such a notion into the girl's head. The idea was ludicrous on the face of it. He was nadelm, in every way his sister's superior.

Which he would prove, as often as necessary.

He considered that his first attempt at bringing this point home had been successful. One year of marriage to Ran Eld's friend had produced ten years of quite satisfactory behavior in Ran Eld's sister. To be sure, it had occasionally been necessary to administer certain—remedial—lessons, but that was expectable, even —enjoyable. Ten years for one was a good investment of time and funds, so he flattered himself.

From the landing above came the lightest of footsteps.

Ran Eld half-crouched in his dim niche, eagerness shortening his breath. The footsteps continued their light path, across the landing, down the remaining stairs. He smiled and dared to lean just slightly out of his hiding place, to better see—

His delm.

He shifted sharply in disappointment, boot heel scraping against marble floor.

Birin Caylon turned. Seething, Ran Eld slipped out of the niche and made his bow.

"Mother."

"My son." She inclined her head, appearing to find

nothing unusual in either the time or the place of their meeting. Indeed, she smiled. "I am fortunate to find you about so early. Break your fast with me, if you have not already eaten. I have completed my study of your analysis regarding San bel'Fasin's offer of partnership and I believe you may be interested in the decision."

So. Ran Eld bowed once more to hide his smile of triumph. "I am, as always, at your service, ma'am," he said and followed her into the dining hall, leaving the door slightly ajar.

Tea had barely been poured when he heard footsteps on the stair, and saw a slim shadow flicker across the half-open doorway. Half a heartbeat later, the front door moaned on its hinges, and snapped softly shut.

Aelliana strode down Mechanic Street, head high and face glowing. She was to train with Trilla this morning, after which she was to lift with Jon himself, who had sworn to put her through an emergency drill like no other.

The door cycled and she stepped into the huge dim cavern of Binjali Repair Shop.

Around the teapot was a cluster of leather-clad figures: Jon, Trilla, Clonak—and a tall man, dark hair clipped neatly back, silver twist swinging in one ear, cat sitting tall on his opposite shoulder.

Aelliana felt her heart lift; she very nearly laughed for the sheer joy of beholding him.

As if he heard her unvoiced joy, he turned, a smile lighting his eyes.

"Hello, Aelliana."

"Daav." Her own smile felt wide enough to split her face. "It's good to see you."

"It's good to be seen," he returned gravely and she did laugh then, standing before him with her face tipped up to his.

"Good comes in odd packages," Jon commented from his stool.

"Jon scolds me for carrying Patch," Aelliana told Daav, reaching up to offer the cat a finger. "He says I'll spoil him."

"The damage has long been done, I fear," he replied as Patch bent his head and allowed her to rub his ears.

"Spoil a cat when there are the rest of us, hungering for a smile!" That was Clonak.

Aelliana finished the cat's ear and stepped forward. "Good morning, Clonak."

"Good-morning, goddess fair! Will you rub my ears?"

She made a show of giving it consideration, head cocked to one side. "No."

"Heart-torn again! Hold me, Daav, I'm bereft!"

"Perhaps if you grew fur on them?" Daav suggested, not noticeably moved by this plea for comradeship.

Clonak glared. "Mock me, oh Captain."

"If you insist."

"The pirates' delm came," Aelliana said, turning back to Daav, "and fetched them home." She grinned, throwing a glance over her shoulder to Jon. "Or mostly."

He snorted. "Ring-and-monkey show."

Daav smiled down at her, one eyebrow slightly askew. "I surmise that they were not clanless, after all?"

"Not—entirely," she said, slowly. "It did seem to be all in a muddle. But the end of it is that they shall come here to work off—work off a debt Delm Reptor feels most strongly is owing, for Jon having given good wages for grunt-work. In the meanwhile, they—the pirates—shall live under Reptor's roof and—and—strive to—amend their difference." She looked up at him. "Or so he said."

"Ah. And do you believe what he has said, I wonder?"

She frowned, chewing her lip. "Yes," she said finally, "I do. He seemed an honest man—and honestly joyed to find them." She lay her hand on his sleeve and smiled. "It was good of you to send him."

Both brows shot up. "I?"

"Well, it must have been you," she said reasonably. "He knew exactly where to come, and asked for me by name. Jon didn't tell him, nor Trilla nor Clonak. I certainly didn't—I hadn't the least idea of how to go about finding their clan! So—"

"When you have eliminated the impossible," Daav murmured, in Terran, "whatever remains, however improbable, must be the truth."

Aelliana blinked at him. "I beg your pardon?"

He grinned. "An observation by a Mr. Holmes, I believe, on the nature of solutions."

"The game is afoot!" Clonak shouted, clattering off his stool with a flourish. He looked to Jon. "I'll get on that maintenance update, if you like."

"Always after the sit-down job," the old Scout grumbled. Clonak laughed and headed toward the office, flipping a casual hand at the rest. Patch jumped from Daav's shoulder and followed.

Across the half-circle, Trilla slid to her feet and tossed Aelliana a grin. "Set for a bit of dancing, pilot?"

"If you have the patience for me," she said. "I am aware I cannot give the challenge you might like."

The other woman laughed as she unbuckled her tool belt. "Oh, and can you not?" She turned to the dark haired man as if she'd heard him speak. "Just a bit of *menfri'at*, Master Daav. No harm in it. Quite of a bit of good."

He inclined his head. "As you say."

He watched them walk away, noting the set of Aelliana's shoulders, the light, confident walk.

"Hard to believe that's the same woman slunk in here half-a-quarter ago and whispered for her ship," Jon commented from his side. Daav looked down into a pair of speculative amber eyes.

"We'll have her brawling in taverns before the year is done," he agreed, watching Aelliana shed her jacket and face Trilla across sub-bay one. "Fine work, Master Jon."

"Now, now, I can't take all the credit. It was a certain young captain set her feet on the path by handing her a bowli ball and telling her to fight."

Daav laughed. "Cow-handed as that? Poor captain."

"Well, as I say, he's young, but his ideas aren't too bad. Usually."

Trilla's first pass was fast and low—rather faster and lower than he would have expected. He felt his own muscles tense as Aelliana slipped gently to the left, sidestepping the attack and spinning, establishing her rhythm and the range of her dance.

"How long has this been going on?" he asked Jon.

"Matter of two days."

"She's good."

"Not bad. The fast stuff don't bother her, but come at her hard, like you're going to do damage and damn me if she won't back down every time." Jon sighed. "Never did hear who beats her."

The crew door cycled and Daav looked around in

time to see Sed Ric bin'Ala and Yolan pel'Kirmin step
through. They came forward, the girl to the boy's
right, stopped and made their bows.

"Captain."

"Children. Pilot Caylon tells me you are joyfully
re-clanned."

Yolan made no answer to that, though the look she
flung him held no amazing charge of joy. The boy
was likewise somber, but replied courteously enough,
"Yes, sir. Thank you, sir."

"Show the captain here your toy, young Sed Ric,"
Jon directed, pointing at the boy's belt. "Look at
this, Daav."

The jang-wire came out with a flash and a snap,
held in the down position, limp and almost pretty.

"Hah." Daav extended a hand. "May I?"

Sed Ric offered the leather handle and Daav slid
his fingers into the loop.

"I believe this may be original," he said and went
back a sudden, silent step, snapping the wire up and
flicking his wrist, *so*.

The limp wire went stiff, becoming an arm's length
of double-edged blade, Daav grinned, shook the blade
carefully and handed the quiescent weapon back to
its owner.

"Very nice, indeed. Where did you come by it?"

"Uncle Lip Ten left it to us," Yolan said, "in a crate
of things he'd gathered, star-hopping. Aunt Fris said
it was junk and wished us joy of it."

"Doubtless Aunt Fris has other virtues," Daav
murmured and Yolan laughed, short and bitter. Over
in sub-bay one, Aelliana spun and kicked, dancing
neatly away from Trilla's snaking grab.

"What—" Daav began, but the question was never finished.

"Aelliana!" Clonak was on a dead run from the office, face, for once, entirely serious. "Aelliana!"

In the circle of the dance, she spun, dropped her stance and came forward.

"What is it?"

"Tower on the line. Fellow on Outyard Five toppled into the mechanics. Autodoc mended the worst, but his heart failed him. Can you lift the spare and the health tech—"

"Yes!" She snatched up her jacket. Clonak was already on his way back to the office.

"Daav." She paused before him, hand on his sleeve, green eyes bright as she looked into his face. "Ride second board for me?"

Adrenaline surged. He grinned. "Yes."

"Thank you," she said, and was gone, running at the top of her speed.

In the next instant, Daav was likewise gone, his shadow merging with hers as the crew door closed.

The delm had decided against a partnership with bel'Fasin.

Oh, she had reasons, and gave them in-depth, her wish, she said, was to instruct him, so that when he was come delm . . .

He scarcely attended her; sat, cold and disbelieving, while she spoke—rambling, meaningless sentences that meant, in final cipher, one thing:

He was ruined.

In his apartment abovestairs, Ran Eld riffled accounts that had been squeezed dry years ago, called up balance sheets and dismissed them, his hands shaking so badly he must make two and three attempts to strike the proper key.

At length, he rose from his desk, poured himself a brandy and wandered the room, wracking his brain for something—for anything—he might sell or take loan against, that would keep San bel'Fasin at bay.

Chapter Twenty-Nine

Emergency repairs at Tinsori Light. Left my ring in earnest. The keeper's a cantra-grubbing pirate, but the ship should hold air to Lytaxin. Send one of ours and eight cantra to redeem my pledge. Send them armed. In fact send two....

—Excerpted from a beam letter from
Jen Sin yos'Phelium Clan Korval to his delm,
written in the first relumma of
the year named Dalenart

THE TECH WENT INTO THE HOLD WITH HIS LIFE UNIT, strapped into the rumble-seat and reported himself ready.

Daav checked the webbing, made certain the unit was properly dogged, advised the tech to take a nap and walked back to his station.

"End," Aelliana said into the comm as he slid into the co-pilot's slot and pulled the shock-straps tight.

"Confirmed," Tower announced half-a-heartbeat later. "Lift at will, *Ride the Luck*."

She shot him a look from eyes more brilliant than emeralds. "Ready?"

"Ready."

"Engage gyros."

✳ ✳ ✳

Jon dea'Cort stood before the command wall in the side bay, working the dials, swearing ferociously at a shower of static. The band caught suddenly, delivering the curt tones of Port Control.

". . . shift lanes immediately. We have an emergency. Freighter X38519, slipshift to alternate path R9. *Tansberg's Folly* on approach, divert to Binjali's sling—"

"Trilla!" Jon shouted.

"On it," came the laconic response as the alert sounded overhead.

"Allow me to provide visuals, Master dea'Cort." Clonak stepped to Jon's side, his hands dancing over the screen-controls, bringing the four most pertinent to sharp life.

"This is Pilot Aelliana Caylon, *Ride the Luck*." Calm as if she were discussing the likelihood of rain. "We have our package and are ready to lift at pilot's two minutes. Mark. Request clearance, Tower. Route computed, checks in line, transmitted . . . End."

"*Markham's Mistress*, change lanes now!" Tower snarled. "Lift at will, *Ride the Luck*. All ships, priority clearance to *Ride the Luck*. We have an emergency . . ."

There was a roar and a shifting whine, which was the gyros spinning to full, and then the muted, held-out throb of power that was lift-off, close by. On the visuals, *Ride the Luck* cleared Solcintra Port and hurtled upward. The radio had a moment free of chatter, into which Trilla's exuberant, "Caught her!" sang savage with delight.

The chatter took up again, grousing about skewed schedules, hovering deadlines, pile ups, back ups and—

"At nearest convenience, will *Ride the Luck* put navcomp on line?" Tower requested with unusual politeness. Clonak gave a shout of laughter and Jon grinned. The pirates, hovering at wall-edge, looked at each other with wide-stretched eyes.

"At nearest convenience," Tower repeated—"Thank you, Pilot Caylon."

There was a gabble of chatter—wonderment, such like: "Caylon? The Tables? *That* Caylon? . . . chel'Mara's ship . . . Flies her like a Scout!"—and then another voice, overriding all the others.

"Aelliana Caylon, *Ride the Luck*, amending filed course. Projected time savings seven-point-three minutes."

"Continue," Tower directed, while the rest of near space held its collective breath.

"We'll be adding a delta vee of 23.8 percent at 14:01.33; and we'll be crossing shipping intersections 14, 15, 16 and 23. At 14:08.14 we will change attitude to 170 degrees exactly and add a delta vee of 33.6 percent plus or minus a tenth. As we hit the tidal effect zone we'll pick up an additional delta vee of 17.04 percent and also be south of the main equatorial shipping lanes so we'll have no clearance problems. My window is 13:59 to 14:03, which at my mark begins in three minutes. May I have confirmation?"

Silence hummed through the lines for a full thirty seconds, broken, at last, by Daav: "Verified."

"In her head!" a Terran-tinged voice whooped from close in. "Working it in her head, damn me for a mudhog! Who's running second—"

"*Ride the Luck*, we have a confirm on that." Tower sounded just the tiniest bit rattled. "You're all go."

The chatter broke over the comm in waves: "Tower fifty-eight seconds behind, running a comp as big as your homeworld!" "I'll drink for free tonight! Caylon at the board, is it?"

There was more of approximately the same, which Jon ignored, glancing instead to the wall of screens.

"What's she got in—"

"The tide!" Trilla cried, leaning over his shoulder to point as Sed Ric and Yolan crowded closer. "She's going to catch the tidal effect at the juncture with planetary grav—"

"She's what?" Clonak cleared a screen and flung the equation into it, fingers blurring as he built the schematic. "I'm damned," he said suddenly. "Jon, look at this."

"I see it. A rare wonder, our math teacher."

It was pretty much textbook then, with one more small adjustment, as Daav kicked them onto an auxiliary approach that put them practically in the 'yard's back door. It shaved another minute and would have been counted very pretty, had it not been overshadowed by Aelliana's stunning bit of work. Jon backed the chatter down and shook his head, Terran-wise, in admiration.

"The woman's unbelievable," Clonak murmured, keying up the replay. "On the run, in her head... I'm in love, Master-mine."

"For the fifth time since yesterday," Jon snorted, elbowing himself a spot at the board. He watched the replay in reverent silence, lost in the beauty of the maneuver. To shave seven minutes—*seven minutes*—off a lift measured and calibrated and understood to the nanosecond, while she was running board, close in traffic, with the possibility of someone breaking out—in her head, as Clonak said...

"I'd sign her first class this minute," Jon murmured,

"and a blight on the regs. Anyone who can fly like that—"

"A goddess," Clonak sighed, sounding more than half-serious. "I claim the privilege of naming her first class, sir, and I am prepared to duel for the honor."

"Yes, but she'll never believe she earned it that way," Jon said, keying the replay to storage. "The book is the path and the math teacher aims to follow it through every twist and cranny."

"We've been avoiding the tidal effect ever since the first ship shed atmosphere," Clonak was almost singing. "Avoiding it! *Compensating* for it! Aelliana Caylon *uses* it and speeds her package on its way! Poor Daav."

"His trick lost in shadow, eh?" Jon grinned. "He won't mind."

"No, I suppose he won't. Anything that improves the lift is joy to Daav, no matter if your grandmother conned it."

Jon started, eyes widening, then going narrow. "There's a notion, though." He turned from the screens and strode down-bay, snagging his jacket from the hook as he went by.

"I'll be back!" he called and vanished through the door, as Trilla, Clonak and the pirates exchanged puzzled stares.

Tech and package off-loaded, *Ride the Luck* rode a holding pattern, waiting for Port Control to sort the scrambled traffic and give them clearance to land.

The pilot had gone to fetch tea from the pantry, leaving the board in charge of her co-pilot, who had reclined his long self at his station, watching the go-lights through half-closed eyes.

304 *Sharon Lee & Steve Miller*

Brief as it was, Daav thought, one ear cocked toward the radio, this lift had thus far been among the most remarkable of his career. Who but Aelliana Caylon could have conceived the notion of using the tidal influence every other pilot in the universe so busily avoided? Who but that same amazing mind could have framed, checked and executed so exciting a new maneuver in the time—

"Daav? You did want tea?"

He opened his eyes with a grin and extended a languid hand for the mug. "It's a lazy second you're burdened with, pilot."

"Yes, certainly." She laughed softly and perched on the edge of her own chair, eyes flicking over screens, lights, readouts.

"It was fortunate you had known of that auxiliary route," she said. "I should have lost us three minutes at the last, lining up the primary approach."

"No more than one-point-five," Daav corrected. "And you had already gained us seven that were utterly unlooked-for."

She moved her shoulders and glanced down into her mug. "I had been working on a notion about the tidals about a year ago," she said. "It wouldn't come together, so I put it aside. Something—shifted—when you showed me Little Jump the other day. And then today, when I saw the numbers and the relationships—" She looked up, pride apparent, though she fought to keep her features composed. "It all just tumbled into place." Abruptly she gave up the struggle for dignity and allowed the grin its freedom. "Pretty, isn't it?"

"A thing of astonishing beauty," Daav agreed, smiling into sparkling green eyes. Those same eyes widened, then moved aside, flashing over the stat-lights.

"You did send Delm Reptor to find the pirates, didn't you?" The look she gave him was quizzical. Daav sighed.

"I suppose I will have to own the act, though I refuse to bear all the blame." He raised his mug to her in light salute. "Jon found who they were."

"Oh." She sipped tea, frowning slightly at the floor-plates.

"That was clever of him," she said eventually. "I had tried, you know, to find their surnames, but I don't expect I was very subtle." Her frown deepened and she raised doubtful eyes to his.

"Do you think we—do you think we did well?" she asked, leaning forward.

Daav raised an eyebrow, caught by her intensity. "Do you think we did not?"

"I—am not certain," she said hesitantly, frowning once more at the flooring. "It had seemed—they were hungry and—and compelled toward thievery—and so young." She glanced up, tawny brows drawn. "I do not—you spoke as if it—the Low Port—as if it were dreadfully dangerous . . ."

"It is," he assured her, with utter sincerity, "dreadfully dangerous."

"Yes! And so it seems that we must have done well, to have caught them away from danger and returned them to safety—and—to kin. Yet . . ."

"Yet?" he prompted softly, when a minute had passed and she said nothing more.

She came to her feet all at once, leaving her mug behind in the arm-slot, and paced to the center of the cabin. There, she spun to face him, fingers twisting and twining til he thought she might never unknot them.

"They left," she said. "They said that they had left because the time was coming when they might be eligible for—for marriage. Neither wished to be married to any other. They spoke to their delm of their desire to be always together, but he was not—not disposed to hear them as more than children. They spoke to him again on the matter, and he was abrupt, saying consanguinity was too near. They went a third time, bearing gene-charts which showed them unlikely of producing a defective . . ." She faltered.

Daav set his cup aside and straightened in his chair. "Their delm spoke of separating them so they might learn to deal with other folk."

"Yes." She bit her lip. "Yes, of course he did. How could he not? To lose the possibility of liaison marriage from two of the younger—he must look to his clan's whole good. I do not fault him—he spoke as he must. But—" She paused; plunged ahead.

"I—I don't pretend to know a great deal about—and of course marriage is—extremely—distasteful—"

"Is it?"

"Yes—and only think how much more distasteful when there is one you—prefer—above all others—I pity them from my heart and wish—I wish we had not stopped to play!"

"For that I shall bear the blame. They looked in desperate case and unlikely to ask for aid. My whole thought had been to force aid upon them—at least as little as a meal." He paused. "Does their delm still speak of separation?"

She sighed. "It is—under negotiation. A trial separation, to determine the—the depth of their devotion. Sed Ric—Sed Ric speaks of being apprenticed to a

cousin on an Outworld, so that Yolan may finish her
pilot's study at home."

"Ah. And Yolan?"

"She cries," Aelliana said, shoulders slumping. "Cries
and looks at him—I cannot tell you how she looks at
him." She frowned at the floor.

"What else may their delm do? They are assets of
the clan, to be used, as all are used, for the good
of all."

"So the Code teaches us," Daav said rather dryly.
He tipped his head, considering her downturned face.

"Is marriage—of course—so very distasteful?" he
wondered softly.

She glanced up, mouth hard. "I do not know that
it must be," she said with precision. "My own—but
that was many years ago."

"From the distance of your exalted age," he said
lightly, misliking the tightness of her muscles and the
way she stood there, tensed for a blow.

She drew herself up, eyes wide. "Next relumma,
I shall have twenty-seven Standard Years," she said
sharply. "I was married the day after my sixteenth
name day."

Too young. Far too young, Daav thought, for one
such as Aelliana. Quivering with something between
pity and outrage, he began a seated bow of apology—
was arrested by her raised hand.

"I had not meant to snap at you, Daav. It is true
that I have—limited—knowledge. Voni—my eldest
sister—marries often and seems quite content."

Marries often, he thought wryly, recalling the drab
street and moldering clanhouse in which she lived.
Contract marriage was an economic necessity for some

clans, true enough. Though in a house with several children of marriageable age—

"You have only married once?"

She inclined her head with brittle care. "It was sufficient." She sighed then, and showed him a palm, as if she wished somehow to make amends for his rudeness. "The clan has the care of my daughter."

She spoke with neither warmth nor interest of her child, as if—

"*Ride the Luck!*" The radio blared and they both jumped. Aelliana flashed forward and slapped the toggle.

"Caylon here."

"Acknowledge filed plan and begin descent," Tower directed. "There is traffic waiting behind you."

"Yes," said Aelliana, glancing at the screen and verifying the equations in her head. "Flight plan acknowledged, descent begins on my mark." She turned her head. Daav was strapped in at his station, fingers dancing over the board. He glanced up, dark eyes bright, and gave her the Scout's go-sign.

"Mark."

It was a solemn crew congregated before the teapot. Jon sat astride his usual stool, Trilla on his right hand, Clonak on his left, Patch lying alert before all.

The door cycled and a tall shadow followed a shorter into the bay. They came forward a few steps, then Aelliana faltered—stopped, face showing pale and wary. Daav paused just behind her left shoulder, eyebrows well up.

"The pair of you," Jon said with a sigh. "Come here, math teacher."

She glanced over her shoulder, up into Daav's face, tension showing in all her muscles. He touched her arm, smiled; she took a deep, shaky breath and went forward.

Directly before Jon's stool, she stopped, hands folded before her, her tall co-pilot at her side.

"Master dea'Cort."

"Hah. I suppose you know what you did today, with that display around the tidal effect?"

She licked her lips, but kept her eyes steady on his. The pulse at the base of her throat trembled like a bird.

"Yes, sir."

"Yes sir, is it? Well, then, tell me."

"Yes, sir." She gulped air. "We framed and tried a piloting addendum under stringent field conditions. The maneuver has tested successfully and I suspect subsequent testings and refinements as the equation is understood and tuned."

"Invented a whole new sentence in the language of local lift," Clonak intoned.

Her chin came up. "If you like."

"Oh, I do like," he assured her, with a flash of his usual deviltry. "Very, very much."

"Pipe down," Jon directed, and lifted a hand, beckoning. "Closer, please, math teacher. I'm too old a dog to bite you."

Doubt showed at that, but she came forward, Daav still at her side, his hand near her elbow, should she have need of support.

Jon turned his palm up. "Right hand, please."

She lay her palm lightly against his. The ancient silver puzzle-ring flashed, as if with defiance. Jon touched it with a reverent fingertip. "Where did you get this?" he asked gently.

"My grandmother left it me," she answered in the same tone, "when she died."

"So. This is fitting, then, since I have it from my grandmother." He reached into his belt and brought it forth.

It sparkled like a nebula: Big, gaudy, garish bit of trumpery. Sapphires, rubies, emeralds, diamond—every one first cut—set in a platinum band meant to cover a finger knuckle-to-knuckle. Jon held it up, let them all see the flash and the wonder of it. Three of them knew what it was. He heard Daav draw a breath.

"This," Jon said, bringing the ring before Aelliana's wide eyes, "is what pilots wore in the long-ago when they took their Jump-ships out to the edge. It was used as a bond of word, as collateral for cargo, as earnest for repairs. A pilot always came back for her ring, that was the wisdom, and most often it was true." He smiled.

"I had this from my mother, who had it from hers, who had it from her father—back more generations than even you can count. It returned to me with my son's body. It's always been worn by a binjali pilot. Favor me, by wearing it now."

For a moment, he thought even so little was too much. Her face blanched to beige, but the eyes—the eyes were beyond brilliant.

She inclined her head, with full respect.

"You do me great honor," she said, voice husking and solemn. "I shall wear it—with joy."

"So." He felt a sweep of pride in her—in the person she allowed herself to become. Tears pricked at his eyes and he slid the old ring onto second finger of her right hand. It seated as if it had been made for her and Jon smiled. He had guessed well, he congratulated himself, in telling the jeweler the new size.

He took his hand from under hers, leaned back on his stool.

From his right, Trilla cheered, joined a moment later by Clonak. Daav lay a quiet hand on her shoulder and smiled when she turned her face up to his. Patch rose and stretched and stropped once against her legs before moving off on more urgent business.

"And now," Clonak announced, leaping to his feet and stretching his hands high over his head, "we celebrate!"

Chapter Thirty

A Healer is one who may look into the heart and mind of one who is in pain, soothe the pain and restore the sufferer to joy.
—From the Preamble to the Healer's Guide

PILOTS LINED UP TO MEET HER; DAAV MURMURED THEIR names in her ear as they bowed: "Hela. Kad Vyr. Mordrid. Nasi."

Aelliana returned every bow, repeating each name in an effort to fix it in memory with the appropriate face.

"Illiopa, Pet Ram, Abi Tod—" The line was coming to an end at last, but Aelliana greatly feared that she had lost some names entirely, and muddled others.

"Frad," Daav murmured on a rather different note. Aelliana shook herself and applied special attention to Pilot Frad.

A bland-faced man nearly as tall as Daav, he bowed respect, coupled with a hand-spelt "binjali." Straightening, he reached out to grip Daav's shoulder and grinned.

"Old friend."

Daav returned grip and grin. "When did you get in?"

"Just in time to catch the most amazing lift I've

312

seen in my poor career, from the vantage of Scout Station."

"Always in the luck."

"Hah!" Frad turned to Aelliana. "Take advice, pilot, and demand the Port Master give you a tenth of the profit she'll realize from selling that tape."

She blinked at him. "Tape?"

"Tried to get a copy myself, but the lines were backed up to next Trilsday. Couple of bars ago I heard a Terran captain offering twenty cantra hard for the first copy reaches his hands before local midnight—" He grinned. "Wants to use it for crew training!"

Aelliana looked to Daav, eyes wide. "He's joking," she suggested, uncertainly.

Daav's lips quirked. "Yes, but it doesn't at all seem like Frad's sort of joke."

"Not a bit of it," that gentleman assured her with utmost gravity. "Given to making pies into the beds of my comrades." He sighed, bland face suffused with sorrow. "Very low sense of humor."

Aelliana chuckled, Frad's name was called by someone across the room and he moved off, raising light fingertips to Daav's cheek in the moment before he was gone.

The small gesture of tenderness awoke an appalling twist of emotion in Aelliana's chest. By custom and by Code, she should have felt shock. That two who were not kin should share such intimacy—to show their depravity in so public a place—It was beyond the pale. If she were Voni, she might well have fainted.

By Code, she should now distance herself from Daav, her surname-less co-pilot, that his corruption not sully her *melant'i*.

Failing of the Code, she lifted her eyes to find his waiting, quizzical and—wary.

Wary—awaiting her censure. It hurt—astonishingly— that he should think her capable—and it was not shock she felt, Aelliana owned in a rush of self-truth, but jealousy, that Frad should be so dear to him.

She smiled and saw the wariness melt.

"Frad was a member of my team," he told her. "The four of us went through Academy together—Frad, Olwen, Clonak and I."

"There you are!" That was Clonak, wading through the crush of Scouts, pilots and hanger-ons that clogged Apel's tiny wine-room. "Jon says it's time to move and let this rabble celebrate on their own. They've made their bows, now they want to talk board."

"True enough," Daav allowed. "Where does Jon want us to go, I wonder?"

"Kinchail's," Clonak said. "Meet us. I'll get Frad." He was gone, melting effortlessly into the crowd.

Daav look down at her from dancing dark eyes.

"Hungry, pilot?"

"Yes!" Aelliana said in surprise and reached out to take his hand.

They sat seven to dinner in the comfort of comrades: Jon, Apel, Frad, Trilla, Clonak, Daav, and Aelliana, with Jon at the top of the table and Aelliana between him and Daav.

It was a merry meal, replete with wine and chatter and dish after dish of delicious things, all ordered by Mistress Apel and shared 'round the table.

The last platter having been taken away, Clonak and Frad embarked on a risque joke contest, into which

Trilla occasionally threw a laconic one-liner. Apel sat quietly between Jon and Frad, sipping her wine and dividing her attention between the band, setting up in the corner opposite, and the entrance way. Jon and Daav were talking quietly.

"A grand, dangerous work, young captain. Happens Liad isn't ripe for hearing it."

"Liad is not altogether happy," Daav admitted, twirling his glass between long, clever fingers. Fascinated, Aelliana watched his hand, struck once more by the ring-marked, empty finger. It occurred to her to wonder if Daav himself had not fallen aside trouble within his own clan, that stripped him of rank-ring and made him eager to aid a pair of clanless pirates.

"Still," Daav said, "Liad must have heard it, soon or late. Truth will be told, sink it as deep as you may."

"We're for company," Apel commented as a drift of leather jackets came through the door. Across the room, the band struck its first notes.

"Music!" Clonak exclaimed, cutting himself off in mid-joke. He bounced to his feet and made one of his extravagant bows.

"Dance with me, peerless goddess."

She stared up at him, feeling Daav's warmth beside her, and the weight of his sudden attention.

"I don't know how to dance," she told Clonak as the band swung into its first number.

"Of course you know how to dance! What has Trilla been teaching you this age?"

"I—"

"We'll show you," Trilla said, pushing back her chair and jerking her head at Frad. "Drafted, mapman."

"Not bad," Frad commented, coming to his feet. "A trifle obvious, but not bad."

Trilla laughed and marched ahead. Aelliana looked up into Clonak's taffy eyes and sighed.

"All right—but no nonsense!"

"Nonsense?" He opened his eyes wide. "When have I ever done less than cherish you?"

"Oh . . ." Aelliana stood, shaking her head at him in Terran fashion. "You are quite ridiculous," she said severely.

"But sincere," Clonak replied, with an evil grin. Taking her arm, he led her out onto the floor.

Learning to dance required as much concentration as learning *menfri'at*. As with the defense system, it was crucial to be aware of the movements and potential movements of one's opponent and to respond correctly. It was made more difficult than *menfri'at*, in Aelliana's opinion, by there being only one correct response—which must be made within the arbitrary rhythm of the music.

Her field of concentration was narrowed to Clonak's body, her own, the music, and the absolute necessity of performing perfectly. She was beginning to sweat with the strain of it, when an unexpected element entered the dance.

"My turn," Daav said calmly and Clonak released her with a preposterous sigh.

Aelliana stood staring up at him, abruptly aware of the others all about—there, Jon and Apel; Frad and a redhead in Scout leather; Trilla with *two* partners, an arm around the waist of each . . .

"Will you dance with me, Aelliana? Or shall I take you back to the table and give you some wine?"

"Dancing is—rather—difficult," she managed, moving closer to him and laying a hand along his sleeve.

"It needn't be," he returned and placed his free hand at her waist, as Clonak had done. "Indeed, dancing can be rather fun—believe me or don't." He grinned. "The first thing you must recall is that the one you dance with is your partner, not your opponent."

She laughed up at him and stepped closer, into the imaginary box Trilla had said she must stay within when dancing. Carefully, she put her right hand on his left shoulder, slid her left hand down to engage his free hand.

"Dance with me, then," she said. "Partner."

He smiled at that, pleasure showing plain. The fingers at her waist tightened; Daav swayed—and they were dancing.

It was absurdly easy. Her body moved without her conscious plan, indeed, it hardly seemed as if she moved at all, but that *they* did, with no separation so gross as *he* and *she*.

The music ended. Aelliana was still, her hand on his shoulder, his at her waist, and they were two now, with she reluctant to stand away.

"The musicians rest, Aelliana."

Daav's voice sounded—odd. The dark eyes that looked down into hers seemed dazzled. Indeed, she felt herself dazzled, wanting only to stand there, touched and touching, and gazing into his eyes, until it was time to dance again.

Abruptly, Daav cleared his throat, swayed back a step, breaking their gaze as his hand fell from her waist.

"Let us return to the others."

There were new faces around the table, and a shortage of chairs. Clonak came to his feet on the bounce. "We contrive," he announced, gesturing toward his empty place.

"My captain to sit here."

Daav lifted an eyebrow, but sat as he was bade.

"So. And my goddess to sit *here*." A hand in the middle of her back propelled her forward, to land with surprised grace on Daav's knee.

"Temporary quarters only," Clonak assured her, and struck a pose. "Chairs or death!" He bustled away, to general laughter.

Aelliana bit her lip. "I—beg your pardon," she stammered, looking down into Daav's eyes. "I shall stand."

"What? Forgo the best seat in the house?" Frad demanded, turning from his redhead with a grin. "Besides, Daav wants sitting on, now and then."

The others laughed. Trilla was between her two former dance partners, an arm around one's shoulders, a hand on the other's knee. The first dancer sipped from a glass, then held it to Trilla's lips. After Trilla had drunk, the first dancer held the glass for the second.

Apel, who was leaning on Jon's shoulder, her cheek perilously close to his, frowned down-table.

"Daav, your partner has no wine."

"Wine for Pilot Caylon!" Frad cried, snatching an empty glass from the table's center. He flourished it at the redhead, who captured a neighboring bottle and poured. Frad leaned over and placed the glass with an authoritative thump. "Good lift, pilot."

His attention was back with the redhead before Aelliana's "Safe landing" was complete.

"Do you wish the chair, Aelliana?" Daav's voice was soft, for her ears alone.

She turned her head, again looking down into his eyes. "I am—afraid—I have never sat on anyone's knee."

"Nor is there reason for you to do so now, if you

don't wish it," he said earnestly. "Stand a moment and allow me to rise."

"I—" She bit her lip, then gave him the truth, as a partner ought. "I think I should like to learn, Daav."

Laughter sparked across his face. "Ah, would you? Then allow me to be your teacher." There was a light touch at her waist—his hand, warm and firm, easing her back until she was sitting sidewise against him, her legs across his.

"Your near arm along my shoulders, if you will," he murmured and she complied; her breast pressed gently against his chest.

She stilled. Daav was warm against her, pleasing in a way that seemed related to the dance, his arm supporting her back, his hand curved over her hip.

"Aelliana?"

Deliberately, she drew a breath, and relaxed into him. Dance-like, indeed, she thought, catching an edge of that same subtle dazzlement. She bent her head, saw the shine of silver along his neck, where the collar gaped loose.

She touched it with a forefinger.

"What is this?" she whispered, her mouth near his ear.

"A chain," he whispered back. She laughed softly and felt him shiver.

"Would you like some wine?" he murmured and with her assent leaned forward. She closed her eyes, savoring the feel of him, the muscles shifting as he bent and her body bending with his—within his.

"Wine," he said. She opened her eyes to take the glass and sip, then offered it to him.

"Wine?" she asked softly, as Trilla's friend had done.

His eyes took fire. She felt—something—quiver through him; felt her heart begin an odd, thick pounding . . .

"Heads up!" That was Jon.

Aelliana felt Daav shift under her as the others leapt to their feet, bowing low to the three who approached the table.

Two men, one woman; one of the men in Scout leather; all bearing themselves as persons of authority. Aelliana gasped, suddenly knowing who they must be. Belatedly, she began to rise.

The man in Scout leather raised a hand. "Never mind, pilot," he said in Comrade. "I'd say you'd earned a comfortable seat and that one—" a casual finger-flip toward Daav—"owes me so many bows he might as well be your chair."

"Commander," Daav said gravely.

The older man inclined his head. "Captain."

"Ah, is this Pilot Aelliana Caylon?" the woman asked, coming forward to stand by Scout Commander. She bowed respect. "I am Narna vin'Tayla, Solcintra Port Master." She reached out and captured the remaining man, who had been speaking strenuously with Jon.

"Pilot Guild Master Per Sea ren'Gelder," she said and the man bowed, quickly.

"We are not here to disturb your celebration," Scout Commander said, with a glimmer of humor. "Master ren'Gelder has an item belonging to Pilot Caylon."

"Yes." Master ren'Gelder made another quick bow, leaned forward and placed a metal card on the table before Aelliana.

"This," he said briskly, "is the license for First Class Pilot Aelliana Caylon. This," he reached inside his jacket and withdrew a data-disk, "is the list of pilots endorsing Pilot Caylon's first class status—" he glanced at his wrist— "as of two hours ago." He inclined his head. "We shall, of course, forward an updated list to *Ride the Luck* maincomp."

Aelliana stared, then bent swiftly forward, reaching for that flat rectangle. Daav's hand shifted to her waist, lending her balance.

First Class: The words leapt out at her, the date of today—or, rather, yesterday—the endorsing pilot—she flipped the card over—

"Acclaim?"

Port Master smiled. "Thus the data-disk. It seems every Scout and master pilot on and around Liad has called to endorse your ascension, Pilot." Her smile widened. "There are several Terran masters in that list, as well."

"I—" It was on the edge of her tongue to protest that she had done nothing, that it had been a mere exercise in—She swallowed, inclined her head, feeling Daav's body solid and sure against hers.

"I thank you," she said formally.

"Custom has now been satisfied," Scout Commander announced, and turned with a sweep of his hand. "dea'Cort, you old ship-jockey, where's my wine?"

She had asked him to escort her to her ship, which was nothing more than a pilot might ask of her co-pilot—or of her partner. He accepted the duty gladly, though he might have served her better by placing her into Clonak's care. His emotions were—not quiescent.

Even now, walking sedately hand-in-hand, he felt

her presence as an intoxicant, so that he fought a mad desire to pull her close, to bury his face in her hair, run his hands over her strong, fragile body, to taste the honey of her skin...

Shuddering, he drew in a deep lungful of dew-early air.

He must not, he told himself, allow this sudden passion rein. A brief night of shared pleasure and a return to easy comradeship on the morrow—that was for some, and no harm in it. But not for Aelliana. For Aelliana, there must be gentleness and a skillful awakening, and night after night of joy—

He gasped, staggered.

"Daav?" Her voice carried concern.

"A trifle too much wine," he said, charging his voice with rue. "No cause for alarm."

Really, Daav, he scolded himself silently, *such unseemly display*.

Beside him, Aelliana drew an audible breath. "Is there anything I must hold from, when I speak with Scout Commander Trilsday? I would not wish to make—to make an error."

"Even if you were likely to make an error," Daav said, glad of the diversion of conversation, "Jon will be with you, will he not? You may rely entirely upon him."

"Yes, of course. It is only..." her voice faded.

He smiled, which she would not see in the darkness. "Be easy, Aelliana. The Commander only wishes to increase the honor of Scout Headquarters by allowing you free run of the World Room."

"And it is very kind in him," she said warmly. "I only wonder how—it is—that people go on in the—in Outspace, when there is no one but one's self to rely upon and the care of strangers must be suspect. Who will I—who insures that error does not occur?"

She begins to understand what the license in her pocket may purchase, Daav thought, *and to see that some of those goods may well be—dangerous.*

"The universe is imperfect," he said, speaking plain truth, which a co-pilot must, in matters of the pilot's safety. "Error occurs. On Liad, the correction of error is social art. In Outspace, it is—a natural force. Those who exercise faulty judgment, die. Those who pilot badly, die. Those who watch, and learn, and have a certain measure of the luck, prosper." He paused, then added, earnestly, "It is possible to be happy, Aelliana. Only be careful, do."

She stopped, her fingers hard around his, and turned to face him in the dark.

"Some pilots take partners," she said, and her voice was not steady.

"Yes."

"Yes," she repeated and after a moment began to walk again, he, hand-linked, beside her.

They came without further talk or incident to *The Luck*. Daav released her hand with a pang and stepped aside so that she might proceed him up the long ramp. At the top, she worked keys and code and the hatch slid open, adding ship's illumination to the dim gantry-light.

In the wash of ship-light she turned to him, close on the narrow landing. Deliberately, she moved closer. Her hand rose to his shoulder, as if they were about to dance.

"Daav?" Her eyes were green, brilliant in the yellow light; her face at once hesitant and resolved.

"Aelliana—" Breath failed him. He stood, quivering, beneath her hand, lost in the brilliance of her eyes.

She bit her lip. "I do not have the pretty words, but I

ask you with all—all honor and—care. I feel that Liad chafes—that you would rather be away. I—I will not be able, I think, to return, once I have gone." Anxiety fogged her eyes for a moment. "No dishonor, not—as Scouts understand honor. Merely, a life that is not—world-bound." She drew a ragged breath, her fingers gripping his shoulder tight. "Will you partner with me, *van'chela*, when I go outworld?"

Almost, he shouted *yes*, and threw everything to the stars: tore Korval's Ring from around his neck and hurled it to the stones below, gathered Aelliana into his arms and bore her within.

Almost.

"I—cannot." He heard his own voice quaver. Aelliana's face went still.

"Cannot?"

"I am promised to wed," his voice—his *sense*—made answer. "My clan has—use—for me." He swallowed, hard in a sand-dry throat, extended one shaking finger and touched her cheek. "You offer—my heart's desire, Aelliana. Believe me."

He did not know if she did. Pain tightened her face and she stepped back, her hand falling from his shoulder. She bent her head quickly, but not before he saw the glitter of tears.

"Aelliana—"

She raised a hand, forestalling him. "It is—I regret," she achieved, with a formal intonation that tore at his heart. She cleared her throat and dared lift her face to his.

"Good lift, Daav."

"Safe landing, Aelliana."

She turned and went into her ship. The hatch cycled, shutting him out of the light.

Chapter Thirty-One

*A lifemating is a far more serious matter than a
mere contract-marriage, encompassing the length
of the partner's lives, even if one should die. One
of the pair must leave his or her clan of origin
to join the clan of the lifemate. At that time the
adoptive clan pays a "life-price" based on the
individual's profession, age and internal value
to the former clan.*

*Tradition has it that lifemates share a "bond
of heart and mind." In view of Liaden cultural
acceptance of "wizards," some scholars have inter-
preted this to mean that lifemates are "psychically"
connected. Or, alternatively, that the only true
lifematings occur between wizards.*

*There is little to support this theory. True,
lifematings among Liadens are rare. But so are
life-long marriages among Terrans.*

—From "Marriage Customs of Liad"

SHE RAN, FOR THERE WAS NO PLACE TO HIDE.

Sick with terror, she hurtled through mazy back
streets, across broad plazas, down endless ship-halls—
and still—and still—It followed.

Its Shadow fell behind her, annihilating the street she had just traversed. Panting, she skidded around a corner, sprinted across a wide thoroughfare and ducked into the gateway of a private courtyard. She dared not rest long, yet rest she must, for her heart was near to bursting, and her sobbing gasps scarcely brought sufficient air to lungs afire with exertion.

She leaned into the warm friendly shadow of the gateway, muscles trembling. Dimly, she wondered how long she could stay this brutal pace and where in the confusion of Port-ways and corridor she might locate a weapon.

Even in the exultation of her terror, she knew that a weapon would not halt the Shadow. It was that which *cast* the Shadow against which she wished, most fervently, to be armed. A being capable of generating so horrifying an Adumbration—*that* she would not face unarmed.

Her breath shuddered through her, echoing weirdly off the close walls of her huddling place. She detected a movement at the edge of the street and pushed away from the wall, steeling herself to run again.

Exhausted muscles betrayed her. She moved one step, two, and folded to her knees at the entrance of the gateway, teeth locked to hold in the shout of despair.

The corner she had turned only moments ago— vanished, eaten by a blackness so absolute that the eyes rebelled and insisted on multicolored lights in the Shadow's depth—a road upon which it was cast.

It hesitated, the Shadow did, and seemed to look about Itself. On her knees atop the paving stones, Samiv tel'Izak held still as might be, hoping against horrified certainty that It would—this once—miss the way.

Half a mile high, It loomed, Its head a twisting

mass of black limbs, Its trunk as wide as a warehouse and the wind that proceeded It was cold, carrying the stink of rotting leaves.

The Shadow turned and half the thoroughfare between It and her huddling place was eclipsed. Wind skirled around her, rank with rot, and overhead she heard a steady, ominous beat, as if enormous wings worked the sky. Samiv raised her arms above her head, pitiful shield though they made, and stared down the diminished street, into the blackness of her Enemy.

But the Shadow did not advance. Above, the beat of wings grew stronger, nearer, until at last it was thunder, driving a dust-laden wind into her inadequate shelter, so that she bent, bringing her arms down to protect her face.

The thunder of wings ceased. She straightened into shadow, blinked to clear her dust-grimed eyes.

A hand gripped her shoulder.

Samiv tel'Izak screamed.

The hatch came down, sealing him out.

Numbly, Aelliana crossed to her station, sat, reached out and triggered initial board check.

Lights flickered, screens glowed: Her ship, coming to life.

Her ship.

She could lift now, this minute; the first class license rode, safe, in her sleeve. There was nothing to tie her here, not clan, nor kin, nor—

"Daav?"

No deep, calm voice answered her whisper; no tall, silent-moving form tickled the edge of her vision. She was alone.

Odd, how badly that hurt. For so many years, *alone* had been everything she wished for.

The board chimed readiness; the screens showed ships, sleeping all around. In screen number six a slim figure walked, shoulders stooped in an attitude so alien it was not until a random light snagged along the silver earring that she knew him.

"Daav!" She snapped forward, palm slapping screen, as if she would reach through plastic, chip and ether—

He reached the top of the row and turned left, vanishing toward...

She didn't even know where he lived.

"Oh, gods."

The board lights blurred out of sense. She wiped at her eyes with impatient fingers, mildly surprised when they came away wet. Tears. Her husband had enjoyed tears; had found a thousand ways to wring them from her, until she refused to weep, no matter how he hurt her.

He had been a master of pain, her husband. But no effort of his genius had produced such agony as this.

The comm light glowed in the corner of her eye. She turned toward it, hope igniting its own agony.

She had his comm number.

Call me, his voice murmured from memory, *if there is need...*

Her hand flicked forward. She snatched it back, brought it, fisted, against her lips and merely sat there, crying in earnest now, for he was lost, sworn to wed and be of use to his clan, whatever and wherever it was. Bound, as even a Scout may be bound, by the knots of kin and duty. To call him now would surely do harm. To beg him for—

What?

A return to the ensorcellment of the dance, when they had moved and thought as one being? To feel his body, strong and lithe, against hers? The gift of his humor and hard common sense? The certain knowledge that, whenever in her life she looked to the co-pilot's station, he would be there, keeping his serene, impeccable board?

She scrubbed at drenched cheeks, pressed the heels of both hands against her eyes in an effort to dam the tears that had become a torrent.

The tears would not be stopped. She leaned forward until her cheek was against first board and there she lay, sobbing into the chill plastic, until, at last, she fell into a gray, uneasy sleep.

It could not be said that Ran Eld Caylon was a man addicted to news. Where current events touched upon Ran Eld Caylon, there his interest was avid. For events centered in other spheres, his interest was—minimal.

Let Sinit ride the news-wire, exclaiming over Council on-dits, the publication of tedious professorial tomes or the undignified stunts of pilots. Enough time for Ran Eld to notice the Council of Clans when he was himself a participant in history. As for the work of professors and pilots—it was difficult to say which bored him more.

So it was by an enormous bit of very bad luck that Ran Eld Caylon on this particular morning, smarting still under his middle sister's continued elusiveness, came face-to-face with The Net.

The Net was Sinit's preferred news service. He had told her time and time over to use the house screen in the library for her viewing, but such was her passion for news that she would use Ran Eld's, in case Voni had prior claim on the communal screen. Mostwise, she remembered to return the setting to Ran Eld's Fund reporter. This morning, she had forgotten.

Ran Eld touched the on-switch and "Caylon" immediately caught his eye, as one's own name is apt to do. Frowning, he perused the story sufficiently to discover that the Caylon found thus newsworthy was one Aelliana, pilot-owner of Class A Jump-ship *Ride the Luck*.

Ran Eld—carefully—sat down.

He then read the newsbit thoroughly, learning such items of interest regarding the pilot as her work upon the ven'Tura Piloting Tables at the tender age of eighteen, which revision was hailed as a boon to pilots everywhere. He learned that Pilot Caylon had owned her ship a bare relumma, having won it in a game of pikit; that her second class license, awarded a few days after her win, had been upgraded by popular acclaim and on the basis of yesterday's amazing rescue, to full first.

He learned that Pilot Caylon flew out of Binjali Repair Shop, Mechanic Street, Solcintra Port.

His hair and face were soaked with dew by the time he reached the platform, high inside the Tree. At least, his hair was.

Daav reached behind his head, snatched the silver ring free and slid it into a pocket. Released, his hair hung in a snarled, sullen twist, trailing spiteful tendrils inside his jacket collar.

He sighed sharply and used rather too much force

to shake his head. Thick, wet stuff lashed his cheeks before spreading into a fan across his shoulders.

All around, the Tree was quiet.

Before him, through a tunnel of leaf and branch, he could see the lights of Solcintra Spaceport, dim against the lightening sky.

"She has her first class now," he said aloud, his eyes on the distant port. "There's nothing holds her but gravity."

Everywhere the leaves hung still, disturbed by not a breath of breeze.

"Er Thom," Daav continued, watching the distant lights grow dimmer. "My brother tells me that when first he saw his Anne—a Terran woman, you know, in a room full with Terrans—that when he first saw her, it was as if there were two women standing there, one within the other. The first—the outside woman, if you like—was well enough—pretty hair and happy eyes . . . beautiful hands. A bit large, of course, and shaped just—Anne-like. But Anne-like was pleasing and Er Thom was pleased."

The red beacon came on at the Port Authority's pinnacle, signaling the change from Night Port to Day. Daav blinked and raised a hand to wipe at the—dew—drying along his cheeks.

"The second woman—he glimpsed her for a heartbeat, understand! The second woman was hardly woman at all, but music, or light, or a rhapsody of both—at once so intricate and so indescribably *correct* that my brother says he felt he could observe it for the rest of his days and neither tire of it nor find it to contain one note—one light-mote—that was not precisely as it should be." Daav sighed.

"The second woman faded in that heartbeat, leaving Anne, to whom he made his bow, and who, in Er Thom's way, he came to love." He turned, facing the Tree's center down the length of the platform.

"My brother tells me that now—now he hears that perfect music all the time—in his heart, so he has it. And when he closes his eyes, he can see that flawless, intricate, maze of brightness that is Anne—that is Anne's inner self. It comforts him, he tells me, in those times when they must be apart, to feel—to know—that he never is alone."

Silence, dead air; a faint, far sense of something—waiting.

"Anne," said Daav, moving one bare step forward. "Anne tells a like tale. Wherever she is, wherever he is, she feels Er Thom's presence, his passions—the universe is not wide enough to dim her perception. He's like music, she says, being a musician. Like a work in progress and a revered masterwork being played both at once. Powerful, she says. Like a heartbeat. She gives me permission to say that Er Thom is become part of her heartbeat—part of her lifeforce, I suppose she means. But it doesn't seem to frighten her. It's joy, she says—they both say. And Er Thom says, 'I wish...'"

Absolute stillness. A silence into which no bird song dared intrude.

Daav took another step forward; stood at the platform's center, hands fisted at his side, trembling badly at the knees.

"At least tell me if it is true," he said, and his voice was trembling, too, "that I am formed as one-half of a wizard's match."

Above, a sharp rustle of leaf, as if a flying mouse had landed. A seed-pod plummeted, striking the planks between his boots with peevish precision. Daav took a breath.

"We danced and it was as if we had been born dancing in each other's arms. I held her and it was sweet—past sweet! And she was caught as tightly as I! *Van'chela*, so she said to me—beloved friend." He went forward another step; another would bring him to the trunk.

"In all of this there was nothing such as my kin describe me—no beautiful mazes, no soul-songs. Even now, she may have lifted—have Jumped!—and I never the wiser, til Clonak called to tell me." He took the last step, raised his fists and lay them, palm-flat, against the trunk.

"Aelliana Caylon," he said. "Clan Mizel."

The bark was rough against his palms, grainy and a little damp. Somewhere in the branches below, a dawn-swallow began to sing.

Daav sagged forward, pressing his cheek against the Tree.

"Samiv tel'Izak does not please you," he whispered. "Aelliana excites no interest. Must I be alone, because Er Thom is not? Shall I tell Bindan that the marriage is canceled, because I have chanced upon one I might love? What shall I do when they cry breach of contract and demand ships and stocks and payments? How shall we keep Cantra's Law, when our ships are gone and we are turned out of our valley? How shall we stay vigilant for the passengers? How will we protect the Tree?"

Nothing, save bark and damp and bird song.

"I should have stayed with Aelliana," Daav whispered, and for an instant it was so: They had the day before them to lay plans and hustle cargo; a course laid Out, and far away...

Madness.

He pushed away from the Tree, walked back and picked up the seed-pod. He stood for a moment, holding it in his hand, then went to the edge of the platform and threw it, as hard and as far as he could.

Chapter Thirty-Two

The pilot's care shall be ship and passengers.
The co-pilot's care shall be pilot and ship.
— From the Duties Roster of the Pilots Guild

A TALL SHADOW CROSSED CLONAK'S LIGHT. HE LAY DOWN his wrench and looked up.

"Master Frad! I hardly expected to see you about so early after such a round of merrymaking!"

The lanky cartographer grinned. "Snatched the words from the tip of my tongue, rascal! What's this you're about? Work? Never say so!"

"I'm a changed man, since my goddess touched my life," Clonak told him piously. Frad laughed.

"Then you're out, comrade. Or wasn't it Daav who escorted the Caylon to her bed last evening? I admit to being a glass or two over-limit, but hardly giddy enough to mistake length for girth."

"Some of us," Clonak said with great seriousness, "worship from afar."

"All of us, unless I misread the matter badly. I've rarely seen Daav so conformable. One might almost think him tame. And the pilot wears her heart on her face."

"Yes, well." Clonak picked up his wrench. "The devil's in the brew, there, old friend. Daav's betrothed."

"No, is he?" Frad stared, then moved his shoulders, answering himself. "Well, but he must be, mustn't he? Korval is none too plentiful, despite the yos'Galan's contribution. Daav's a sensible fellow—full nurseries are certain to be a priority with him. Merely, he had held himself aloof such a time . . . Well. Who is the intended?"

"Samiv tel'Izak, Clan Bindan, as my father has it."

"So? I've flown with the lady, as it happens. Piece of roster work for the Port. *She* unbends, eventually, but her delm's ambitious."

Clonak sighed. "My father said that, too."

"Hah." Frad glanced about. "Are we the only two about? Surely Jon hasn't left the care of the Yard to yourself?"

"Jon's presence was required at the Port Directors meeting. Trilla called in a few minutes ago to say she'd be . . . late."

Frad grinned. "Well, and it was a pretty pair she had with her last night."

"Pretty enough," his friend agreed. "And willing. I have not yet seen my captain or my goddess, but, then, I hadn't expected them."

"So, it is you alone! Well I happened by."

"Why, so it is," Clonak returned with an evil grin. "You might actually be of use, you know, instead of nattering about and holding me from my appointed task. But you never were much of a hand at repair."

"Ho, a challenge! What have you here, a vector engine? Stand aside, sirrah, and give a master room to work!"

Sleep ebbed, leaving a headache behind. Aelliana sat up creakily in the pilot's chair, and rubbed her gritty

eyes. The message-waiting light was on and she touched
the amber stud, her heart lifting in hope. Had Daav—?

The communication was from the Port Master's
office, verifying completion of roster work for the Port,
and recording a transfer of three cantra paid into the
account of *Ride The Luck*, Aelliana Caylon, Pilot.

She sat back, tears rising, then took a breath, saved
the message to ship's log and opened a line to the
Pilot Guild's bank. Three cantra earned by ship and
pilots, ciphered thus: one share to the ship, one share
to the pilot, one share to the co-pilot. She would
transfer Daav's share at—

Hands on the keys, she froze. Transfer his cantra?
Yes, surely. And what was his surname—his clan?
What, indeed, was the number on his pilot's license?

Aelliana sighed, shut down the connection and stood.
Very well. First, a shower. The rest of the day, with its
various necessities and pains, would proceed from there.

As it happened, the repair required a team. They
barely had the casing open when the crew door cycled.
Frad looked round in time to see a nattily-dressed man
of about his own age step cautiously within.

For a long moment he stood on the threshold, holding
the door back on the tips of his violet-gloved fingers.
Then, warily, he came into the bay, mincing lightly, as if
he feared soiling the soles of his exquisitely tooled boots.

"Oh, la!" Clonak murmured, catching sight of the
stranger. "A bird of paradise!"

"Perhaps he is a buyer," Frad suggested.

"Much more likely a seller," returned Clonak. "His
gloves match his lace."

Frad sighed.

Twelve paces into the shop, the stranger paused, his sleek, well-kept head tipped to one side, gloved hands clasped loosely before him, as if expecting at any moment to see an abject lackey hurrying up to beg his pardon. Indeed, for three heartbeats, by Frad's count, he tarried, apparently awaiting this phenomenon. At last, disappointed in his patience, he turned his head and spied the two at work on the vector-engine.

One glove rose with studied elegance. One finger pointed. "You there," he stated. "Fellow."

Above the engine, Clonak snorted. "I haven't been 'fellow' to some dog wearing lace in the daytime since I was twelve years old."

"Well, then," said Frad, putting down his probe and reaching for a rag. "I suppose he means me."

Wiping his hands, he walked silently toward the dandy. At precisely the proper distance for speaking with strangers, he stopped and bowed, Adult-to-Adult.

"Good day, sir," he said, also in the mode of Adult-to-Adult. "How may I serve you?"

The dandy had eyes of purest cerulean, large and spaced appealingly, one on either side of his pert little nose. The eyes widened now, with, Frad supposed, insult, and the rather thin-lipped mouth turned down.

"I will speak with the owner of this establishment," he announced, with no "if you please" about it. Frad moved his shoulders.

"Alas, the owner is away."

The frown became definite and a gleam of displeasure was seen in the pretty eyes.

"When," he demanded, "will the owner return?"

"He did not say," Frad returned, unremittingly courteous. "Is there some way in which I might assist you?"

"Perhaps," the dandy allowed and drew himself up, fixing Frad with a very stern stare, indeed. "I," he announced, "am Ran Eld Caylon, Nadelm Mizel!"

"Aha!" Clonak said soto voce from just beyond Frad's shoulder. "That explains the matter perfectly!"

Nadelm Mizel directed what he doubtless wished to be a quelling glance at the source of this lamentable frivolity. However, the glance disintegrated even as it arrowed toward the miscreant. The thin mouth tightened convulsively, as if the nadelm might be ill, and the blue eyes skittered back to Frad.

"You will produce Aelliana Caylon," he ordered. "At once."

Frad raised his eyebrows, face displaying earnest, if laborious, intelligence.

The nadelm frowned heavily. In a mode perilously close to Superior-to-Inferior, he stated: "You will cause Aelliana Caylon to come before me, instantly. I have good reason to believe she is here."

"Aelliana Caylon," Frad repeated, in a tone of wonderment. He glanced to Clonak, who stood lovingly stroking his mustache. "Aelliana Caylon?"

"The ven'Tura Tables," Clonak told him kindly, and looked to the nadelm. "He's a bit of a block, you know, but a very good fellow, nonetheless. He would have remembered, in an hour or three. But, there, it's our turn, and we are wasting your time!" He struck a pose. "Cantra yos'Phelium!"

The nadelm glared at a point just short of Clonak's chin. "I am not here to play Biographies!"

"You're not?" Clonak demanded in fair imitation of idiot bemusement. "Well, whatever are you here for? I must say, buttercup, it is not at all the thing to be drawing people away from their work to answer your tease, and then refuse to take your turn! Too shabby!"

"*I beg—*" Ran Eld Caylon raised angry eyes to Clonak's face and hastily averted them. "Master Binjali will hear of your insolence, my man!"

Clonak clapped his hands. "Now, that I should like to see!" he cried. "Indeed, sir, you must stay and await Master Binjali. I insist upon it! Come, let me give you some tea—and perhaps a day-old bun, if the cat has left any whole—to ease your wait!"

The dandy drew himself up, splendid in violet lace and tight black coat. "Sir, I see that you must be drunk."

"Oh, no," Frad said soothingly, feeling matters had gone far enough. "Indeed, sir, he's hardly ever drunk this early in the day. Unless, of course," he added fairly, "he's still in his cups from last night."

The nadelm fixed a stare fraught with awful menace on Frad's face. "Do you refuse to bring Aelliana Caylon or Master Binjali to me at once?"

He gave it consideration, taking lengthy counsel of the ceiling. "Yes," he said finally, meeting the angry blue eyes blandly, "I do."

"Very well." Ran Eld Caylon inclined his head. "I then instruct you, as the owner's nadelm, to seal *Ride the Luck* and bring the keys to me."

Frad merely stood there, face bland, posture conveying polite attention.

"I had said," Pilot Caylon's nadelm snapped, "you will seal *Ride the Luck* immediately and fetch the keys to me!"

"I had heard you the first time," Frad said calmly. "I am of course desolate to find myself unable to accommodate you, sir, but I am not authorized to seal an owner's ship."

"So. I shall then await the proprietor of this establishment." *And it will*, his tone stated, *go ill for you then, fellow!*

"Proprietor can't seal a patron's ship, either," Clonak said cheerfully. "Port proctor's what you want, buttercup—but I'd advise against it."

"I do not recall soliciting your advice," the nadelm informed him icily.

"Yes, but it happens to be excellent advice," Frad said. "Matters such as sealing a ship fall firmly within the Port Master's honor and it is to her that you must apply."

The blue eyes raked his face with a look meant to inspire terror. Frad lifted an eyebrow, face showing no sign of the fury leaping within. Really! This—*popinjay*—held rank over Aelliana Caylon? Liad grew less sensible each time he returned.

"Very well," Ran Eld Caylon said at last. With neither bow nor courtesy, he turned and stamped toward the door, to the detriment, as Frad could not help believing, of his boot-soles. Fingers on the push-plate, he turned to glare.

"Ship and owner had best be in this Yard when I return with the proctors!" With which awful threat he exited.

Clonak collapsed against Frad's chest, wailing with delight.

"Why, why, oh *why* would you not let him stop for Master Binjali?" He gasped, clutching the taller man's shoulder for support. "Only think how lovely it would have been to dust him and water him and turn him to face the sun—" He subsided into howls of merriment.

Frad patted his head absentmindedly and set him straight on his feet. "All right, darling. Get a grip, do, and think why Pilot Caylon's nadelm wants to seal her ship."

"Random act of cruelty," Clonak said promptly. "Did you see that mouth? Spoilt. Ill-tempered, too. And those shoulders, all held thus!" He demonstrated the rigidly level shoulders, screwing his face up in a very passable imitation of the nadelm's look of outrage.

"Yes." Frad stared at the floor, thinking. The nadelm had been *angry*. One would almost suppose him to have not the least understanding of yesterday's flight. And yet, it *was* Liad and local custom was plain: A nadelm had the right to order a lower-ranked clanmember—unless the delm intervened.

"She probably forgot to give him his proper grace at breakfast," Clonak commented, moving back toward the vector-engine, "and he's taken a pet. You know the sort. Something else will annoy him between here and Port Authority and he'll forget all about the proctors."

"Yes," said Frad again, and sighed lightly. The Port Master would make very short work of Ran Eld Caylon's pretensions—which was no guarantee that the nadelm would not return to Binjali's. He was, in Frad's opinion, already on the outer edge of sensible and a scold received of the Port Master would not likely return him to reasoned judgment.

"Did Jon say when we might expect to have the joy of beholding his face?" he asked, shaking off a sudden chill and walking back toward Clonak and the repair.

Behind him, the crew door cycled wide.

"Four minutes sooner and you'd have met the personage!" Clonak shouted gleefully.

Aelliana frowned, looking from him to—Frad, Daav's especial friend, who had been at their table last evening. "Personage?" she asked.

Clonak thinned his mouth, scrunched up his shoulders, and announced, in haughty accent: "Nadelm Mizel!"

She felt her knees go to rubber, staggered and snatched herself upright.

"Ran Eld, here!" she stared at Clonak, who had let his caricature fade into a look of genuine dismay. "Why?"

"He wished to see you," Frad said calmly.

"Wanted to seal your ship," Clonak added. "Told him he needed the proctors for that. Last seen, he was on his way to Port Master, where it's my belief he'll take delivery of one of her thundering scolds."

"He wanted to seal my ship," Aelliana repeated, blankly. "Ran Eld knows nothing about my ship! I—" She swallowed, looked up into Frad's face. "It was on the news wires," she whispered. Her heartbeat was a hollow roaring in her ears. "Yesterday's lift."

"I expect it was," he said, voice neutral. "You seem unwell, pilot, is there—"

"It's nothing . . ." She gasped, pressing damp palms together. "I—forgive me. I must think."

The two Scouts exchanged glances.

"Pull up a stool and think away," Clonak said, almost serious. "Shall I bring you a mug of tea, goddess?"

"Thank you, no," she managed and went numbly toward the clustered stools. She hoisted herself up on the first she came to and closed her eyes, hands gripped along the edge of the seat. After a moment, and another mute exchange of worry, the Scouts drifted back toward their work.

Ran Eld. Aelliana ground her teeth to keep them from chattering. Ran Eld, *here*—demanding her presence, demanding her ship be sealed. Her heart wanted to scream that it could not be so. Her mind was made of sterner stuff.

Fact: She was discovered.

Fact: Ran Eld would exact his price. Perhaps he would even beat her, as he had in the days just after her marriage, to reinforce her subservience.

Aelliana shuddered. She had no illusions regarding her ability to withstand such treatment: She would surrender *The Luck's* keys willingly, if they were the coin that bought an end to her punishment.

Options. One: Run. Leave now, lifting for the Liaden Outworlds, and hope the luck smiled sufficiently for her to find cargo and contract before her outlawed condition became known.

Objections: She would be leaving Jon dea'Cort and all his shifting crew open to Mizel's Balance. A very creditable case of kin-stealing could be shown to the Council of Clans, in settlement of which Jon might easily lose his Yard, while Daav, Trilla, Clonak and Frad might find themselves called clanless...

No. She would not call disaster down upon her comrades.

Option Two: Submit to Ran Eld's wishes and hope, in time, to appease him sufficiently that she might live in tolerable peace.

Objections: Prior testing proved this application failed of success.

Option Three: Go home and put her case before the delm.

This was risky. Historically, Mizel championed her

heir in any dispute. On several occasions, such as the matter of Aelliana's marriage to Ran Eld's friend, Mizel had allowed herself to be guided entirely by her son's advice and refused to hear any other.

Balancing history was an indication that of late the delm had softened toward her middle daughter. If she were clever enough to show the profit a working ship might bring to the clan—many times over the single gain of a sale . . .

An imperfect solution, but the best she could fashion, for the best good of herself and her comrades. The clan's fortune had not been—robust—of late, despite Voni's marriages. Mizel might very well be receptive to the addition of a new source of funding.

Aelliana opened her eyes, slid off the stool and crossed to the busy Scouts.

Two pair of eyes immediately lifted to her face.

"I am going home," she said, and wished her voice sounded steadier; that she felt more certain of a happy outcome. "You may tell my brother so, if he should come again. I—he will not trouble you further."

Clonak cleared his throat. "Trust me, goddess, he was no trouble to us at all, despite that Frad would not allow him to await Master Binjali."

"You might stay an hour or two," Frad put in. "It seemed to me that your nadelm was—very angry. Perhaps it would be best to allow him time to cool."

She looked at him straightly. "Ran Eld does not cool, thank you, pilot. If he has—if he has reached so high a pitch as you say, it is—best—that I return home and put the matter before the delm."

"Hah." Frad looked at Clonak. "Local custom."

"Local custom," the pudgy Scout repeated, but

there was a frown between his taffy eyes. "Still it might be better, Aelliana, to stop until Jon returns. Or Daav does."

"That's the card you want!" Frad said, leaning forward. "Call on Daav's assistance, pilot. Surely, he—"

"No!" she said sharply. Frad blinked and flicked a look to Clonak, who nodded and reached for a rag.

"Then I will come with you," he said, with unClonak-like firmness, "and see you safe before your delm."

"No, you shall not." She drew herself up and mustered a glare. "You do not understand how spiteful— should my brother consider you have thwarted him, he will do his utmost to ruin you." He continued to wipe his hands, entirely uncowed by the prospect of ruin. Aelliana bit her lip.

"Indeed, Clonak, you must not come with me. I—my nadelm several times has ordered me to—to absent myself from the company of Scouts. I have not obeyed and it would . . ." She faltered.

"It would," Frad took up, "make matters immeasurably worse, were you seen to be championed by a Scout." He shook his head, mournfully. "Pilot, take advice. You want Daav for this. He can mend the thing in a thrice."

"No," she said again, and reached into her pocket, pulling out the bank envelope and thrusting it into Clonak's hand. "If you would, however, see that Daav receives this, when he does arrive for his shift? It is his share of yesterday's lift-wage. And . . ." She yanked the chain over her head, ship keys jangling as she pressed those, too, on Clonak.

"Please, ask Jon to hold these for me. I will—say that I will come for them—myself, or . . ." She drew a hard breath. "Or my co-pilot may claim them, should he have need."

Clonak stared at the items in his hand. "Aelliana..."

"No," she said for a third time. "Truly, friends, it is better so. I will—Good lift, pilots." She turned and ran, not waiting for their well-wishing in return.

Chapter Thirty-Three

Kin and love
Comfort
Home.

—From "Collected Poems"
Elabet pel'Ongin, Clan Diot

SHE SOUGHT THE SHIP'S HEALER, WHO LISTENED, PROBED, and laid salve upon her pain, so that all was well. Until she slept again.

Twice more, Samiv tel'Izak sought the Healer. The third time, he denied her.

"I eradicate the memory of the dream, Pilot, but, when you sleep, you dream again. To eradicate the memory which *causes* the dream—that I might do. But in a situation such as yours, where the pain-matrix or referents to the matrix will be shortly re-encountered, eradicating the older memory—and what defenses you have thus far built—serves you ill, and the Guild counsels against it."

"And what cure does the Guild counsel?" she inquired, voice grating in weariness.

"An old cure," the Healer said softly, "and a harsh one. Confront that which gnaws at your soul, stare into its face and achieve what Balance you may."

Harsh, indeed. She left the Healer and sought her immediate superior. She informed that serious and ship-wise pilot that lack of sleep and stress of spirit made her an active danger to ship and crew; that the Healer had no succor.

Her superior did duty, cancelling what remained of her contract, which was required, as a matter of ship's safety, and would show in her permanent Guild record. He also commended her for exemplary service and expressed willingness to see her under his command at any time in the future, which would also find a place in her record, and fell on the full side of Balance.

Samiv signed the separation paper, removed her effects from quarters and twelve hours later was walking out of Solcintra Guildhall, pack slung over a shoulder, and her heart cold with dread. Confront her fear, indeed.

And then there was one's delm to consider.

Step by step, Aelliana forced herself home, hands fisted in the pockets of her old blue jacket.

Her feet faltered at the corner of Raingleam Street. She drove herself onward, shaking.

The delm. It was her right, as one of Mizel, to ask a hearing and justice of the delm. She could not be refused this.

Her hand touched the gate and her knees locked, so that she stood for an entire minute, unable to go on.

The delm, she told herself. *Lay all before the delm . . .*

Her hand moved, the gate swung open. She entered Mizel's front garden, closed the gate behind her and walked, step-by-step, to the door.

Three wooden steps to the porch; a touch of her hand to the lock pad.

"Good afternoon, Aelliana." The luck was out. And yet it was her right, to ask, to be heard, by her delm.

She bowed, so low that her forehead touched her knees, and straightened only somewhat, eyes fixed humbly on the faded pink stone of the foyer floor.

"Good afternoon, brother," she murmured, though the words seemed like to choke her.

"So respectful," he commented, rising from his chair in the stair-niche. "Indeed, the very portrait of subservience, drawn with rare skill. I confess myself charmed—but no longer deceived."

She did not raise her head. She did not move. Barely did she breathe. Ran Eld's boots came into her range of vision: They were dusty and scuffed; the right bore a stain of oil along the instep.

"You keep to your character?" he inquired, voice poisonously sweet. "But perhaps you are correct! We are so open here that anyone might chance to see, should you choose to fly your true colors! I suggest we adjourn to the parlor. After you. Sister."

"I have—urgent—need to see the delm," Aelliana said, staring, staring, at that scuffed, stained leather. "Pray conduct me to Mizel at once."

"The delm is from house," Ran Eld purred. "She returns tomorrow, midday." There was a pause, in which she felt his gloating like rancid grease across her skin. "The parlor, sister. Of your kindness."

There was no help for it. Shoulders slumped, eyes lowered, steps mouse-light across the old stone floor, Aelliana entered the parlor. Ran Eld's footsteps gritted noisily behind her. He crossed the threshold and closed the door with a bang, striding to where she waited in the center of the room, eyes on the nap-worn carpet.

"Look at me!" he shouted, augmenting the order with a savage yank of her hair.

She ground her teeth, imprisoning the cry, and met his eyes.

"So . . ." Satisfaction settled in her brother's face. "Have you truly forgotten the old lesson, Aelliana? Do you no longer recall what I had done to you, the last time you challenged me?"

"I remember."

"Ah, she remembers! But where is the failing note in the voice—the twisting together of the fingers? She remembers, but appears to discount the memory. Perhaps she takes comfort in the Delm's Word! What was that promise, Aelliana?"

She stared at him, recalling all of what he had caused to be done to her. He had boasted of it, after, and spoken of such things as made it certain that he and the contract-husband had spent many delicious hours, planning how best to harm her.

"You know well what the Delm's Word was," she told him, and heard the acid in her voice with dismay.

"Ah, but of course I know!" Ran Eld returned, in high good humor. "But you will tell me, Aelliana, because I have commanded it. As nadelm, it is my right—indeed, my duty!—to command you. Surely, you cannot have forgotten that."

She took a careful breath, trying to still her body's shaking, which was all of long-pent fury and hatred, and nothing whatsoever of fear.

"The Delm's Word," she said, neutralizing the acid note with an effort, "was that I had fulfilled my duty to the clan and need never marry again."

"Yes, that is what I thought," her brother said, with

a smile. "Never *marry* again. I may be able to keep to that, when I am delm." His face hardened. "In the meanwhile, I learn from the news wires that you are a holder of real property which you have neglected to report to the clan." He moved an elegant, heavily-ringed hand. "Step to the desk, if you please."

She went forward to the tiny letter-desk, stood blinking down at the paper laid there, at the pens, bare-tipped and ready.

Bill of Transfer, the words shouted from the page. *I, Aelliana Caylon Clan Mizel, hereby transfer all right, profit and holding in the starship Ride the Luck to Ran Eld Caylon, Nadelm Mizel to be his personal property to dispose of or profit by . . .*

"No."

"No?" Incredibly, Ran Eld sounded merely amused. "But you are grown bold!" He smiled viciously into her eyes as she looked up. "You will sign this paper, Aelliana, and this . . ." He pulled a second from the pile on the letter-desk and thrust at her face.

She danced aside, flicking the paper from between his fingers. Another transfer, this one of her Ormit Shares. She dropped the paper onto the desk.

"Not that one either," she said, her voice shaking. "I sign nothing until I have spoken with the delm. If she is from House, I ask that you put me in contact with her. If she is not to be disturbed, I will wait upon her arrival."

Ran Eld's eye had snagged on the glitter of Jon's ring.

"What's this?" he asked, snatching her wrist. "A love-token? Relinquish it."

Her throat closed with outrage. She forced herself to stand quiet in his grip, as Trilla had taught her, waiting for her moment.

"Come along, Aelliana! Have it off!" His fingers tightened. "Or shall I take it off myself?"

"You may not have it," she said, striving for Daav's tone of calm reason. "I earned it and it is mine."

"You *earned* it?" her brother jeered. "In that wise, it is wages, and we had long ago decided what was best done with your wages, hadn't we?"

So they had, and her wages had bought her nothing. Aelliana looked into her brother's eyes and saw that he would never be placated, that no harm he visited upon her would ever be enough to Balance his own fears and failings.

Fool, she told herself. *Why did you not listen to your comrades and stay away?*

Ran Eld jerked her hand forward and reached for the ring. She clenched her fist, braced and twisted free, all as Trilla had taught her.

"I will return when the delm is at home," she said, backing toward the door.

Ran Eld lunged, fist raised, which would have been enough, at some forgotten, rageless point in the past, to have her on her knees, begging his forgiveness.

Aelliana swept sideways, coming 'round in a deceptively graceful spin, her right hand, weighted with Jon's ring, rising, to whip, pilot-quick and anger-hard, across her nadelm's face.

The blow kicked him backward, dazzled by pain. His hand went up, came down—there was blood— blood! And Aelliana was at the door—through it—hair streaming behind her.

Ran Eld leapt, snatched—caught not hair, but jacket, yanked—

She came around fast, landed a blow to the side of his head, twisted free of his staggered grip and flung into the foyer.

Ears ringing, he hurtled after, grabbing for an arm.

She eluded his fingers like mist, one foot flashing out to touch his knee.

Pain.

He screamed, lurched and went down, flinging out a hand too late to break his fall—

But soon enough to catch her ankle, destroying her balance, and sending her crashing beside him on the gritty marble floor.

He rolled, using his weight to hold her, cuffing her face a time or two, while beneath him she fought with silent ferocity—teeth, fists and feet. His cheek was clawed from eye to chin while he struggled to pin her arms, and when finally he accomplished that—she kneed him.

He grunted, gasped—and she twisted, pitching him aside, flashing to her feet, turning—

There was a sound, as of a particularly sturdy vase being forcibly broken. Aelliana swayed—and crumpled to the floor, left cheek rubbing grit.

"Ran Eld!" Voni's voice quavered. "Brother, can you speak?"

Cautiously, he rolled to his back and blinked up into her horrified face.

"I can speak," he managed, somewhat breathlessly.

She swallowed. "Your face..."

"Yes, I don't doubt she marked me well. She certainly meant to do so." He sat up, then wished he hadn't. Blearily, he considered Aelliana's still shape.

"She went mad," he said, for Voni's benefit. "I gave

nadelm's instruction and she—struck me." He took a breath, wincing at the pain.

"She ran for the door," he continued. "To have her show such a face to the world—I tried to hold her. She—"

"I saw," Voni said hoarsely. "She was—an animal. I have never—" She gulped. "She must have gone mad. I—Shall I call a Healer?"

A Healer? Ran Eld's stomach turned to ice. A Healer would immediately perceive the cause of Aelliana's revolt—and report it to Delm Mizel. Who would doubtless have many difficult questions to lay before her son and heir.

He licked his lips.

"No," he whispered, then, more strongly, "No. We shall—we shall put her in the sleep learner."

Voni blinked. "The sleep learner, brother? But—"

"The sleep learner," he said firmly, while the idea took root and grew before his mind's eye. An overlay of intensive direct-learning might very well befuddle Aelliana's remembrance of this confrontation. Perhaps, were the session long enough, she would forget the matter altogether.

"She has broken with the Code," he told Voni. "It is our duty to reinitiate her to proper behavior—and that before the delm returns. Only think of our mother's distress, to find Aelliana as you saw her just now—a beast, raising fists against her kin."

Voni looked to Aelliana, lying like a broken doll, her cheek pillowed on stone. "How—"

"The two of us can drag her to the study," he said. "Give me your arm and help me to rise."

She did, flinchingly, and refusing to look at his face.

He shambled over to Aelliana and used his foot, none too gently, to roll her over.

"Take her right arm," he directed Voni, bending for the left. Bruises were rising amid the cuts on Aelliana's face, he saw with satisfaction, and the left cheek was badly scored. She would be well-served if he denied her use of the 'doc when she emerged from the sleep learner.

"Pull," he told Voni.

Squeamishly, she did.

He pushed the timer to the top, selected maximum intensity and yanked the abort button from its socket. In the act of closing the lid he paused, reached down and snatched up his sister's limp hand.

The heavy ring sparkled in the dim light as Ran Eld twisted it brutally free. *Earned* it, had she?

He let her hand fall and slammed the lid home.

"The Code of Proper Conduct," he typed into the program queue. "Volume One, Number One, Page One, Word One. Continue sequentially until timer disengages function."

"Accepted," the sleep learner signaled. "Touch the blue button to initiate the learning session."

Ran Eld touched the blue button.

"Shouldn't—we—have put her in the 'doc, first?" Voni asked uncertainly. "Her face was—was swollen, brother, and—and raw, where she—"

"Mere bruises," he said airily. "There will be time to tend them when she's schooled. Besides, I have need of the 'doc."

Voni gulped and inclined her head. "Of course."

Chapter Thirty-Four

The Learning Module is intended for use as a supplement to conventional learning. It is not intended to replace conventional learning, nor should it be utilized in this manner.

The best use of the Learning Module is in review of old material, in order to sharpen details in the Learner's mind. The Module also has value in laying baseline information, upon which the Learner will then build.

IMPORTANT INFORMATION: The Learning Module utilizes intense, direct-brain stimulation to impart pre-programmed information. Direct-brain stimulation is painful, even dangerous, to some individuals. Always run a compatibility test before logging into a full Learning session.

In no case should a Learner undertake more than one six-hour session of moderate intensity within one twenty-eight-hour period. Cerebral vesication may result from overuse of a Learning Module.

—From the manual for Learning Module No. X5783

"DAAV."

He started, wine splashing in his glass, and guiltily looked up.

"Your pardon, *denubia*. I—fear my thoughts were elsewhere."

"As they have been," Er Thom said, with some asperity. "Perhaps I am inconvenient. I can easily go and come again, after you have rested."

"No, there, don't take a pet—There's a good-natured, biddable fellow!"

Only Daav knew the effort it cost Er Thom to keep the smile from his lips and continue to stare sternly.

"Well, and what am I to think, when I have your person, but neither your eyes nor your thoughts?" His face softened. "What troubles you, brother?"

Daav glanced down, put the glass away and looked back to his brother's eyes.

"Well, if you will have it, Aelliana Caylon desired me to partner with her, when she is ready to forsake Liad forever. And I was tempted, brother. Indeed, I was only now striving to recall why it was I denied her—I should say, denied myself."

"Hah." Er Thom set his glass aside. "I had thought you Pilot Caylon's co-pilot and comrade. Do you tell me your feeling goes more deeply than that?"

"Well," he moved his shoulders, still unwilling to meet his brother's eye, "we both know me for a volatile brute. Likely I should have grown bored in a relumma or two and wished for the comforts of home."

There was a small silence, before Er Thom said dryly, "Very likely."

Daav looked up, extended a rueful hand. "Now,

darling, don't, I beg, tell me to stand away! You know I cannot do so, without ruining Korval."

"But I was not going to tell you any such thing," Er Thom said softly. "I only wondered why you had not at least spoken to Pilot Caylon before settling upon the tel'Izak."

Daav closed his eyes. "Because she was not then a pilot," he said, imposing calm upon his voice. "The first parameter in a spousal search is *pilot,* as you well know. She had never even been tested." He opened his eyes and reached for his glass.

"The initial winnowing gained us the names of several promising thirteen-year-olds—yet *Aelliana Caylon* had never been tested!" He took a hard breath and made an effort to soften his voice.

"Had Vin Sin chel'Mara been less a fool, she would be untested at this hour. Fortune smiled, brother, that she held a problem to which the ship provided a solution—could she but achieve Jump."

"And has she?" Er Thom wondered.

Daav moved his shoulders. "This afternoon, should she have the inclination." He smiled wryly into his brother's skeptical face. "Never bet against the Caylon."

"I will remember," Er Thom said. Then, very gently indeed, "*Shall* you stand away from the tel'Izak, Daav?"

He shook his head wearily. "For what gain? Aelliana is for Outspace, as soon as she finds her courage. She sees me as partner, darling, not husband. Indeed, she speaks of the married state in the most—abhorrent—terms possible. Her own mating was too early and—illmade, as I hear it." He sipped his wine, and added, quietly. "Damn them for clumsy fools."

"Ah," Er Thom said, and said nothing else.

Daav sat with his legs thrust out before him, apparently studying the tips of his boots, now and then sipping wine. Abruptly, he straightened, put his glass aside and looked up, black eyes bright.

"I love you, brother."

Er Thom blinked, for this was a thing little said between them. As well say, "We breathe the air, brother." Still—

"I love you, Daav."

"Yes, with all my faults! I shall strive not to shame you." He smiled, wanly, but with good intent, and pointed at the sheaf of papers Er Thom had brought with him.

"Let us assay your difficulty again, eh? I promise to give you my eyes and my thoughts."

"Fair enough," Er Thom replied and picked up the first.

". . . three hundred and fifty-eighth edition of the Code of Proper Conduct, published under the aegis of the League for the Purity of the Language, Kareen yos'Phelium, Clan Korval, editor and chair.

"The first edition of the Code of Proper Conduct was compiled during the Exodus by a committee made up in equal part of the Solcintran Houses, the *dramliz*, and the pilots. Transcribed in the margins of expired trade manifests, the document ran approximately 85 pages and was little more than a protocol for shipboard life.

"The second edition, circulated twelve years after planetfall . . ."

Sleep learning is a peculiar undertaking. Neither asleep nor awake, one drifts in and out of phase, sometimes "hearing" the instruction; other times upheld by a wave of image, emotion and language; still other times, simply—elsewhere.

There are periods of lucidness within this shifting trance. One can, for greater or lesser periods of time, think, independent of the program. One can take stock, analyze—react.

So it was that Aelliana drifted out of elsewhere and into a discourse on the history of the Code. She was aware, also, of pain, but it was a thin sensation, all but lost in the thunder of instruction.

Learning Module, she thought, eyes open against the blackness within the unit. *But, why am I Learning the preface to the Code?*

She moved her right hand along the wall of the unit—and found the hole where the end-session toggle should have been.

Ran Eld, she thought, experiencing a rather unnerving desire to laugh. *Does he think being Code-wise will make me less insistent upon seeing the delm?*

Any desire to laugh faded, then, as memory provided the instant; the feel of her hand cracking across her brother's face.

Oh, gods.

Ran Eld had put her in the Learning Module and taken away the deadman switch. He meant her stay until he let her out. And he meant her to have Learned proper respect by the time she was allowed to emerge.

Or he meant her to be dead.

People could die of brain-burn. There had been a student—not, mercifully, one of hers—who had tried to use a Learning Module to cram for a critical test.

Six hours in the Module, the needle set at maximum intensity . . .

The thought jellied and slid away, lost in momentary thunder: ". . . newly-formed Council of Clans . . ."

Aelliana went—elsewhere.

One's delm was not amused.

"You are plagued by ill dreams," she repeated. "And the Healers are unable to succor you."

Samiv bowed. "In essence, ma'am. The Master at the Solcintra Hall had nothing better than the cure given by the Healer on *Luda Soldare*: look upon the face of that which frightens me and make—a peace." She drew a careful breath, aware that Bindan had very little tolerance for weakness even when an alliance with Korval Itself was not at risk.

"The Healers inform me, ma'am, that this is an old, ungentle cure, but efficacious."

"I see." Bindan's frown had not eased. "One is unaccustomed to counting you timid, and so naturally the question arises: what has birthed this enormous fear? Korval? I did not hide from you that he is odd. His entire clan is thus and has been, clear back to Pilot Cantra.

"Korval's *melant'i* is impeccable—they have sworn to insure your health and comfort and to return you safely to your kin at contract's end. If it is himself . . ." She lifted a shoulder. "I grant he is no beauty, but I had always thought you too intelligent to let a pretty face matter more than honor and obedience to your delm."

"It is not," Samiv said, trying to think clearly through the haze of weariness, "that one wishes to cry off the marriage. Only that one desires the delm's permission to—to call upon Korval beforehand, that the cure may begin with all speed."

Bindan moved a hand in negation. "In three days' time, you shall be his wife. Enough time to roust your terrors after the contract is in force."

She had expected nothing else, yet she was so *very* tired, more than half-ill with fatigue...

"If the delm pleases. Korval had said he—wished to stand my friend. I do not think he would hold it a miss-throw, did I take the matter to him and..."

Bindan's palm hit her desk with a sound like a whip crack. She surged to her feet and Samiv effaced herself, bowing low, but it was too late to redeem the error.

"You *dare*! Upon what date was tel'Izak given into Korval's care? I remind you that tel'Izak belongs to Clan Bindan and that Bindan solves for you!"

"Yes, ma'am," Samiv murmured, head bent to her knees. "Forgive me."

There was silence. Samiv held the bow a heartbeat longer, then straightened, slowly, head pounding. Her delm sighed.

"You are tired," she said. "Go to your room and rest."

Rest. Samiv folded her lips firmly over a wild desire to laugh.

Rather, she bowed respect for the delm, "Ma'am" and retired, as ordered, to her room.

Daav ate sparingly of a meal composed chiefly of gall and wormwood, accompanied by fine vintage vinegar.

At the conclusion of this solitary feast, he rose and rang for Mr. pel'Kana, and instructed that august person that he was not at home to callers.

He then retired to his private apartment abovestairs, where he fussed about for some little time, pretending to put things in order, before finally sitting down at his work table.

Lovingly, he fingered over bits of wood and odd pieces of ivory, choosing at last a rough round of bronwood. Carving would reveal soft black and bronze swirls that would show well, so he thought, against her hair. It would also emit a subtle scent that he was certain must please her.

She might wear it, when she went Outworld.

He held the wood in his hand, feeling the weight and the shape of it, considering how best to carve the comb he saw so clearly in his mind's eye. He pulled a paper pad forward, picked up a pen and sketched quickly. Laying the wood aside the sketch, he felt a stir of pleasure.

"Yes," he said, and reached for the roughing blade.

He had been some time at this project when a muted chime sounded. Glancing up, he saw it was his private line thus demanding his attention.

He lay the wood and knife aside, his heart inexplicably beginning to pound, for surely it was only Er Thom, calling to ask if he would care to eat Prime at Trealla Fantrol.

"Yes?" he inquired, touching the stud. Frad looked at him with unwonted seriousness.

"Hullo, darling. I'm afraid we've made a muddle of things."

The dome would not open.

Aelliana fought down the urge to beat at it with her fists—a waste of her strength—and of time.

Time was her enemy. The longer she stayed locked into the program, the more certain the chance of damage or death. She could not know that Ran Eld meant her to die—his intent was meaningless to the equation of destruction she saw looming before her. Unless—

Her thoughts staggered; reformed beneath the voice of the program:

". . . heir or assignee of Captain Cantra yos'Phelium shall be acknowledged to hold the rank of Captain and bear the burden of the passengers' well-being . . .

". . . shall continue until such time as the Houses of Solcintra or that ruling body which may succeed it revoke, cancel or otherwise make null and void this . . ."

The thunder began to fizz; she felt her bruised attention slip and thankfully crossed over to that other place which was neither sleep nor waking.

". . . It never occurred to me that she *didn't* know who you were," Frad said. "We tried to get her to rouse you, but she'd have none of it, and—forgive me—it began to seem like bed-sport gone awry. In any wise, darling, here's Jon telling us she came to him the first time fresh from rough usage, and if you're looking for the villain, I'd advise you to lay money on the nadelm." He made a wry face.

"As it happens, you have money to lay. The pilot left a cantra for you here."

Daav remembered to breathe. "A cantra?"

"Your share, so she tells it, of yesterday's work-fee."

He closed his eyes. "Gods."

"Just so. Now you see what comes of mumming innocents. Do you go?"

"At once." He shook himself and looked into Frad's bland, efficient face. "A car, at the main gate of Korval's Chonselta Yard, in an hour."

Frad inclined his head. "Done."

...direct stimulation. The Learning Module utilizes direct-brain stimulation...

Conceive the brain as a series of relay stations, engaged or not engaged by thought. The Learning Module targets those stations currently disengaged, fills them sequentially and moves on, in theory allowing each station sufficient opportunity to recover from this assault upon its sensibilities. The Learning Module does not approach those stations engaged in cognition, or those concerned with life support.

Within the darkness of the void, Aelliana reached forth her thought and created a star.

And around this star, she placed a world which ran in elliptical orbit, its rotation rate once in eighteen hours, time of orbit transit, four hundred and eighty-five Standard Days.

To the world, she gave a moon, and to the moon a spin three hundred and four days in duration, while it circled its principal once every twenty-two hours.

She held the little system in her mind, painstakingly calculating each orbit, weighing each relationship, adjusting mass and pull and finally, the spin-rate of the little moon.

When all was stable, balanced and beautiful, she added a second world.

Somewhere, there was thunder. Her concentration wavered, the worlds faltered in their carefully-calculated courses. She caught them, replaced them, checked—rechecked—the relational equations; reconsidered certain mathematical alliances and necessities.

The thunder receded.

In time, she added a third world.

Then a fourth.

She populated the second world, strung space stations like Festival lights, ringed the system with beacons and waystations, created satellites and traffic patterns.

In her head, the numbers danced, the equations pure as poetry.

She spun an asteroid pod, skated it 'round the sun, calculating trajectories, stress breakage, possible strikes upon populated areas.

There was no thunder. There was no Code. There was her creation and the vital necessity to keep all in balance—to calculate and continue to calculate, each nuance and effect.

Aelliana—was.

Ten minutes to change from house clothes to the formal costume appropriate for one delm's official call upon another. Daav knotted the silver ribbon in his hair, caught up his cloak and was gone, the door to his apartment snapping closed behind him.

Dragon's Cub was free-berthed beyond the formal gardens. It was barely more than a Jump-buggy, but it would do very well for this particular mission. He would worry about assuaging his gardener's injured feelings once he knew Aelliana was well.

He was moving down the main hallway at just under a run, when Mr. pel'Kana stepped out of the smaller receiving parlor.

"If Your Lordship pleases."

Daav shook his head. "I am in great haste. Pray make my excuses to whomever has called."

But Mr. pel'Kana did not bow obedience. Rather, he extended a hand, fingers curled in supplication.

"Please, Master Daav," he said, softly. "I think you will want to speak to the lady."

He blinked, catching himself in mid-stride. "Lady?"

Aelliana? Had she discovered him after all and come to ask his aid, while Jon and Frad and Clonak fretted for her safety? He changed course and swept into the parlor.

Samiv tel'Izak spun away from her contemplation of the mantle—or possibly of Korval's shield, hung above it—and came three steps toward him, one hand outflung.

"Please," she said, voice none too steady in the mode of Comrades. "Please, I—you must help me."

Chapter Thirty-Five

The cops called young Tor An to bail me out,
which he did, right enough, and all according to
co-pilot's duty. When we were free of the place,
he read me such a scold as I haven't heard since
nursery. Puppy.
    He was right, too.
—Excerpted from Cantra yos'Phelium's Log Book

HE CHECKED, AND IN THAT MOMENT TOOK NOTE OF HER face, which was strained, pale, with black circles under her eyes, her muscles etched in exhaustion.

"Samiv, what has happened?" He hardly thought, answering Comrade with Comrade.

"I . . ." Her eyes filled and she glanced aside, blinking. "Forgive me."

"Freely—and you must return the grace at once. I am in desperate haste. Word has come that—one to whom I sit co-pilot may be in peril. I must be gone in moments."

She was a pilot: Guild rule was as natural to her as breath. Her eyes leapt to his.

"Of course, you must go at once! I will—" She gasped, eyes widening.

"Hold, you say *the Caylon* is in peril?"

Daav lifted an eyebrow. "And who told you, I wonder, that I am the Caylon's co-pilot?"

She moved a hand. "The tape was on in the Guildroom when I came through. In what way is she imperilled?"

Daav felt his face tighten. "An illegal attempt was made to seal her ship. Last report was that she had gone to treat with the party involved. Who is known to have beaten her in the past."

He had not thought it possible for Samiv to pale further.

"I see," she said, flatly. "Who flies with you?"

"There is only myself here, and to tarry even for my *cha'leket* seemed wasteful of minutes."

"Which I have now wasted for you." She moved forward, resolute. "By your leave, I will sit your second. If the peril is extreme, I may be of use."

And so she might be, he allowed, *if Aelliana* . . .

"Quickly, then," he said, and spun toward the door.

Ran Eld did not come down to Prime, but was served in his apartment, as was his custom when the delm was from home. Voni sat at the head of the table, as was *her* custom when the delm was from home, though she displayed appetite for neither her dinner nor the game of correcting her junior's manners. But, thought Sinit, it might be that she pined for her favorite target of ridicule.

Sinit considered asking after news of Aelliana's return. Indeed, she spent some minutes as she drank her soup, examining phrasing appropriate to the task. In the end, however, nothing seemed quite safe enough

to venture. She did not think either Voni or Ran Eld
knew of the amazing and adventurous life Aelliana
lived, over on the other side of the world, as neither
was an aficionado of the news wires, and they would
not, Sinit vowed, hear of it from her.

It was of course, terribly exciting to learn that
Aelliana *regularly* flew with Daav yos'Phelium, as
reported on the pilot's wire. Sinit had taken advan-
tage of her trip to the library that afternoon to look
Daav yos'Phelium up in the newest edition of the
Book of Clans.

Korval Himself sat co-pilot to Aelliana, which was
honor to Mizel, but Voni would only see that Korval's
attention belonged to her and Aelliana had stolen her
rights. Ran Eld would say something vile and perhaps
slap Aelliana for rising above her place. Ran Eld *did*
strike Aelliana, Sinit had seen him do so, twice, no
matter if the delm chose to hear of it.

"This dinner is vile!" Voni snapped from the head
of the table. "Really, the cook takes liberties with my
good nature when the delm is from home!" She rose,
flinging her napkin into her soup bowl.

"*You* may continue, if you can stomach such swill!"
she told Sinit. "I shall retire to my room. I have a
headache. Pray, disturb me for no one!"

Sinit looked up at her. "All right. May I have your
popover, then? Mine was excellent."

"Repellant brat," Voni uttered, and swept tragically
from the room.

Straight from the lawn they lifted, the little craft
hurtling upward with no such niceties as gradual
acceleration. Korval flew a brutal course, at a trajectory

only a Scout would think sane. Samiv kept her board, exhaustion dissolved by adrenaline.

"Can you tell me now," he said softly, hands quick and certain on his controls, "what it is I must help you resolve?"

She swallowed, eyes on the readouts, and it helped, someway, not to have to meet his gaze as she said it.

"I . . . dream. Frightening dreams. The Healers—send me to face my terror."

There was a small pause. "Which is myself?"

"No." She licked her lips. "I—believe—it is your Tree." She took a breath, fighting tears that came all too easily, these last days. "I resigned my contract on *Luda Soldare*—I could not sleep, my reactions are—in question. I could not endanger the ship . . ."

"Of course not," he agreed and it was uncannily comforting, hearing that said in his deep, rough voice. Samiv closed her eyes briefly, opened them again to the necessity of her board.

"One's delm desires the alliance, of course. I—I would ask your leave to—before the lines are signed—to approach the Tree and—and assure myself that it is—only—a tree."

"Ah. But it is not, you know, *only* a tree." He was silent for a moment, then, "Is your delm aware that you have brought this to me?"

She looked over to him; saw only the side of his face, and the quick, sure hands on the board.

"My delm is—certain—the dreams will abate, once the contract is signed."

"I see." He sighed, and flicked her another of his bold, uninforming looks. "Your board to me, if you will. Thank you. In regard to our present mission—there is a firearm in the pocket beside you. It would be best to check it now, so there are no surprises, if you must use it."

She stared at him, at the eyes that told her nothing. "You think—"

He moved his head from side to side. "We may find that all is well, in which case we will merely be called upon to drink tea and display our manners."

Samiv pulled the gun from its nest. "But you do not expect that."

"I don't," he said gently. "All my life, I've been plagued by hunches. From time to time, one does prove to be merely indigestion." He cast her a glance that seemed rather too full of amusement. "Korval *is* mad, you know."

Samiv looked down and cracked the gun.

Somewhere in the beatitude of equations, a chime sounded. Sometime later, there was light.

Aelliana detached a portion of her attention from the problem of the retrograde planet and raised heavy arms, stiff fingers groping against—nothing.

The dome of the Learning Module was open. It took a moment to understand the significance of that.

She was free.

Free belonged to the subset of things which are precious beyond rubies.

Aelliana flung herself up, crying out as her body simultaneously reported every bruise she had gained from her encounter with her brother, and the additional information that she was hideously thirsty.

The room reeled. She clawed the staggered data into sense, lurched toward a low table, hefted a heavy vase full of wilting flowers and lurched back to the Learning Module.

Flowers and solution went into the program box, which fizzed, smoked and popped. She raised the vase in both hands, swung it at the control dials. Her first attempt failed to connect; the force of the missed blow kicked her legs out from under her and she went face-first into the carpet.

Gagging, she clawed her way to her knees, got her hands around the vase once more and smashed at the controls.

The blow connected, hard enough to dent the faceplate. Aelliana whimpered, the controls twisting in and out of perspective. She raised the vase, staring at the main dial, forcing herself to see it through the images that flickered and flashed before her mind's eye. The dial steadied and she swung with all her might.

Glass broke, instrumentation screamed, shrilly, and went silent.

Aelliana dropped the vase, hung onto the edge of the Learning Module and lurched to her feet, staring round at a room that spun out of sense, objects pulsating, edges attenuating into nothingness, the image of a star system she had never seen superimposed over everything and she struggled—struggled to recall. Something. Something—important.

It was dim in the room . . . dark outside the gaping window. Something. Numbers, strung together in the shape of a personal comm code, and a deep, beloved voice, whispering from memory, "Call me, Aelliana, should you have need . . ."

There was a comm in the study. She knew that.

Over—over by the window. Yes. She could see the window, through the pulsating stars. First one foot...

She fell over a table, lost her balance and hit the floor amid an avalanche of bric-a-brac. Panting, she got to her knees, oriented herself and crawled the rest of the way to the window. Once there, she pulled herself upright with the aid of a built in bookcase, put her hand flat on its top surface and inched forward, feeling for the comm.

Her fingers touched cool plastic. She bit her lip. Numbers. Daav's comm code. All she need do was code the number into the comm, here beneath her hand. Daav would help her.

Thought formed. There was danger. Danger in using the house comm. Scouts. Ran Eld. Ran Eld would harm Daav.

She must not call.

Chapter Thirty-Six

I ran co-pilot for Garen 'til she broke her skull, and the ship came to me, complete with a full load of trouble. I was young enough then to believe my skull was too hard to break—opted to run solo, and take care of the troubles as I met them.

I wasn't looking for a co-pilot the night I found Jela, though I was old enough by then to know I could die. What I wanted was a glass and a roll in the blankets—one glass, one roll and an early lift out, headed for the Rim with a load of don't-you-care.

Funny, how even simple plans so often fail to work.

—Excerpted from Cantra yos'Phelium's Log Book

SINIT WAS CURLED IN THE ROUND CHAIR IN THE FRONT parlor, reading. Chonselta City Library had only today placed on its shelves *In Support of the Commonality of Language* by Learned Scholar Anne Davis and Sinit had been fortunate enough to engage it.

Language and the roots of language had their places in the larger art of anthropology and she read with absorption. Indeed, she read with so much attention to the work that it was not the first, but the second sounding of the doorchime that roused her.

Blinking, she uncurled, taking care to mark her place, and pull on her houseboots. She straightened her tunic on the way to the entry hall and tucked her hair behind her ears.

The bell sounded once more.

From above-stairs came the noise of a door opening, feet thumping along thin carpeting, and Voni's voice, wondering: "Whoever could be calling this late in the day?"

Sinit opened the front door.

The taller of the two visitors bowed as the porch light came up, cloak shimmering around him: *Visitor to the House*, Sinit read, and inclined her head.

"Speak."

Black eyes looked down at her from a stark, clever face; his dark hair was pulled back and secured with a silver ribbon, an end of which lay across his shoulder. A twist of silver was in the right ear; there a flash of slick enameled colors as he brought his left hand up in the age-old gesture and showed her.

Tree-and-Dragon.

"I have the honor to be Korval," he said in the Mode of Announcement. He gestured toward his companion. "Pilot Samiv tel'Izak."

Sinit barely attended. Korval. Korval *here*, in the company of a second pilot, who must surely be another of Aelliana's comrades. Yet, if they were come here—

"But," she blurted, looking from his eyes to the smooth, careful face of his companion. "Aelliana is not to House, sir—pilot. I had thought—*surely*—she is at—at Solcintra?"

They exchanged a glance, the two on the porch, and Sinit caught her breath, afraid suddenly, though not of them.

"Please," she said, backing away and pulling the door wide. "Please, come in. I—"

"Sinit, whatever are you doing?" Voni demanded peevishly from above. Sinit spun, squinting through the dimness toward the landing.

"These gentles are here to speak with Aelliana, sister. Pray, ask her to come down."

There was a moment of shocked silence, then the sound of footsteps, going swiftly back up the stairs. Sinit felt her knees go weak.

"She must have come in while I was reading," she said, shakily, and pushed the door closed. "Doubtless, she will be here in a moment to greet you. Would you care to step into the parlor, gentles? Refreshment..."

Upstairs, a door slammed and the footsteps that pounded hastily down were not Aelliana's. Sinit saw the man know that; saw him convey the knowledge to his comrade with the twitch of a well-marked black brow.

"Callers for Aelliana?" Ran Eld's voice was breathless, but, then, Ran Eld was very little used to running. Sinit went two steps back and to the side, instinctively seeking the shadow of the back hallway. She looked up and directly into the eyes of Pilot tel'Izak. The pilot held her gaze a moment, then turned her head away.

"Who is—ah." The questioner had gained the foyer—a slender and be-ringed young man in a houserobe much too ornate for his surroundings. Samiv frowned as he came into the light. There were marks of paler gold on the man's face, as if he had been scratched and had recent recourse to an autodoc. From the edge of her eye, she saw the halfling door-keeper fade one more step toward the safety of the hall-shadows.

"I am Nadelm Mizel," the gaudy young man said, inclining his head slightly. "May I know your business, sir, ma'am?"

Korval silently extended his left hand. The Tree-and-Dragon flashed. The nadelm froze, as well he might, then bowed again, ornately.

"The House is honored to receive Korval. How may I serve you?"

Korval did not deign even to incline his head. "I would speak to the House's daughter Aelliana, sir."

"I regret that is not possible," Nadelm Mizel said.

"Ah, I see." Korval said quietly. "In that wise, I will speak with Mizel Herself."

The nadelm spread his hands, rings glittering. "It is my misfortune to disappoint you twice, sir. Mizel is from House."

"That is unfortunate," Korval agreed gravely. "When will she return?"

Relief loosened the haughty shoulders. "Tomorrow midday, by my best information. Shall you call then? Or perhaps Mizel may call upon you?"

"Perhaps we need not embrace either alternative," Korval said, as the elder sister—she who had skittered from the landing—came carefully down the stairs to stand at her nadelm's side. He ignored her.

"When," Korval inquired, "will it be possible to speak with Pilot Scholar Aelliana Caylon?"

The nadelm's lips thinned. "Indeed, sir, Aelliana

is the veriest fluttercap! One never knows when she might appear."

In the shadow at the edge of the hallway, the halfling girl jerked—and was still.

Samiv flicked a glance at Korval, but his eyes where all for the nadelm.

"I have never found her thus," he said, meditatively, and the black eyes moved, pinning the elder sister. "Of your kindness, ma'am, bring me Aelliana, or tell me where I might find her."

The woman fluttered, foolish blue eyes darting this way and that. "Truly, sir, I don't—but it is as Ran Eld says! Aelliana is—she is—" She faltered, staring wildly at her nadelm. "She is—"

"At study," the nadelm said forcefully. "It would be perfectly useless to try and rouse her, sir. Leave your card, and I will see she receives it, when she is sensible again."

Fool, thought Samiv and looked again to the hallway.

The halfling was gone.

"I am prepared to wait," Korval said, fixing the nadelm in his eye, "until Scholar Caylon has completed her study."

The other man's eyes slid aside. "It may be—some time."

"I understand," said Korval. He laced his hands together and moved his eyes to the hall table, his face composed into an expression of gentle meditation.

"See here," Nadelm Mizel said sharply, "you can't just stand in our entrance hall all night—"

The black eyes moved. Gravely, Korval inclined his head.

"Your concern does you credit. I hasten to assure you that it is entirely within my scope to stand in your entrance hall all night—and all of tomorrow, if necessary. However, Pilot tel'Izak would perhaps welcome the use of a chair."

"Thank you," she said, with a composure she was far from feeling. "I am perfectly at my ease."

The nadelm's face tightened in anger. "I do not think you have entirely understood that you are standing within Mizel's own House. I do not—"

"Delm Korval!"

He turned. The halfling who had admitted them to the house skittered to a halt at the mouth of a sidehall, brown eyes wide with terror.

"The Learning Module," she gasped and Daav felt ice down his spine.

"Show me," he said.

She turned and fled back down the hall, he striding after her.

"Halt!" shouted Nadelm Mizel, face suddenly gone pale. "I forbid you to enter any further into Mizel's house!" He flung after Korval and Samiv spun into his path, hand up.

"Hold!"

Snarling, he pushed her aside. She staggered, caught herself and swung before him once more.

"Hold!" she ordered again, gun out and quite steady on his belly. "Proceed at your peril."

The learning module was empty, the brain-box shorted, the timer shattered, the master controller smashed. The session dial had stopped at five hours. The concentration slide was pushed to the top.

"It makes no sense," the halfling stuttered. "Why would Aelliana wish a maximum intensity review of the Code?"

Excellent question. And he was very sure that the answer was—*Aelliana* had not. Daav took a deep breath and ran the Scout's Rainbow quickly, bringing both terror and fury down to manageable levels.

"We will be certain to ask her that," he said to Sinit Caylon's frantic face, "when we find her. Have you looked anywhere else? Her rooms?"

"No, sir."

"Do so," he instructed her. "I will see what else may be found here. Quickly. If she has indeed been in the sleep learner for so long a time, she will be—disoriented."

Brain-burned, he amended to himself as Sinit ran from the room. He swallowed against resurgence of terror and began methodically to search the room.

He lingered for a moment by an overturned gidget table, frowning at the trinkets scattered across the rug, then passed on, satisfying himself that delirium had not moved Aelliana to shelter beneath the furniture.

Eventually, he came to the end of the room. There was a comm on the floor beneath the closed window. He bent to pick the unit up and felt a cool breeze kiss his cheek. Straightening, he moved to the window, put his hand flat on the tall center pane and pushed.

The window swung open, soundless on well-oiled hinges. Daav leaned over the sill, a Scout's trained eye picking out the route she had taken through the meager garden, the marks at one consistent height along the length of the worn wooden fence, where she had likely set her shoulder, for balance, and for orientation. The gate at the bottom of the yard stood open, rocking slightly in the night-breeze.

✳ ✳ ✳

"Pirate!" Nadelm Mizel shrieked, his face flushed and twisted in rage. "I will see you ruined, outcast and ridiculed! I will—"

Rapid footsteps sounded in the hallway and the half-ling flashed by, raced across the foyer without a sideward glance and flung up the stairway, two steps at a time.

"Sinit!" howled the nadelm, but Sinit did not answer.

"Voni!" the nadelm shouted then. "Call the Peace-keepers."

But Voni was sitting on the lower step, head resting on her knees.

Furious, he raised a ring-crusted hand, as if he would strike her. Samiv called his attention to the gun, and he froze, rings glittering—tawdry things for the most part, she saw, all sharp edges and shine.

Except for one. And how had such a tasteless dirt-stomper as Nadelm Mizel come by a Jump-pilot's cluster? she wondered. Such things were priceless—clan treasures, to be locked safe away and brought forth once a twelve-year to marvel upon.

"Samiv." Korval's voice was in her ear. "I have found her trail. She does not appear—well," he said, and she felt a thrill of horror run her spine. "We must overtake her before she comes to more harm."

"Yes," she said. "Go you first while I keep this one—"

The front door clanked and swung ponderously open. A round-faced woman in a travel cloak stepped into the foyer—and froze, as she took in the scene before her.

She swept forward then, raising her hand, so that the Clan Ring was plain to see.

"I have the honor," she said icily, fixing Samiv in her eye, "to be Mizel. You will explain yourselves."

* * *

It was difficult to talk; words she did not mean to say fell in abundance from her lips while words she desperately wished to say failed to form themselves.

Still, she had made the taxi driver understand—at least, he drove her to the Pilot's Guildhall in Chonselta Port. She did not think she had precisely asked him to do so, but it was—enough.

"The orbit of the retrograde planet will develop a wobble in approximately ten thousand years," she told him as she fumbled the cantra-piece out of her pocket, "and will fail entirely in eleven thousand."

"Then it's nothing either of us need be concerned of," he replied, pressing the coin firmly back into her palm, and bending her fingers over it, one by one. "Plot a straight course for the dorm, now, pilot. Time to sleep it off."

"If you are outside a major gravity well you may ignore the pel'Endra Ratio and proceed," Aelliana said gratefully, fingers locked around the cantra.

"I fully intend to proceed, and as quickly as may be," he said. "Hull's cool, pilot. Out you go."

She managed to disembark and stood trembling on the walkway. The taxi's door began to descend and she said, "Don't tell him you saw me."

The door sealed and the taxi moved slowly away.

Aelliana turned carefully, there being nothing to hold onto here on the walk. She focussed on the doorway, ignoring the random flashes and flarings that had nothing to do with the street before her. Focus established, she moved forward, sliding her feet along the sidewalk, to maintain what balance she might.

She only fell twice before she gained the door.

Chapter Thirty-Seven

Duty is not indulgent, nor does it seek vengeance.
— Proverb

"SHE'S NOT HERE, SIR!" SINIT'S VOICE CAME DOWN FROM the upper floor, closely followed by Sinit herself.

"Mother?" She reached the foyer and made her bow. "Good evening, ma'am. Ran Eld had said you were not expected until tomorrow."

"Well I came tonight," Mizel said coldly. "Are you in a league, Sinit, with pirates who come armed into a clanhouse?"

"Pirates?" Sinit frowned. "Truly, ma'am, Delm Korval and Pilot tel'Izak have called for Aelliana, but she is—she is not to House."

"Learning so, they hold the nadelm at gunpoint. Entirely understandable." Mizel extended her hand. "You will relinquish that weapon to me."

"Forgive me," Samiv said firmly, "but I will not. This person shoved me and then threatened to strike me. I fear for my safety in his presence. More, I fear for Pilot Caylon's safety." She looked up, and Daav saw fury in her eyes. "Did the Caylon wear a Jump-pilot's ring?"

"Yes."

Nadelm Mizel took a step back, hand creeping toward his pocket.

"Show it!" Samiv cried. "Show your delm what you wear on your hand!"

"I do not take orders from you!" snarled the nadelm.

"But you do take orders from me," Mizel said, and extended her hand once more. "Let me see this ring, Ran Eld."

Reluctantly, he pulled the cluster from his hand, and laid it in her palm.

"It is a foolishness, ma'am—a bit of paste. I—"

Mizel stared at her palm. "How came you by this?"

The nadelm stood speechless.

"Ran Eld! I ask how you came to have this ring. An answer, if you please."

"It was Aelliana's," the elder sister moaned from her crouch on the bottom stair. She looked up, showing a wet and ravaged face. "He took it off her hand. I saw him. Just before he sealed the lid on the Learner."

It was a slow night at Chonselta Guildhall. Rab Orn and Nil Ten were playing pikit in the common room and Keyn was over in the corner, reading. Beside the occasional hand-bid from the card players, the only noise came from the Port comm, a continuous babble so familiar to the three pilots that none consciously heard it.

Nil Ten sighed. "Fold," he muttered, throwing his cards down in a heap. "Glad we're not playing this for cantra."

"We're not?" asked his partner, wide-eyed and the first pilot laughed, looked up and gasped.

Her face was a mottle of cuts and bruises, so swollen the pupil-big eyes could scarcely open. Her hair was snarled in a hopeless knot. She was trembling, visibly and continuously.

"What—" Rab Orn turned in his chair to see, and froze.

"Daav's the card I want to play," the apparition stated, her voice like sand being ground into stone.

"Merciful gods," that was Keyn. She got up out of her chair and came forward, peering into the newcomer's battered face.

"It's the Caylon," she breathed. "I saw her last evening, at Solcintra, when the Guildmaster gave over her license. Sitting on Korval's lap she was and happy as you please."

"It is the duty of the pilot to protect ship and passengers," Aelliana Caylon said gravely. "It is the duty of the co-pilot to protect pilot and ship."

The three exchanged glances, then Keyn reached out and touched the other woman's shoulder. "That's right, pilot. Guild rule, plain as plain." She took a deep breath. "Come along with me, and let's get you to a 'doc, eh? Everything's going to be binjali..."

"Binjali." The slitted black eyes locked onto Keyn's face, one trembling hand rose, fumbled and fastened 'round the pilot's wrist.

"Jon dea'Cort." Keyn stared and the Caylon said again, voice rising. "Jon dea'Cort. The retrograde planet will release a hysteresis energy effect proportional to the velocity and spin of Smuggler's Ace, cheese muffins, Daav, efficient function! Call, call if you need me, Aelliana!"

"That's plain." Nil Ten jumped up, oversetting his

chair, walked over to the comm and punched in a rapid code. The screen blanked as the unit on the other end chimed, three times, four, five...

"Binjali's."

Nil Ten inclined his head to the old pilot in the viewer. "Master dea'Cort. Nil Ten pel'Quida, Chonselta Guildhall, sir. We have one of your crew here, in distress."

Mizel raised her head, lines showing hard about her mouth and she looked to her son.

"Aelliana's father," she said, speaking in the Mode of Instruction, "wore one of these. Other than himself, it was his clan's whole treasure. This ring will ransom a Jump-ship, will it not, Korval?"

"Indeed," Daav said gravely, "that was the purpose behind its making. Ma'am, I beg your pardon. The timer and intensity meter on the Learning Module are frozen at such levels as must cause me extreme alarm. I have found the course Aelliana charted, out the window and through the back gate. She—she is very likely brain-burned, ma'am, and I fear for her life if we do not go after her at once."

"Yes." Mizel looked up at him. "I am correct in thinking that your personal name is Daav?"

"It is."

"So." She held out the Pilot's Cluster. "You will safeguard this and return it to my daughter when you find her. I will do—what is discovered to be necessary—here. Pray inform me of—your progress. Should she return here—" Her mouth tightened. "But you will know where she is most likely to go."

Daav inclined his head, slipping the ring into the

inner pocket of his cloak. "If she should return here, ma'am, leave word with Master dea'Cort at Binjali Repair Shop, Solcintra Port." He glanced over to Samiv, who slipped her gun away.

"Will you help me search?"

"I demand the honor," she replied, and followed him down the hallway.

He tracked her down the alley, following the path her shoulder had smoothed against splintered fencing. He found the places where she had fallen, the places where she had crawled until she found a fence post, an arbor or a tree to cling to and drag herself up to her feet.

The alley was intersected by a street; on the other side there was no sign of her passage. He and Samiv recrossed the street, she went right and he to the left, looking for a hint, a footprint, a thread.

A thread.

A snag of bold blue, caught in the rust of a sign pole. He cast out, moving in a gradually widening circle around that whisper of hope, but found nothing else. Defeated, he returned to the pole.

Had the Peacekeepers seen her, ill-balanced as she was, and born her away to their Guildhall? But, surely, she would told them her name, her clan?

Or, he thought with a shiver, perhaps not. Brain-burned, she might not recall such things.

Where would she go, if she were able to recall herself?

Binjali's, no doubt.

But in such a condition as he had seen, falling flat when there was no wall to support her? She might, he supposed, flag a taxi, but Aelliana rarely had more than a few dex in her pocket...

The hum of a motor brought him to a sense of his surroundings and he turned to see a cab moving slowly up the street. Apparently the cabbie noted his interest, for the vehicle pulled to the curb and the passenger door rose.

"Service, your Lordship?"

"Information," he said, bending down to look at the driver. He pulled a cantra out of his pocket. "I am in search of a friend—a fair-haired lady, very slender. Green eyes. She would have perhaps been confused in her direction and—unsteady on her feet—" The cabbie stiffened, but said nothing. After a moment, Daav murmured.

"You have seen her."

The man moved his shoulders, leaned forward to make an adjustment on his board. "I saw her," he said, and the look he gave Daav was hard and straight. "Took her up-city. Set her down at Commerce Square."

Commerce Square? The opposite direction of the Port. Daav frowned, considering the man's face, almost tasting the lie. And yet...

"You must forgive me if I ask again," he murmured, hearing Samiv coming down the walkway from his right. "I am the lady's co-pilot and I fear she is—very ill. Perhaps she was not—precisely as I had said. Perhaps she had been hurt, eh? And you think you are looking at the cause. I beg you tell me if you took her to Port. I tell you plainly that I fear for her life, should she board ferry for Solcintra."

The cabbie hesitated, then. "I'll see your hands."

Wondering, Daav held them out. Korval's Ring

gleamed in the cabin light. The cabbie stared a long moment, then raised his eyes.

"That wouldn't have done the damage I saw. You want stones for that kind of work." He sighed and looked away. "I took her down to the Pilot's Guild, and I'll tell you right now she wasn't making no sense."

Mizel looked at the deeds of transfers in her hands. Two deeds of transfers, each from Aelliana Caylon to Ran Eld Caylon: one for an Ormit Shares account, one for a spaceship named *Ride the Luck*. Both were signed.

Neither signature was Aelliana's.

"Voni has already confessed to signing these in her sister's stead," Mizel said, her eyes still on those damning papers. "I have seen, I think, enough. While it is possible that your sister Aelliana has survived your use of her—while it is possible, though not probable, that she has survived *intact*—the delm cannot but see that your actions are consistent with a deliberate and knowing desire to take what was not rightfully yours, counting no cost too high. Not even your sister's death."

Mizel raised her head and stared at the man standing before her desk. A man dressed for travelling and not in the first style of elegance. The cloak was serviceable but shabby. The shirt and trousers had been made for him, but some time ago. The boots—would be a difficulty for him. He wore no jewelry. His face was pale.

"Mizel does not sanction kinslaying. Having shown yourself capable of such horror, the delm is unable to do otherwise than declare you dead. You will leave this house now. At once. You will never return. You have no call upon Mizel. You are clanless and outcast."

The man before her bowed his head.

"Because you were once my son, I give you somewhat to take away with you. The clothes you stand in. A cantra-piece." She reached into the desk drawer, removed the keepsafe that had belonged to her mother and the half-gone box of pellets. "A weapon."

Ran Eld looked up, face wet with tears. She put gun and ammunition on the desk. After a moment, he picked them up. Mizel inclined her head and stood.

"I will escort you to the door."

He walked silent beside her down the hall, silent across the foyer. When she opened the door, he turned, but she averted her face and in a moment heard him walk down the steps, whereupon she closed the door and locked it.

Duty done, Mizel gave way to Birin Caylon, whose son had just now died, she lay her cheek against the inner door—and mourned his passing.

Chapter Thirty-Eight

He found it in a desert, so he told me—the only living thing in two days' walk. A skinny stick with a couple leaves near the top, that's all it was then.

I don't remember the name of the world it came from. He might not have told me. Wherever it was, when his Troop finally picked him up, Jela wouldn't leave 'til he'd dug up that damned skinny stick of a tree and planted it real careful in an old ration tin. Carried it in his arms onto transport. And nobody dared to laugh.

—Excerpted from Cantra yos'Phelium's Log Book

"YES," THE DOORKEEPER AT CHONSELTA HEALER HALL sighed, stepping back to allow them inside. "Jon dea'Cort had said you would be here and that it was out of his power to prevent you." He closed the door and beckoned. Silent, they followed him down a short hallway and into a small parlor.

"There is wine on the sideboard, and filled bread. Hall Master will be down to speak to you very soon. In the meanwhile, I am asked to convey to Pilot yos'Phelium the Master's most urgent plea for serenity. We have novices in-Hall." He bowed and left them, the door swinging shut on his heels.

In the center of the room, Korval sighed, then turned, looking down at her from eyes as giving as obsidian.

"Shall you wish refreshment, pilot?" he asked, with a gentleness she would not have expected, from such eyes. "Seat yourself, I beg. I have used you cruelly this evening, when you are already in pain through my ineptitude. At least, let me bring you a cup of wine."

"Thank you," Samiv said, moving to a doublechair and sinking into the soft cushions with bleary gratitude. "I believe I will sit, but I do not think wine . . ."

The door swung open and a white-haired woman in plain shirt and trousers stepped into the chamber. She bowed, briefly.

"Chonselta Hall Master Ethilen. Pray, Pilot tel'Izak, do not trouble yourself to rise. Recruit your strength." She turned her face toward the man in the center of the room.

"Well, Korval?"

"Not well, Master Ethilen," he replied. "You have Aelliana Caylon in keeping here. The report I have of her condition from the pilots at Chonselta Guild is—terrifying. I will see her, of your kindness."

"Alas."

Samiv saw Korval's shoulders tense, though his voice was as calm as always.

"She had wanted me, said the pilots at Guildhall. I would show her she is not abandoned by one in whom she placed trust. I am her co-pilot. I have this right."

"Masters Kestra and Tom Sen are with Pilot Caylon. I cannot allow interference of their work at this juncture. The report you have from the pilot's guild-fellows

appears overstated. It is in her best interest that her
co-pilot allow himself to be satisfied with this prelim-
inary information and retire to Solcintra."

"I—"

"Korval, you are blinding the House," the old woman
said sternly, and held up a hand. "Yes, I See that you
are attempting to control yourself, and I thank you
most sincerely for the effort. Without it, my shielding would not be sufficient to allow me to stand in
the same room with you and converse. However, no
amount of converse will deliver you to Pilot Caylon's
side this evening. Believe me in verymost earnest."
She sighed and lowered her hand.

"Daav, go home. Come again tomorrow. She will
love you no less then."

There was a moment of silence charged so strongly
Samiv felt the hairs rise on her arm. Then, Korval
swept a bow to the old Healer.

"Tomorrow, Master Ethilen, I am not denied."

She inclined her head.

Samiv got her feet under her and rose, muzzy-
headed and aching.

"Pilot."

She looked up into a face utterly without expression.
Korval offered his arm.

"Allow me to take you to your delm."

She sat in the co-pilot's chair, but her board was
dark. Korval flew, silent, as he had been since leaving
Healer Hall.

"Samiv," he said, and she started, though he spoke
gently.

She straightened against the webbing and looked

to him, seeing the side of his face, the quick, clever fingers, moving among his instruments.

"Yes, pilot?"

He glanced over to her—lightless eyes in a hewn-gold face—then went back to his board. "I wish you will tell me true. May you?"

She licked her lips. "Yes."

"Good," he murmured. "I wish to know if you, of your own will and heart, desire this marriage which is promised to your delm."

Of her own will and heart. A Scout's question, phrased as if one's own will and heart had place within the weavings of kin and duty. And yet . . .

"If I were—my own delm—I would not seek the marriage," she said slowly, feeling along those unaccustomed threads of personal desire. "I—forgive me . . ."

"I had asked," he said softly. "There is no need to ask forgiveness for truth, among comrades, eh?"

"Just so." She took a breath, hands fisted on her lap. "Truly, Korval, I find I—like—you much more than ever I—But I do not think that we should—that we should—*suit*," she finished, somewhat helplessly.

"Ah." More silence, and she sat back into the chair. It came to her to wonder what her delm might think, could she hear Samiv in such a conversation with her affianced husband, and hiccuped a laugh.

"Are you able to bear some little of your delm's displeasure?" he asked abruptly. "I swear that I will take all that I might to myself. But she is bound to be displeased with you."

"She is displeased with me now," Samiv said blearily. "I was never to have come to ask your aid, you know."

"I see. In that wise, I believe we may win you free

of the Tree's attentions, pilot. You need only stand firm and quiet. And swear me one thing."

She blinked. "What shall I swear?"

He looked at her, one dark brow up. "Come to me, when your delm's anger has cooled, and let us finish Balance between us."

"Korval, there is nothing owing. I—"

"I must beg you to allow me to know the extent of my own debt," he interrupted, all stern-voiced and by-the-Code. Samiv strangled a rising giggle and managed to incline her head.

"As you will, sir. When I may, I will come to you, in order to complete Balance. My word upon it."

"Thank you," said Korval, and flicked up the comm toggle.

"*This* is your notion of propriety?" Delm Bindan demanded. "Of withholding from scandal? Of safety and respect for Bindan's treasure? I suppose it a mere trifle for you, Korval, nothing higher than a lark! Certainly, go to the opposite end of the world for your mischief, force yourself into a clanhouse, hold a nadelm at gunpoint, subvert the youth and steal away the second daughter! Amusing in the extreme, I make no doubt! Certainly, Delm Guayar thought the news delicious. He called while I was yet at breakfast to share it with me. I could have hidden my face!

"And *you*—" She turned her eyes to Samiv.

"I have only respect," Daav murmured, "for the honor and the fortitude of Samiv tel'Izak, who stood staunch, as a troth-wife must and—"

"Troth-wife!" Bindan spun. "If you dare believe, after last evening's escapade, that I will allow one of

Bindan to risk herself and her honor in support of your mad whim—Good-day, sir! Your man of business will hear from mine."

Had he not been frantic to return to Chonselta, he would have laughed aloud. Clonak's father had done his work with admirable thoroughness. And, doubtless, he thought wryly, enjoyed every moment of it.

He bowed to Bindan's outraged face. "Good-day, ma'am. Pilot. Sleep well."

"If your Lordship," Bindan's butler murmured from the doorway, "will attend me. I will escort you to the door."

Charged with unexpended adrenaline, Daav strode across the glade, laid both palms against the trunk and glared up into the branches.

"You may give over terrorizing Samiv tel'Izak," he said, voice shaking. "She and I will not wed."

The bark beneath his hands warmed. "Yes, very good!" he snarled, snatching his hands away. "Approve me, do! What shall it mean to you, that a fine pilot was all but destroyed for your whim? What shall any of us mean to you, who has seen us all die—from Jela to Chi! Breed-stock, are we? Then hear me well!"

He was in the center of the glade now, with no clear notion of how he had gotten there, hands fisted at his sides, shouting up into the branches as if the ancient, alien sentience cared—had ever cared—for his puny, human anguish.

"I shall lifemate Aelliana Caylon, if she will have me, and if you dare—dare!—frighten or in any way discontent her, I will chop you down with my own hands!"

His words hung for a moment, and were gone, swallowed by the still, warm air. Daav took a breath—another—deliberately relaxed his fists...

In the height of the branches, something moved.

He tensed, recalling the torrent of trash that had greeted Samiv tel'Izak, thinking that the Tree could easily and with no harm to itself loose a branch onto his unprotected head, thus disposing of a breed-line that had failed of its promise.

The noise grew louder. Daav crouched, ready to leap in any direction.

And fell to his knees as dozens of seed-pods cascaded around him.

Chapter Thirty-Nine

The heart keeps its own Code.

—Anonymous

THE DOORKEEPER SHOWED HIM TO A PRIVATE PARLOR, served him wine and left him alone, murmuring that the Master would be with him soon.

The wine was sweet and sat ill on a stomach roiled with fear. He set it aside after a single sip and paced the length of the room, unable to sit decently and await his host.

Behind him, the door opened, and he spun, too quickly. Master Healer Kestra paused on the threshold and showed her hands, palms up and empty, eyebrows lifted ironically.

Ignoring irony, Daav bowed greeting, counting time as he had not done since he was a halfling, throttling pilot speed down to normality, though his nerves screamed for speed.

The Healer returned his bow with an inclination of her head and walked over to the clustered chairs. She arranged herself comfortably in one and looked up at him, face neutral.

"Well, Korval."

He drifted a few paces forward. "Truly, Master Kestra?"

She waved impatiently at the chair opposite her. "I will not be stalked, sir! Sit, sit! And be *still*, for love of the gods! You're loud enough to give an old woman a headache—and to no purpose. She's fine."

His knees gave way and, perforce, he sat. "Fine."

"Oh, a little burn—nothing worrisome, I assure you! For the most part, the Learner never touched her. She knew her danger quickly and crafted her protection well. She created herself an obsession: an entire star system, which required her constant and total concentration—I should say, calculation!—to remain viable." She smiled, fondly, so it seemed to Daav. "Brilliant! The Learning Module will not disturb rational cognition." She moved her shoulders.

"Tom Sen and I removed the obsession, and placed the sleep upon her. We did not consider, under the circumstances, that it was wise to erase painful memory, though we did put—say, we caused those memories to feel *distant* to her. Thus she remains wary, yet unimpeded by immediate fear." Another ripple of her shoulders.

"For the rest, she passed a few hours in the 'doc for the cuts and bruises. I spoke with her not an hour ago and I am well-satisfied with our work."

Daav closed his eyes. She was *well*. He was trembling, he noted distantly, and his chest burned.

"Korval?"

He cleared his throat, opened his eyes and inclined his head. "Accept my thanks," he said, voice steady in the formal phrasing.

"Certainly," Kestra murmured, and paused, the line of a frown between her brows.

402 Sharon Lee & Steve Miller

"You should be informed," she said, abruptly, and Daav felt a chill run his spine.

"Informed?" he repeated, when several seconds had passed and the Healer had said no more. "Is she then not—entirely—well, Master Kestra?"

She moved a hand—half-negation. "Of this most recent injury, you need have no further concern. However, there was another matter—a trauma left untended. Scar tissue, you would say."

"Yes," he murmured, recalling. "She had said she thought it—too late—to seek a Healer."

"In some ways, she was correct," Kestra admitted. "Much of the damage has been integrated into the personality grid. On the whole, good use has been made of a bad start—she's strong, never doubt it. I did what I could, where the scars hindered growth." She sighed lightly and sat back in her chair.

"The reason I mention the matter to you is that I find—an anomaly—within Scholar Caylon's pattern."

Daav frowned. "Anomaly?"

The Healer sighed. "Call it a—seed pattern. It's set off in a—oh, a *cul-de-sac!*—by itself and it bears no resemblance whatsoever to the remainder of her pattern. Although I have seen a pattern remarkably like it, elsewhere."

"Have you?" Daav looked at her. "Where?"

Master Healer Kestra smiled wearily, raised a finger and pointed at the vacant air just above his head.

"There."

It took a moment to assimilate, wracked as he was. "You say," he said slowly, "that Aelliana and I are—true lifemates."

Kestra sighed. "Now, of that, there is some doubt.

The seed-pattern was found in the area of densest scarring." She looked at him closely, her eyes grave.

"You understand, the damage in that area of her pattern was—enormous. Had a Healer been summoned at the time of trauma—however, we shall not weep over spilt wine! I have—pruned away what I could of the scar tissue. At the least, she will be easier for it—more open to joy. That the seed will grow now, after these years without nurture—I cannot say that it will happen."

He stared at her, seeing pity in her eyes. His mind would not quite hold the information—Aelliana. She *was* his destined lifemate—the other half of a wizard's match. He was to have shared with Aelliana what Er Thom shared with his Anne... She had been hurt—several times hurt—grievously hurt and no one called to tend her, may Clan Mizel dwindle to dust in his lifetime!

He drew a deep breath, closed his eyes, reached through the anger and the anguish, found the method he required and spun it into place.

He was standing in a circle of pure and utter peace, safe within that secret soul-place where anger never came, and sorrow shifted away like sand.

"And who," Kestra demanded, "taught you that?"

He opened his eyes, hand rising to touch his earring. "The grandmother of a tribe of hunter-gatherers, on a world whose name I may not give you." He peered through the bright still peace; located another scrap of information: "She said that I was always—busy—and so she taught me to—be still."

"All honor to her," Kestra murmured.

"All honor to her," Daav agreed and rose on legs that trembled very little, really. "May I see Aelliana now?"

* * *

The room was sun-filled and fragrant, with wide windows giving onto the Healers' extensive gardens. She stood in the open window, looking out on the rows of flowers—a slender woman in a long green robe, her tawny hair caught back with a plain silver hair-ring.

He made no noise when he entered, but she turned as if she had heard him, a smile on her face and her eyes gloriously green.

"Daav," she said, and walked into his arms.